Garnet Wolseley

The Life of John Churchill, Duke of Marlborough, to the Accession of

Queen Anne

Vol. 1

Garnet Wolseley

The Life of John Churchill, Duke of Marlborough, to the Accession of Queen Anne
Vol. 1

ISBN/EAN: 9783337324612

Printed in Europe, USA, Canada, Australia, Japan

Cover: Foto ©Raphael Reischuk / pixelio.de

More available books at **www.hansebooks.com**

THE LIFE

OF

JOHN CHURCHILL

DUKE OF MARLBOROUGH

TO THE

ACCESSION OF QUEEN ANNE

BY

FIELD-MARSHAL VISCOUNT WOLSELEY, K.P

ASH HOUSE IN THE YEAR 1750

VOLUME ONE

FOURTH EDITION

LONDON
RICHARD BENTLEY AND SON
Publishers in Ordinary to Her Majesty the Queen
1894

I dedicate this Book

TO THE

MEMORY OF MY MOTHER,

WHO TAUGHT ME TO READ.

PREFACE

— ⊷ —

WHEN Virgil undertook to sing of 'Arms and the man,' he knew well that an account of the 'arms'—the actual campaigns—would fail in interest without a study of 'the man' himself. Following afar off so great an example, I have striven in these volumes to bring before my readers the man John Churchill whilst I relate the Duke of Marlborough's feats of arms.

There is, both at home and abroad, ample material for the history of his wars in Queen Anne's reign, but there is little to be found which bears upon his domestic life, or illustrates the inner working of his curiously constituted mind.

After a careful study of my subject, I found it would be impossible to make the reader understand Marlborough's character and actions without giving a brief account of the picturesque period in which he lived and of the people with whom he associated.

It is not easy, therefore, to condense the story of his life, and I would disclaim all intention of competing with the writer of the following stanza, who won the prize of five hundred pounds which the Duchess of Marlborough offered for the best poem commemorating the deeds of her great husband :

> ' Five hundred pounds, too small a boon
> To set the poet's Muse in tune
>   That nothing might escape her,
> Were I to attempt the heroic story
> Of the illustrious Churchill's glory,
>   It scarce would buy the paper.'*

In these volumes the dates are given according to both the old and new styles. When at home, Marlborough invariably used the former, and when abroad, the latter.

I need hardly add that this book has been written at the odd moments of leisure in a busy life, on board ship, in camp, and often at long intervals of time when on duty abroad and in the field.

WOLSELEY.

June 4. 1893.

---

* *Notes and Queries*, 2nd series, vol. iv.. p. 153.

EAST END OF ASH HOUSE, 1890.

CONTENTS OF THE FIRST VOLUME

CHAPTER III.

EARLY BOYHOOD AND EDUCATION.

CHAPTER IV.

ARABELLA CHURCHILL.

CHAPTER V.

CHURCHILL BECOMES AN ENSIGN IN THE FOOT GUARDS.

CHAPTER VI.

THE CHARACTER OF THE ROYAL BROTHERS.

CHAPTER VII.

THE RELIGION OF THE RESTORATION PERIOD.

CHAPTER VIII.

THE COURT AND MORALS OF THE RESTORATION.

CHAPTER IX.

CHURCHILL SERVES IN TANGIER.

CHAPTER X.

JOHN CHURCHILL'S PERSONAL APPEARANCE.—HIS INTRIGUE WITH THE DUCHESS OF CLEVELAND.

CHAPTER XI.

THE SECOND DUTCH WAR, AND HOW IT CAME ABOUT.

CHAPTER XII.

THE CHARACTER, AIMS, AND AMBITIONS OF LEWIS XIV.

CHAPTER XIII.

THE FRENCH ARMY OF 1672.

CHAPTER XIV.

WILLIAM OF ORANGE: HIS CHARACTER.

CHAPTER XXVI.

ENGLISH PREPARATIONS FOR A WAR WHICH THE KING HAD NO INTENTION TO DECLARE.

CHAPTER XXVII.

CHURCHILL EMBARKS FOR ACTIVE SERVICE IN HOLLAND.—THE PEACE OF NIMEGUEN.

CHAPTER XXVIII.

THE POPISH PLOT.

CHAPTER XXIX.

CHURCHILL GOES WITH JAMES TO SCOTLAND: THEY RETURN TO ENGLAND.

CHAPTER XXX.

JAMES IS AGAIN SENT TO SCOTLAND, AND THE CHURCHILLS GO WITH HIM.

CHAPTER XLII.

THE CHURCH OF ENGLAND AND JAMES.—HE TRIES TO RE-ESTABLISH POPERY.

CHAPTER XLIII.

CHURCHILL BEGINS TO INTRIGUE WITH WILLIAM OF ORANGE.

CHAPTER XLIV.

LORD CHURCHILL ADVISES JAMES NOT TO FOLLOW AN ANTI-PROTESTANT POLICY.

LIST OF ILLUSTRATIONS

CONTAINED IN THE FIRST VOLUME

THE LIFE OF JOHN CHURCHILL, DUKE OF MARLBOROUGH

CHAPTER I.

MARLBOROUGH'S BIRTH AND BIRTHPLACE.

The registry of his birth—His horoscope—Situation of Ash House, his birthplace—Axminster and its church—The Axe River—Musbury and its church—The Drake Family—Lord Boteler—Ash House burnt—Mrs. Churchill's 'groaning chair'—Ash House Chapel—Marlborough's lineage—The Manor of Churchill.

'Those will not look forward to their posterity, who never look backwards to their ancestors.'—BURKE.

Tнıs is the facsimile of an entry* in the badly-kept and sorely-neglected parish register of the very old church of St. Mary's, Axminster. The year is noted on the margin, as there was apparently no room for it elsewhere. There

* This entry has been examined most carefully, and the following reading of it has been corroborated by those well skilled in deciphering this old written character. 'John the Sonne of Mr. Winstone Churchill was Babtized att Ash the 2th Daye of Jun in the year of our lord god.' As mentioned above, the year 1650 is added on the margin of the page.

is also a marginal reference to a note written on the cover in 1780 by the Vicar, the Rev. B. Symes. This note refers to the entry, not only of John Churchill's baptism, but also to that of his sister Arabella, two years before, in which her surname and the Christian name of her father are incorrectly spelled: it is as follows: '*For Churchwell read Churchill; for Weston read Winston; and for Aishe Haule read Ash Hall. The person whose baptism is here so simply recorded was afterwards the illustrious Duke of Marlborough, Prince of Mindleheim, Generalissimo, etc.'*

The date given is Old Style; had it been rendered according to the New Style, it would have been June 12, 1650. This christening took place, when the child was a week old, in the little detached chapel belonging to Ash Hall. The ceremony was performed by the Rev. M. Drake, Rector of Musbury, the parish in which Ash stands.*   It is not clear why the entry of this baptism was made in the Axminster instead of in the Musbury parish register, where most of the baptisms and marriages celebrated in Ash Chapel are recorded, but it may have been because the church of St. Michael's, Musbury, was closed at the time for extensive repairs, and for the addition of what is known as 'Drake's Aisle.'

John Churchill was born in Ash House, about 1 a.m. on Sunday, $\frac{26\text{th May,}}{5\text{th June,}}$ 1650. Many have asserted that he could not have been born there as the house was then in a ruined condition from injuries sustained during the Civil War. But although it was in a dilapidated state, his parents did certainly live there in 1650, and there he was born. Mr. Prince, the author of 'Worthies of Devon,' was then seven years old, and lived at Newenham Abbey, close by Ash Hall. He was related to Mrs. Winston Churchill's family, and Marlborough's maternal uncle, Sir John Drake, was his godfather; in writing, therefore, about the birth

---

* The Rev. Matthew Drake was a distant relative of the Drakes of Ash.

of his illustrious playmate, Prince wrote of circumstances personally known to him. He refers to the companion of his boyhood as 'The present Right Honourable the Earl of Marlborough, whose birth at Ash, in the parish of Musbury, hath greatly honoured our county of Devon.'*

The date of John Churchill's birth has been variously recorded, but that given above may be relied on. Two of his autograph letters bear out this statement. It was his invariable practice to use the 'New Style' when writing from abroad, and the 'Old Style' in letters written at home. In one of these two letters, dated 6th June, 1707, and written in Flanders, he says : 'This day makes yᵣ humble servant 57.'† The 6th June, N.S., in the eighteenth century, corresponded with the 26th May in the seventeenth. The other letter was written at home, and its date, the 26th May, 1710, was 'Old Style.' In it he states that day to be his sixtieth birthday.

A manuscript book in the British Museum, by Partridge, the well-known contemporary astrologer and almanack-maker, gives Marlborough's 'Scheme of Nativity.' According to it, he was born 58¼ minutes after midnight, 25th—26th May, 1650. In a note to this horoscope it is said that had he come one hour later into the world he must have been beaten at Blenheim.‡

His birth was in the darkest period of the rebellion, when Cromwell was made Captain-General of all the forces of the Commonwealth, and when chivalrous Montrose was hanged in Scotland. King William III. was born some five months later. Thus the same year gave England two of her most remarkable history-makers—two men destined

---

* Page 564, quarto edition of Prince's 'Worthies of Devon.' Prince was an accurate historian of his own locality.

† This letter is in the Earl Stanhope's possession.

‡ Mr. Henry Jenner, of the British Museum, has been good enough to work out this horoscope astrologically. Of it he writes : 'It does not seem at all characteristic ; it has avowedly been "rectified" as to time by working backwards from some event in Marlborough's life.'

to be in after life most intimately associated, and to take prominent parts in that great but vulgar drama of the Revolution.

The traveller who visits the birthplace of Marlborough will not be rewarded by any striking scenery. But association will give interest to a spot not otherwise remarkable. If I dwell on the surroundings of the house in which he spent the first ten years of his eventful life, it is because I feel that his strong personality has power to lend charm to a humble landscape, and dignity to a homely valley.

Ash House lies about two miles south-west of the drowsy, stone-built little town of Axminster, and about one hundred and fifty by road from London. It is well situated, though, like most English dwellings of the same period, it stands low. It is on the left or eastern bank of the river Axe, from which it is distant some five hundred yards. Originally a simple oblong block, facing north-west, it was partly burnt during the civil wars, which about 1642, began to surge westward into Somerset and Devon. Axminster was occupied alternately by the troops of both sides, between whom there were frequent encounters. The town stands on a hill, at the foot of which runs the Axe, a bright and rippling stream. The narrow streets of the present little town creep up from the river to the high ground, once a British, and afterwards a Roman station. From earliest times the site had been occupied as a stronghold. In Saxon days the town was called Brunenburgh, and the great battle of that name was fought close by nearly a thousand years ago.

Early in this century most of the old houses were destroyed by fire, and few now exist that Marlborough could ever have seen. The Grand-Duke Cosmo III. passed through the town in 1669, and describes it as a collection of about two hundred houses, mostly of mud, and thatched with straw. He refers to its manufacture of woollen cloth, and remarks upon the pleasing harmony of its bells. The church, dedicated to the Virgin and St. John the Baptist, is mainly of the thirteenth century, but part of an earlier structure, notably one doorway, remains which was built by King Athelstan to mark the burial-place of those who fell in the battle. Within the church lie many of Marlborough's maternal ancestors, the Drakes of Ash.

On many a surly winter evening, as the boy John Churchill sat listening for the latest news of Cromwell's doings, he must have heard the curfew-bell toll its slow and solemn admonition from this massive, square-towered belfry. Two centuries later the narrator of his deeds was busy in searching the records of that church's register for information about the Duke of Marlborough, and in copying from its pages the entries of sums expended by the church-wardens to supply General Churchill's troops with guides and transport during another, though much less serious rebellion.

To reach Ash House from Axminster, you follow for about two miles the winding, narrow road—the Fosseway of the Ancient Britons—which runs from that little town through the village of Musbury to Axemouth.* Near Ash House the river flows lazily over a gravelly bed through a deep fertile valley. The smooth, luxuriant meadows of luscious grass, often covered with flights of seagulls and curlews driven inland by stress of weather, afford rich grazing to herds of red Devonshire cattle. These choice fields have belonged in turn to Celtic, Roman, Danish, Saxon and Norman invaders.

In the seventeenth century the lower waters of the Axe abounded with salmon, but none run up now, though its bright, gleaming pools and rippling, sun-coloured shallows, still afford the trout-fisher good sport. No troublesome bushes entangle his casting-line, for the mower's scythe sweeps the very edge of its shelving banks. The peaceful, meandering stream is at certain seasons a chosen

---

* The Fosseway was used by the Romans to connect Ischalis and Moridinum. It was said to run · from the south-west to the north-east into England's end.'

haunt of wild duck and widgeon, and a happy nursery
of water-hen and bald-coot. After many a sunny reach
of placid, slowly-running water, the Axe discharges itself
noiselessly into the sea, some four miles below Ash
House. The dominant characteristic of the scenery is
smiling tranquillity. There is a harmony in the tone and
colouring of this essentially English landscape that is
most restful to the eye. The rich green of its herbage
contrasts pleasantly with the deep red of its stone-
strewn ridge-and-furrow. The fields, small, and curiously
irregular in shape, have been fenced in by the patient
industry of generations, with huge, hedge-topped banks
which in places rival the dykes of Holland. The grass-
covered ramparts of many a Flemish city may well have
reminded Marlborough in after-life of these great fences
of his own native valley. These thick, robin-haunted
hedges are well studded with small-sized trees of oak,
elm, sycamore and beech. But there is certainly no
oak now there that could have existed when the great
Alfred, or his equally-great though less-known grandson
Athelstan, hunted in the extensive forest then surrounding the royal residence at Axminster.

Deep hollow lanes, perhaps dating back to Druidical
times, wind their tortuous way in all directions. Snug
homesteads surrounded by small crofts or great orchards,
and 'bosomed high in tufted trees,' find shelter there from
the winds of winter, while thatched cottages, covered with
honeysuckle and other creepers, sleep on in the sunshine.
Time would seem to have no value for these good Western
folk, and the air of drowsy idleness which pervades both man
and beast, appears, as it were, to be stamped upon the very
face of nature herself. It is a vision of languid rest, and
even the clouds seem to move in a lazy and objectless
fashion. Stillness, fitfully broken by the song of birds and
the lowing of kine, reigns supreme in the ripe maturity of
this fruitful valley. Here gentle nature breathes content,
and the well-fed herds, and the pleasant humming of bees

in the fruit-laden orchards, bespeak a land flowing with milk, honey, and cider.*

Looking south from Ash House, about three-quarters of a mile down the valley, you see the little stone-built hamlet of Musbury, with its narrow street of detached cottages, and small, trim gardens. It is built upon a spur of the rounded hills which there form the eastern side of the Axe Valley. High above the village is the parish church of St. Michael's, whose square tower forms a conspicuous landmark in the neighbourhood. There, many of the Drake family lie buried, and some interesting monuments exist to their memory. One represents three couples, husbands and wives : the men in armour, all in ruffs, and cleverly painted in the fashion of the day. The hands of each figure are joined in prayer, and in front of each couple is an open book, inscribed with this Royalist text : 'Let the Lord arise, and let His enemies be scattered.' In part of the church still known as ' Drake's aisle,' the windows are of the same character as those in Ash House, and like them doubtless came from the ruins of Newenham Abbey.

Early in the fifteenth century the estate of Ash, Aish, or Esse, as the name was variously spelled, passed by marriage into the Drake family, from a junior branch of which came Sir Francis Drake, the great navigator.

Sir John Drake of Ash, Marlborough's maternal grandfather, was a Cavalier, and commanded the quota of militia raised in Axminster. He died in 1636, leaving a widow and a large family, one of whom—Elizabeth—was Marlborough's mother.† His eldest son, Sir J. Drake, knight

---

* Duke Cosmo complains of the badness of the roads, abounding in mud and water, but he remarks upon the ' spacious meadows for feeding cows in which this district abounds.'—The London edition of his travels, 1821.

† This Sir J. Drake is buried in Musbury Church, where a art of his tombstone still exists. He was married in the church of St. Giles-in-the-Fields, $\frac{18}{25}$ 5, 1616. His family consisted of eight sons and five daughters.

and afterwards baronet, was also loyal to the King, but on bad terms with his Puritan mother, to whom Ash was left absolutely.* He lived at Trill, then known as the ' Tenant's House,' and about half a mile south-east of Ash.†

Lady Drake, his mother, a stanch Parliamentarian, lived at Ash until her death in 1666.‡ She left the place to her grandson, passing over her son. She was the eldest daughter of Lord Boteler (sometimes spelt Butler§), of Bramfield, Herts, by his wife, who was sister of George Villiers, Duke of Buckingham, the favourite of James I., and of his son Charles I. ; hence the cousinship between Marlborough and Barbara Villiers, the infamous Duchess of Cleveland, of whom more anon. Another daughter of Lord Boteler married James Ley, second Earl of Marlborough, a fine chivalrous gentleman, who was killed in the naval battle off Lowestoft, in 1665. His title became extinct in 1679. It was in consequence of this distant connection that Lord Churchill took the title of Earl of Marlborough.

In 1644 the Roundhead Lady Drake sent to the officer commanding the rebel troops at Lyme to ask for a detachment of soldiers to garrison her house of Ash. Lord Powlett, then in command of the King's forces at Hinton-St. George, being told of this, marched forthwith upon Ash. He effected an entrance through the window of the chapel, which then joined the house, and put to flight the

* During Lady Drake's widowhood, her son, Sir John, was not allowed access to Ash Chapel. We find from the parish registers that all his children were baptized in his house at Trill, or in Musbury Church, whilst all Winston Churchill's children were baptized in Ash Chapel.

† He was in 1643 godfather to John Prince, author of ' Worthies of Devon.' See Davidson's ' History of Newenham Abbey,' p. 221.

‡ She died ¹ᵘₐ 10. 1666. and was buried in Holyrood Church, Southampton.

§ This family had also representatives in Bedfordshire, and one of the Botelers from that county was Lord Mayor of London in 1515.

The first Lord Marlborough of the Ley family was a lawyer who became Chief Justice. and afterwards Lord High Treasurer.

Roundheads before they had had time to finish the defensive works they had begun.* The King's troops upon this occasion did great injury to the house, and burnt part of it. Enough, however, remained for Lady Drake to live in, and shortly afterwards, about 1646 or 1647, her daughter Elizabeth with her Cavalier husband, Mr. Winston Churchill, joined her, and, being destitute, were glad to find a home, even in that ruined place.

In 1647 Lady Drake demanded, and soon afterwards obtained from the Cromwellian Government, the sum of £1,500 as compensation for the damage done to her house and chapel by the Royal troops.† After the Restoration, the house was repaired, and two wings added, by Marlborough's cousin, Sir J. Drake, Bart., who thus converted it into an E-shaped building, with the open part of the letter facing north-west. The Drakes had some control over the neighbouring abbey of Newenham, and its ruins seem to have been extensively drawn upon for the mullions and other cut stone required for these additions. Sir John Drake enclosed the park with a wall, dug fishponds, and stocked the gardens 'with a great variety of choice fruits, etc., so that now it may vie for beauty and delight with most other seats in those parts.'‡ In 1778 the stables and offices were destroyed by fire, the house itself was injured, and upon the death of the last Lady Drake, in 1782, it was dismantled as a gentleman's residence. What remained of it was converted into the farmhouse which we now see.

Amongst the old furniture then sold was the 'groaning chair,' in which Mrs. Winston Churchill was delivered of her son John. It had been highly valued in the Drake family as an heirloom 'home to the time of Lady Drake's

---

* 'Axminster during the Civil War,' by Davidson.

† Roberts, in his 'History of Lyme Regis,' says this money was voted to her by the burgesses of that place in August, 1648, from the rents and profits of Lord Powlett's lands, sequestered by the rebel Government.

‡ Prince's 'Worthies of Devon.'

death.'* Such an article of furniture was common in many parts of England during the seventeenth century, when 'groaning cake' and 'groaning ale' were as customary at births as plum-cake now is at weddings.

The existing farmhouse of Ash is evidently the southern wing, that represented by the upper stroke of the **E** in the former plan of this 'antient and gentile' family mansion. It is in the Tudor style of domestic architecture, and built of the gray limestone of the neighbourhood. Some few windows of the same fashion have recently been added. The present owner, an Axminster grocer, has only lately purchased the farm. All immediately around the house is commonplace and unlovely. There is an air of dirt and decay about the grim old place and its rickety, badly-thatched barns. It is about a hundred and eighty yards from the main road, with which it is connected by a mean farm lane. The original drive quitted that road much nearer the village of Musbury, making a wide sweep to the south and west of the house. The visitor reaches the present hall-door through a dirty straw-yard, where even the old watch-dog who sniffs your heels has an air of having seen better days that is in general keeping with the place.

In a large orchard behind the existing farmhouse stands a little slated building of the same perpendicular style. It was once the family chapel, and formed part of the house, but it belongs to an earlier date than the home of the Churchills, for the Bishop of Exeter had licensed it in the fourteenth century. It continued to be used as a chapel until the Hall was dismantled, when it was ignobly turned into a cider-house.

> 'Thus in this poor world of ours,
> Noblest things find vilest usings.'

___

* This groaning chair was purchased by Sir J. W. Pole, of Shute, in 1782, when the property was sold by the trustees. This is taken from a note in the handwriting of the well-known antiquary, Mr. John Crouch, on a copy of Polwhele's 'History of Devon' (1793), now in possession of General Sir Redvers Buller, of Downes, Crediton.

Carved in stone over the door are the Drake arms, with the baronet's bloody hand, showing that the chapel, as well as the house, was restored after 1660, the year in which the baronetcy was created. The chapel is now divided into two storeys, the upper a wretched apple-loft, whilst in the lower stands a cider-press. The fifteenth-century piscina still remains, also a little old oak panelling in the loft; but dirt, neglect and decay are now the chief characteristics of what was once a shrine of holiness.

There Marlborough and most of his brothers and sisters were baptized, and there, just a century later, Lord North, the Minister, and as some have it, the half-brother of the King, married Anne Speke, the daughter and heiress of the last Lady Drake by her second husband. Both Marlborough and North were the favourites of their respective sovereigns, and in their day of power both wielded great authority. One name recalls the story of victory and national triumph; the other, of failure, folly, and defeat.

Of the fish-ponds with which Ash was once provided, one still remains, and the site of the old level bowling-alley can even yet be traced in the adjoining orchard. Not long ago some of the old bowls were found in the fish-pond. Near the chapel is a fine old walnut-tree, under whose spreading branches the handsome boy Churchill may often have played, and watched the pink apple-blossoms of the neighbouring orchard flutter down into the fish-ponds, or whirl about in the soft wind of a Devon summer. Descending some stone steps, you reach the now neglected garden, where box borders hem in the ill-kept flower-beds, and where herbs and weeds struggle for supremacy. The lichen-covered fruit-trees, gnarled and bent, are in keeping with the high moss-tufted and crumbling walls by which they are enclosed.

Standing on these garden steps, the threshold of Marlborough's forgotten birthplace, what heart-stirring memories of English glory crowd upon the brain! Surely, the imagination is more fired and national sentiment more roused by a visit to the spot where one of our greatest countrymen was born, and passed his childhood, than by any written record of his deeds. This untidy farmhouse, with its neglected gardens and weed-choked fish-ponds, round which the poor, badly-clothed boy sported during his early years, seems to recall his memory—aye, even the glory with which he covered England—more vividly than a visit to Blenheim Palace, or a walk over the famous position near the village of Hochstadt on the banks of the Danube. The place, the very air, seems charged with reminiscences of the great man who first drew breath here. Yet there is nothing in the scenery of this placid valley to justify the theory that man's mind takes a tone and colouring from its early surroundings. The fair valley, rich with farm produce, seems essentially peaceful and incapable of producing men of the sword. It is difficult indeed to realize that its smooth, grassy banks were once torn by the feet of contending armies, that its hillsides rang with the clash of swords and the din of war, and that nigh ten centuries ago thousands of Norse warriors trampled its rich meadows, as they fled to their ships before the victorious Saxons. The little stream which circles round what was once the park, or, as it was still styled in the Restoration epoch, the 'barton,' of Ash House, has been known as the 'Warlake' ever since that Saxon victory. It crosses the Axminster road near Ash House, at a spot still called the 'King's Field.'* We learn from local folklore, that until recently the children of the neighbourhood prattled of the time when that brook ran red with the blood of Norse warriors, and that there was hardly a grown man between Axminster and the sea who, if obliged to cross the Warlake by night, was not sensible of a certain creeping feeling of superstitious terror.†

---

* It is common in Devonshire to use the word 'lake' for brook.— 'Book of the Axe.'

† 'Book of the Axe.'

But the place may remind us still more of later times, when Royalist and Roundhead, gay Cavalier and prim Puritan, stalked through the land in such grim contrast. The sight of this once goodly country house revives stirring memories of gallant Drakes and Powletts and other neighbouring squires who fought and suffered for their luckless and unworthy King, and their very names remind us of the long struggle between ruler and people in this distant corner of England. Local tradition is still full of stories about the handsome, ill-starred son of Lucy Walters, who landed hard by with a handful of followers, and whose abortive career presents such a contrast to that of his early friend and comrade, Jack Churchill, who knew not failure. In this spot we recall Monmouth's rebellion, in the suppression of which Churchill took such a leading part, and we pass naturally from the fate of Monmouth to the 'Bloody Assize,' ordered and directed by Churchill's merciless master, whose memory is to this day execrated in these south-western counties. Thus a visit to Ash House is like opening a page of history inscribed with the names of kings and princes and mighty warriors, and looking at the hill across the river, we reflect that in 1688, it was there that Orange William met John, Lord Churchill.

Born here ten years before the Restoration, Marlborough's earliest recollections were of civil war. Stories of hard-fought fights had inflamed his young imagination. Sites of camps, new and ancient, lay thick around his home, and the old folk, far and near, were wont to amuse their children with war stories and legends of Saxon heroes and of Danish invaders. Brought up amongst those who had fought for the King, his young companions were the sons of Cavaliers who had charged at Naseby or bled at Edgehill. The stories of these events were then household words in every neighbouring Hall; and the dented breastpiece and notched sword hanging in the parlour, bore silent witness to hard blows given and received for unfortunate Charles. Taught by a ruined Cavalier father to hate the canting Puritan, and to ridicule and despise his vulgarity, the chivalry of the unselfish Royalist appealed all the more strongly to the heroic sympathies of the boy, while the remembrance of the overwhelming misfortunes of the picturesque Royal martyr appealed to his imagination and excited his compassion. Whatever effect the peaceful character of the surrounding scenery may have had upon him, the atmosphere of his early home could not fail to foster a love for war, to arouse within him a healthy personal ambition, and to tinge his young dreams with military enthusiasm.

Biographers sometimes think it necessary to prove their heroes to be of ancient lineage, and long pedigrees are accordingly invented by ingenious heralds to substantiate the existence of mythical ancestors. But the vexed question of John Churchill's genealogy will not be entered upon here, for it is impossible to connect him positively in any direct way with the long list of forefathers allotted to him by many historians. Indeed, it seems doubtful if his descent in the male line can be traced with any certainty beyond his grandfather, Mr. John Churchill, though there can be no doubt, that, like most of England's greatest leaders, he sprang from a family that had long been reckoned amongst the landed gentry of the Kingdom.

In the list of landowners near Bridport, in 1330, we find the name of 'John Chirchille,' who was doubtless one of his ancestors.* In Wilts and Dorsetshire, families of that name had long been settled.† Mr. Awnsham Churchill, the celebrated bookseller and publisher in the reigns of William III. and Anne, was a kinsman of Marlborough, and Sir John Churchill, Master of the Rolls, was his father's first-cousin.‡ Many Churchills had been knights of the

---

* Appendix to Sixth Report of Historical MSS. Commission.
† Hutchin's 'Dorsetshire'; Anthony Wood; Collinson's 'Somerset-shire,' vol. iii., p. 57.
‡ Sir John, born about 1620, married Susanna, daughter of Edmund

shire, which generally implied that they were men of birth and position, and the name of Elias de Churchville appears in the list of Edward II.'s Parliament, as 'manucaptor of Rogerus de Xonaunt, Knight of the Shire,' returned for Devon.*

The family would seem to have come originally from Somersetshire, and probably derived its surname from the hamlet of Churchill, in the parish and manor of that name. Some biographers, not content with dilating upon the assumed ancient lineage of Marlborough, insist upon his French origin, because of the strong similarity between courcil and Churchill. They ignore the fact that the name is composed of two very common Saxon words, frequently found joined together in all parts of England, churches being often built upon hills. No combination of two words could be more natural than that of 'Churchill;' indeed, no fewer than four parishes and one hamlet in England are so named. It has its counterpart in Churcham, Churchdown, Churchover, and Churchston. A common family name in Dorsetshire is Churchnaye — 'naye,' or as it is sometimes written, 'nayre,' being the South-country word for ham, or hamlet. Crichel (Circel) is evidently the same word as Churchill. Long Crichel, Dorset, is written in the 'King's Book' *Kyrchil Longa*. Churchill is, and was, by no means an uncommon name, and looking to its derivation, it is unlikely that all who bear it come from a common stock. The poet Churchill came of an Essex family, and there are other families of that name who can trace no connection with Marlborough or any of his forbears. Of these families, one was settled in the seventeenth century at Crawley, in the parish of Chardstock, Dorset; another at Crewkerne, Somerset, near Lyme Regis. A Churchill family now resides at Colliton House, Dor-

---

Prideaux, and died in October, 1685. He was godfather to Henrietta, Marlborough's second child. There was also another Churchill at the Bar, who died in April, 1709, as M.P. for Dorchester.

* Palgrave's 'Parliamentary Writs.'

chester, where there still hangs a picture of the Colonel Joshua Churchill who joined Monmouth when he landed.

Luttrell records: 'Yesterday one Deborah Churchill, sometime since found guilty of murder, was carried in a coach to Tyburn, and there executed for the same.' Among the twenty 'poore Weomen' paid to 'walke' at the funeral of Charles II., we find one 'Ann Churchill.'* In reference to the Duke of York's partiality for John Churchill, Legge, and Hyde, Lord Halifax writes: 'He ought to consider those who had ancestors, as well as those who had none.' Sir J. Reresby describes those three favourites as 'being scarce Gentlemen.'† But in the Oxford matriculation papers of Marlborough's father, the grandfather is described as 'Generosus,' which may be deemed as equivalent to what we now mean by 'Esquire.'‡

The manor of Churchill, in Somersetshire, did not apparently belong to anyone of that name, until Marlborough's cousin, the Master of the Rolls, bought it, in 1652, from Mr. Richard Jennyns, the father of Sarah, Marlborough's wife.§ It had only been about a century in possession of her family, Ralph Jennyns, her great-great-grandfather, having purchased it in 1563.‖ At Sir J. Churchill's death it passed to one of his daughters, and

---

* Warrants for funerals in the Lord Chamberlain's office.

† 'Reresby Diary.' 28, 2, 1683.

‡ At Oxford the term 'Armiger' was not, it appears, then bestowed upon anyone under the rank of a knight's eldest son. A knight's younger son and all the sons of country gentlemen were described as 'generosus.' The entry in question runs thus: 'Winstonus Churchill Londõ fil. Johis Churchill de Glanvile Wootõ in Com. ꝗd. Gen. an. nat. 16.' The ꝗd. (predicto) is evidently a clerical error for 'Dorsetiensi.' This information has been kindly furnished by Mr. F. Madan, of the Bodleian Library.

§ Mr. Green, in his history of this manor, describes it as consisting of 20 messuages, 20 cottages, a windmill, 20 gardens, 20 orchards, 200 acres of land, 60 of meadow, 250 of pasture, 60 of wood, and 300 of gorse and heath. Common pasture for all manner of cattle, and free warren in the appurtenances of Churchill.

‖ He bought it from Sir Wm. Lo, or Lowe. See the 'Manor of Churchill,' by E. Green, F.S.A.

through her to her husband's family. It was thus but a very short time in possession of any member of Marlborough's family.

The manor of Great Mintern, in Dorsetshire, where Marlborough's father and grandfather had lived, was not their freehold property, but was only rented from Winchester College.*

* The original lease was granted to Marlborough's grandfather in 1642, and it was renewed by Mr. Winston Churchill, Marlborough's father, in 1660.

CHAPTER II.

MARLBOROUGH'S MOTHER, FATHER, BROTHERS, AND SISTERS.

The violent temper of John Churchill's mother—His father at Oxford, in the Civil War, and afterwards in Dublin — 'Divi Britannici '—Sir Winston's ten children.

MARLBOROUGH's mother was Elizabeth, daughter of the stanch Cavalier Sir John Drake, by his Roundhead wife, Eleanor Boteler. She was clever, but her talents did not compensate for the sharpness of her tongue and the violence of her temper. Her great son inherited his mother's ability, but, happily for him and for England, not her irritable disposition. After his marriage she had many serious encounters with her imperious daughter-in-law, which led to unpleasant family jars. A letter from Dublin in June, 1668, contains an amusing allusion to the fiery, jealous tone of the letters she sometimes wrote to her husband when he was in Ireland. She twitted him for not coming to England occasionally to see his wife, as, she asserts, his colleagues were in the habit of doing. This letter says : ' Sir Winston's lady saluted him with such a tempestuous epistle, as if the only reason he sought not the same liberty was because he was more delighted with his divertizements than obliged by his business to continue here.'*

Marlborough's father, Winston Churchill, was born in 1620, and lived at Mintern, near Dorchester. He was the

* The Carte Papers, Bodleian Library.

son of Mr. John Churchill, of Wottan Glanvile in the same county, who was a member of the Middle Temple, and one of the Deputy-Registrars of the Court of Chancery.* Mr. John Churchill had married Sarah, daughter of Sir Henry Winston, of Standiston, Gloucestershire, from which connection the name of Winston came into the Churchill family. He is said to have made money at the Bar, and the Duchess of Marlborough, in describing her husband's family, states — with some exaggeration certainly — that, when Winston married, his father was able to give him property worth £1,000 per annum. Winston, she adds, was no favourite with his father, who bequeathed his property to his grandson John, her husband, only giving his own son Winston a life-interest in it. In 1678, when seriously in debt, Winston induced his son John to break the entail, in order to raise money on the property to pay off his liabilities.†

In 1636 Winston Churchill, then only sixteen years of age, was sent to St. John's College, Oxford.‡ There he soon acquired a reputation for sedateness, talent, and application, but for some unexplained reason he did not remain long enough to take a degree. He quitted the quiet of a Collegiate life when England was already on the brink of that great civil war which for many years ravaged her most fertile districts, destroyed many of her cities, castles and country houses, and laid low thousands of her noblest and manliest sons. The Churchills, father and son, remained loyal to their King. Winston became Captain of Horse, and took part in many a hard-fought encounter. He distinguished himself at the battles of Lansdown Hill and Round-

---

* He was admitted to that society on $\frac{13}{23}$ 3, 1613. See 'The Manor of Churchill,' by E. Green, p. 6.

† MS. paper by Sarah, Duchess of Marlborough, in the Spencer House Collection.

‡ The following is the entry of his matriculation, as given in Coxe. '1636, April 8. Winstonus Churchill Londin' fil. Johās Churchill de Glanville Wooton in com.tiō Gen. an. nat. 16.'

way Down, at the siege of Taunton, and at the defence
of Bristol.*   For the active part taken by father and son
against the Parliament, heavy fines were imposed upon
both.   The father's fine was £440, the son's £4,446.†   The
former was paid, but the latter was so much more than the
son, Winston, could afford, that he was compelled to surrender his property to the Commonwealth.   Thus rendered
houseless through his loyalty to the King, he was glad to
avail himself of his mother-in-law's invitation to share with
her the possession of Ash House, her ruined home near
Axminster.   There he lived with his young wife until his
property was given back to him at the Restoration.

During this forced retirement of twelve years at Ash
House most of his children were born.   It was a period full
of portentous excitement for all Englishmen, especially for
those who, like Winston Churchill, had staked their all in
the cause of the King.   He had the good fortune to be fond
of books, and was consequently able to find occupation in
literary pursuits and in the personal education of his
children, for which duty he was eminently qualified.   It
was from him, at this time, that his son John acquired the
rudiments of education.

At the Restoration Mr. Winston Churchill sat in Parliament for Weymouth.   Fond of science, he became in 1661
one of the earliest members of the Royal Society, then

---

* These names are mentioned in the grant of augmentation of arms
—now at Blenheim Palace—given to Winston Churchill in 1661 ; but
these names are indistinct, and those of other battles in which he took
a part are entirely illegible.

† 'On the 9th April, 1646, John Churchill, of Dorset, late one of the
Deputy Registrars in Chancery, prayed in regard he was aged, of infirm body, and unable to travel, that he might be admitted to make a
composition by deputy.   Following this, in July, he stated he had resigned his office to his nephew, John Churchill, of Lincoln's Inn ; and
then came John Churchill, of Lincoln's Inn, and answered for the
payment imposed on his uncle John, of Wotton Glanville.   On the
28th August the fine was fixed at £440.'   The Royal Composition
Papers, 2nd ser., vol. xiii. ; 'The Manor of Churchill,' by E. Green,
F.S.A.

in its infancy. In recognition of his loyalty, an augmentation of arms and (what was then by no means
common amongst the smaller gentry) a crest were conferred upon him by special warrant.* This was a very
cheap way of rewarding loyalty, but, when the privilege of
bearing arms at all was confined to a few, it meant more
than it sounds to modern ears. As some sort of recognition for all he had lost through his fidelity to the King,
he was appointed one of the commissioners of the Court
of Claims, created by patent to hear the appeals of the
Irish against the Cromwellian Settlement, and to distinguish
between the ' innocency and the nocency ' of all concerned.
This court sat at the King's Inns in Dublin, where the Four
Courts now stand.† The date up to which cases were to
be heard was May, 1661, afterwards prolonged for some
years more.‡ The first case was heard in February, 1662,
and the court did not close its proceedings until the beginning of 1689.§ Many of the cases brought before it
were heartrending in the extreme. Impoverished gentlemen claimed back the properties of which they had been dis-
possessed by Cromwell because of their loyalty to the King.
The doors of the court were daily crowded by famished
soldiers and by tattered peers and squires in absolute want.
A few had their lands restored to them ; but in most cases
those who had sided with the regicides were allowed to retain
the castles and the baronies, which, robbed from the loyal
Irish, had been given to them by Cromwell as the reward of
their treason. It was about this time that Sir Winston took
as his motto ' Faithful, but unfortunate '; for he, too, in a

CHAPTER II.

1650.

29/1, 1660/1.

5, 1661.

7, 1663.

2, 1661.

---

* This warrant of 29/1, 1660/1 is registered in the Heralds' College.
It was then he assumed the Spanish motto of ' Fiel pero desdichado '
—faithful but unfortunate.

† Kennet's ' Register of Events,' 14, 3, 1660/1.

‡ Some of the Cromwellian Settlers who had obtained forfeited lands
were ruined by the decisions of this court.

§ It may be of interest to know that the weekly allowance granted to
these commissioners for board and lodging in Dublin was £4 2s. 1½d.
each.

Chapter
II.

1660.

small way had been similarly made to suffer in England. How the boy John Churchill must have pondered over these words in Dublin, when he saw daily in those men who appeared before the Court a striking illustration of how often steadfastness in faith and loyalty led to penury, and in how many cases wealth and titles had been won by treason and perfidy! It was a bad lesson to be learned by a youth at the most receptive period of life.

ﾟ 1, 166ﾞ.

22·1) 1662-3.
1·2)
1ﾟ 9, 1664.

Recalled to London by the King's order in January, 1663,* Winston Churchill had conferred upon him the distinction of knighthood, and the following year he was made Junior Clerk Comptroller of the King's Household.† He again went to Ireland in January, 1665-66, to sit on the same commission as before.

'Brother Churchill,' writes one of his colleagues, 'was particularly severe upon the Duke of York's agents.'‡ Why he should have been so is difficult to determine.

In 1675 he published a dull, but by no means an unlearned, book, under the curious title of 'Divi Britannici.' It proves him to have been a man of great research, skilled in heraldry, and well read in ancient history. It contains the lives of the English monarchs from the earliest times, and dwells forcibly upon the Divine right of kings to rule their subjects absolutely. It also gives some interesting information about the armorial bearings of our reigning houses.§ In the dedication of this book to Charles II., he says it was 'begun when everybody thought that the

* Fourth Report of Historical MSS. Commission, p. 247.

† Records of the Board of Green Cloth. We read of him as a visitor to the Bodleian Library on 4, 10, 1665.

‡ In the Report of the Carte MSS. by Russell and Prendergast, published 1871, there is a curious story of a fight between Sir Winston Churchill and Captain Thornhill at the chambers of the former in King's Inn, Dublin.

§ Anthony Wood describes this book as 'very thin and trite.' Lord Macaulay, in his lofty, offhand fashion, refers to it with pitying contempt. The work is described on the title-page as 'Being a remark upon the lives of all the Kings of this Isle from the year of the world 2855 unto the year of grace 1660.

CHAPTER
II.

1660.

monarchy had ended, and would have been buried in the
same grave with your martyred father,' and ' when none
of us that had served that blessed prince had any other
weapons left us but our pens to show the justice of our
zeal by that of his title.'

When James II. came to the throne, Sir Winston Churchill
was continued in his position as ' Eldest Clerk Comptroller '
of the Green Cloth, and he represented Lyme Regis in Parliament during the whole of that King's reign. He was
shortly afterwards promoted to be Second Clerk of the
Green Cloth in ordinary. He died in 1688, and was buried $^{27-\frac{4}{5}}$, 1687-8.
in St. Martin's-in-the-Fields, Westminster. He had very
little to leave his widow, and nothing to leave any of his sons,
having been in straitened circumstances for some years before
his death. The entail having been broken by arrangement with his son John, as already mentioned, he left
the leasehold of Mintern and all his personal property to
his widow, with a request that she should bequeath it at
her death to their third son, Charles, from whom he had
borrowed money to pay his debts.*

Mrs. Winston Churchill bore her husband twelve
children. Their names were as follows :

1. Arabella, born in Ash House, and baptized in Ash
Chapel, $\frac{28-\frac{3}{10}}{}$, 1648. She died in 1730.†

2. Winston, who died young.

3. John, born at Ash, $^{2\frac{6}{5}-\frac{3}{5}}$, 1650, and baptized in Ash
Chapel, $\frac{3}{12}$ 6, 1650 ; died 1722.

4. George, born at Ash, $\frac{28-\frac{3}{10}}{}$, 1652-3 ; baptized $\frac{11}{24}$ 5,
1653 ; he died $\frac{8}{19}$ 5, 1710.

5. Ellen, baptized in Ash Chapel, $\frac{30}{9}-\frac{12}{1}$, 1652-3.

6. Mary, born $\frac{10}{17}$ 7, 1655 ; baptized $\frac{27}{9}-\frac{5}{8}$, 1655 ; buried
$\frac{4}{11}$ 5, 1656.

7. Charles, born $\frac{2}{12}$ 2, 1655-6 ; baptized seven days
afterwards.

* Mintern was held on lease from Winchester College. His wife,
Lady Churchill, died in 1697. The probate to her will is dated
$\frac{1}{11}$ 3, 1697.

† The name in the parish register is spelt ' Churchwell.'

8. Mountjoy: died young.

9. Jaspar; died young.

10. Theobald, born in Dublin, and baptized in St. Bride's Church, $\frac{11}{21}$ 1, 1662-3.*

There were two other daughters, Dorothy and Barbara, who died in infancy.

Of these only one daughter—Arabella—and four sons—John, George, Charles, and Theobald—lived beyond childhood.†

In small county families like the Churchills of those days, it was the common ambition of parents to provide for their sons in the army and navy, and, if they had any Court influence, to place their daughters in some royal household. Sir Winston and his father had suffered much for their King in the 'Great Rebellion,' and at the Restoration, Charles II. and his brother, the Duke of York, felt bound to do something for them in return. As soon as Arabella was old enough to leave the paternal roof, Anne Hyde, Duchess of York, took her as a maid-of-honour. How she very soon became the mistress of that Duchess's husband will be told in another chapter.

John, the eldest son who reached the age of manhood, is the subject of this history. George, the second son, was provided for in the navy, where the Duke of York, as Lord High Admiral, had, of course, much patronage. He served as a volunteer at sea in the Dutch war of 1666, and in after-years displayed both courage and ability as a sailor. His ship, the *Newcastle*, was the first which joined William III. in 1688. In the following year he was given command of a squadron employed on the coast of Ireland during the Duke of Schomberg's unfortunate campaign in that country, and when in command of the *St. Andrew*, he took a distinguished part in the victory over the French at Cherbourg

---

* Noble says he died in 1685.

† The use of more than one Christian name had not yet been introduced into society.

and La Hogue. He withdrew from the navy when Captain Aylmer was made Admiral over his head. This supercession followed soon upon his eldest brother's disgrace, and was probably in consequence of it. When Marlborough had been restored to favour, George was appointed Lord Commissioner of the Admiralty, and he retained that position until Lord Pembroke became Lord High Admiral. Lord Pembroke was succeeded by Prince George, Queen Anne's husband, who, without doubt to please Marlborough, promoted George Churchill to be Admiral, and made him one of his Council. During the six following years, thanks to his brother's influence, he was virtually the supreme master of the navy. He sat in Parliament during the greater part of his life, but, crippled with gout, he was forced to relinquish all public duty in 1708. At one time he was seriously suspected by the Junto of giving information, through Prince George, to the Queen, of the Whig doings and intentions, but when told of this Marlborough said: 'It is not true, for the Queen does not like him, and seldom speaks to him.' It is much to his credit that he died poor, in an age when most public men robbed the State. This is all the more remarkable, because he had long held highly-paid offices, and had never been married. He died in his fifty-eighth year, and his epitaph in Westminster Abbey contains these words: *3. 5, 1710.* 'Invictissimi ducis Marlburghii frater non indignus.' He left all he possessed to his illegitimate son, George Churchill, and to his nephew, Francis Godfrey.

Charles, Sir Winston's fourth son—the third who lived to grow up—became page to Christian, King of Denmark, at thirteen years of age, and at sixteen Gentleman of the Bedchamber to Prince George.* He was a keen soldier and an able infantry leader. Had he not been overshadowed by his brother's fame, he would have left

---

* In the papers of the Lord Chamberlain's office are recorded several lawsuits for debts owed by him, that lead one to believe he was extravagant.

behind him a well-deserved military reputation. At the battle of Landen he made his nephew, the Duke of Berwick, a prisoner, and was allowed 20,000 guilders for his ransom.* He took a distinguished part in the battle of Blenheim, in recognition of which his brother sent him home in charge of Marshal Tallard and other French prisoners of distinction. He was at different times Governour of Kinsale, of Guernsey, of the Tower, and of Brussels. He rose to be a Lieutenant-general, and was Colonel of the Coldstream Guards, but resigned when he was given to understand at the accession of George I. that his services 29, 12, 1714. were no longer required. He died much regretted by those 9, 1, 1715. who knew him, and is buried at Great Mintern. He married a daughter of Mr. Gould. She afterwards married Lord Abingdon, and the Dorsetshire property passed with her from the Churchill family. Charles had no children by his wife, but he left an illegitimate son, Charles, who became a General, Governour of Plymouth, Groom of the Bedchamber to the King, and represented Castle Rising in Parliament for many years.† This son was a friend of Sir Robert Walpole's, and married his natural daughter by Moll Skerrett.‡ By her he had one daughter, married 1796. to the first Earl Cadogan, who divorced her. He also had a natural son by Mrs. Oldfield, the actress.§

The youngest son, Theobald, entered the Church. He never obtained preferment, but was at one time chaplain

---

* Warrant of 2nd March, 169⁷⁄₆.

† 'I hear Colonel Churchill is gone to your city. I don't know what he may pass for among you : if assurance will recommend him, he never fails of that quality, though he can behave himself with as much good manners as anybody where his impertinence meets with no encouragement.' Letter from Mrs. Delany, dated 22, 8, 1725. See her Life, vol. i., p. 117. He was born in 1679, and died 1745 at Bath, where there is a monument to him in the abbey. He is immortalized by his friend Hanbury Williams.

‡ Sir R. Walpole afterwards married this Moll Skerrett.

§ Mrs. Oldfield, born 1683, died ²³⁻¹⁰⁄₁₁, 1730, aged forty-seven.

to the Royal Dragoons when his brother John was its
Colonel.*

* He matriculated in Queen's College, Oxford, when fourteen years
of age, 2, 3, 167$\frac{9}{}$; B.A. 1680, and M.A. 1683; died 3, 12, 1685, and
was buried in St. Martin's-in-the-Fields. The following genealogical
tree is copied from one found in the Rolls Office amongst the domestic
papers of James II.'s reign. The bundle is marked in pencil : 'Heraldic
peerage between 1664 & 1668.' It is also endorsed '1687.'

Jasper Churchill, of Bradford, Dorsetshire.	Alice, d. of John Claxton, of Herrington, Dorsetshire.	John, Ld. Butler, of Broomfield.	Elizabeth d. to Sr George Villiers, of Brokesby, & sister to George, Duke of Buckingham.

John Churchill, of Mintern, Dorsetshire.	Sarah, d. & coheir of Sir H. Winston of Standish, Gloucestershire.	Sir J. Drake, of Ash, in Devonshire.	Ellen, d. & coheir.

Sir Winston Churchill, of Great Mintern.	Elizabeth Drake.

John, now Lord Churchill.

CHAPTER III.

Marlborough's boyhood—His life in Dublin—Goes to St. Paul's School—His education and bad spelling—Knowledge of French.

JOHN CHURCHILL was his father's second son, the eldest having died in infancy. We know little of his boyhood, and have none of those anecdotes of his early days that are so common in the biographies of great men. His father, an earnest student of history, was his earliest instructor, and from that loyal soldier he drank in a love of England and a deep respect for its history, laws and liberties, which influenced his whole subsequent career. His first regular tutor was the Rev. R. Farrant, Rector of Musbury parish, a man noted for piety and scholarship, and remarkable for having refused a bishopric.* During the ten or twelve years young Churchill spent at Ash House, he learnt from this worthy man the rudiments of knowledge as usually taught at that time to the sons of English country gentlemen, and he acquired that sincere love for Protestantism which was ever his strongest conviction, and one of the most remarkable features in his character. At no period of his career, however, was there any bigotry in his

---

* 'The Lives of the Two Illustrious Generals,' etc., etc., p. 6. This reverend gentleman (M.A. Oxon.) was in every way fitted for the office of Bishop. He died in 1662, having been given the living of Musbury in 1656 by Sir J. Drake, of Trill House, in succession to Edward Griffin, expelled by the Puritans.

religion, and he leaned rather towards the broad, liberal, Protestant teaching of the Church, than to the narrow theology and ceremonial of its High Church section. In the following pages it will be shown how much this Protestant feeling, acquired in boyhood, influenced his conduct at the great crisis of his life and at what may be termed the most important point in the history of the English Constitution.

When Sir Winston went to Ireland in 1662 as a commissioner of the Court of Claims, he took his wife and family with him. They lived in Bridge Street, Dublin, then a fashionable quarter, though now one of the most squalid in that city. Their neighbours were Sir P. Davys, the principal Secretary of State; John Chevers, whose son was created Viscount Mount - Leinster by James II.; Sir E. Burrowes; Patrick D'Arcy, a famous Roman Catholic lawyer and member of the Confederate Irish; Derrick Westenra, the well-known Dutch merchant; the Marquis of Antrim; and Sir Hercules Langford.*

In Dublin, John Churchill attended the City Free School, an old foundation for some twenty children of poor freemen. The master was the Rev. Dr. W. Hill, Fellow of Merton, Oxford, who only received eighteenpence a quarter for each scholar, in addition to a fixed salary of £15 per annum.† He was, however, allowed to live in the school-house rent free, and to take in by private arrangement a few better - class boys as day - pupils, amongst

---

* Private letter from Sir Bernard Burke, Ulster, who informed me that the following gentlemen sent their sons to the City Free School, viz., Sir N. Purdon, Colonel O. Wheeler, A. Campbell, A. Adair, F. Rogerson, etc.

† Dr. Hill, known as ' the famous Hellenist,' was born in Warwickshire in 1619. At one time he practised as a physician. The school-house—of which some walls still remain—stood on the eastern side of Schoolhouse Lane, which is extremely narrow, and runs north from High Street to Cook Street. The schoolhouse only fell about 1846. The great and learned Archbishop Usher had been educated at this school.

whom were young Pooley, afterwards Bishop of Cloyne,
and Nat Foy, afterwards Bishop of Waterford. Young
Churchill did not, however, remain there more than a
year, for he returned with his father to London towards
the end of 1663, and became a pupil in St. Paul's School,
of which Samuel Cromleholme was then headmaster. How
long he was at St. Paul's is not known, but, as the school
—which was closed at Midsummer 1665 on account of the
plague—was destroyed in the Great Fire the year after,
and was not apparently reopened until 1670, it would
seem that his school education must have ended in 1665,
near the date of his fifteenth birthday. In that same year
his father went back to Dublin to resume his duties as a
Commissioner of Claims.

In the Rev. G. North's copy of Knight's ' Life of Colet,'
now in the Bodleian Library, where the ' De Re Militari ' of
Vegetius is entered as one of the books then possessed by
St. Paul's School, there is the following MS. note* : ' From
this very book, John Churchill, scholar of this school, afterwards the celebrated Duke of Marlborough, first learnt the
elements of the art of war: as was told me, George North,
on St. Paul's day, 1724-25, by an old clergyman, who said
he was a contemporary scholar, was then well acquainted
with him, and frequently saw him read it. This I testify
to be true.— G. NORTH.'† Most schoolboys would find the
Latin of this work difficult to construe, but the book contains
passages of a character to account for the pleasure with
which a boy of a strong military bent would pore over
its pages, even though he might not be able to turn all
its sentences into good English. In the dedication to this
' Life of Colet,' it is said: ' We have lately lost two

---

* The Rev. G. North was Rector of Codicote. This MS. note is at
page 483 of the above-mentioned work in the Bodleian Library.

† This note has been recently verified in the Bodleian Library by Mr.
R. B. Gardiner, one of the masters of St. Paul's School ; he wrote an
article on the subject in *The Pauline* from which I have taken this
information.

persons of the most exalted station that our school (St. Paul's) could glory in, viz., the Dukes of Marlborough and of Manchester, from whom, as we have many instances of favour, we might, if they had lived longer, have expected more.'* In an Apposition speech delivered by Christopher Hussey in St. Paul's School about 1702, there is the following allusion to Marlborough : 'Hic Malburius denique ab ipso Cæsare Gallos domare et a Gallorum injuriis vicinas gentes tueri didicit.'+

From all this, we are justified in assuming that Marlborough had at least an elementary knowledge of Latin, in addition to the stock of learning he picked up from his father, from the Rector of his parish, and at the schools he attended. When we further remember that in early life he could converse fluently in French—which hardly one of all the King's Ministers could do—we feel that when his enemies pronounced him to be 'grossly illiterate,' they grossly maligned him. As with Hannibal, so with Marlborough, much of our knowledge regarding him comes to us from his enemies. The Jacobites detested him because he assisted William at the Revolution. His rivals in public life envied his success, and hated him for it. It was necessary for the existence of the Government which destroyed him to disparage his talents, and writers employed to vilify him sought to make him ridiculous because he could not spell. His spelling was unquestionably bad, and he often subscribed himself in early life, 'Your lordchipe's humbell servant.' But in his time there was no recognised standard of spelling, and if he failed in this respect, it was in company with Lord Chancellor Somers and a host of other well-known and even learned contemporaries.‡ The letters of Pepys abound with mistakes in

---

* See the edition of 1724.

+ *The Pauline*, of June, 1892, p. 117.

‡ Somers wrote 'bin' for been, 'coold' for cooled, 'don' for done, 'dor' for door, 'gon so farr,' 'Munday,' 'wee,' 'mee,' 'busines,' 'wine,' 'restlesse,' 'oppurtunity,' etc. In many contemporary letters from men

spelling. and even in our own time we have had many instances—Wellington and Napoleon, for example—of great men who could never learn to spell properly. His grammar and style were quite as good as those of James II., or Queens Anne and Mary, and most of the history-makers of their time.

To allege, therefore, that he was conspicuously illiterate and ignorant, is to misstate facts.   He left behind him a most voluminous official correspondence, from which the reader can judge for himself on this point. One of his friends, a good judge of literary work and style in the reign of Anne, when recounting the wits and writers of his time, says : 'Others I forbear, because tho' a thousand Occasions testify their Abilities, their Modesty hath hitherto concealed their Works and Names : only give me leave to add, it is the Opinion of some good Judges that if the Duke of Marlborough would give us his own Memoirs, we should find he could Write as well as Fight like Cæsar.'*

His knowledge of French has been questioned, because

of position we find the following : 'Pepell.' 'prisoner.' 'rable,' 'peces,' 'quiat.' 'imbassadors,' 'to judg.' 'Chanseler,' 'whare,' 'interest,' 'acompaned,' 'pertickelery.' 'exterpreted,' etc.   I have taken these examples at hazard from some letters before me.   That bad spelling was not a failing peculiar to the English of Marlborough's day the following copy of a letter from the French Duchess of Portsmouth is a good proof.   Although her virtue was not what it might be, she was a well-born lady, belonging to the Court of the 'Great Monarch.'   This letter is addressed to 'Mr. Sidney.'   'De Paris ce 8 de mar 1689. Ge sais toute les bonté avec lesquelle vous aves parlles de moy monsieur dont ge vous suys infiniment obliges. Vous saves combien toute ma vie ge esté dans vos interais. et de vos amie de mon caute ge ne suys poingt changé et lonne peut prandre plus de part au toussse,' etc. Many other of her letters, with equally bad spelling and grammar, are in Mr. Alfred Morrison's collection of autographs.

* Dr. H. Felton's 'Dissertations on reading the Classics and forming a just style, written in the year 1709.' He draws a constant distinction between the writings of men of quality and of scholars, and says there is as much difference between their writings ' as there is in the behaviour of a dancing master and a gentleman.'

in one of his letters to Robethon—the faithful agent of the House of Hanover—he gives as an excuse for writing in English, that his secretary, 'poore Cardonale, is sicke.'* This is a very unfair accusation, for many who speak the language fluently, would shrink from writing it, and it is absurd to suppose that one who had served so long in the French army under Frenchmen entirely ignorant of English, like Turenne, should be unable to converse freely in French. In one of his letters from abroad he criticises the imperfect manner in which someone had spoken French in his presence, which of itself should convince the most unbelieving that his knowledge of the language was considerable. Bishop Burnet writes of Marlborough that he was 'bred up in the Court with no literature.' Evelyn refers to him as 'well-spoken and affable, and supports his want of acquired knowledge by keeping good company.' Lord Chesterfield, always cynical about him, says, he was 'eminently illiterate, wrote bad English, and spelt it worse,' and that 'he had no share of what is commonly called parts; he had no brightness, nothing shining in his genius,' meaning presumably that there was no sparkling wit in his conversation. In a discussion with Burnet upon some historical point, he displayed so incorrect a conception of the subject, that the Bishop asked him the source of his information. He replied that it was from Shakespeare's plays he had learnt all he knew of English history.† Such an expression may be regarded as a figure of speech not intended to be taken literally, but still the story has been often quoted as a proof of his ignorance. At any rate, it does not prove his ignorance of history, but rather his knowledge of Shakespeare, which then was and still is, more rare and valuable.

We learn from the published papers of Flamstead, our first Astronomer Royal, that Marlborough was one of the

---

* Macpherson, vol. ii., note to page 29.

† This anecdote is told by Dr. Warner in his 'Remarks on the History of Fingal,' on Bishop Burnet's authority.

hundred and forty gentlemen who had been his pupils. Flamstead states that he employed these ' young gentlemen ' in his ' night observations, to tell the clock, to " write for " him, and in other duties and work that he could safely trust them in.'* He says he was compelled to take in these pupils to help him to pay skilled assistants and to purchase instruments. Under such a master it may be fairly assumed that Marlborough learned something of mathematics and astronomy.

With the exception of his bad spelling, then so common a failing, I do not find in the vast correspondence he left behind him any particular evidence of a marked want of education. He was not even then esteemed highly educated, nor was he well read in either ancient or modern literature; but his knowledge of French gave him access to a wide field of literature, which was at that time closed to most Englishmen, and even to many men of letters. But whatever may have been his lack of book knowledge, he had within him the divine spark of genius, that heaven-sent gift which, when allied to wisdom, makes men great ; no study can produce it, and no learning can compensate for its absence. It is the rarest of all gifts, and few, if any, have had it in larger measure than Marlborough. But his genius was slow in development, and his great force of character, as well as his mental power, matured leisurely. Even his handwriting was better at forty than it had been at five-and-twenty. As the slowest growing trees produce the hardest timber, it would seem that the genius which takes most time to develope is usually of the highest quality. Marlborough only began his career of victory at fifty-two, and, in the words of Bolingbroke, his ' was the perfection of genius matured by experience.'

---

* Bailey's ' Account of Flamstead,' p. 49.

CHAPTER IV.

ARABELLA CHURCHILL.

Female virtue in the Restoration epoch—The position of a Royal
mistress—Arabella's children—Duke of Berwick—James deserts
Arabella—She marries and has more children.

THERE is a wide gulf between our standard of female virtue
and that of the Restoration epoch. This is brought home
to us by the fact, that an upright, God-fearing gentleman
like Sir Winston Churchill, should have wished to see his
only daughter established as a Maid of Honour at a Court
where Charles II. was King. But in those days it was no
slur upon a lady to become the mistress of a prince, nor
did her family suffer in reputation. Lord Arlington, in a
letter of advice to the beautiful Miss Stewart, refers to the
position, which he thought she had accepted, of mistress
to Charles II., as one to which 'it had pleased God and
her virtue to raise her.'* It is said that the parents
of Louise de Kéroualle, Duchess of Portsmouth, sent her
originally to Versailles, in the hope that Lewis XIV. would
thus favour her. Sir E. Warcup records with pride in
one of his letters, that his daughter, a Maid of Honour
to Queen Katherine, 'was one night and t'other with the
King, and very graciously received by him.'† The mistress
to a royal prince was courted by all who had access to

* De Grammont, 'Memoirs.' Miss Stewart never did become the
King's mistress.
† Granger, vol. iv.. p. 338.

her. Other women envied her good fortune, and her family looked upon her as a medium through whom Court favour, power and lucrative employment were to be obtained. In allusion to the statement that Marlborough owed much of his success in early life to his sister Arabella, Hamilton, who knew thoroughly the French and English Courts, writes, ' Cela était dans l'ordre.' In common with others of his time, he assumed that ' the favourite of the King's mistress, and brother of the Duke's mistress, was in a fair way of preferment, and could not fail to make his fortune.'* Edward Villiers was made Earl of Jersey because his sister was the acknowledged mistress of William III., and it was taken as a matter of course that ' la maîtresse en titre ' should obtain honours and advancement for the members of her family.

Arabella Churchill joined the household of Anne Hyde, Duchess of York, about four years after the Restoration. She soon lent a willing ear to the importunities of the amorous Duke, best known in history as James II. Where or in what year the intrigue began, is not quite certain ; but it was probably at York, to which place James and his Duchess went in August, 1665. James had the redeeming trait of being extremely fond of golf and field sports. He rode well, and kept a large number of horses. The country near York being then very open, he amused himself with coursing. Upon one occasion a large party on horseback accompanied him, the Duchess alone being in a carriage, attended by her Master of the Horse, who was also her lover, the handsome Robert Sidney.† Arabella, who was a bad horsewoman, rode a spirited animal, which presently bolted and threw her. James gallantly dismounted to help her, and, struck by the grace and beauty

---

* De Grammont, ' Memoirs,' p. 310, Bohn's edition, 1846.

† He was son of Lord Leicester and brother of Algernon, who was beheaded. James says in his ' Memoirs ' that this Robert Sidney, and not Charles II., was the father of the unfortunate Duke of Monmouth. See Macpherson, vol. i., p. 76.

of her figure as she lay half unconscious on the grass before him, his susceptible heart took fire, and ere-long she became his acknowledged mistress.

She was tall, slight, and well proportioned. Her pale face was not pretty, but neither was she the hideous skeleton which De Grammont describes. Indeed, some of her contemporaries speak of her as good-looking.* In disposition, she was lazy and inert.

She bore four children to the Duke of York. The eldest was Henrietta, Lady Waldegrave. The second was James, Duke of Berwick, whose name will frequently occur in these pages. The third was Henry FitzJames, born in August, 1673, created by his father Duke of Albemarle, and by Lewis XIV. Grand Prior of France; a useless and debauched drunkard, who died in 1702. The fourth was Arabella, born in 1674, who became a nun, and died at Pontoise in 1704.†

The Duke of Berwick saw active service in many countries. He rose to a high position in the French army, and is best known amongst the famous marshals of Lewis XIV. as the Englishman who, in command of a French army, defeated the English and Spanish armies under the command of the Frenchman, Lord Galway, at Almanza. Berwick was killed by a round-shot in 1734 at the siege of Philipsburg. Unlike his renowned uncle, he gave liberally to those about him, and distributed large sums in secret charity. He died poor in an age when most men of high position amassed fortunes. If, however, he despised wealth, he loved glory. A devout Catholic, he made no parade of his religion. A sincere though moderate Jacobite, he was at all times ready in after-life to fight for his half-brother, the 'Pretender.' Marie Louise, Queen of Spain, said of him:

---

* There is a portrait of her at Althorp.

† See *Notes and Queries*, 2nd series, vol. iv., p. 488. In O'Callaghan's 'History of the Irish Brigade,' p. 106, it is stated she 'lived to the age of ninety, and died in February, 1762.'

'C'est un grand diable d'Anglais sec, qui va toujours tout droit devant lui.'

James soon deserted Arabella Churchill for Catherine, daughter of the witty Sir Charles Sedley, of Eylesford, Kent. This was the lady whom Marlborough's parents wished him to marry. The discarded mistress lived in comparative poverty and obscurity until she married Colonel Charles Godfrey in 1677.* She died in 1730, and was buried in Westminster Abbey, near the ' Quire door,' in the grave of her brother, George Churchill.

William III. awarded her a pension of £1,000 a year from the revenues of the Irish property given to James II. when Duke of York.† But she never received this left-handed jointure, as an inquiry by Parliament into the grants of land made so profusely by William resulted in an order to sell all James's Irish property for the benefit of the public. She left, by her husband, one son, Francis, and two daughters. The elder, Charlotte,‡ became Maid of Honour to Queen Mary II., and secretly married H. Boscawen, afterwards created Viscount Falmouth.§ The other married Mr. E. Danch, M.P. The son Francis served in the Foot Guards during several of Marlborough's campaigns in the Netherlands.¶

Arabella Churchill lived to see her old lover deposed and

---

* He had served with Marlborough as a Captain in the Guards. He died at the age of sixty-seven, in 1715, in Bath, where there is a monument to him in the abbey.

† The property upon which Arabella's pension was charged was known as Newcastle, in Co. Limerick. See O'Callaghan's ' Irish Brigade,' p. 106.

‡ She was born 1678, and died in March, 1754, in her seventy-sixth year.

§ His mother was sister of Godolphin, the Lord High Treasurer. This marriage was not owned for several months ; why, I know not. Historical MSS., Coke Papers, vol. ii. of 1888, p. 403.

ǁ Of Newington House, Wallingford. This old Oxfordshire family is now, I believe, extinct.

¶ He was for several years Colonel of the Bedfordshire Regiment, and died ₁⁴₁ 10. 1712.

die in exile. The man she married fought against him, and for years she must have followed with peculiar interest the progress of a great war, in which her brothers fought for England and her traitor son served in the ranks of England's enemies.*

* Horace Walpole says he had often seen her, and had once been in a room with her when he was a boy and she in her dotage.

CHAPTER V.

CHURCHILL BECOMES AN ENSIGN IN THE FOOT GUARDS.

Churchill becomes a page to the Duke of York—Becomes a favourite
with James.

THE compulsory break in the studies of young John
Churchill, caused by the closing of St. Paul's School, may
very possibly have hastened his introduction to Court life.
Upon leaving school his father obtained for him the
position of page to the Duke of York, in recognition of
Sir Winston's fidelity to the royal cause. It is said that
application was in the first instance made to the Duke of
Beaufort to take the boy, but as there was no vacancy in
the Badminton household, Sir Winston applied to the
Duke of York, who granted his request.*

James had a royal fondness for military display. To
inspect a handful of troops in Hyde Park, and to see them
march past in all their feathers and fine clothes, was
one of his most cherished enjoyments. The young page
usually accompanied him upon these occasions, and was
thus able to indulge that taste for everything military
which had grown up with him from earliest childhood.
He evinced the utmost interest in these parades, and
soon learnt to answer quickly and clearly all questions
upon drill details. James was highly pleased with his
precocious military knowledge and love for matters to
which he himself attached so much importance. When

---

* Seward's ' Anecdotes,' vol. ii. Also Noble.

asked upon one of these occasions what he intended to be,
'A soldier,' was the ready answer, and availing himself of
the opportunity, he begged the Duke to give him a commission in the King's regiment of Foot Guards, then on
parade before them.* His wish was gratified; and in the
autumn of 1667 he was given 'a pair of colours,' that is,
made an ensign in that distinguished corps, and was posted
to the King's company, vice John Howard, compelled to
retire because of the new law which forbade Roman
Catholics to hold any office under the Crown.

Thus began the career of this penniless boy. His own
and his parents' poverty brought home to him, as it so
often does to young men in similar circumstances, the
necessity for hard work on his part. It was the spur in
his side which made him put forth all his strength to win in
the race of life. How many able men owe it to their easy
circumstances that they have passed away, without raising
even a ripple on the sea of fame! It is difficult, we are
told, for the rich man to enter the kingdom of heaven;
it is no less difficult for him to become great in the profession of arms, where a life of hard work and anxious
care, often endured under great privations, must always
be the initial step on the road to distinction. It is surely
for this reason that younger sons are more apt to succeed
as soldiers than their brothers who are heirs to fortune.
The ambition born of poverty is generally for riches and
the comforts they ensure; but a noble nature seeks wealth
rather as a means to an end, that end being honour and
renown.

To what extent John Churchill was indebted for his first
start in life to his sister's influence with her royal lover, it
is difficult to say. She had been James's mistress for nearly
two years, when her brother entered the Foot Guards,
and though it is not improbable that she had something to

* This regiment was subsequently called the 1st Regiment of Foot
Guards, and, having in this century, like all the foot regiments in the
army, dropped its number, is now known as the Grenadier Guards.

do with his advancement, still, nothing could be more natural than the nomination of a handsome young royal page of engaging manners to a place in the Household Troops. Even in our own time, prior to the abolition of purchase in the army, the Queen's pages received free commissions in the Foot Guards.

It was about this time that James began to entertain for him that warm regard which lasted to the moment when the ensign, become a General, quitted his service for ever. James much disliked having about him men who were not Catholics, and his liking for young Churchill must have been deep and strong to make him forgive the determined Protestantism of his favourite.

It has been often said that the Duchess of York fell in love with her handsome young page, and much of his success in early life is thus accounted for. There is, however, no trustworthy authority for this imputation.*

It is interesting to note to what trifling and accidental circumstances the greatest reputations have often owed their origin. How frequently has the course of history been turned aside by some apparently unimportant Court intrigue or by some chance like the finding of Moses by Pharaoh's daughter! How many leaders of men have owed their first opportunity to some trivial occurrence or some fortunate connection with those in power! The period produces the man, chance assists him, and then if real greatness be in him, he dominates his generation and influences posterity. Some hold to the pleasant belief that the golden moment of opportunity must come sooner or later in life to each one of

---

* Anne Hyde died 1671. Mrs. Godolphin, who had been her Maid of Honour, gives the following touching description of her death : ' She was full of unspeakable torture and died (poor creature) in doubt of her religion, without the Sacrament or Divine by her, like a poore wretch ; none remembered her after one weeke, none sorry for her ; she was tost and flung about, and everyone did what they would with the stately carcase.'—' Life of Mrs. Godolphin,' p. 13.

us.   Be that as it may—and it is a debatable theory which finds little acceptance with the unsuccessful—it is amongst the first qualities of the man of genius to recognise his chance before it is too late, to see, as Clough puts it:

' 'Midst all the huddling silver, little worth
The one thin piece that comes, pure gold.'

CHAPTER VI.

The talents and vices of Charles II.—His immorality and want of principle—His leaning towards Roman Catholicism—His amiable traits — The Arts flourish in his reign—The character of James — His bigotry, cruelty, and immorality—Churchill brought up in their depraved society—Churchill's Protestantism.

CHAPTER
VI.

1670.

To understand thoroughly the surroundings amidst which Marlborough grew into man's estate, it is necessary to have a clear conception of the Restoration Court. To know what an army is worth, we take stock of its commander ; and to form any useful estimate of society during the reigns of Charles II. and of his brother, we must know what were the habits, tastes, and morals of those princes. What was their character and disposition? Were they English gentlemen in thought, word and deed; honest, and truthful? Did they love England for England's sake, or only for their own selfish ends? Were they better or worse than their father and grandfather, the mere feeble imitators of the sturdy, manly Tudors? It was wittily said of them that Charles could do well if he would, and that James would do so if he could.* But the character of the elder brother is difficult to describe, for it was made up of many different and conflicting qualities. Quickwitted and clever, he had acquired abroad a knowledge of foreign affairs such as none of his Ministers could lay

Said by Buckingham : Burnet, vol. i., p. 288.

claim to, with the exception of Clarendon and Temple. His natural aptitude for the study of character often enabled him to see through the cleverest machinations of those he employed. But ease and pleasure were the great aims of his unkingly life. Come what may, his one and fixed determination was to live in undisturbed possession of that crown which his father had lost by the adoption of violent and unconstitutional measures. Having secured the throne, life thenceforward was to him a species of comedy, a practical joke. Sensualist, idler, and cynic, he scoffed at religion, and believed neither in the honour of men nor in the virtue of women. If every man had his price, experience led him to believe that every woman had hers also. The ironical dealings of fate tickled his fancy; the foibles and ambitions of men amused him, and their wrangles over trifles afforded material for his careless and witty raillery. Tenacious of what he deemed his kingly rights and prerogatives, he was utterly without ambition; devoid of any semblance of patriotism or principle, wrapped up in love of self, he cared nothing for the feelings or wants of others. His only aspiration was to rule as he chose, without interference from Parliament or Minister, and whilst so doing, to wrest from the passing hour every possible personal enjoyment. In pursuit of that enjoyment there was no temptation that he sought to resist, no vice or villainy from which he shrank. As long as he was allowed to saunter lazily through life in possession of the throne, he felt no sting of shame, although the Dutch fleet burnt his ships in the very Thames. The wail of a nation dishonoured but not overthrown, troubled him nothing. If the plague decimated his subjects or the flames destroyed his capital, why should such national misfortunes affect him? As long as the taxes supplied money for himself and his mistresses, why should he distress himself? The avarice and extravagance of these women, however, drained his coffers, and compelled him to depend upon Lewis XIV. for the money

he dared not ask from a Parliament of English gentlemen.*

During his unworthy reign, public as well as private
honour and virtue were laughed to scorn by all the Court.
He left his soldiers and sailors unpaid, and every department of Government became rotten to the very core.

The royal brothers were both unblushing libertines. The
intrigues of Charles were known not only in Whitehall,
but in the country generally. His indifference to the
affairs of State was also notorious, and was thus recorded
in contemporary doggerel :

> ' And when he was beat,
> He still made his retreat
> To his Clevelands, his Nells, and his Carwells.'†

He disliked wars, not because he shrank from bloodshed, but because they meant stir and trouble. At heart
he was a coward, a fact which, together with his love of
ease, kept him from such heroic ventures as brought his
father to the scaffold, and subsequently sent his brother
into exile. His heart was too hollow to admit of any manly
respect for the most faithful public servant. The sturdy
honesty of Clarendon was to him as nothing in the balance
with the caresses of a Barbara Villiers or the smiles of a
Louise de Kéroualle. He was a treacherous friend, an
accomplished dissembler, and Barillon's letters to Louvois
show him to have been devoid alike of truth and self-
respect. His idea of happiness was apparently to sit
munching sweetmeats and dried pears in the midst of
rollicking rogues and wanton women. To his low, craven
nature it mattered nothing that he should be hated by all
that was honest at home, and despised as the puppet and
pensioner of Lewis by all that was honourable abroad. He

---

* ' A prince like a pear which rotten at core is,
   With a Court that takes millions, and yet as poor as Job is.'
                                        —From a contemporary song.

† Marvell's ballad on the Lord Mayor and Aldermen.

knew Oates to be a perjurer, yet he paid this false accuser of
Catholics from his own private purse with money obtained
from Lewis upon this stipulation amongst other things,
that he should declare himself a Roman Catholic.

Like his brother, he leaned towards absolutism in government, and consequently towards the Roman Catholic religion which fostered it. Unlike James, however, he would
risk neither his head nor his throne—not even his ease—
for either. A voluptuary in every sense of the word, he
was too fond of lazy comfort to be either brutal or vindictive; but, unlike his brother, he was endowed with
as much good nature as a selfish monarch, destitute of
heart, could possess. Yet he had many qualities which
attach men to princes, and which made him generally
popular. His good humour was inexhaustible. Like
most indolent men, he was familiar with all, easy of
access, affable, and so intolerant of formality and ceremony that it was no easy matter to make him play
the King at any time. Entirely devoid of haughtiness
or insolence, he allowed those about him to laugh at his
foibles, and seldom resented even the wit and satire they
pointed at ' Old Rowley,' as they had familiarly nicknamed
him.* Dryden wrote:

> ' In loyal libels we have often told him
> How one has jilted, the other sold him;
> How that affects to laugh, how this to weep.'

Although his wicked, melancholy face did not bespeak
amiable qualities, his natural disposition was soft, weak,
pliable and gentle. He had a smile and a cheery greeting
for everybody. It was no part of his easy, indolent philosophy to cherish animosity or to register wrongs. He forgave with extreme readiness. Weak, careless, and hating
business, he was steadily consistent in his determination
to die King of England. He would do nothing to risk his

---

* This nickname was given to him after a stallion of that name
which was one of his favourite race-horses.

crown. He had tasted the bitterness of foreign exile, and was determined never again to set out upon what he laughingly referred to as 'his travels.' When he found it necessary to yield to a popular demand, he did so with grace, but without inquiring whether it was just and right. He loved to tell stories of his many adventures when in exile, and he told them well, with an accuracy of memory that made his courtiers wonder he did not also remember how frequently he had related them before.

Fond of music and the stage, he may be said to have introduced the opera into England. The whole life of Charles II. proves that it is as hard for a man to be entirely bad as it is to be perfectly good.* Yet in such a reign and under such a King the arts and sciences flourished! The painters Lely, Huysman, Wissing, and Sir G. Kneller owed much to his patronage and protection. It was when England had been reduced by his treason to the lowest level of national degradation that Milton published his 'Paradise Lost,' Newton his 'Principia,' and the Royal Society was founded. Stranger still, during his reign some of our most valuable enactments were added to the Statute Book, proving that although good laws may be made under the worst rulers, they do not necessarily imply good government. Those passed in this reign were rather concessions to expediency than the fruit of an enlightened statesmanship.

James possessed none of his elder brother's ability, wit, or geniality. Nature had designed him for an inquisitor; the accident of birth made him a King. In manner he was ungracious; he accepted as a right, and with no sign of courteous recognition, the cordial greetings with which he and his brother were welcomed at the Restoration. The vicissitudes of his youth, his travels abroad and visits to foreign courts, had afforded him exceptional opportunities for the acquisition of practical knowledge of public affairs. But from poverty and ad-

* Machiavelli.

versity, often the best masters, he had learnt nothing, and he returned to England as fully possessed, as his father had ever been, with a belief in royal prerogative and in Divine right. We cannot believe him to have been the coward his enemies assert, though he possessed the cruelty which so frequently accompanies cowardice.* A contemporary, who knew him well, said: 'He is every way a perfect Stewart, and hath the advantage of his brother: only that he hath ambition, and thoughts of attaining something he hath not, which gives him industry and address even beyond his natural parts.'† James was a bigot of the worst type, though some may think that his honest belief in the dogma he wished to force upon his people somewhat redeems his bitter and cruel fanaticism. His disposition was detestable—a mingling of cruelty with vindictiveness, of obstinacy with bigotry and stupidity. To a follower of Argyle brought for examination before him, he said: 'You had better be frank with me, for you know it is in my power to pardon you.' 'Though it is in your power, it is not in your nature to pardon,' was the prompt reply.‡ When James once remonstrated with his brother upon the smallness of his military escort, Charles cynically answered: 'No man in England will ever take my life to make *you* King.'§

Portraits of James represent him as a man of a long and gloomy countenance, though some of his biographers assert that his complexion was fair and his manners sprightly. He was somewhat above middle height, and had a good figure, 'very nervous and strong.'‖ In

* See Burnet, vol. iii., p. 57, for a description of the extent to which James is responsible for the cruelties perpetrated by Jeffreys in 1685.

† Shaftesbury.

‡ Dalrymple. The prisoner's name was Ayloff or Aylif. He was a lawyer, connected by birth with the families of Hyde and Hatton. He had been concerned in the Rye House Plot, and fled to Holland in consequence. He accompanied Argyle to Scotland in 1685.

§ King's 'Anecdotes,' p. 61; Macpherson's 'History,' vol. i., p. 424.

‖ Clarke's 'James II.'

life and morals he was quite as dissolute as his brother, but with less discrimination in the selection of his mistresses. He was apparently as insensible to their beauty as Charles was to their manners, breeding and intellect. Louise de Kérouaille told the Duchess of Orleans that Charles had said of his brother : 'You will see that when he comes to the throne he will lose his kingdom through over-zeal for his religion, and his soul for some hideous creatures. He has not taste enough to choose good-looking women.'*

In the early days of Charles II.'s reign, before it became certain that Queen Katherine would have no children, the religious convictions of James were of little moment to the English people. But when he became the recognised successor to the throne, his adherence to the proscribed faith, and the presence of priests in his household, attracted the hostile criticism of all classes. According to his notions of royal prerogative, the people had few rights ; certainly none to interfere with the religious beliefs of their rulers. The reigns of both brothers were little more than persistent intrigues with the French King against the rights and liberties of the English people. It suited the foreign policy of Lewis XIV. that, whilst subsidising Charles and James to enable them to reign without a Parliament, he should also pay the English Protestant faction to oppose them in everything. This subtle policy was designed to keep England weak, and unable to interfere with his designs on Holland and Flanders. But whilst thus scheming to have England at his mercy, he little dreamed that he was all the time blindly working to bring about the very consummation he most dreaded. His deep-laid machinations eventually

---

* The clever Duchess of Orleans, writing to the Duchess of Hanover, says : 'Si la prophétie du dernier Roi d'Angleterre est vraie, le bon Roi Jacques ne pourra pas même faire un bon Saint.' She goes on to insinuate that during his stay in Dublin, 'il y avait deux affreux laiderons avec lesquelles il était toujours fourré.'—' Correspondance de la Duchesse d'Orléans,' vol. i., p. 94.

ended in the closest possible alliance between Holland and
a strong and united Great Britain and Ireland, under his
most dreaded enemy, William of Orange.   In fact he
played into the hands of that great Protestant leader,
who hated France as relentlessly as Hannibal had hated
Rome.

The more thoroughly we realize the public corruption
and private depravity of English Court life during the
twenty-eight years previous to the Great Revolution, the
more difficult it is to believe in the virtue of any woman
or the honesty of any man educated in that polluted
atmosphere. Yet it was amidst those surroundings that
John Churchill, the trusted servant of both Charles and
James, passed his years from boyhood to early middle
age.   His faults no doubt were many, but the reader who
studies his character will freely acknowledge them to have
been the faults of the age he lived in—whilst his sturdy
Protestantism, the honesty which caused him to refuse
great bribes with which he was more than once tempted,
and his many other good qualities, were all his own.   In
the virtues of public and private life he was far ahead of
his fellow courtiers, and few of his contemporaries passed
as unsullied as he did through the temptations which surrounded his early manhood.

Though Churchill lived at this Restoration Court and
was certainly no saint in his relations with women, he
still kept himself free from many of the other vices then
so common in society.   He neither drank nor gambled,
and doubtless his strong religious feeling had much to
do in keeping him above the low debauchery indulged
in by most of his Court associates.   In our days of extreme liberality in matters of faith and even of morals,
it is not easy to realize how largely the question of creeds
and of rival Churches entered into public and private
affairs in the seventeenth century.   The most serious
charge brought against Marlborough — his desertion of
James in 1688 — had its origin in the firmness with

which he clung to Protestantism, and in his determination to support the law which had made it the State
religion of England. Indeed, notwithstanding his many
lapses from virtue, and much that he did which was out of
harmony with our ideas of a pure Christian life, the more
closely we study his character, the more clearly we see,
that with him, a love for Protestantism was a guiding
principle, to which even his craving desire for power and
renown was always subordinated. The sincerity of his
conviction was proved by his steadfast resistance to King
James's wish, that he should embrace the Roman Catholic
faith—a resistance fraught with peril to his prospects of
advancement.

CHAPTER VII.

THE RELIGION OF THE RESTORATION PERIOD.

Protestantism disliked by Charles II.—His indifference to religion
—His letter urging his brother Henry to hold firmly by the Protestant Faith—He pretends to be a strong Protestant—James, on
the contrary, puts his religion before all other interests—His
bigotry.

THE religion of Charles II.'s Court was little more than a
mixture of superstition and freethinking, and, as regards
those who then governed England, this reign may be well
described as the era of no God. The teaching of the
Bible was only mentioned to be laughed at. But whilst
vice and public immorality reigned supreme at Court,
there was still a strong religious leaven amongst the
people. The Protestantism of that epoch was not an
inspiring belief, yet it was a living power in the land.
It influenced the conduct and the lives of men, and even
the scoffing Court dared not openly ignore, still less
despise it. King James defied it, and lost his throne in
consequence. The heroic spirit of the praying Puritans
survived the Commonwealth, and the earnest, zealous faith
of those who had died for the Reformed Religion, was
still an important factor to be dealt with by the rulers of
England.

The struggle between Charles and his people about
religion, and also about the political freedom which Protestantism brings with it, began soon after the Resto-

ration. It quickly became evident that neither of the royal brothers had much sympathy with the faith to which their father clung through life, and even Charles was soon suspected of a leaning towards the Church of his mother.* The great majority of his English and Scotch subjects were Presbyterians and other Nonconformists, but because of their deep-rooted hatred of Popery he had from the first treated them with great severity. Throughout his reign he favoured Roman Catholics as far as he dared, to the disgust of his Protestant subjects, and in spite of the protestations of his Parliament. The religious feeling was, however, too strong for Charles, and he had to bow before it. The result was a proclamation in 1666, by which all priests and Jesuits were banished the kingdom, and all Roman Catholics forbidden the possession of arms. So strong and general was the belief of unreasoning people that London had been set on fire by the Papists, that the King was compelled in the following year to dismiss all Roman Catholics from the Army and Navy.

It is desirable that the reader should have a clear conception of how this question of Romanism and Protestantism stood in England when Charles, and subsequently James, occupied the throne. Had the absolute indifference of Charles II. to all sacred matters, and his bias in favour of the Queen-mother's faith, been thoroughly known to the English people [in 1659-60, it is very doubtful whether he would ever have been crowned at Westminster. He dreaded lest the influence of his mother, backed up by her wily confessor, Montague, should induce either of his brothers to join the Church of Rome. Any such untoward event then, would, he knew, operate most injuriously upon his chances of being brought back as King of England. The following letter, dictated by expediency, and not by any love of Protestantism, shows how strongly he felt upon this point. It

§ 11, 1666.

§ 9, 1667.

* Sir R. Bellings was sent to Rome in 1662 to assure the Pope that Charles II. was a Roman Catholic in heart, and wished to enter that communion and to bring back England to it.

was written to his brother Henry from Cologne, the 10th November, 1654 :

'DEAR BROTHER,—I have received yours without date, in which you mention that Mr. Montague* has endeavoured to pervert you in your religion.' Charles then refers to the commands he had given him on this subject, and warns him against listening to his mother. Should he, however, turn Romanist, he 'must never,' he says, 'think to see England or me again ;' that ' all the mischief that may befall me, you will be responsible for ;' that his perversion will not only ruin the family, but also 'your King and country. Do not let them persuade you either by force or fair promises ; for the first they will neither dare nor will use, and for the second, as soon as they have perverted you they will have their end, and will care no more for you.' This remarkable letter ends thus : 'If you do not consider what I say to you, remember the last words of your dead father, which were, to be constant to your religion, and never to be shaken in it ; which if you do not observe, this shall be the last time you shall ever hear from, dear brother, your most affectionate brother, CHARLES R.'†

The same influence which had impressed Prince Henry, was also brought to bear upon his brother James. It was from his mother and her priests that his mind received the bent towards Roman Catholicism which led him eventually to sever his connection with the Church of England. In heart, he was, at the Restoration, already a Roman Catholic, though ' many weighty reasons at first obliged him to conceal that change from public view.'‡ Before the Restoration Charles never lost a chance of pretending to be a strong Protestant. When a deputation of Scotch ministers went to the Hague to congratulate him on the approaching Restoration, he arranged they should discover

---

* His mother's—Queen Henrietta's—confessor.
† Kennet's ' History of England.' vol. iii., p. 320.
‡ ' History of the Revolution,' by the Jesuit Orleans, p. 232.

him on his knees, thanking God that he was a 'covenanted'
King.* When he landed at Dover, the Mayor presented
him with a Bible, and, as he took it, he said solemnly that
' it was the thing he loved above all things in the world.'†
Indeed both brothers returned to England avowedly as
sound members of the Established Church. But in his
heart, Charles II. cared nothing for any religion, though
a sort of superstitious reverence for the 'ancient faith
of England' had been early implanted in him by his
French mother. He hated and despised the religion of
those who had murdered his father. The Puritan was
the standing joke of his court, and in his opinion ' Presby-
tery was not a religion for gentlemen.'‡ Roman Catholicism, on the other hand, with its doctrine of Divine Right,
was, he thought, the faith proper for all loyal courtiers
and men of breeding. The Catholics were so loyal, and
talked so pleasantly of that absolute authority for which he
longed, that he naturally felt himself drawn to them. On
the other hand, the Protestants lectured, and, still worse,
wearied him by their incessant attacks upon the Pope and
his followers, and especially upon his brother James, to
whom he was attached.

Charles was willing openly to join the Roman Catholic
Church, provided he could do so with safety to himself;
James put his religion before all earthly considerations.
For it, if necessary, he was prepared to die. Above all
things, he longed, with the proverbial zeal of the neophyte,
to see his Church restored to its former power and position
in England. In a letter to his daughter Mary, he gives
his reasons for leaving the Church of England.§ He
refers to himself as having been a keen Protestant, and
says—untruthfully beyond all doubt—that during his long

---

* Calamy states this on Oldmixon's authority.
† Pepys, 25, 5, 1660.
‡ Burnet, i., p. 184.
§ ' Lettres et Mémoires de Marie, Reine d'Angleterre,' edited by the
Countess Bentinck. La Haye. 1880.

foreign exile no priest had ever spoken to him on the subject of religion. The statement of Father Orleans, already quoted, is certainly opposed to this declaration. James did not openly avow his change of faith until 1672, although very soon after the Restoration he was generally regarded as the friend and advocate of English Catholics.* In his own memoirs, he says it was about the beginning of 1669 that he sent for the Jesuit, Father Simons, and told him he wished to join the Church of Rome. He wished to do so secretly for policy' sake, but he could not arrange matters with the Pope, and the Catholic party were too anxious to secure the King's brother as an openly avowed convert to consent to secrecy. Writing in 1679 from Brussels to his faithful servant, Lord Dartmouth, James says:

'And pray once for all never say anything to me againe of turning Protestant ; do not expect it, or flatter yourself that I shall ever be it. I never shall, and if occation were, I hope God would give me His grace to suffer death for the true Catholike religion as well as Banishment. What I have done, was not hastily, but upon mature consideration, and foreseeing all and more than has'yett happened to me, and did others enquire into the religion as I have done without prejudice, prepossession, or partial affection, they would be of the same mind in point of religion as I am.'†

Like most Protestants who join the Church of Rome, James fell completely under priestly influence. He failed to apprehend the Protestant instinct of the English people —their innate love of liberty, and their absolute hostility to his religion. It was universally felt that his zeal for the repeal of the Test Act was prompted by no regard for liberty of conscience, but rather by a desire to protect and favour the Romanists. His efforts to bring about the

---

* Pepys.
† Historical MSS.: The Earl of Dartmouth's Papers, eleventh report, appendix, p. 36.

repeal of that Act were especially unfortunate at a time when foreign Protestants were pouring into England to avoid the religious persecution with which all Roman Catholic rulers then pursued them. It was evident that it was not equality, but supremacy, that James sought to obtain for his newly adopted faith. He did nothing by halves, and on the point in question, displayed the usual earnestness of the proselyte. Like all men of weak character, he mistook obstinacy for firmness, and he set himself to resist what he described as the 'yielding temper which had proved so dangerous to his brother, and fatal to the King his father.'[*]

Such were the princes who ruled the Court in which Marlborough was educated, and such were the religions of those who composed it. Marlborough in early life was brought so much into contact with these royal brothers, that the scepticism of the one and bigotry of the other might conceivably have exercised much influence over his mind; but this was not so. The bigotry of James was certainly an important element in Marlborough's early career, but nothing could shake that great soldier's faith, which remained to the last as the sheet-anchor of his soul, sure and steadfast.

* Macpherson, vol. i., p. 152.

CHAPTER VIII.

THE COURT AND MORALS OF THE RESTORATION.

The women of the Court of Charles II.—The men drank and
gambled—The ingratitude of Charles.

Men and women are generally what they are taught to be
by the prevailing views, opinions, and aims of the society
in which they have been brought up, and in the midst of
which they live ; and in order to estimate fairly the moral
worth of man or woman of this time, we must measure it
by the standard of morality which then prevailed.

Katherine, the neglected Queen, ungainly in appearance
and commonplace in intellect, designedly surrounded herself with uncomely ladies. The Duchess of York, on the
other hand, strove to make her household remarkable for
beauty, brightness and engaging manners. Sir Peter Lely
has made us familiar with the beauties of Charles II.'s
court, ladies whose 'sleepy eye bespoke the melting soul,'
and whose charms were emphasized by the low-bodied
gown of the period. Anne Hyde was no beauty herself, but her bearing was good and her air distinguished.
She was sensible and endowed with plenty of natural
wit, which imparted a charm to her personality. She
wisely shut her eyes to the infidelities of her coarse-
minded husband, while the Queen loudly proclaimed
her wrongs, and irritated Charles by her bitter remon-
strances.

With the Restoration began a period of open licentious-

CHAPTER
VIII.
——
1670.

ness at the English Court unparalleled in any previous reign. Even the common, conventional and superficial decencies of civilized life were ignored there. Numbers of pretty women sought to charm and fascinate the King and the gallants who surrounded him. No statesman or man of business exercised any influence within that dissolute circle. Charles, devoted to his mother's country, and to everything French, brought home with him at the Restoration, the fashions, Court etiquette, and vices of Versailles. French profligacy soon became as fashionable in London as French lace or Parisian silk stockings. Card-play for high stakes became the everyday occupation of both sexes. In some of the Princess Anne's letters to Lady Churchill, she deplores her favourite's ill luck at cards. In one letter she states her own winnings at dice, the previous evening, to have been three hundred pounds; half of which, however, she lost the following morning. In another she says: 'I have played to-day, at Court, hand to hand with the Duchess of Portsmouth, and have won three-score pounds.'*

Modesty, the old outward sign of feminine virtue, was no longer reckoned an inward grace, and even regard for common decency was stigmatized as prudish. Chastity was held up to scorn, and faithless husbands made faithless wives. The outspoken Pepys says of the Court ladies: 'Few will venture upon them for wives. My Lady Castlemaine will in merriment say that her daughter (not above a year or two old) will be the first mayd in the Court that will be married.'

Men drank deeply, and quarrelled over their cups and cards. Street brawling and practical jokes, often ending in bloodshed, were the common amusements of the young men about town. The drinking encouraged at Court became the fashion amongst all classes. Men in society were esteemed in proportion to the quantity of liquor they could carry, and

* The games commonly played were 'ombre,' 'basset,' and 'thirty and forty.'

drunkenness in a gentleman was scarcely deemed a fault. This was indeed 'a mad, roaring time, full of extravagance, and no wonder it was so, when the men of affairs were almost perpetually drunk.'* We read of orgies at which the Lord Chancellor, the Lord Treasurer, and other dignitaries, drank themselves into a quarrelsome frenzy, and ended by stripping to their shirts.† We are told of a wedding-party where the Lord Chief Justice and another judge got drunk, and passed the evening in smoking and giving toasts.‡ The plays reflect, in their coarseness, the manners, morals, and language of the day. The perfect courtier was wittily described as 'a man not weighted by either honour or temper,' and the boon companions of Charles II., who swore and brawled and drank and gambled, fully answered that description.

In George Villiers, Duke of Buckingham, we have a good example of a popular and successful courtier of the period. He had been brought up with Charles and his brothers, and the habits, manners, and views of all of them were very similar. He scoffed at public opinion, and took pleasure in outraging all recognised decency. Volatile by disposition, he surrendered himself to every passing whim, mistaking 'profligacy for pleasure, and prodigality for magnificence.'§ He was witty, fond of literature, a gallant soldier, but entirely ignorant of all useful military knowledge. Above all things, he was a staunch and loyal Cavalier, firmly believing that the King could do no wrong. He cared nothing for sacred or spiritual things, though nominally a member of the Established Church of England.

Such were the intimates of the King, and yet so strong was the innate loyalty of his people, that nothing short of the obstinate folly of his bigoted brother could finally

---

* Burnet.   † Sir John Reresby, 1686.   ‡ Evelyn.

§ This saying was by Philip, Duke of Orleans, nephew of Lewis XIV., and afterwards Regent. He was, like his father, a truly vicious man in a vicious age. He scoffed at religion, but was a devout believer in astrology : 'A godless Regent trembling at a star.'

estrange it. The enthusiasm with which Charles was hailed at the Restoration, is partly accounted for by the fact, that England had grown weary of Cromwell's iron rule. Men did not forget that he was a usurper; and he never forgot it himself. Besides, the tragic death of Charles I. had thrown a glamour of romance over the royal House of Stewart, which served to stimulate the loyalty of men, and to captivate the sentiment and sympathy of women. Hence it was that Charles II. had been welcomed with every outward demonstration of joy. He was described, in contemporary verse, as:

> 'The first English born
> That has the crown of these three Kingdoms worn.' *

In an outburst of loyalty and of joy at their relief from the military despotism of Cromwell, the people freely gave to Charles nearly all the power they had sternly refused to his father. They did so without any formal pledge on his part that he would respect their political freedom. And having thus surrendered themselves, he repaid their generous trust by scheming to make over their souls to the Pope, and their bodies to the French King.

* Waller.

CHAPTER IX.

CHURCHILL SERVES IN TANGIER.

Tangier, and military service there—The garrison left in great want
—Marlborough returns home, and the place is finally abandoned.

To a handsome youth like John Churchill, the Court of
Charles II., though a hot-bed of temptation, must have
been also an Elysium of bliss. But to one of his temperament it was far from satisfying, for his ambition soared
above mere pleasure. Court amusements soon palled upon
him, and the daily routine of a subaltern's life in London
became irksome to his adventurous spirit. He longed to
distinguish himself in some other field than Whitehall, and
to excel in some occupation more noble than dancing.

Tangier had lately been added to the dominions of the
British Crown as part of Queen Katherine's dowry. It was
important as a place of arms against the pirates who infested
the Barbary coast, and as possessing the only harbour for
nine hundred miles on the Moorish shores of the Mediterranean. For some twenty years an English garrison was
kept there, and we then finally abandoned it for economical
reasons. Whilst our occupation lasted, it was to our officers,
what Egypt has lately been, a drill-ground for practical
soldiering. Men fired with the love of danger, and wearied
with the sham nothings which form so large a part of a
soldier's occupation in peace, found there some scope for
their daring and their military talents, and also learned
something of the meaning of real war. To Tangier our

young ensign accordingly went in search of adventure and distinction. The date of his going is somewhat uncertain, but it was most probably about the end of 1668 or the beginning of 1669. He served as a volunteer with the 'Governour's,' or, as it was often called, the '1st Tangier Regiment,' now known as 'The Queen's' or 'Royal West Surrey.'

The garrison usually consisted of four battalions of Foot and one strong troop of Horse, or about 3,100 men in all.* But when Churchill arrived, it had fallen to a total of only two battalions and one weak troop of Horse—in all, not more than 1,500 or 1,600 men.

History repeats itself constantly in our military annals. We are told periodically that our army is 'going to the dogs.' The Tangier papers contain many complaints in the same strain against the quality of the recruits sent to complete the establishment of the garrison, depleted by disease and death. We find the gentleman in charge of the guns, ammunition, etc., loud in his complaints of the uselessness of the gunners sent to him.

'The firemaster,' he reported, 'is certainly a most ignorant person as to the knowledge of any ingredient except brandy.'† In the following December Colonel P. Kirke, writing on the same subject, says: 'Of thirty-three gunners there is not ten knows the gun from the carriage, and now that Mr. Povey is gone, there is not two men in town understands the art of gunnery.'‡

---

* This troop of Horse was subsequently enlarged into a regiment of Mounted Infantry, then styled Dragoons. It is now a cavalry regiment, and known as 'The Royal Dragoons.'

† Historical MSS.: Dartmouth Papers, p. 61.

‡ Ibid., p. 72. Mr. Thomas Povey was ' Paymaster and Exchanger of Moneys,' as well as in command of the guns and munitions of war. He had been M.P. for Bossiney in 1658. To economize the number of sentinels at night, recourse was at one time had to watch-dogs, which were posted at some of the most exposed points. In one of the orders sent from home in 1664, we find the Governour urged to 'abolish as much as you can that national distinction of " English," " Irish," and " Scotch " ' amongst the soldiers.

Tangier was a troublesome and, what is worse, according to English opinion, an expensive possession. It entailed an annual drain upon the home exchequer of over £70,000, for which outlay England obtained no direct return.*

The affairs of the place were managed, or rather, jobbed, by the Tangier Committee, of which Pepys was a leading member. Money voted for Tangier was too frequently spent by the King on his own pleasures, and the garrison was in consequence often reduced to great straits both for money and provisions. Whilst Churchill was there, the soldiers were left for seven months, and later on, for nine, twelve, and even sixteen months without pay; they were overworked, and they more than once became mutinous. In 1665 the soldiers were reported to be dying from want of proper food.+ The sickness and mortality at last became a scandal, and alarmed those at home even in that age, when human life was little regarded, and when our soldiers were far less cared for than at present. Tangier was, however, useful to Charles and his brother in providing employment for some to whom they were indebted, and for others whom they wished out of the way. It was jocularly said to be to the King what a spendthrift had called his timber, 'an excrescence on the earth provided by God for the payment of debts.'‡

For the military reader it may be well to add, that having blown up the Mole we had nearly finished, we abandoned Tangier in 1684 as a useless and costly possession. The portions of the walls and other defences that are evidently

---

* 'History of the Queen's Regiment,' by Colonel Davis, p. 88.

† Pepys, the man of business, always on the look-out for opportunities to make money, is said to have realized a considerable amount by his contract for victualling this garrison. On 4, 6, 1672, there were 1,540 men in the garrison, when it was reported to the authorities at home that there was only enough biscuit left for eight weeks, beef for twenty-one weeks, whilst there was nine weeks' oatmeal due to the troops. In the following month the report was that they only had biscuit for three and beef for sixteen weeks.

‡ Pepys.

of British construction may still be distinguished, and the remains of English-built houses in the citadel still rear, as if in defiance, their high-pointed gables above the flat roofs of the Moorish dwellings around them. The place is but little changed since Churchill's day, as civilization and progress are still unwelcome visitors there, and even the presence of eleven Consuls has hitherto failed to combat its picturesque barbarism.

We know little of Churchill's doings at Tangier, beyond the fact that he was constantly engaged with the enemy. who closely invested the place. He took part in frequent sallies made by the garrison, and showed remarkable daring in numerous skirmishes with the Moors, whose enterprise often took the form of cutting off, by means of cleverly laid ambushes, those who ventured to straggle beyond the British lines. Churchill was thus able whilst still a boy to test his nerve, and to accustom himself to danger and to the curious sensation of being shot at. He returned home in the winter of 1670-71, and rejoined the household of the Duke of York.

BARBARA DUCHESS OF CLEVELAND

CHAPTER X.

JOHN CHURCHILL'S PERSONAL APPEARANCE.—HIS INTRIGUE
WITH THE DUCHESS OF CLEVELAND.

The character of Barbara Villiers—Churchill banished from Court as the
result of his intrigue with her—The prejudice of Swift and Macaulay
in their estimate of his character—The lessons we seek to learn
from the study of his career—His ambition He fights a duel His
business-like qualities.

THE portraits of John Churchill at this period of his life
represent him as strikingly handsome, with a profusion of
fair hair, strongly-marked well-shaped eyebrows, long
eyelashes, blue eyes, and refined and clearly-cut features.[*]
A wart on his right upper-lip, though large, did not de-
tract from his good looks.   He was tall, and his figure
was remarkably graceful, although a contemporary says:
'Il avait l'air trop indolent, et la taille trop effilée.'[†]
His bearing was noble and commanding, and one who
particularly disliked him tells us, that 'He possessed the
graces in the highest degree, not to say engrossed them.'
He adds, that his manner was irresistible either to man or
woman.[‡] The truth was, he knew how to be all things to
all men.   Kings, courtiers, and private soldiers alike were
captivated by his gentle demeanour, his winning grace.

* In the Duke of Buccleugh's collection there are two beautiful
miniatures of him as a very young man, a copy of one of which is
given in these volumes.
† De Grammont, 'Memoirs.'
‡ Chesterfield Letters.

He understood Court life thoroughly, 'caressed all people with a soft, obliging deportment, and was always ready to do good offices.'[*]

Such in appearance and manner was this gifted young soldier and courtier, who, bedecked with ruffles and point lace, waited in the ante-rooms of Whitehall. He soon became a general favourite with the ladies of the Court, of whom none was more fascinating than Barbara Palmer, better known as the Duchess of Cleveland, one of the King's many mistresses, appropriately called in the language of the day, 'the chargeable ladies about the Court.' She was second cousin to Marlborough's mother, and her husband had been recently created Earl of Castlemaine. Her portraits represent her as exquisitely beautiful, with the soft, almond-shaped eyes and languishing expression which Lely painted so well. 'Everything she did became her,' writes the susceptible Pepys. Depraved from early youth, she had for two or three years before her marriage carried on an intrigue with the Earl of Chesterfield. At the age of eighteen, she married Roger Palmer, a Roman Catholic of the Inner Temple, and son of a Middlesex knight, but within the first year of her married life she renewed her relations with her former lover. In the course of the same year she went to Holland with her husband, who was the bearer of a large present in money from the English Royalists to Charles II., and there began her intimacy with the King, by whom she had several children.

She was the most inconstant of women, and had lovers of all degrees, even whilst openly recognised as the King's mistress; but far from allowing him a corresponding privilege, she always pretended to be violently jealous of his attentions to other women. She was a gambler and a spendthrift, imperious in temper, and far from wise.[†] Her cousin, Mrs. Godfrey—sister of Marl-

CHAPTER
X.
1671.

Born 1643;
died 1709.

½ 1, 1659.

½ 12, 1661.

---

[*] Burnet, vol. iii., p. 267.
[†] In 1668 Charles purchased Berkshire House for her. It stood on

borough's mother—was the governess of her children by
the King, and is said to have designedly thrown her handsome nephew, John Churchill, in her way. The result
was, as anticipated by the lady, an immediate intrigue
between them. This affair became known to Charles
through the Duke of Buckingham, who had quarrelled
with Barbara Palmer, and wished to ruin her in the
King's favour.* Aware of her intimacy with Churchill,
he bribed her servant, and so contrived that the King
found the young guardsman in her bedroom. This was
too much even for the easy-going Charles. A scene
occurred, which has been variously described, and the
result was Churchill's temporary banishment from the
Court.† This intrigue must have begun shortly after
Churchill's return from Tangier, and it was renewed
annually during his winter visits to England throughout
the Dutch war, from 1672 to perhaps as late as 1676.

Those who, like Dean Swift and Lord Macaulay, bring
to their study of Marlborough's life a strong prejudice
against him, deal severely with this episode, and dwell
upon it with all the unction of the Pharisee. They make
no allowance for the temptations to which he was exposed,
for the thoughtlessness of youth, or for the character of

the site now occupied by Bridgewater House, the street leading to
which is still called Cleveland Row in her honour. Her ordinary
salary from Charles seems to have been about £14,000 a year, but she
obtained large sums from him besides. In the year 1682 she appears
to have received about £34,000. See Camden Society paper on Secret
Services of Charles and James.

* This George Villiers was born 30·1, 1627, and died 16 4, 1688.
He was the 'B' in the 'Cabal.'

† This story is told by De Grammont, and by Barillon, the French
Ambassador, in his letters to Lewis XIV. It is repeated with many
imaginary details by the scurrilous Mrs. Manley, in that 'jumble of
obscenity and falsehood,' the 'New Atalantis.' In referring to this
book, upon which Macaulay and other detractors of Marlborough rely
for many of their stories about him, Lord Campbell says: 'Swift, as a
slanderer of private character, is to be placed in the same category
with the author of it.'

the beautiful and depraved woman—so many years his
senior—who lured and tempted him. They affect to
regard his youthful indiscretion as a crime, to be judged
without mercy, and this appears all the more unjust,
when we consider that his subsequent career exhibits him
as the most faithful of husbands, the most moral of men.

No man's character should be judged by a bare record
of his early love affairs, whether they were innocent or
otherwise. Time, circumstance, opportunity, the nature
of the temptations experienced, the amount of moral
strength in the man, the power or weakness of his religious
convictions, and above all, his natural temperament, all
should be duly weighed before judgment can justly be
pronounced.

From the days of Moses to those of Napoleon the lives
of mighty men abound in useful moral lessons. But we
do not read their story in order that we may gloat over
those failings which attest their mortal origin, gratifying
though such a course might be to our own vanity. What
we want to know from the study of a great career is, what
the man was like, what was his mode of life and thought,
what motives guided and prompted him, and what convictions, what circumstances, influenced his conduct and
action? In his dealings with men and with nations, was
he actuated by self-interest, or by faith in God, by honour,
truth, justice, loyalty and patriotism? What did he do
for England? That is the measure by which all great
Englishmen must be measured. We seek to discover
the extent to which he directed or his genius influenced
the events which constituted the history of his time. Was
it the man who made the events, or the events which made
the man? Did he shape a course for history to follow,
after the manner of the great leaders of all ages? or was
he content, like the ordinary political leader of the present
day, to wait upon events and to manipulate them for his
own or his party's benefit? In calm weather a small man
may steer the ship of State safely through the rocks and

shoals which must always beset public life. But it is only the courageous and lofty spirits, such as Cromwell, Marl-borough, Washington, Napoleon and Pitt who can create the circumstances required for their own genius to work in. They alone can ride safely through the storms and upheavals which their policy necessarily occasions.

It is not to censure his amours, to despise him for his niggardliness, or to hate him for his double-dealing, that we wish to study Marlborough's character and to follow his career. We do so because we desire to learn the secret of his success, and to discover the motives of his actions. We wish to know how he so contrived to carry public opinion with him for nearly ten years, that he was able to direct our foreign policy, and to shape our history. Had he failed in this, not even his genius for war could have won for England that fore-most position in Europe to which he raised her. When the whole civilized world rang with his name, when kings and princes sought his advice and were proud to obey his orders, we still more want to know what was the spirit within him that urged him on. There must have been some strange power in the man who was able to endow his country with such power and influence whilst he ruled her and guided her destinies.

The intrigue of a young subaltern in the Foot Guards with the King's mistress was an event which made some stir in society, and was even deemed worthy of mention by the French Ambassador in his official despatches. It un-questionably had an influence upon Churchill's subsequent career, and further reference to it will be made in the chapters which deal with the Dutch war. One of his failings at this period, was a tendency to indiscretion in speech, which led him at times to talk of his intimacy with the Duchess of Cleveland; and although we are told, that, with her usual audacity, she took no trouble to correct him for doing so, it added to his difficulties with the King.*

* De Grammont's Memoirs.

This intrigue, however, was not to him what it would have been to most of those about the Court. Even at that early period of life Churchill allowed his passion neither to run away with his reason, nor to triumph over his better judgment. His dealings with women never took the form of reckless debauchery, and the cool, calculating side of his character seems to have saved him from becoming the slave of pleasure. Self-contained from early manhood, he began life with the determination to make a name for himself in the world. A craving for distinction has wrecked the careers of many second-rate men; but it is the ruling principle with most of the best as well as with many of the worst amongst us. Sages have denounced ambition as beneath the dignity of the true philosopher; holy men have condemned it as dangerous to the soul; and a great poet has pronounced it to be the last infirmity of a noble mind. We have, however, Shakespeare's authority for calling it 'the soldier's virtue,' and in Churchill's case, it assuredly was the tonic which saved him from that deterioration of mind and body which follows inevitably upon a life of idleness and luxury.

Duels were at this time of common occurrence, and few gentlemen who lived much in London were able to entirely avoid them. In these affairs of honour, the seconds fought as well as the principals. In the summer of 1671 Churchill fought with Captain Henry Herbert, afterwards Lord Herbert of Cherbury.[*] The cause of quarrel in this instance is unknown, but Herbert was apparently in the wrong, for the King and the Duke of York were both angry with him when the affair came to their ears. Young Churchill was twice run through the arm, he wounded his antagonist in the thigh, and the affair ended in Churchill being disarmed.[†]

---

* We read of a Captain Henry Herbert serving afterwards in France and Holland with Sir Harry Jones's Regiment of Horse, but it is not quite certain that this was the same man.

† Hatton, 'Correspondence,' vol. i., p. 66.

John Churchill had early chosen a military life as the career best calculated to afford him opportunities for distinction, and a wide field for his ambition. A seat in Parliament was always open to him, but it presented little attraction to the young soldier, who had no turn for politics. Personally attached at this time to his royal benefactor, he served James with zeal and loyalty, but had there been no other motive for this, his own interest alone would have dictated it. It soon became evident that Queen Katherine was not destined to become a mother, and the life of the King was known to be precarious. In the ordinary course of events, therefore, it was tolerably certain that his vigorous brother, James, must soon succeed to the throne. What a vista of ambition this prospect must have presented to Churchill! James was fond of him, and to be the King's favourite, in those times, meant power and wealth. To him it meant even more, for he knew it would afford him opportunities for the exercise of those powers which he already felt stirring within him.

During the reign of Charles he took little part in public affairs, never gave his advice unless asked for it, and always counselled moderation.* Wisdom alone would have prompted this line of conduct, and, in any case, the quality of his mind was more suited for the direction of foreign policy than for dealing with small questions of social and local interest. It was not that he lacked either method or business-like qualities, for the care he bestowed upon the minutiæ of camp discipline, upon the food and comfort of his soldiers, and upon the management of his slender means, are clear proofs of his aptitude for business.

* Burnet.

CHAPTER XI.

Death of Monk—Lewis XIV. determines to capture Holland—The first Dutch War—'Peace of Aix la Chapelle'—Marlborough's victories over France pave the way for the French Revolution—The wars between England and Holland—Treaty of Dover—The question of our flag in the narrow seas—Louise de Kéroualle becomes Mistress to Charles—England and France declare war against Holland.

UPON his return from Tangier, young Churchill rejoined the household of the Duke of York, and when not in waiting, did military duty as Lieutenant in the King's Company of the 1st or Royal Foot Guards. He attended with his Company at the funeral of 'Honest George,' Duke of Albemarle. That stout soldier and stern patriot, who had long been ailing, died in January, 1670, after many

a hard tussle with Death. He had been a trusted leader when England occupied a proud position of authority, and he had lived to see her hour of humiliation in which the Dutch fleet thundered at the very water-gate of the Kingdom. In him Charles II. lost a soldier who had given him his crown, and the people an honest patriot whom they had fully trusted.

Churchill was now to see active service in the Low Countries, destined, some thirty years later, to be the theatre of those great achievements with which his name will be for ever associated. The campaign which afforded him this opportunity, is known in history as the 'Second

Dutch War,' and had its origin in the ambition of
Lewis XIV.   The annexation of both Flanders and
Holland to France was one of the great aims of his life.
His first attempt upon these provinces was made in 1667,
when he suddenly marched an army of 50,000 men into
Flanders.   The people of Amsterdam had heard of the
recent victory of their old allies the French over their
enemies the Spaniards, with the utmost delight.   But
this feeling changed into one of dismay, when they realized
that the French frontier had been suddenly pushed forward
to their very doors.   The alarm soon spread over Europe.
In England the old national hatred of France was inflamed,
and fear was even felt for the great cause of religious liberty.
Dutch enterprise might interfere with our commerce, but
the rapidly growing power of France seemed to menace
our national independence.   The outcome of this apprehension, was the Peace of Breda between England and
Holland, and also the celebrated Triple Alliance between
Holland, Sweden and England.   The Catholic no less than
the Protestant States determined to thwart the growing
pretensions of the French King, and he found arrayed
against him a force before which, without allies, he felt
he must bend.   It was a cruel blow to his insatiable
ambition, but under the circumstances, peace was a necessity, and the Treaty of 'Aix la Chapelle,' was concluded 2, 5. 1668.
between France and Holland.   In his heart, however,
Lewis only regarded this peace as a truce that would
enable him to prepare the better for another Dutch war
on a far larger scale.

The struggle so begun in 1667, was not really brought
to an end until the battle of Waterloo, but when it had
lasted for a period of forty-six years, the Peace of Utrecht
secured a long lull in this stupendous conflict.   It was in
the last ten years preceding this celebrated peace, that
Marlborough won for himself his imperishable renown.

It is interesting to trace how surely the disasters which
befell France in Queen Anne's reign, led, step by step,

to those scenes of rapine and bloodshed which, nearly a century later, culminated in the destruction of the Bourbon dynasty. France under her old race of kings, never recovered from the blows dealt her by Marlborough. The series of wars waged by Lewis from 1667 to 1713 against the Dutch and their allies exhausted France quite as much as did the subsequent wars of Napoleon. So great, in France, became the demand for soldiers during the early years of the eighteenth century, that in many localities the fields were left untilled, and whole districts passed out of cultivation. The very life of the nation was sacrificed to the inordinate ambition or the selfish carelessness of its Kings, until at last the people could stand it no longer. The down-trodden population of an exhausted country, a people deprived of every right that is the natural inheritance of civilized man, rose at last in desperation. Their fury knew no bounds, and, in the cruel fashion of mobs, they swept from France everything that could recall a system and institutions which had at once ruined and degraded them.

Between the English and the Dutch, there had been many wars in the sixteenth century, in which the ostensible cause of quarrel was often little more than the haughty demand of England that the ships of all nations meeting British men-of-war in the Channel, should lower their flags, and in some instances, their topsails, in recognition of the ancient right which England claimed as mistress of the 'Narrow Seas.' But these wars really sprang from the commercial rivalry of the two great maritime nations, and from their respective efforts to secure the monopoly of the Indian trade. Lewis XIV. had always watched with extreme satisfaction these wars for naval supremacy between the two great Protestant Powers. Every ship sunk on either side, was, he felt, a gain to the French navy. Holland for her part was wont to regard France as her best friend, and she continued to do so until the first Dutch war opened her eyes to the true nature of Lewis's intentions.

Although thus forced to make peace, Lewis at once began to prepare for a renewal of the struggle, fully determined, when all was ready, to choose an auspicious moment for the recommencement of hostilities. In the meantime he sought to strengthen himself all round by treaties with his neighbours, bribing some with money, and all with promises. England, with her impecunious King, was of course easily dealt with. Charles wanted money for his mistresses, Lewis wanted the alliance of England to help him in his intended conquest of Holland. To complete the bargain, Lewis sent his sister-in-law, Henrietta, Duchess of Orleans, to England, to arrange details with her brother Charles II. They met at Dover, where a treaty called after that place was soon arranged between them. For a lump sum down, and a liberal annuity as long as the war against Holland should last, Charles agreed to declare war against the Dutch, and to furnish a contingent to help Lewis. Poor England! Plague, pestilence, fire, and famine had already sapped her strength, and now the unworthy Sovereign she had recalled from exile, sold her honour and her interests for gold! Only ten years before thousands of loyal subjects had flocked to welcome their King as he landed at the very spot where he now betrayed them. Crowds of men and women had lined the beach and cliffs of Dover to greet him with shouts of joy, and this was the return he made them for their warm-hearted welcome!

Lewis XIV. was an adept in the art of bribery. All through his long reign he expended great sums on the purchase of ministers and princes whose co-operation he required at the moment. At the beginning of the 'second Dutch war,' he bought up the active support, or at least the neutrality, of those rulers who, from dread of his rapidly-increasing power, might have been inclined to side with Holland. Charles, as already mentioned, was one of those so bribed, but in his dealings with him, Lewis was under no delusions. Although he had bought the King, he well knew that Charles and the Roman Catholics about the Court were the only allies he could count upon in England, and that the English hated him, his policy, and his country. Charles had recently told Colbert that he himself was the only friend to France in all England, and that his subjects preferred even Spain.* Lewis could not hope to secure more than the neutrality of this freedom-loving people by bribing their ignoble King, and he soon found it necessary, in dealing with a nation so full of insular prejudices, to meddle as little as possible in their home affairs. They passionately resented any interference from without in their internal administration, though few concerned themselves about foreign affairs. In order to keep Charles up to his engagements, Lewis thought it desirable to provide him with a new mistress, a Frenchwoman, entirely devoted to French interests. For this position he selected pretty Louise de Kéroualle—for years afterwards known to Londoners as 'Madam Carwell.' She belonged to an old Breton family, had been for some time about the Court of Versailles, and now came to England, nominally as Lady-in-waiting to the Duchess of Orleans, but in reality for the purpose of captivating the fancy of Charles. He fell a victim to her winning ways, and she soon succeeded to all the power and influence which Barbara Palmer had previously exercised. For nearly fifteen years, Lewis XIV. may be said to have directed the foreign policy of England through her. The wretched creatures who were ministers under Charles II. were bribed through her agency to subordinate British interests to the territorial aggrandisement of France. She was created Duchess of Portsmouth, and largely pensioned by her royal lover.†

* Dalrymple, vol. i., p. 104.

† The author of 'Hudibras' thus refers to the King's selection of a new queen of the harem:

'Takes a gay Tit from France to mount,
The cast-off of a Paris Count,
With apple-face and slender *waste*,
All over jilt, but looking chaste.'

In the winter of 1671-72, Lewis XIV. at last felt himself strong enough to carry out his deep-laid plans for the destruction of Holland, as agreed upon with Charles II. His preparations had been carried on very quietly, and all was now ready for this infamous undertaking. The terms agreed upon in the Treaty of Dover were confirmed in another written compact of February, 1672. England and France were simultaneously to declare war with Holland, and to act in concert, neither Power to make peace without the other's consent. The English claim to supremacy at sea was to be openly recognised by Lewis, and every vessel in the French navy was to strike her flag whenever she met an English ship of war. The fleets of the two nations were to act together under the orders of the Duke of York, or of any other British admiral whom Charles might select. England was to furnish for service in Flanders a contingent of 6,000 troops under an English general, who was to obey the orders of the French Commander-in-Chief in the field. He was, however, to be senior to all other French generals employed there. As long as the war lasted, Lewis was to pay all the expenses connected with this contingent, and to allow Charles an annual stipend of £240,000, besides paying him £200,000 down—half when the war began, the remainder some months afterwards.

It had been the intention of Lewis and Charles to declare war with Holland as early in 1672 as the weather would admit of field operations in the Low Countries. Before doing so, it was for every reason desirable that England should be represented at the Hague by a man prepared to do the bidding of the despicable clique who then ruled England. It did not suit their purpose that the high-minded and upright statesman, Sir William Temple, should remain there as Minister. He was consequently recalled, and Sir George Downing, Bart., 'a rougher hand,' was sent to replace him towards the end of 1671.* Still earlier in the

* Ralph.

year, Mr. H. Coventry had been sent to Sweden to announce officially, that England had withdrawn from the 'Triple Alliance.'*

Even in the seventeenth century, it was considered a breach of international decorum to declare war without at least some alleged cause of quarrel. Our grievances against Holland were of the flimsiest nature. The East India Company had some undefined claims for the detention of English subjects—detained with their own consent—in Surinam, after that country had been ceded to Holland. This, and the old dispute about the 'honour of our flag,' which we paraded whenever we wanted a pretext for complaint or quarrel, were practically our only grievances, and these Sir G. Downing was ordered to urge at the Hague in an unfriendly spirit.

It was alleged that the Dutch fleet had not 'vailed bonnet' to a royal yacht, the *Merlin*, which had been sent the previous autumn to bring home from Holland the Ambassador's wife, when Sir William Temple was recalled. But, in order to cook up this grievance against Holland, her captain had been specially ordered to sail through the Dutch fleet, and open fire on all ships that did not at once strike topsails to his flag. This he did upon his return voyage, and so great was then the national vanity on the point, that his conduct was generally approved. To heighten the national feeling, he was sent to the Tower on reaching London 'for not having sufficiently asserted his right.'+

The honour of our flag in the English Channel had been from time immemorial a recognised article of English national faith.‡ The 19th clause of the Treaty of Breda

---

* It was Mr. H. Coventry who, with Lord Holles, concluded the Treaty of Breda with Holland in 1667, after our naval humiliation that year.

† Lord Arlington's letter of 7, 9, 1671.

‡ Admiral Lord William Howard in 1554, Sir John Hawkins in 1597, Sir William Monson in 1604, Sir Thomas Mansell in 1620, and Blake in 1652, had all at different times opened fire upon French or

prescribed the honours which Dutch ships should pay to the
King's flag, and in the treaty with Holland of 1674, the
limits within which these compliments were to be paid, were
defined as 'from Cape Finistère to the middle point of the
land Van Staten, in Norway.' Many a sea-battle originated
in the exaction of this proud claim, and much blood was
shed in its peremptory enforcement, but it gave us a weighty
influence amongst nations, and blood has often flowed in a
cause of less national concern.

When our grievances against Holland were formulated
in Council, one of those present remarked, that the Dutch
would tear Sir G. Downing to pieces if he dared to urge
them, but the King, who was present, cynically remarked,
'Well, I'll venture him.'* As predicted, the Dutch were
very naturally incensed by the flimsy nature of our alleged
grievances, and furious at the manner in which Downing
pressed them, so much so that he became alarmed for his
personal safety, and fled from the Hague without waiting
for an answer.†

The frivolous complaints preferred by Sir G. Downing at
the Hague were reiterated by Charles in his declaration of
war. Louis XIV. scarcely condescended to give any reasons
for declaring war beyond telling the world that he 'was
dissatisfied with the Dutch.' His conduct in this matter
was perhaps more dignified than that of his ally, although
his explanation was equally insulting to Holland. These
declarations of war recall the wolf's complaint against
the lamb, in the well-known fable. Lewis complained of
Dutch insolence, and especially of a medal struck imme-

Dutch ships, because they failed to pay our flag the compliments we
then claimed and insisted upon.

* He had been Cromwell's Ambassador at the Hague. His home
was East Hatley, Cambridgeshire.

† Sir C. Lyttleton in a letter of 12. 2, 167½ says: 'Sir G. Downing is
in the Tower for coming away in so much haste, and contrary to the
King's direct orders to him under his own hand. It is believed he was
afraid the people would attempt upon him.'

diately after the Peace of Aix-la-Chapelle, on which Holland was represented as victorious, with a legend stating that she had 'secured the laws, reformed religion, assisted, defended and reconciled Kings, vindicated the liberties of the ocean, and established the tranquillity of all Europe.' This pardonable outburst of Republican braggadocio was, in the main, fairly true, but it was declared by Lewis to be an insult to him and to France, which nothing but war could wipe out. At the same time Lewis pretended to the Pope that the war was intended to further the interests of the Catholic Church.

'No clap of thunder in a fair, frosty night could more astonish the world than ' did this declaration of war by England and France.* No one in Holland believed that we really meant war until our attack upon the Smyrna fleet, with which very doubtful operation we opened the campaign. The Prince of Orange and his party were for compliance with the English demands, in order to split up the alliance between Charles and Lewis, and with a view to unite the two Protestant powers of England and Holland. against the ambition of Lewis. On the other hand, the Republican party, under the De Witts, wished for an alliance with France, and recommended abject submission to the demands of Lewis. They disowned the offending medal, and broke up the die. Holland, thus divided, was well nicknamed the ' Disunited Provinces.'

* Page 17 of Sir W. Temple's Memoirs (1 vol., 1700).

CHAPTER XII.

THE CHARACTER, AIMS, AND AMBITIONS OF LEWIS XIV.

Lewis as a statesman and a soldier—He longs to annex Holland and by doing so to destroy a dangerous hotbed of Protestantism and liberty—Revocation of the Edict of Nantes.

For this second Dutch war a magnificent army, thoroughly organized and well furnished with every appliance of the day, had been provided. The preparations had extended over four years, and no expense was spared to make them complete. Lewis XIV. was not remarkable for military genius, but as a King, history readily accords him the title of 'Great.' His ideas were grandly conceived, and his aspirations were lofty. His aim was to make France the greatest Power in the world, and her capital the greatest of all cities. He loved to adorn it with palaces, splendid buildings, and museums, and to enrich his libraries and institutes with rare books, pictures, and works of art. He was statesman enough to provide himself with an army and navy sufficiently strong to defend this accumulated wealth against all possible enemies, for he knew enough of history to be well aware that amassed riches constitute a danger rather than a strength to the country which neglects to provide for their effective protection. His title to the Crown was undisputed, and he controlled the destinies of France as completely as Napoleon did in the day of his glory. An absolute monarch, he had a large revenue at his disposal, and splendid troops and ships to do his bidding. Endowed with great natural talents, his industry was untiring. His clear judgment made itself felt in every department of the State, whilst art, science and literature flourished under his immediate protection. A sincere and ardent Roman Catholic, he believed himself to be the instrument designed by God to root out heresy from the earth, whilst a boundless ambition urged him to attempt the imposition of his despotic will upon Europe. Of these two aims the latter was, however, the nearer his heart, and it was he who first gave shape and reality to that longing for the Rhine as a frontier, which subsequently became a recognised article of French faith.* His ambition was to emulate Charles the Great, and to unite under his sway all the civilized States of Europe. The imperial crown was to be joined to the crowns of Spain and France, and the Mediterranean was to be converted into a French lake. His territorial greed was insatiable, and he may be said to have originated the policy which Napoleon adopted, of making France great by the absorption of neighbouring provinces. The weakness of Spain seemed to invite him to add Flanders and Holland to his dominions. Spain was no longer to be dreaded : she had ceased to be an effective force in Europe, and had become little more than a geographical name. Her splendid infantry, but yesterday the terror of her enemies and the admiration of all nations, was no more, and her commerce had waned and disappeared with her fighting strength. Her King was weak both in mind and body, and Lewis, knowing that he could not live long, wished to have everything ready for the occupation of the Spanish Netherlands whenever his death should take

---

* As a sentiment, however, this longing for the Rhine frontier may be said to date back to Philip the Fair. It was Richelieu who devised the scheme of making France the mistress of the world, and the recognised centre of all learning and cultivation. This aim was adopted by Mazarin, and became the corner-stone of Lewis XIV.'s political system.

place. The previous possession of Holland would greatly
facilitate this operation, and hence the anxiety of Lewis to
effect its early conquest.

But the acquisition of Holland was not an object which
met with universal approval in France. Ministers warned
Lewis that the destruction of Holland would mean the
aggrandizement of England's naval power and commercial
wealth—in fact, the transfer of trade from the Scheldt to
the Thames. This argument, however, had little weight
with Lewis. He knew too well how completely Charles
and James relied upon him for money to render them independent of the Parliament they hated. Charles could
look to no other quarter for help, since Parliament would
only vote money for specified objects, on conditions which
both brothers deemed derogatory to the dignity of an
English King. James, the heir to the Throne, with all the
zealous hurry of a recent convert, was burning to restore
the Roman Catholic worship in all its ancient splendour,
and it was from France alone that aid could be expected in
such a cause. Lewis was therefore justified in his calculation, that come what might, he could reckon upon
Charles II. At his own back, was the compact power
of France—then the greatest and richest of European
kingdoms—and he could see no reason why his ambitious
aspirations should not be fully realized, as indeed they
surely might have been, but for William III. and John
Churchill.

Apart from his craving for territory, Lewis longed to
destroy the Dutch hotbed of Protestantism and liberty. He
believed that the existence, and still more the prosperity,
of this heretical republic, was a dangerous example to the
subjects of all kingdoms. Protestantism implied liberty of
conscience and the civil rights of man, as opposed to the
absolute will of an hereditary King. In Holland and in
England, where it had taken firm root, there had grown
up a spirit of political independence which taught men to
realize that they too had rights as well as the princes,

bishops, and nobles in whom power and privilege had hitherto been exclusively vested. When therefore the United Provinces presumed to incite other States to adopt their views upon civil and religious liberty, it is easy to understand how hateful Holland and her institutions became to a despot of Lewis XIV.'s aims and temperament. The conquest of Holland was, therefore, doubly necessary to his aims. It would not only open the door for him into the Spanish Netherlands, but it would enable him to eradicate this pernicious religion.

Lewis XIV. was absolutely unscrupulous, and regarded neither home law nor foreign treaties. Punctilious in all matters of etiquette, he loved to pose as the central figure in his superb Court, but truth, honour, and justice found no place in his home policy or dealings with foreign nations. As with the powerful rulers of all epochs, he only regarded treaties as binding when it suited him to respect them.

As a ruler, he thought he could do no wrong. He believed that the hearts and thoughts of Kings by Divine right, were under the special guidance of Him who made them, and that it was sinful in a subject to resist the will of his Sovereign Lord. Courtiers, whose property and lives were in his hands, accorded him a reverence more suited to a deity than to a mortal. By nature vain, and through habit fond of flattery, they played upon his weaknesses, and confirmed him in the belief that his power came from above, and that he was not as others are. That a man so educated should have been able to make France what he made her, is a strong proof of his ability.

The most foolish as well as the most wicked act of his reign, was the revocation of the Edict of Nantes, which amounted to a declaration of war against every Protestant State, and against every Protestant man, woman, and child. It was the turning-point in his reign. Thenceforward his successes became fewer and fewer, and what was worse, the victories he did win, no longer strengthened his power or increased his fame. France grew poorer and poorer without any compensation for the privations of her people; and when, at the beginning of Queen Anne's reign, Marlborough took the field against her and her only ally, Bavaria, Lewis drank the cup of failure and humiliation to the dregs.

CHAPTER XIII.

THE FRENCH ARMY OF 1672.

Lewis a great Army Reformer—General Martinet—Louvois—Organization of all civilized armies then—Strategy—Crime.

IN one respect at least, Lewis XIV. resembled the great
soldiers of every age—he was an army reformer. His
keen instinct taught him that the army opposed to reform
must fall behind in the race for fighting efficiency, and he
was quick to take advantage of all the inventions of the
day which in any way affected the implements or methods
of warfare. Whatever science could do to improve the arms
and equipment of soldiers, he adopted with alacrity. He
did not shrink from new ideas or new inventions, because
they had not been taken up by some rival nation. He
was wise enough to act in accordance with the advice
of experienced generals, and to recognise, that among the
privileges of royal birth, a knowledge of war is not
necessarily included. He never carried his royal infalli-
bility into such matters, nor did he presume to override the
opinions of real soldiers experienced in the field, and the
result was, that his army was dressed, equipped, drilled, and
trained in accordance with the most advanced military views
of his day. He possessed that gift rare in kings, the common-
sense to understand that courtiers flatter. When they told
him that he, being a Prince, must know how armies should
be organized and how soldiers should be drilled and trained
better than Turenne or Villars he knew that they lied.

But Lewis, although not a great soldier, was a great man. Long practice at peace reviews and military displays had made him a first-rate authority on all the theatrical side of an army, but he did not therefore conclude that he was competent to advise about war, or the organization of an army for war. He habitually sought and acted upon the advice of experts, whether in matters of science, of civil government, or of war; and as we shall see later on, when upon one occasion he was over-persuaded to run counter to the advice of his experienced generals, failure was the result.

He often made mistakes, but he had the rare merit of not fearing to employ able men. Vanity and a deliberately-adopted policy, caused him to claim for himself the credit of every great success achieved by his army. To make his people believe that all victory emanated from himself, tended, he thought, to magnify the dignity of his kingly office. This love of false glory, though foolish, did no harm to his country, for he strove to avoid the crime of committing the fortunes of France and the lives of her soldiers to incompetent hands. Despots like Napoleon are prone to surround themselves with mediocrities, for they fear to create rivals for popular applause. But a wise hereditary sovereign has no reason for any such fear, and can afford to employ the best material he can find.

The troops of France were at this time the finest in Europe, and her frontiers bristled with fortresses, the creation of the first engineer of his age, the modest and loyal Vauban. Whilst preparing for the invasion of Holland, the ablest officers of Lewis, men of tried war-experience in Hungary, Flanders, and Portugal, were hard at work with the drill and instruction of the troops. A new and well-ordered mobility and a facility of manœuvre was taught, whilst a greater precision in the performance of military duties was strictly enforced. Discipline was brought to a high state of perfection. The instruction of the infantry was intrusted to General Martinet, whose name is still a synonym for unrelenting strictness in the punctual performance of all duties, no matter how small and apparently unimportant.*

Until Lewis reformed his army, there was little discipline amongst the superior officers. This he was determined to correct, and when the three marshals, De Bellefond, De Créqui and d'Humières refused to serve under Turenne because he was not a member of the Royal Family, he promptly dismissed them from the army.† By degrees, he taught his officers to attach more importance to military rank and to military efficiency, than to birth, and in these and other reforms he was ably served by his great bullying bourgeois minister. It was really Louvois who compelled the nobles in the army to submit to the same discipline as officers of inferior birth, and it is related of him, that on remonstrating with a nobleman about the unsatisfactory state of his company, he said, ' When one is an officer, it is necessary to take a decided line, sir. You must either declare yourself a courtier or apply yourself to your duty !'‡ Birth had then, as property has now, ' its duties as well as its rights.'

In the field, the King made it a point to take especial notice of all meritorious officers, no matter how humble their origin. In fact, he was the first to recognise and encourage the 'professional soldier.' His generals were consequently the ablest in Europe, and his army was excellent in all respects. Such a power in such hands may well have inspired the dream of making France the dominant Power in Europe.

---

* It was Martinet who replaced the pike with the bayonet. This new weapon had a wooden handle which fitted into the muzzle of the musket. The first regiment to receive the bayonet was ' le regiment de Fusiliers créé en 1671 appelé depuis Regiment Royal d'Artillerie.' In this second Dutch war he introduced the use of copper pontoons. He was killed at the siege of Doesburg in 1672.

† After an interval of about six months, when they had eaten well of humble pie, the King forgave them and restored them to their former position in the army.

‡ Madame de Staël.

Among other reforms, Lewis clothed his army in uniform. He began this at first only with his Guards in 1665, but he soon afterwards applied the system to all regiments. Before that date, the captains clothed their own troops and companies. Strange to say, with the exception of the wigs worn by officers, the dress of some European armies in the seventeenth and in the early part of the eighteenth century, was better suited for the work soldiers have to do, than it is at the present moment. Frederick the Great's absurd ideas of what soldiers should look like on parade, have been the curse of armies ever since.

The organization of European armies at this time was as follows: A regiment of Horse consisted generally of two or three squadrons of three troops each, and each troop had a captain, a lieutenant, a cornet, and about fifty troopers of all grades mounted on big, clumsy 'war-horses.' In the Dragoons—the Mounted Infantry of to-day—the regiment had four squadrons of similar strength, but their horses were small and light—seldom above fourteen and a half hands high. Every cavalry and infantry regiment had a colonel, a lieutenant-colonel, and a major. Mounted troops fought in three ranks. Their defensive armour consisted of a back and breast piece, and a pot-helmet, but about fifteen years later these were mostly laid aside. The infantry battalion was usually divided into from ten to seventeen companies of fifty men each, one company being grenadiers. Each company had a captain, a lieutenant, and an ensign. The grenadiers carried grenades and a short musket, called a fusil. The other companies consisted each of about thirty matchlockmen, twelve pikemen, and four men armed with the fusil, and a bayonet which in shape and size corresponded with the dagger-bayonet of our new magazine rifle, except that its wooden handle fitted into the muzzle.* Every infantry soldier wore a sword, suspended to a broad buff-leather belt, to which

---

* In the 'Dictionaire Etymologique, à Paris, 1694,' is as follows: 'Baionnette. Sort de Poignard : ainsi appelé de la ville de Baïonne.'

also, for all men with fire-arms, were fastened little cylinders of wood or tin, each containing a cartridge. The infantry fought six deep, with the pikemen in the centre and the musketeers, or matchlockmen, on the flanks. The pikeman was equipped with an iron pot-helmet, a gorget, and breast and back piece; his pike, exclusive of the steel head, measuring sixteen feet long.

Holland and Flanders, then the battlefield of Europe, abounded in strong places. Almost all that was known of strategy, was gathered from the practice of war in the Low Countries, where campaigns consisted of little more than sieges, the passage of canals and rivers, the construction and occupation of fortified positions, and endless marches and counter-marches. Although it was the rule to make war support war,* still, it was considered necessary in an enemy's country to establish magazines of provisions within the zone of operations, and when an army was pushed beyond any such zone, further supplies were collected and fresh magazines formed. No army, as a rule, dared to cut itself off from its magazines, and such an operation as Marlborough's march into the heart of Bavaria in 1704, was an unheard-of enterprise. Biscuit, as a ration instead of bread, had not come into use, and the system of exacting contributions from a country in proportion to its agricultural resources, now so well understood, was then unknown. Armies were either fed from magazines of provisions, or lived chiefly on plunder. Woe betide the province through which a hostile army passed. The horrors of war were real indeed, and the records of black deeds too often perpetrated by men in search of food, may well make us shudder.

Crime has only too frequently accompanied armies in the field, and the foreign soldier in particular has seldom shown much respect for the feelings or property of the invaded. But it does not become us to throw stones at our neigh-

---

* An expression that originated with Julius Cæsar, and not with Napoleon, as is so commonly imagined.

bours on this score, for although the British soldier is
usually humane and merciful, still, upon some memorable
occasions, he behaved infamously to the people of captured
towns in the Peninsula. British generals, too, have been
compelled in certain instances, as an urgent matter of
military policy, to lay waste whole districts, to burn villages,
and to snatch all means of subsistence from their inhabitants.* We are given to thanking God with great
unction that we pay for everything we take, and that we do
not live upon an invaded country as other nations do. The
fact is, that it answers better to pay for all we want, as
by doing so we obtain it more easily and expeditiously; but
wherever this system of paying for supplies has failed, our
commanders in the field have never hesitated to take them
by force. No prejudices on this score ever affected men
like Cromwell, Marlborough, or Wellington.

The armies of Lewis XIV. acted upon the system which
was and is common in war—they took what they wanted.
The difference between his time and ours is, that, as a
rule, the supplies are now taken upon a well-understood
system, through the agency of the enemy's local authorities,
whilst formerly, individuals took very much what they
required, and in so doing, often destroyed more than they
obtained.

It may be said that Marlborough was the first General
of the Lewis XIV. period who reduced the commissariat
service to a regular system. It was, however, a common
thing, at the opening of a campaign, to enter into regular
stipulations, or treaties, as to the districts which were to be
recognised as at the disposal of each side for purposes of
contributions. The manner in which the parties sent to
levy them should behave was clearly defined by written
agreement, and it was usually stipulated that, 'No body of
men, under a certain number, were to advance into their
enemy's country beyond the limits agreed upon, under the

* The French ravaged the Palatinate in 1674, and again in 1689.
Marlborough ravaged Bavaria in 1704.

penalty of being treated as freebooters.' By such steps
many disorders and enormities were prevented.*

Those who wish to understand the strategy of this period
should study the campaign of 1691 in Flanders. It is a
fair example of the formal and cautious strategy of the
time. The wars of those days were wars of sieges rather
than of battles. The investment of a place implied carefully constructed lines of circumvallation and contravallation,
as in the days of Cæsar. Commanders loved to surround
themselves in the open country with great continued lines,
designed to defend some frontier or to bar the progress of
an adversary. A battle was seldom more than an incident
in the attack or defence of a fortress, or of some long line
of field-works.

This was the period immediately preceding that in which
the genius of Turenne's great pupil infused new life, energy,
and concentrated direction into military operations. The
movements of William and of Luxembourg in 1691 illustrate
how a nation's money could be squandered in projects
which led to no decisive result; how a people could be impoverished to no purpose by generals wanting that true fire,
that natural instinct, which rises above the rules of the
military theorist. It was the day of the drill-sergeant and
the formalist, when war was a methodical, but costly,
game, of which the rules could be learnt from books.
Roads were improvised across country to enable armies to
move mathematically in columns at carefully regulated
intervals from one position to another, often not more than
five, six, or eight miles distant. Each side gave 'check' in
turn, or by clumsy expedients and countermoves sought to
secure what was deemed to be a strategic advantage in
these slow and ponderous manœuvres. From first to last
in the campaign of 1691 there was not one spark of
military genius. What havoc would Marlborough, Frederick,
Napoleon, or Wellington have made had any one of them
commanded on either side !

* Vattel. p. 366.

In subsequent campaigns, Marlborough may well have chafed when compelled to serve under the Kurfursts, Margraves, Landgraves, Herzogs, and other Erlauchts and Durchlauchts, their sons and their nephews, who by right of birth held command in the allied armies of the period; but, indeed, many a military genius has since then smarted and endured in a somewhat similar position, and States have had to suffer in consequence. Many of these right gallant princes mistook, as their descendants still at times mistake, the theatrical properties and the 'stage business' of an army for real warfare. Their Highnesses of Waldeck and Vandemont, of Nassau Saarbruck and Nassau Friesland, of Wurtemburg and Pumpernickel, all good fighting soldiers, believed that they were endowed with the genius of command because they were princes.* How must sorrow and amusement in turn have possessed Marlborough when compelled to listen with respectful gravity whilst their Serenities laid down the law to him upon strategy and tactics! What gall and wormwood it must have been to a soldier of his stamp to find himself serving as a subordinate to a 'wooden-headed' courtier like Bentinck!

The military punishments of the day were not only severe, but cruel. When the allied army was encamped at Cour, south of the Sambre, a French incendiary was caught in the act of attempting to blow up the powder in the artillery park. He was tried by court-martial, and sentenced to have his right hand cut off and burnt before him, and then to be burnt alive himself. This inhuman sentence was duly carried out, and the reverend chaplain who describes the execution refers to it as 'the punishment he deserved.'† Such was the custom of war in those days.

---

* To the English ear the titles and position of some of these German Serene Highnesses sound curious. When the Treaty of Vienna decided the contingents to be furnished by these potentates, one, 'Reuss-Schleiss-Lobenstein,' was to supply twenty soldiers . . . to the army of the Bunde.'

† D'Auvergne's 'History of 1691 Campaign,' pp. 116 and 123. Carlton in his memoirs mentions this also.

The treatment of prisoners-of-war is well described by Mrs. Davies, the woman soldier who served so long in Flanders under Marlborough. Having fallen into the hands of the French during a skirmish in 1694, she says that the English prisoners were well treated, because the wife of James II. took a deep interest in them. They had clean straw every night to lie on, and each man was given five farthings a day for tobacco, a pound of bread, and a pint of wine, and all were allowed to retain their own clothes. But the poor Dutch prisoners had nothing beyond half a pound of bread per diem, and were kept 'almost naked in filthy dark prisons without other support.'*

On the sea also little regard was shown for human life. The English claim to sovereignty over the waters of the English Channel was stoutly maintained during this reign, and gave rise to many bloody encounters. In 1694 Sir Cloudesley Shovel found in the Downs a Danish man-of-war which omitted to strike her flag to his, as in custom bound to do. He reports that, having ordered her captain three times to do so without effect, he directed the *Stirling Castle* to bear down upon her, and compel her obedience. This was done by pouring a broadside into the Dane, who returned the fire and then 'quickly struck his flag.' But 'there were several dead and wounded on both sides.'†

In 1672 the French frontier on the side of the Low Countries was protected by the fortresses of Dunkirke, Bergues, Lille, Courtray, Oudenarde, Ath, Tournay, Douay, Charleroi, Philippeville, and Rocroi. Early in that year, under the cover of these places, a large French army was collected on the river Sambre, near Charleroi. Including the contingents furnished by the Elector of Cologne and the Bishop of Münster, the army numbered nearly 140,000 fighting men, and it was well supplied with artillery and bridge equipment. In name, Lewis was the Commander-in-Chief, but in fact, the operations were directed by Turenne

---

* 'Life and Adventures of Mrs. C. Davies.' p. 25.

† Lexington Papers. Report dated from the *Neptune*. ⁴¹ 8, 1694.

and Condé, with Luxembourg as a subordinate, whilst Vauban conducted the sieges.

Pierre de Groot, the Dutch Ambassador in Paris, soon discovered the intentions of the French King, and the purpose for which he had collected this large army. He believed all opposition to be so hopeless, that he recommended De Witt to submit, and make the best terms he could to avert the coming blow. The faction of the Grand Pensionary seriously weakened Holland, and the base plots of Charles and of Arlington and Clifford, as already said, secured to France the co-operation of England. Spain's weakness was France's opportunity, and the influence of French gold was felt on every side.

CHAPTER XIV.

The hatred between Lewis and William—William's appearance and
disposition—His ability as a Commander.

> ' He is a great observer, and he looks
> Quite through the deeds of men ; he loves no plays,
> As thou dost, Anthony ; he hears no music ;
> Seldom he smiles ; and smiles in such a sort,
> As if he mock'd himself, and scorned his spirit
> That could be mov'd to smile at anything.'

CHAPTER
XIV.

1672.

No two contemporaries, perhaps, have ever hated each other
more cordially than Lewis XIV. of France, and the Prince
of Orange, afterwards King William III.   Many circumstances conspired to intensify this feeling.   The French
King had wished William to marry his illegitimate daughter,
Mademoiselle de Blois ; but the proposal met with an
indignant refusal from William, who said : 'The princes of
Orange married the legitimate, but never the illegitimate,
offspring of great kings.'   Lewis was furious.   He never
forgave what he took as a personal insult to himself, and
William in after-life strove in vain to efface his remembrance
of this incident.

William of Orange was the only issue of the marriage of
the Stadtholder William, with Mary, Princess Royal and

4, 11, 1650.   daughter of Charles I.*   A seven-months child, born eight

* She died of small-pox during a visit to England in 1660, and was
buried in Henry VII.'s Chapel.   She prided herself so much on being
Princess Royal of England that she never allowed herself to be called
by her husband's title.

days after the death of his father, he was constitutionally weak, and through life suffered much from dyspepsia. There can be little doubt, that much of the moroseness for which he has been censured, was the result of a weak digestion. He is said to have borne a strong resemblance to his mother, and if so, she must have been a very plain woman. Gaunt and frail, with round sloping shoulders, he was of medium height, and ungraceful carriage. His high forehead and large aquiline nose, were, however, somewhat relieved by bright, piercing eyes, which bespoke cunning, and seemed to penetrate the thoughts of those with whom he conversed. Thin, closely-compressed lips, and a squareness of jaw and chin, indicated a firm resolve and a will that was not to be trifled with. His general appearance, by no means striking, might indeed be called insignificant. He lacked presence, and his ungracious and almost boorish manner was the reverse of winning. He laughed most ungracefully, a serious fault in man or woman, and his chronic cough irritated those he conversed with. Cold, calculating, and parsimonious, his distant and reserved deportment seemed to repel all friendship. To the casual observer he did not look the hero he undoubtedly was, though there was yet something almost noble in his face. He entertained a truly royal dislike to contradiction, and, though above all petty meanness, was an arch intriguer and a thoroughly good hater.

It is not easy to describe the Prince, whom in their hatred of Popery, the English people afterwards elected to be their King. That he was one of the great men of the earth, none but the prejudiced will deny. But many of his best qualities were dimmed by a cold and unsympathetic nature which found its expression in a repellent manner, and hindered him from exercising any personal influence over those whom he sought to lead. Men followed his plans and appreciated their cleverness, but could feel no enthusiasm for their gloomy author. Yet cold as he was to Englishmen, he loved Holland and its people with the depth and sincerity of the man of one great absorbing idea. To raise the renown of his fatherland and to bring down that of France, was the wish nearest his heart. In him a noble, manly spirit was ever in conflict with the sickly, frail body that contained it. He was absolutely unscrupulous, as evidenced by the superlative deceit to which he resorted in 1688. But his was no mere personal or ignoble ambition, for its object was the freedom and greatness of his country; and when he fought for Holland, the struggle was also for the liberty and Protestantism which Lewis XIV. sought to destroy. The cause of the Reformation was the cause of freedom, and it was evident that both must stand or fall together.

William was self-contained, proud, and ambitious as Lucifer; a statesman, a diplomatist, and yet, above all things, a devoted patriot. So able was he as a negotiator, that his allies, it was said, reaped as much benefit from his diplomacy as his own subjects. His courage was rather of the Wellington than of the Cæsar type, for as a leader, he lacked that depth of human sympathy, that sense of comradeship, which some master-minds inspire, and which cause them to be followed with blind devotion. There was none of that animal magnetism about him, with which some leaders are so charged as to infect all who come within the zone of their influence. He had no power to attract men to his cause by any personal spell or glamour, and he was more calculated to inspire confidence than enthusiasm. His was an unemotional fanaticism, so dumb that the crowd gave him credit for none at all. He was incapable of those generous emotions of the heart which must be at least simulated, if not possessed by men who aspire to influence and lead others. The fire that burnt within him was intense, but it sent forth no flame and imparted no heat to others. The glory which surrounds his name in history is solid and lasting, but it is not the military glory he so ardently coveted, and worked so hard to achieve. The name of but one brilliant victory adorns his epitaph; yet he can never be forgotten in the Holland he saved from extinction, or in the England he rescued from priestcraft and despotism. William of Orange must be remembered in these islands with sincere gratitude and admiration as long as men prize civil and religious liberty. To him we owe, if not actually our liberty, at least our present system of Parliamentary sovereignty. Since he dethroned James II., it is no longer the will of a more or less despotic Sovereign, but the will of the people, which directs the policy of the kingdom. No great man had a larger number of bitter enemies in his lifetime, but in history, few have found more able, more brilliant advocates than William III Yet to a large extent, his were the principles and policy so unblushingly propounded by Machiavelli. He drew the broadest distinction between the honour of a gentleman in his private capacity, and in his management of public affairs. The teaching of the astute Italian may or may not influence the conduct of politicians of to-day, but it did strongly and undisguisedly influence the proceedings of statesmen and rulers in the seventeenth century, and particularly those of the King to whose initiative we owe the Union of England and Scotland, and many of the institutions upon which our greatness has since been built up.

Too sickly when a child for much study, he had nevertheless acquired a considerable amount of knowledge through the care of a fond mother, and after her death, through the watchful solicitude of his grandmother. He learned to speak Dutch, German, French, and English, and to understand Latin, Italian, and Spanish. He was well versed in the science of government, and he had a fair knowledge of mathematics, which he studied with pleasure. He disliked all music except the drum and trumpet. He cared nothing for either poetry, literature, or dancing, and with the exception of painting, the fine arts generally had no more charm for him than they had

for Marcus Antoninus. He admired fine pictures, but took
no interest whatever in those who painted them, nor,
indeed, in artists of any kind. By education a Calvinist,
throughout life he proved himself a friend to Protestants
of every denomination, and stoutly opposed all religious
persecution. Those who knew him well, tell us that he
was a pious predestinarian, and 'constant in the private
worship of God.'* During the visit he paid to his uncle's
Court in 1669, he made a favourable impression upon all
he met. Very abstemious then, he resented being forced
to drink at supper with the King and his tipsy companions.† Contemporary writers described him as having
'a manly, courageous, wise countenance,'‡ and as possessed 'of the most extraordinary understanding and
parts.'§ Sir William Temple, writing of him in 1668, says,
he had no vice, and refers to his good plain sense, his habit
of rising early, his dislike of swearing and dissipation, and
his love of study and of hunting. He dwells also upon his
charity, religious zeal, and ' desire ' (rare in every age) 'to
grow great rather by the service than the servitude of his
country.'

Whilst still in his teens, his sound common-sense enabled
him to see through the French King's designs, even before
the experienced statesmen of the day. He seems, as a youth,
to have regarded the growing power of France as a menace
to the safety of Holland, and as a danger to religious and
political liberty. He had implicit confidence in himself,
and from early boyhood all he said and did proclaimed his
intention to follow in the footsteps, and to emulate the
renown, of his forefathers. No danger appalled, no difficulty daunted, no reverse could dismay, and no success
demoralize this self-contained, unbending, unlovable Cal-

* Burnet.
† Reresby's ' Memoirs,' p. 83.
‡ Evelyn's ' Diary,' vol. i., p. 409.
§ ' Lord Arlington's Letters,' vol. ii., p. 310.
‖ Sir William Temple ; see Mackintosh, p. 312.

vinist. He was absolutely devoid of personal vanity; he was not vindictive, and even when young, was reserved as he was prudent. His aptitude for business was considerable, and, endowed also with great tenacity of purpose, he dealt seriously with all the affairs of life. These were the qualities which gave to previous Princes of Orange so much weight and authority in Holland. In writing of William's progenitors, an English author of the day says, that, Henry IV. excepted, they were on his mother's side only sovereigns, but on his father's such as deserved to be so.*

Such was the Prince now called to rule over Holland and direct her destinies. Her future was in his hands, and never did some four millions of freemen commit their fortunes to safer keeping. Whatever were his failings, we forget them in our admiration of his single-minded, all-absorbing love of country. His devotion to what he felt to be his duty, and the noble courage with which, in Holland's darkest hour, he fought for what he believed to be right, are enough to obliterate from the pages of history all record of his faults. He was ungracious, but he always rode foremost in the battles he waged for the independence of a country far dearer to him than life.

William and Lewis differed in character as night differs from day on all points save one, and that was ambition. William, unostentatious in all he did, loved war for itself: Lewis, who was no soldier, loved it only for the gratification of his personal vanity, and as a means of effecting his ambitious projects. Though almost always defeated, William was well versed in the theory of war, and to him the camp was a real home, where, sickly as he was, it was a pleasure to him to share with his soldiers the fatigues and privations inseparable from active service. King Lewis, on the other hand, was strong and robust. Vain of his personal appearance, he loved the theatrical side of war, and had a childish relish for its 'pride and circumstance.'

* 'Feasts of the Gods,' written in 1708.

He gloried in the 'triumphs' so readily accorded him by a vainglorious people and a sycophant Court. No amount of adulation was too much for him, even when he knew it to be false. He made war like a king on the stage, surrounded by well-dressed courtiers; William did so seriously, as a real soldier in the midst of camps and fighting comrades. William would have scouted the minister who should presume to style him 'the Great'—a title which Lewis assumed from the day of the insignificant skirmish

which marked his prosaic passage of the Rhine. William would have laughed at the man who, courtier-like, pretended to regard that operation as an important feat of arms. To Lewis, France doubtless owes much of the reputation that gained for her the title of 'Great Nation'; but we cannot forget that it was he who sowed the seed which in course of time grew into the noisome weed of revolution. Had he never lived, the names of Marat and of Robespierre might be still unknown, and France might have been spared the humiliations inflicted upon her by Marlborough and Wellington.

To William, Holland owed her independence. To his far-seeing genius and well-balanced judgment, Europe was indebted for the 'Grand Alliance,' which was the means of confining France for nearly half a century within her ancient limits. Entrusted by his countrymen with the defence of Holland, he soon came to be recognised as the champion of European liberties. But he never learnt to know or understand the English people, and hated their system of government by party. Always regarding English politics as insular, provincial, and unimportant, he neglected them, and thereby created many enemies in his new kingdom. His ways and manners and estimate of things were not theirs. No community of sentiment existed between the ruler and the ruled, for they were strangers each to the other. Esteemed and liked, if not loved, in Holland as Stadtholder, he was as King in England disliked by all classes. It was nothing but

England's dread and hatred of Popery that kept him on the Throne, so supremely uncongenial was he in every way to the people. He never associated with his English courtiers, whilst he loved to boose in the society of his own countrymen. He took no trouble to conceal either his warm regard for the Dutch adventurers whom he had imported, or his contempt for the English statesmen of the day. It must, however, be frankly admitted, that he had good reason for this feeling towards his new subjects.

CHAPTER XIV.

1672.

CHAPTER XV.

HOLLAND'S POWER OF RESISTANCE.

She trusted to her wealth—With a strong Navy she neglected her Army—Greed of wealth and mercantile pursuits had made her men effeminate.

HOLLAND, with her comparatively small population and contemptible army, was apparently powerless to meet the coming storm, although her commerce was great and her coffers were full. The theory so strongly held in England, that wealth can save a nation when threatened with extinction, is the greatest and most dangerous of all our present-day delusions. It received a severe shock in 1870-71, when rich France fell before poor Germany, but it still helps to soothe the politician in moments of anxiety as to the unpreparedness of his country to defend itself if seriously attacked. During peace, money enables a wise Government to prepare and organize the army and navy required for the national safety. With it, guns, ships, ammunition and all warlike stores can be obtained, and reserves provided. All this can be done by the Minister who is sufficiently wise, patriotic, and courageous to tell his countrymen the whole truth as to the condition of their defensive forces. But if—as in the case of Holland in 1672—this be not done in time of peace, if the provision of a suitable army and navy be postponed until the country is attacked by an enemy strong by land and sea, its accumulated wealth will avail it nothing. The attack will be made so rapidly, and most likely, so unexpectedly—as it was by France in 1672—that the unprepared nation will have no time to pull out its purse, still less to spend its contents to any useful purpose. As is generally the case at such a time in all civilized States, there were then in Holland many who refused to believe in the reality of the danger, and who persisted in crying, 'Peace, peace!' when war was even at their door. Regardless of the warnings they had received from their own Minister in Paris, they seemed anxious to believe only what was pleasant, and, up to the last moment, refused to admit that invasion was even a possibility. Strong at sea, the Dutch had allowed their army to dwindle into feeble insignificance. To save money, it had been so reduced in numbers, that when the French poured into Holland, some 25,000 very indifferent troops were all that could be found to meet the invaders. Even these, mostly old men disused with long peace, were badly trained and equipped, and lacked confidence in themselves and in their officers.* During the long period of eighteen years in which Holland was ruled by De Witt, age had carried off the experienced officers to whom she owed her freedom, and the many foreigners she had in her ranks could not be expected to take any deep interest in the cause of Dutch independence.

The Dutch mercantile marine numbered about twelve hundred ships, and to watch over what was then regarded as a colossal trade, Holland had ministers at all the great courts, and consuls in all the principal seaports of the world. Her commercial capital, Amsterdam, had become the richest of cities. The provinces of Holland alone contained 3,000,000 souls, and the other states were peopled in like proportion. In fact, the sterling qualities of the Dutch had raised a down-trodden Spanish province, into a State which, in many respects, rivalled the first in Europe. Forestalling the policy of England during the last three-quarters of the nineteenth century, Holland was content to be strong,

* Sir W. Temple's Memoirs.

at sea, whilst the army maintained for defence against invasion, was contemptible in numbers and poor in quality. The mercantile classes, by whom she was governed, were quick to perceive how necessary a strong navy was for her circumstances and position, but the need of a land army was not so apparent. They looked at the question from an exclusively maritime point of view, and all possibility of invasion had been eliminated from their calculations. Her merchants could not by any arguments be got to believe, that France would be unrighteous enough to invade their country without warning, or to attempt the overthrow of a nation that had given her no recent cause of offence. Thus it was, that their defensive forces were neglected, whilst they devoted all their energies to the accumulation of wealth, and to what may be termed domestic and party politics. Their sailors were as good as those of England, but the generation of landsmen which had grown up while the Louvestein faction ruled Holland, were more fitted to handle the yard-measure, than to wield the pike. Engrossed in money-making, they had forgotten the art of war on land. A long peace had lulled them to sleep, and they had false visions of a strength and security which they did not possess. They constructed dikes to keep out the sea, but they neglected the fortifications which should keep out the enemy. Greed of wealth was slowly killing that public spirit upon which alone a healthy naval and military discipline can ever be maintained. 'Oh shopcraft, how do you effeminate the minds of men!'* Holland deliberately elected to trust for safety to paper treaties, and to the good faith of the States which signed them, rather than incur the cost and inconvenience of an army sufficient to make those treaties respected. The States-General deliberately entrusted the command of their fortified places to the unmilitary sons of peaceful burgomasters and city deputies, who, when summoned by some handful of French regular troops, generally surrendered without firing a shot.

* 'The Siege of Mons,' a comedy of 1691.

In this first move of Lewis's game for universal dominion, William, as Stadtholder, was forced to the front, a position he held until his death, and which thenceforward was occupied by Marlborough. In these early Dutch wars, Charles II. and his brother James were bribed to assist the French, and until the peace of Utrecht, England held the balance in the game. When she remained neutral, or still worse, when her King was paid to fight against Holland, all hope of liberty and free thought in Europe seemed futile. And for several years it seemed as if Lewis must win.

CHAPTER XVI.

Naval battle of Sole Bay—Noble death of Lord Sandwich—Churchill promoted for his service upon that occasion—He goes to Holland with Monmouth—Monmouth's parentage—De Witt : his murder—Lewis makes the great mistake of taking the advice of his civil minister instead of his generals.

CHAPTER
XVI.
———
1672.

THE time selected by Lewis XIV. for the conquest of Holland was singularly propitious. Spain, grown weak, and ruled by a half-witted King, was content to send some six thousand troops to Ostend, with orders for them to act, if necessary, in the defence of the States-General. The Emperor Leopold was fully occupied with his endeavours to calm or crush the spirit of his Hungarian subjects, whom his intolerance had driven into revolt. He had neither the leisure nor the money—even if he had the inclination—to enter into any alliance for the protection of rebellious Holland against France. According to his views, the Dutch richly deserved punishment, whether as subjects who had risen against their lawful rulers, the princes of his house, or as irreconcileable enemies of his religion. He was consequently easily induced to sign a secret treaty with France, in which he undertook to remain neutral during the coming war.

It was during this war that Churchill first pushed himself to the front, and it is to be noted, that like most great generals he first attracted the notice of his superiors by reckless daring, contemptuous indifference to danger, love of enterprise, and unconcealed craving for personal distinction. It was in the early campaigns of this war that he learnt from Turenne and other able French commanders that military science, which others may have known as well theoretically, but in the practice of which few have equalled, none have surpassed him.

During the winter of 1671-72, the English Admiralty made great exertions to fit out a fleet to act in spring with that of France, as agreed upon with Louis XIV. The dockyards were alive with workmen, and satisfactory progress was made. By the month of April, sixty vessels of the line and twenty fire-ships were assembled at the Nore, under the command of the Duke of York. The *Prince*, a ship of one hundred guns, carried his flag, whilst that of Lord Sandwich, the second in command, flew from the *James*, a ship of similar size. When this fleet put to sea, many gentlemen joined it as volunteers. This was a common and a praiseworthy custom in the days when a large proportion of soldiers were required on board every ship of war. Indeed, so usual was it that society questioned the courage of the lazy idler of good family who stayed at home, whilst his friends and brothers were boarding hostile ships, or fighting in some deadly breach abroad.* In our day it is the fashion to sneer at those who so thirst for distinction and revel in danger, that they volunteer to share the privilege of fighting for their country whenever and wherever they can secure it. But the soldier's heart warms to the volunteer, for the spirit of the hero is everywhere the same. The freemasonry of daring ignores all differences in rank and birth, and makes all brave men comrades, be they princes or peasants, soldiers or men of peace.

The French fleet, just half as strong as ours, put to sea at the same time under Count d'Estrées, and joined the Duke of York's command early in May, off St. Helen's in the Isle of Wight. Over three thousand troops were dis-

May 5, 1672.

* 'Memoirs of Captain Carlton.'

tributed as Marines throughout the English fleet. The Duke of York's flagship carried the King's Company of what is now the Grenadier Guards, in which John Churchill was ensign, Edward Picks lieutenant, and Sir Thomas Daniel captain. The orders given to the Duke of York were to find and destroy the Dutch fleet. He put to sea, but, as the weather was bad, he made for Sole Bay, near the little Suffolk town of Southwold, twenty-six miles south of Yarmouth.* Whilst at anchor there, Lord Sandwich, the experienced second in command, reported to the Duke, that the fleet generally, seemed more anxious to feast than to fight, and were consequently seriously exposed to surprise 'as the wind then stood.'† The fiery landsmen who accompanied the fleet chafed at his habitual caution, the outcome of knowledge and experience, and hastily concluded—as young men are apt to do—that his prudence arose from want of enterprise and daring. It was even hinted that Lord Sandwich lacked the courage of the English gentleman, the mettle of the English seaman. Evelyn says that both the Duke of Albemarle and Sir Thomas Clifford —neither knowing anything of seamanship—had looked upon his cautious skill as closely allied to fear. Sandwich was painfully aware of these suspicions, and the fact preyed heavily upon his mind. Before leaving London to embark he said: 'I must do something, I know not what, to save my reputation.'‡ He seems to have made up his mind to die in the first action, and, by the gallant manner of his death, to show how cruelly and unjustly he had been suspected. He detested this war with Holland, for he knew it to be an unholy war, prosecuted for un-English objects by King Charles and the 'infamous crew' who were his ministers.§

The prediction of Sandwich came true. The English

* It is about 125 miles from London.
† Kennet.
‡ Evelyn's 'Diary' of 31, 5, 1672.
§ Campbell's 'Lives of the Admirals,' vol. ii., p. 187.

and French fleets were surprised at anchor by De Ruyter,

the greatest naval commander of his day. A bloody battle
ensued, and at sundown both sides claimed the victory, the
Dutch with most reason on their side. The hero of the
day was the gallant but suspected Sandwich, who, by his
noble conduct and skilful seamanship, saved our fleet
from the disaster which neglect of his warning had made
imminent. His was a glorious death, fighting the enemy
all round as long as his ship would float, and refusing to
leave her even when in flames. De Ruyter, in his report
of the battle, wrote, that of the thirty-two actions he had
fought, this was the hardest.*

We have no record of the part which John Churchill
played in it, but he must have done well, for he was
promoted over the head of the lieutenant of his own com-
pany, to be captain in the Lord High Admiral's regiment, $\frac{12}{16}$ 6, 1672.
of which the Duke of York was colonel.† This regiment
was intended for sea-service, and was the first in which all
the men were armed with muskets. Churchill's promotion
over the heads of many seniors was naturally attributed
to Court favouritism. The young ensign was known to
have distinguished himself at Tangier, but he was also
known as a lover of the King's mistress, and as a member
of the household of the Royal Admiral, the father of his
sister's children. Lieutenant Picks, of the King's Com-
pany, in a letter written some months after the battle, $\frac{23-19}{10}$, 1672.
complains that he has been passed over for promotion,

---

* A very fair account of this great but indecisive battle is given by
James II. in the Macpherson Papers, vol. i., p. 60.

† It had been raised in 1664; Sir William Killegrew was colonel, and
Sir Charles Lyttleton lieutenant-colonel. It was composed of six companies, each of 200 men. In 1689 William III. incorporated it in the
2nd Regiment of Foot Guards, now the Coldstream Guards. Four
captains of this regiment were killed at Sole Bay, and Churchill was
promoted to one of the vacancies. Sir C. Lyttleton, writing about
the battle from Languard $\frac{14}{4}$, 6, 1672, says, 'Mr. Churchill that was
ensigne to ye King's Company' was promoted to be captain.—
Hatton, 'Correspondence,' vol. i., p. 92.

although twelve years in the army, and adds with ingenuous simplicity, that he was prepared to make a present of four hundred guineas to Sir J. Williamson—a Lord of the Admiralty—to whom his letter is addressed. He urges it is hard that he, the lieutenant, should be forgotten, when 'Mr. Churchill, who was my ensign in the engagement, is made a captain.'*

Charles now appointed his illegitimate son, James, Duke of Monmouth, to command the contingent with which he had agreed to furnish the French King for his invasion of Holland. Born in 1649, Monmouth was only twenty-three years of age when he embarked to assume this important position. His mother was Lucy, daughter of R. Walters, Esq., of Haverford West, in the county of Pembroke. She was a very abandoned woman, but her origin was not so mean as James II. and Evelyn would have us believe.† The latter describes her as 'a browne, beautifull, bold, but insipid creature,' 'whom I had often seene at Paris; she died miserably without anything to bury her.' The King met her, before the Restoration, in Holland, where, under the name of Mrs. Barlow, she was the mistress of handsome Robert Sidney, afterwards colonel of the 'Holland Regiment,' now the 'Buffs' or East Kent Regiment. It is by no means certain which of the two, the King or Sidney, was Monmouth's father, though his portraits show the heavy eyelids of the Stuarts. Evelyn says he was more like 'handsome Sidney' than the King, and James II. says the same. But James was an interested party, and his evidence must therefore be taken with caution. In any case, Charles recognised him as his eldest illegitimate son, and married him to the great heiress, Lady Anne Scott, whose name he took.‡ He was bred a Catholic, but, having

---

* Hamilton's 'Grenadier Guards,' vol. i., p. 166.

† Her family were entitled to arms.

‡ He had been for years known as Mr. Crofts, from the fact that Lord Crofts, one of the King's boon companions, took charge of the child when the unfortunate mother died from debauchery in Paris.

no strong religious principles, he soon found it to be to his
interest to pose before the English people as a stanch Protestant. His doing so at a time when the country was in
the anti-Popery ferment caused by the announcement that
James had joined the Church of Rome, gave him at once a
great position with the people. He was well made, and
his handsome, manly face was full of expression and charm.
His address was engaging, and his manner distinguished.[*]

> ' Of all the numerous progeny, was none
> So beautiful, so brave as Absalom.' [†]

But though he thus possessed every advantage of person
and manner, his mental and moral qualities were essentially
commonplace.

The French King joined his army at Charleroi in May.
He took with him many waggon-loads of silver coin, of
which he fully knew the efficacy in a war, in which most of
the enemy's commanders were ready to be bribed. He expected to work as great wonders with this money in the
reduction of Dutch fortresses, as with his vast siege-train
of heavy guns, and we know that Rheinberg, which could
have stood a long siege, was surrendered without resistance
by its Irish governor after some discussion as to the amount
he was to receive for his treachery. In two months Lewis
had overrun and conquered the three provinces of Gelder-
land, Over-Issel, and Utrecht, had taken over fifty fortified
cities or fortresses, and had captured more than 24,000
prisoners. The fall of Rheinberg, Wesel, Orsoy, and Burich
spread dismay everywhere, and in the States-General, confusion reigned supreme. The Dutch funds fell to an alarming extent, the provincial bonds went down 70 per cent.,
and East India Stock to 25. The Hague mob became wild
with fury, and De Witt and his colleagues were forthwith

For a long time the boy passed as Lord Crofts' son. When he was
beheaded, his widow married Charles, third Lord Cornwallis.

[*] De Grammont; Evelyn; Pepys; De Sévigny.

[†] Dryden's ' Absalom and Achitophel.'

accused of treachery.'*   Both the brothers De Witt were attacked, and the Grand Pensionary was slightly wounded.†

In this great crisis all classes turned to their Prince as the one man who could save them.   He was one of those to whom men instinctively turn when their hearts 'fail them for fear.'   In every city of the Republic the people clamoured for the revocation of the 'Perpetual Edict,' and, notwithstanding the opposition of the De Witt faction, the States-General revoked it.   This was the death-blow to the power and influence of the Louvestein party.   A mob, the most unjust of judges, the most cruel of executioners, is always ready, in its passion and ignorance, to kick the man who is down, and with all the more rancour if he has previously been its favourite.   De Witt soon learned the actual truth of this, for no terms of abuse or execration were now too strong to be hurled at him.   He wished to resign, but William would not allow him to do so.   Every fresh success of the French army, intensified the popular feeling against their former idol.   He was rash enough to ostentatiously face their wrath upon the occasion of his brother's release from prison, and was brutally trampled to death and torn in pieces by the mob from whom he had derived his power.   So died ignominiously a demagogue of rare ability who wished to see his country great, provided he was its ruler, and to see her free, provided her freedom was secured by the theories of government in which he was a fanatical believer.   Upon one thing he was determined: Holland should be exposed to every risk, sooner than he should fall from power.   He was a party man in the worst sense; yet he was brave and had convictions in defence of which he was prepared to risk everything. For the sake of power and office he was content to ally

---

* We can all remember the 'Nous sommes trahis' of the French in 1870.

† Of those who assaulted him, one was a man of good position, for whose life great intercession was made.   The refusal to forgive him heightened popular feeling against De Witt.

himself with the avowed enemies of his religion and of his
country.

When the invasion actually took place, Holland was rent with party strife. The power of the Prince of Orange was crippled by constitutional restrictions, and still more, by party intrigues and the bitter personal animosity of De Witt himself. The nation had no recognised head; and without a supreme ruler, Holland could not be saved. Many of the richest families abandoned their homes in despair, and fled for safety to Amsterdam and Hamburg, and so great became the general panic, that the States-General ordered the removal of the national archives from the Hague.*

Although the murder of De Witt was brutal and cowardly, it was, at the moment, of great national advantage to Holland. De Witt, always anxious to thwart William's military plans, to criticise his proceedings, and to excite popular opposition to his policy, would, so long as he lived, have made the young Prince's difficulties insuperable.

A month before De Witt's murder, William had been made Captain and Admiral-General by acclamation. He was now created Stadtholder. He brought to bear upon his new public duties all the knowledge of war it was possible to obtain from books. Taking a sound military view of the situation, he urged the immediate abandonment of all the small fortified places; first, because he knew they could not hold out if invested, and secondly, because their garrisons, useless where they were, would if collected together constitute an important addition to his field army. Ignorant of war, like all political assemblies, the States-General would not consent to this proposal, and these little garrisons, unable in any way to check the French invading columns, were captured one after the other. Maestricht and the chief towns of Brabant, which had been lately strengthened, alone held out.

The rapid progress of the French arms had a great effect upon the English people, and their anger rose high.

* Welwood's 'Memoirs,' p. 222.

Charles, who had himself become somewhat disturbed at the magnitude of the French success, ordered the 'Royal English Regiment' to leave the immediate theatre of operations for Ypres and Courtray, and desired Monmouth to return home. Nevertheless, in November he raised a second English regiment for service with the French army. It was drawn from eight other battalions, the Company from the 'Lord High Admiral's' Regiment being under the command of Captain John Churchill. Many men of good family took service as private soldiers with this new corps in the hope of distinction, and in order to obtain commissions as officers. Churchill's company marched from London to Canterbury early in November, and a month later embarked at Dover for Calais. The day after its disembarkation at that ancient city, it marched to join the French army, but soon took up winter quarters in Arras and Douay.

The campaign of 1672 had been disastrous to Holland. The Dutch levies could not stand before the well-trained regular French troops. The fate of the country hung in the balance, and Holland hovered on the brink of final extinction. Even the stout heart of William seemed at times to fail, and he spoke of saving himself the anguish of witnessing the final conquest of his country by meeting death 'in the last ditch.' To save what remained of Holland, he persuaded the people to open the dykes and flood the country, preferring to see it submerged, rather than become a French province. With the exception of the islands of Zealand, the distant Province of Friesland, some higher land between Amsterdam and Rotterdam, and a few towns and fortresses which elsewhere rose like islands from the general inundation, Holland was in possession of the French army and the sea. At this supreme moment, Lewis offered to guarantee to William the sovereignty, under the protection of France and England, of what remained of Holland. But he answered proudly, 'I will never betray a trust, nor sell the liberties of my country which my forefathers have so long defended.' When all around him despaired of the Commonwealth, he alone was calm and determined.

Had Lewis now acted upon the advice of Turenne and Condé, instead of upon that of his civilian Minister, Louvois, nothing could have saved Holland. Neither the genius and courage of her young Stadtholder nor the patriotism of her people would have availed. Turenne and Condé had urged Lewis, when he crossed the Rhine, to refuse ransom for his Dutch prisoners, and to employ them on the Languedoc Canal and in razing the fortifications of the cities he captured. If left standing, those works must be occupied, and to find garrisons for them, would seriously reduce the fighting strength of the field army. They pressed him to retain only a few of the most important fortresses as points of strength, and if necessary, of refuge, and as safe depots for stores, etc. Upon this purely military question, the civilian Minister's advice was followed; and whilst William got back all his best soldiers at so many guilders a head, the strength of the French army in the field was so reduced by the garrisons required for some fifty captured places, that Turenne found it difficult to collect even 10,000 men for active operations.*

* In nearly all the histories of Marlborough, it is stated that he took part in the capture of Orsoy, Rheinberg, Wesel, Emmerich and Utrecht, but those places fell in the months of May and June, when he was serving with his company on board the Duke of York's flagship.

Winter quarters in the seventeenth century—Churchill's daring attack
—Turenne calls him the Handsome Englishman—England forces
Charles II. to make peace.

In the seventeenth century the roads throughout Europe
were too bad to admit of military operations on a large
scale between the beginning of November and the end of
April. This was consequently a period of enforced in-
action; and whilst it lasted, the troops left the field and
went into 'Winter Quarters,' in the towns and villages. It
was a common practice for a large proportion of the officers
to obtain leave, and spend the winter with their families
at home. Captain Churchill did this during the winter
of 1672-73, and continued the practice in subsequent years.

The campaign of 1673 opened with operations which,
begun during the winter months, extended well into spring.
The hardships endured by the troops on both sides were
excessive, and the losses from exposure were heavy. The
Elector of Brandenburg, beaten at all points by Turenne,
asked for peace, which was granted and signed in April, and
the imperial troops, having suffered enormously, retreated
into Bohemia.

This year Lewis made great efforts to put an army in the
field, large enough to complete the subjugation of the United
Provinces. Maestricht was invested on the 7th of June, and

trenches were opened some ten days afterwards. The French King, who was present, although he hated tedious operations, set a brilliant example to his officers by a patient endurance of the trying fatigues and wearing labours which are inseparable from large siege operations. The attack was conducted by Vauban, who for the first time made use of parallels provided with large places-d'armes, capable of holding considerable numbers of men for the protection of the batteries.* The place, which was regarded by both sides as one of great importance, was held by a garrison of about 5,000 men. The Governour, M. Fariaux, a Frenchman in the Dutch service, was a soldier of experience and determination, and the defence he made did him much credit.

A week after ground was broken the siege works were sufficiently advanced to justify an attempt to effect a lodgment in the covered way. Charles had specially recommended Monmouth to the care and consideration of the French King, and the latter, anxious to please his royal pensioner, selected his son for this service of honourable danger. It is indeed stated, that the attack was postponed, so that it might take place during Monmouth's tour of duty as ' General of the day.'† Lewis took up a position ‡ 6, 1673. in the trenches to watch the result. The assaulting column, composed of detachments from several regiments, was augmented by numerous volunteers thirsting for honour and distinction, and amongst the number was Captain Churchill, who accompanied Monmouth. The attack was eminently successful, the counterscarp was gained, a lodgment was effected, and the Half-Moon in front of the Brussels gate was stormed, and occupied after half an hour's hard fighting, during which the enemy sprang two mines.

The next day, between noon and one o'clock, when

* This plan is said to have been first adopted by an Italian engineer in the service of the Sultan at the siege of Candy.—' Siècle de Louis XIV..' chap. ii.

† ' Memoirs of John Sheffield, Duke of Buckingham.'

Monmouth was about to dine, news reached him that the Dutch were preparing for a sortie. He at once sent to Lewis for reinforcements, and hastened with Churchill and others to the Half-Moon, which had been taken the previous evening. Before he reached it, the enemy sprang a mine which killed several of its garrison, and under cover of the confusion the Dutch sallied out in considerable force to retake the work. The attacking party, composed of some of their best troops led by the Governour, soon found themselves in the midst of the working party, engaged in strengthening the lodgment which Monmouth had made the day before. Fariaux pushed home his attack with gallant determination, and, helped by a shower of hand-grenades, drove off with heavy loss the French and Swiss troops who formed the guard over the working party. Some musketeers who came to assist, could do but little, and the Half-Moon was almost entirely reoccupied by the Dutch, when Monmouth and Churchill, with twelve private gentlemen of the Life-Guards and a few others — all volunteers — reached the trenches.* At a glance, Monmouth took in the critical state of matters. The advantage so dearly won the day before seemed on the point of being lost. Instead, therefore, of making his way to the front by the circuitous route of the trenches, he leaped the parapet and led his small party across the open against the Half-Moon, in the face of a heavy fire. His party was small, for when he started for the scene of action, most of the gentlemen volunteers with the army were asleep in their tents, having been in the trenches all the previous night. Those actually with Monmouth, besides the twelve Life-Guardsmen, were Lord Arlington, Mr. Charles O'Brien, Mr. Villars, Lord Rocking-

---

* The names of these twelve gentlemen volunteers of the Life-Guards are given, as copied from the public records, in Cannon's 'Historical Records of the Life-Guards,' p. 41.

ham's two sons with their kinsman Captain Watson, Sir T. Armstrong, Captain Churchill,* Captain Godfrey, Mr. Roe, the Duke's two pages, and three or four more of his servants. The Life-Guardsmen, throwing away their carbines, drew their swords, and all made for a barricade of which the enemy had taken possession.+ The opening through it was so narrow that only one man could pass at a time, and there several were killed and wounded. Mr. Villars was sent back to head-quarters to urge forward reinforcements—the need of which was very apparent. Monmouth and his party, helped by a few French musketeers who now joined from the neighbouring trenches, held their ground until 500 fresh troops arrived, who soon cleared the Half-Moon. Churchill was amongst the many wounded, Lord Arlington had a shot in his thigh, and Sir Harry Jones, also a volunteer, was killed at Monmouth's side.‡

This adventure was one of the most important events in John Churchill's early life. It brought him prominently forward; his courage was talked of in the army, and his reckless daring became a common topic with the gossips in the antechambers of Whitehall. Lewis XIV., who witnessed the affair, thanked him publicly on the spot for the valuable service he had rendered, and promised to recommend him to the favour and protection of his own Sovereign.

* Arlington, in his letter to the Secretary of State, which I have mainly followed in this description, spells the name 'Cherchelle,' being evidently the way in which he heard it pronounced by the French officers then about him. This letter is dated ' From the campe before Maestricht, Jun. 26 (73).'—Foreign Office State Papers: France, No. 285, 1673—Rolls Office.

† By an order dated London, $\frac{29}{30}$ 5, 1674, twelve carbines, to replace those thrown away upon this occasion, were to be issued from ' Our stoares remaining within the office of Our Ordnance.'

‡ He commanded a regiment of Horse, which at his death was given to Monmouth.—Hatton. ' Correspondence,' vol. i., p. 108.

In this affair, the French lost about 100 officers and 1,000 men, but it was such a success for the besiegers, that the townspeople soon forced the Governour to make terms, and after thirteen days of open trenches, Maestricht surrendered. The garrison, including 1,000 Horse, marched out the next day, ' wᵗʰ bag and baggage, drums beating, Colours flying, match lighted, bullet in the mouth, &c., with pieces of canon and two mortar pieces.'*

But a change now came over the French dreams of conquest, and Lewis began to understand the real difficulties of the enterprise in which he had embarked. The roads were under water, the fields had been given back to the sea, and the towns alone remained above the flood. He liked glory, but he liked to win it easily, and he was not prepared to seek it in operations more suited to beavers and water-rats, than to Regular troops. Like the fair-weather creatures in red coats--I must not call them soldiers—who hurried home from the Crimea when hardships and privations began, he preferred the comforts of Versailles to campaigning fare in a flooded country ; so, leaving Turenne to complete the conquest of Holland, he returned to Paris to receive the congratulations of his courtiers. Condé said of him very truly, that he had not the soul of a conqueror in him.

Europe now began to awake from the slumber into which it had been thrown by the diplomacy, the subsidies and the bribes of Lewis. William of Orange, on his part, left no means untried to arouse England and other countries to a sense of the dangers to which they were exposed by the inordinate ambition of the French King. His efforts were not in vain, for in August, Spain and the Empire guaranteed Holland against further attack, and most of the German princes followed their example. It was with the utmost difficulty that Turenne held his own against the

* Letter of Charles Hatton to his brother of ²⁶·⁵, 1673.—Hatton, ' Correspondence,' vol. i., p. 108.

host of enemies who now confronted him, and in Monte-cuculi he met an antagonist who was not to be trifled with.

When the troops went into winter quarters at the end of this year's campaign, Monmouth returned to England to be made much of by his reputed father, who loved him as much as that selfish creature could love anything, accompanied by Churchill, who met with a most flattering reception at Court. Monmouth told the King that Churchill had saved his life at the siege of Maestricht. His own immediate master, the Duke of York, made him successively Gentleman of the Bedchamber, Master of the Robes, and in the course of the winter, he was promoted to be lieutenant-colonel in the 'Admiral's Regiment of Foot.'*

Throughout this eventful campaign of 1673, Churchill had shown a determination to obtain distinction, cost what it might. He knew that for him, advancement in life was only to be secured by hard work and reckless daring. He could not hope to be pitchforked into high command like Monmouth, who was a Lieutenant-General at the age of twenty-three. Churchill had only himself to depend on, and he knew it. He deliberately played the game of 'neck or nothing' at which so many ambitious men have staked their lives—all they had to play with. How many gallant English gentlemen have found graves in every part of the earth who have gambled away their lives at this same lottery! If Churchill had not been brave by nature, he was one of those who would have been so from pure calculation, for he knew that there was no royal road to fame, though there might be to promotion. Moreover, he was amply endowed with that readiness of resource and calm-

---

* He paid six thousand crowns for the post of Gentleman of the Bedchamber, which amount, some say, was given to him by the Duchess of Cleveland. Sir Charles Lyttleton was the full colonel of this Regiment, which was afterwards incorporated in the Coldstream Guards.

ness in danger—perhaps the most valuable of military instincts—which can only be tested in the field. Thus he succeeded to his heart's content, and won the great distinction of being noticed by Turenne, who nicknamed him the 'handsome Englishman,' and is said to have foretold for him a brilliant career. Upon one occasion a Dutch column attacked an outpost, from which the French colonel in command retired precipitately without fighting. The post was of sufficient importance to render its recapture necessary. Turenne wagered a supper and some wine, that his 'handsome Englishman' would retake it with half the number of men who had lately formed its garrison. The Marshal won his bet, and Churchill became the hero of the hour.

There had grown up in Europe during the autumn of 1673, a very general feeling of hostility to the French designs on Holland. The intriguing Bishop of Münster and the Elector of Cologne separated themselves from the cause of Lewis, and in October Spain declared war against France. England and Holland 'had been at war without being angry,' and there was a general cry for peace, and for the immediate recall of the British troops from Flanders. The subsidies granted by Lewis did not nearly cover the cost of the fleet maintained in the exclusive interests of France, and Charles was more than usually in need of money, which he knew he could only obtain from Parliament. Our seamen fought without heart, and dreaded their friends and allies the French, more than their foes the Dutch. Discontent at home was rife, and Charles was said to fear the embodiment of the militia, as much as he did invasion.* In the preceding year, public opinion had forced him to send a special mission to remonstrate with Lewis, and to impress upon him, that, in the English people's existing mood, he could not be allowed to complete the conquest of a country

* Sir W. Temple's Works, vol. ii., p. 375. London, 1750.

which they regarded as the home of freedom and of Protestantism. The members of the mission, however, had no sympathy with this English feeling, and took care that Lewis should not be seriously hampered by any action of theirs, while, at the same time, they urged William to accept the terms Lewis had offered him, Buckingham frequently repeating to him, 'Do you not see that the country is lost?'

Parliament gravely censured Charles for his conduct in this business, and in November petitioned him against the Dutch war and the French alliance. They would not brook the continued employment of British troops in so unholy a cause. Monmouth's contingent was consequently broken up, and his own regiment was brought home in November. It was plainly stated in Parliament, that further supplies would not be voted, unless, indeed, the Dutch should refuse honourable and reasonable terms. Charles prorogued Parliament to prevent its further action in this matter, but when it met again in the following January, he was made to feel that he must make peace forthwith. Spain had thrown herself entirely into the cause of Holland, and now threatened to declare war against England, unless Charles made peace. The war had already cost our merchants the trade of the Northern seas, and war with Spain would cost them the trade of the Mediterranean. These considerations brought Charles and his advisers to their senses. Sir William Temple was sent for, and the negotiations for peace were confided to his skilled diplomacy. Few of our public men have combined as he did, such a strong, sound, national statesmanship, and so keen an appreciation of public affairs and knowledge of men, with so deep a love of literature and of philosophical research. Once again, in the interests of the State, he was obliged to exchange the quiet of his library in the country for the bustle of diplomatic intrigue in the city.

4. 11, 1673.

Terms of peace were soon arranged with the Spanish Ambassador in London, and a treaty was signed at Westminster in February. The questions of Surinam and of the 'flag,' were satisfactorily settled. The States of Holland undertook that not only single Dutch ships, but whole fleets, should strike their Colours and lower their topsails to any fleet, or even to any single vessel, which carried the King of England's flag, as had been the custom in former times. Thus ended the most unpopular war we had ever been engaged in—a war from which England could reap neither honour nor material advantage.

CHAPTER XVIII.

THE TEST ACT.—CHURCHILL BUYS AN ANNUITY.

The Duchess of Cleveland gives him £4,500, with which he buys an annuity.

QUEEN KATHERINE had miscarried in 1669, and all hope that she would ever become a mother, was now finally abandoned. It then became evident that the Duke of York must, in the ordinary course of nature, succeed to the Throne, unless some strong measures were taken by Parliament to exclude him. Ashley, who led the Protestant party, together with Buckingham and others, talked of bringing in a Bill to legitimatize the Duke of Monmouth and to declare him the King's heir. Although this measure did not meet with general approval, all Protestants were agreed that a law should be made to prevent any Roman Catholic from sitting on the English throne. Many cruel enactments had been already made to exclude Roman Catholics from office, and many good and loyal men had been thus driven from the army and the navy; but with the King's connivance, James had hitherto succeeded in evading these laws and their penalties, and continued to hold the office of Lord High Admiral and the command of one or two regiments. Though he well knew how hateful Popery was to the English people, he lost no opportunity of parading his change of faith before them. It was a curious trait in his character, that he appeared to glory in outraging public opinion on this and other points upon which the people felt earnestly. He deeply offended Parliament and the people, by the announcement of his intended marriage with the beautiful Roman Catholic Princess. Mary of Modena.* This marriage, and the long squabble between Charles and his Parliament regarding the illegal 'Declaration of Indulgence,' led to the introduction of a new Bill, so stringent, that James would have no alternative but to recant his faith, or to quit the public service. This new law, known as the Test Act, was primarily aimed at James, and was intended to exclude him from succession to the throne.

Both Houses of Parliament were bent upon passing it notwithstanding the strenuous opposition of the King and his friends. Speaking in the Commons, Churchill's father said, 'No song, no supper'—no Test Act, no supplies—and this soon became the popular cry. The Bill meant that James must resign all his public offices. The King wanted money for his duchesses, as his pension from France did not even cover his war expenses. Poor, ease-loving Charles was driven into a corner; but he must have money, and, as he could only obtain it by compliance with the wishes of his Parliament, he had to yield. His 'faithful Commons' at once voted him over a million and a quarter sterling towards the expense of carrying on the war. James was either too honest or too much in fear of his confessor, to comply with the provisions of the Test Act. He was

* She landed at Dover $\frac{21}{11} \cdot \frac{11}{2}$, 1673. She was fifteen, and James forty years of age. She had been reared in a convent, and so badly taught there, that until her approaching marriage was notified to her, she had never even heard of England. Upon meeting her husband, this infant bride conceived the utmost dislike to him, a feeling which in after years gave way to the most genuine affection. Her life was a sad and stormy one. Joined to an unwise and obstinate bigot, she had soon to realize the miseries of Court life in all its worst forms. Her husband, given to coarse amours, made her early life miserable; her frequent miscarriages, the hatred of the English people, and the cruel lies and suspicions to which she was exposed, robbed her life of all brightness or pleasure.

consequently compelled to resign all his public offices, that of Lord High Admiral included.

The passing of this infamous Act had a most important bearing upon the life of the Duke of York, and consequently upon the career of John Churchill, as the fortunes of the two men, master and follower, were inseparably linked together until the plot began which ended in the Great Revolution.

Churchill spent the winter at home, and again fell a victim—doubtless a willing victim—to the wiles of his kinswoman, the Duchess of Cleveland. Extravagant in her style of living, she squandered on every passing whim the large sums of money bestowed upon her by the King. Her young lover, Jack Churchill, was poor, and she is said to have been most liberal to him. She had purchased for him the position of Gentleman of the Bedchamber to the Duke of York,* and she is supposed to have now bestowed upon him, as a new mark of her affection, the sum of £4,500; but the authority for this statement is the Earl of Chesterfield, who never lost a chance of repeating any gossip that told against the fame or reputation of the man whom he disliked. But whether the Duchess did or did not supply the money with which an annuity was purchased in 1674, it is certain that Churchill came into possession of it about this time. The ordinary courtier of the period, who had suddenly found himself in possession of so much money, would have gambled with it, or spent it on some form of pleasure. But this strangely-constituted

---

* In a note on Burnet, Lord Dartmouth asserts that the Duchess had told one of her near relations, who had repeated the story to him, that Marlborough had received a great deal of her money 'for very little service done.' Nearly all commissions in the army and all the posts at Court were then paid for, the out-going man generally obtaining the money. About this time Sir William Temple refused the position of Secretary of State, because, amongst other reasons, he could not afford to pay down the £6,000, then the price of such an office. The King nominated whom he chose, but the man turned out received the amount at which the position he lost was commonly rated.

young man, was already thinking more of the future than of the present. Bitter experience had taught him the miseries of poverty, and he determined to purchase an annuity, so that, come what might, he should at least feel himself above the daily sting of want. The money was accordingly handed over to Lord Halifax, who, in consideration thereof, settled £500 per annum upon him for life.*

His action upon this occasion showed a strength of character, and a rare power of looking ahead. This uncommon quality can be traced through all the public and private events of his life, his marriage alone excepted. His position had been one of dependence upon Royal favour, but the annuity gave him a new start. His friend Bishop Burnet says : 'He had no fortune to set up on ; this put him on all methods of acquiring one.' The Bishop also says, that money had as much power over Churchill, as Churchill had over his master, James. Many have sunk beneath the weight of poverty, whom such an annuity would have helped to success, possibly to eternal fame! Want of money had engendered in Churchill that strict attention to economy from which parsimony is so often bred. Long practised frugality degenerates easily into penuriousness, and that again into miserly habits and avarice. It did so in his case, and afforded grounds for the biting invective of the Swifts and Manleys of his own day, and of the Macaulays, Thackerays, and other romance-writers of the present century.

Books have been written with the express purpose of proving, that, however great Marlborough may have been, he was a monster of ingratitude, and only rose to power by low and infamous methods. That he should take money from the woman he intrigued with, is often denounced as the worst and most ignoble action a gentleman could be capable of. But this was not the opinion entertained of

---

* The original documents connected with this transaction—dated 1674—are amongst the papers at Blenheim.

the transaction by his contemporaries. It was regarded as quite natural that a handsome, young soldier should be selected by the mistress of the King as one of her lovers, and that, penniless as he was, she should make him large presents. There is no foundation for Mrs. Manley's story that when the Duchess became poor, the lover to whom she had been so generous in the day of her power, refused to lend her a few pounds when she lost at basset.* It was truthfully said of him, that from his youth up he had sucked the milk of courts, and that his grace of manner and unfailing courtesy were not unalloyed with a spirit of intrigue and duplicity which has always been a stumbling-block to his warmest admirers. But throughout this intrigue with Barbara Palmer, he did nothing more than was done by many others, by Monmouth for instance, who when in exile lived chiefly upon the bounty of his mistress, Lady Wentworth. Yet Monmouth has not been held up to everlasting obloquy. No English gentleman of to-day would act as Marlborough and Monmouth did, but their conduct was not regarded at the time as either disreputable or unusual, and it is by contemporary law and custom that we must judge them, and not by our own code of morality and honour.

* Even Macaulay, unscrupulous as he is in his accusations against Marlborough, rejects this story, although he did not hesitate to draw from the infamous writings of Mrs. Manley much of his information on other points which he gave the world as history. De Grammont says that one of Barbara Palmer's daughters whom Charles disavowed was Marlborough's child. This must refer to her daughter Barbara, who became a nun in Pointoise. Not counting Barbara, she had two daughters and three sons by Charles.

CHAPTER XIX.

CAMPAIGN OF 1674.—THE BATTLE OF ENTZHEIM.

The English Army largely reduced—Churchill made Colonel of a regiment in the French service—The English contingent under Turenne distinguishes itself—The fighting of the English troops in the Little Wood at Entzheim.

ALTHOUGH Charles had been forced by his people to make peace with Holland, he had no intention of breaking with his paymaster, the King of France. Parliament insisted upon the reduction of the army, and even threatened to disband the Guards. To avoid further discussion of the question, the King promised to send the Irish regiments back to Ireland, and said that he had already given orders to disband the Horse and Foot he had raised for the Dutch war. This, when carried out, reduced the strength of the army in England to about 6,000 men.*

In the treaty with Holland, it had been privately stipulated, that the British regiments in the French service should be allowed to die out by stopping the supply of recruits, and leave had been given to the Dutch to raise troops in

---

* Horse	1,000 men
The King's and Coldstream Regiments of Foot Guards	
—36 companies in all	2,160 ,,
The Duke of York's Regiment (in France) . .	550 ,,
The Holland Regiment	600 ,,
Twenty-nine Garrisons	1,522 ,,
Total .	5,832 men

Hamilton's 'Grenadier Guards,' vol. i., p. 193. The use of the fife was introduced into the English army this year.

England. Charles failed to carry out the first part of this engagement, for not only did he still encourage recruits to enlist in those regiments, but he actually pressed men for that purpose. The British troops remaining in the French service, were Monmouth's Regiment of Horse, and one Scotch and one English brigade of Foot.* Thus, the campaign of 1674 exhibited the unpleasant spectacle of British soldiers fighting one against the other in the ranks of the two contending forces by order of their Sovereign. But what did he care ?

During this winter, King Charles asked his friend Lewis to appoint Churchill to be Colonel of the Regiment of English Foot which, by a private arrangement between the two monarchs, was to be regularly taken into the French service. In a correspondence on the subject, Louvois refers to Churchill as too much devoted to pleasure for this position. A man was wanted, Louvois said, who would give as much attention to the regiment as a lover would to his mistress. Churchill went to Paris in March to urge his case, and was presented at Court by the English Ambassador, who also pressed upon the French Minister of War the request of King Charles. The request was granted, and in April Churchill became Colonel of the 'Royal English Regiment' vice Lord Peterborough, resigned.† The nucleus of 'Churchill's' Regiment, as it was thenceforward called, had been formed by drafts of fifty men from each of the three companies of the Foot Guards before their return home from Holland.‡

* Of these, the Royal Scots is now the sole representative in our army. Sir George Hamilton's, Churchill's and Monmouth's regiments of Foot formed part of these two brigades. Colonel N. Littleton commanded Monmouth's Regiment of Foot, which was disbanded in 1697.

† See letters of $\frac{18}{28}$ 3, 1674, and of $\frac{31}{28}$ 3, 1674, from the English Ambassador, Sir William Lockard, at p. 87 of 'Lord Stanhope's Miscellanies,' and F. O. State Papers, No. 289, 1674—Rolls Office. Marlborough's commission as Colonel of this regiment is still in existence. It is signed by Lewis and countersigned by Tellier.

‡ War Office Entry Book, No. 512A—now in Rolls Office. This regiment was disbanded in 1697.

In the campaign of 1674 the French no longer swept everything before them as they did at the beginning of the war in 1672, for the Dutch army had been educated by William into self-confidence. The people had taken heart, and had become united, whilst abroad as well as at home, it was realized that in the young Prince of Orange, Holland had a ruler on whom she could rely. His faith in himself, in his cause, and in his country never wavered, and he was determined to fight to the bitter end. The year opened well for the Dutch, for the ill-success of the French in the previous year had also given heart to the wavering German princes. Lewis seeing that he could not hold all his conquests, and at the same time make way against so many enemies, fell back from his position on the Rhine, and, abandoning all Holland except Grave, took up the line of the Meuse from his own frontiers to Utrecht. This retrograde movement, carried out before the completion of his triumphal arch at Port St. Denis, must have been galling to his pride. The French plan of campaign was, that Condé with an army of about 40,000 men should face William, whilst Turenne with another army of about half that strength was to march into the Palatinate. Churchill's and the other English regiments in Lewis' pay, formed part of the latter, and none of Turenne's troops were oftener engaged, or gained more honour. We are told on good authority that the French Marshal himself, as well as his German adversaries, attributed much of his success to their firmness and courage.[*] In the month of June, Churchill took an active part in the battle of Sintzheim,[†] and again in October in the very hardly contested battle of Entzheim. The Duke de Bournonville, who commanded the Imperial army, crossed to the left bank of the Rhine at Mayence on the 1st September, with 30,000 men and thirty guns, and marched up the river to a position between Spire

---

[*] Sir William Temple's Works, vol. i., p. 392.   London, 1750.

[†] The British regiments of Hamilton, Monmouth and Lord Douglas also took part in it.

and Philipsburg. There he encamped, and began to prepare for the siege of the latter place. Turenne, learning that the bridge of boats which De Bournonville had begun to construct over the Rhine near Loussen, about six miles below Philipsburg, was nearly finished, sent out the Baron de Montclar with 1,200 Horse and 500 Dragoons to observe the enemy. He also sent forward Colonel Churchill to the defile of Rhinzabern with 500 Foot. The Governour of Philipsburg had been ordered to fire six guns if the enemy repassed to the right bank of the river. Upon this signal Montclar was to charge the enemy's rearguard, and Churchill was to support him. If four guns only were fired, it was to be taken as an intimation that the Imperialists were advancing towards Turenne's army, and in that case both Montclar and Churchill were to hasten back to camp. No signals were given, however, for owing to the close and wooded nature of the country, De Bournonville managed to cross to the right bank on the 21st September without being seen, and the movement was discovered too late to secure the French any advantage. The Imperialist General's plan was to march up the right bank and again cross the Rhine at Strasbourg. Turenne tried to forestall him, but failed to obtain possession of the place, and the Imperialists were enabled to cross there on the 26th September.* They also passed the river Breusch on the same day, and took up a position upon it near Entzheim, to the west of the Ill. This virtually gave them command of Upper Alsace, where provisions were still abundant, and whence they could invade France with ease. De Bournonville's army was already 40,000 strong, and the Elector of Brandenburg with 20,000 more was expected to join it in a fortnight. Turenne, on the other hand, had only about 22,000 men, in a country whose supplies had been exhausted by his troops, now two months in occupation of it. He

* Napoleon finds great fault with Turenne for this serious mistake. Mémoires de Turenne, suivis du précis des campagnes par Napoléon. 1877, p. 456.

was charged to cover Hagenau and Saverne, both weak, but important places. His position was difficult and dangerous, and it was clear that he would have to quit Alsace when the Brandenburg contingent joined the Imperialist army. Retreat would entail the loss of Brisac and Philipsburg, the provinces of Lorraine and Franche-Comté would be retaken, and Champagne would be laid waste. This would mean the destruction of the allies of France in Germany, which of itself would give a serious shock to the military reputation of Lewis XIV.

Turenne, the great soldier, full of imagination and expedients, did not flinch. He clearly saw that his only resource was to attack De Bournonville before the Brandenburg Elector joined him. Having given his fatigued and over-marched soldiers a rest of three days in camp at Wantzenau—where the Ill joins the Rhine—he made a night march towards the enemy on the 2nd October. It rained heavily all the night, and the roads were deep in mud, but, notwithstanding this and other difficulties, at four p.m. the following day, his advanced guard reached Achenheim, a village at the junction of the Mutzig with the Breusch. Churchill and Montclar, whose march had also been retarded by the heavy rain and badness of the roads, rejoined the army just as it reached the river Breusch. Turenne at once pushed forward with some cavalry to reconnoitre the enemy, sending his Dragoons and about 1,500 British Foot under Lord Douglas to occupy the village of Holtzheim, beyond the little southern arm of the Breusch. In the plain, south of that river, he found the enemy—facing north—in occupation of a crescent-shaped position, with the village of Entzheim in the centre of the curve. De Bournonville's position was strong, but it was too far back from the Breusch. He did not even occupy the fords and bridges, but left a space between the river and his front line wide enough for the French army to form upon. His right rested on the 'Great Wood,' about fifteen hundred yards in width, which here skirts the left bank of the Ill.

This wood was swampy and much cut up by watercourses. His left rested on the southern arm of the Breusch, between which and the river itself there is a marshy, thickly-wooded space about twelve yards across. Immediately in front of his left, was the 'Little Wood,' which he stupidly neglected to occupy until Turenne boldly pushed troops into it. It was about twelve hundred yards long and seven hundred wide, and was, in fact, the tactical key of the position. Throughout the battle the great struggle was for its possession, and in it Churchill's English mercenaries were engaged all day, and there occurred the chief loss on both sides.

The village of Entzheim was surrounded by a ditch, bordered with hedges, which formed a rectangular parallelogram about six hundred yards long and four hundred wide, while ravines and hedges stretching out from it to both flanks added much to its strength. The position was strongly occupied with Foot and bristled with guns; while the hedges, orchards and vineyards near the village, and along the front of the position, screened the defenders, and even their mounted troops, from view.

Turenne quickly perceived the mistake his enemy had made in not holding the line of the Breusch. He saw that, if he could but get his army across the river during the night, there would be room to deploy it into fighting formation between the river and the Imperialist position, and he believed that he could do this, possibly without even De Bournonville's knowledge. His enemy's army was numerically stronger, but it lacked the cohesion, and consequently the power, which the homogeneity of the French army gave to it. He was the sole commander of King Lewis' army, and his word was law. The army opposed to him was, on the contrary, made up of contingents from many electorates and provinces, commanded by their own princes, each of whom was more bent upon his own special aim, than upon common Imperial interests. Such a condition of things always leads to bickerings and jealousies, often to grave complications which weaken the fighting efficiency of confederate forces : and Turenne's experience told him that he might count much upon the want of agreement known to exist among the many Serene Highnesses in the Imperial army.

Making all allowances, however, for the extent to which his knowledge of the enemy's army and of its generals seemed to warrant him in undertaking an enterprise that he would not have dared to attempt against Montecuculli, it can hardly be said that Turenne was justified in the attack upon which he now resolved. To cross an unfordable river and attack a superior force strongly posted behind it, was to defy all military theory. None but a master in the practice of war knows when to discard theory; and the instinct which prompts him to do so at the right moment, is the hall-mark of real military genius. It is this instinct which chiefly distinguishes the true general from the theorist, who though, perhaps, a clever writer upon war, could never be converted into a leader of men. The operation in question was one which embraced so many elements of danger and of failure, that it was only as a last resource that a general with an army of very inferior strength could have been warranted to make the attempt. That Turenne was not punished as he ought to have been, is, however, a strong argument in his favour, and proves how well he had gauged the weakness of his enemy's army, and the character of its commander.

All through the night, Turenne's troops, column after column, filed in silence over the bridges on the Breusch, and through the fords in the little southern arm of that river, and by daybreak on the following morning, the 4th October, the whole French army was formed in battle array, with its right resting on the village of Holtzheim. The Imperialists made no attempt to interrupt this difficult and dangerous night operation. Turenne, who had been in the saddle all night, moved forward his army in two lines as soon as it was light, and formed up, with his right resting on the 'Little Wood' and his left on the village of Lingelsheim.

The French army numbered about 22,000 fighting men, with thirty guns,* that of the Imperialists consisted of about 35,000 men and fifty guns.

The morning opened with a thick fog, which soon turned into a heavy downpour of rain lasting all day. As the troops took up their appointed positions in line, Turenne moved about from one command to another, and showed himself to his men, who caught from him that electric feeling of confidence with which he never failed to inspire them, and for which, as well as for his peculiar gaiety of manner on the day of battle, he was renowned. It is unnecessary to follow the events of the day in detail, for the British troops were exclusively engaged at one point, the 'Little Wood.' Twice it was taken, and the French and English driven from it with horrible loss. After the second repulse, a violent storm suspended the fighting for awhile; but the temporary cessation of slaughter seemed only to intensify the fury with which Churchill's and the other British regiments returned to the attack for the third time, over piles of dead and dying. The battle, fought throughout in drenching rain, lasted from 9 a.m. until darkness separated the combatants and ended the mutual cannonade which was kept up, as long as the gunners on each side could see an enemy to fire at. The French and English in the end remained masters of the 'Little Wood,' but only after a vast expenditure of human life. Although technically the French won, it was in every way an indecisive battle. The French, who had been on the march in rain and mud for nearly forty hours before the battle, were too tired and hungry to pursue, even had they known of their opponent's retreat or

---

* The French regiments were not nearly up to their establishment. The squadron was only about 120, and the battalions not more than 600 strong each. This was an epoch of strong squadrons and strong battalions.

of his heavy losses. Both sides fell back simultaneously
as soon as darkness covered their movements, each ignorant
of the fact that his enemy had retreated. Turenne felt
that his men must have repose and food, and of these he
could only be certain by falling back behind the Breusch,
where he had left his supply trains and baggage. The
courage displayed by the troops on both sides in the
' Little Wood ' was remarkable, but the battle was not
creditable to either of the commanders engaged. The
rashness of Turenne's passage of the Breusch and of his
attack on the Imperial Army, has been already commented
on. But De Bournonville's whole scheme for the battle
was bad, and its execution was still worse. Fearing a
renewal of Turenne's attack the next day, he abandoned his
position during the night, repassed the Ill, and reoccupied
his old camp at Illkirch, to which he had sent back all his
impedimenta towards the end of the battle. In this
hurried retreat he abandoned two guns, a large quantity of
ammunition, and left more than 3,000 dead unburied on
the battle-field. His wounded—most of whom died from
neglect on the following day—were fully as numerous as
his dead. He did not even take the trouble to gain intelligence of the French movements after the action. Had
he known that Turenne had fallen back on Achenheim, he
might have held his position and claimed the victory, for
the twelve squadrons of Horse and four of Dragoons, left by
Turenne to hold the battle-field when he retreated, might
have been easily driven back. During the action the
French took some standards, eight guns, and other trophies.
They lost 2,000 killed and 1,500 wounded.

Churchill, writing to Monmouth some days after the
battle, tells him that his regiment was hotly engaged, and
lost ten officers—five killed and five wounded—out of a
total of twenty-two.*

* In Monmouth's Regiment of Horse eight officers were killed and
most of the others were wounded; in his Regiment of Foot two officers
were killed and two wounded. — General Hamilton's ' History of
Grenadier Guards,' vol. i., p. 194.

The English Ambassador reports that Lewis XIV. 'commended the courage of the King my master's subjects in that action.'* Turenne had his horse shot, and his aide-de-camp, Duras, Lord Feversham's brother, had three horses killed.†

The news-letters from Paris of this autumn describe how late the French army was in taking up its winter quarters.‡ The want of forage was much felt, and heavy storms made life under tents peculiarly trying. A correspondent, writing from Paris in December, mentions that he daily expects Colonel Churchill's arrival. His chief item of news is that the French expect to have two hundred thousand men in the field for the next campaign. Lord Duras, who had just returned from the army, is, he says, 'still here or at Court, where he is like to stay till he hath lost his money, for they play much there.'§

P. 12, 1674.

Turenne's winter campaign, which followed, is amongst his most brilliant achievements, and its details, which are not attempted here, are extremely valuable to the military student as a splendid example of what is technically known as the offensive-defensive.

* Fourth Report of Historical MSS., p. 238.
† Historical MSS., Appendix to Seventh Report, p. 492.
‡ Rolls Office, F. O. State Papers, France, 1674.
§ *Ibid.*

CHAPTER XX.

CHURCHILL SERVES WITH THE FRENCH ARMY.

He spends his winters at home—Turenne's character—Charles receives large sums from Lewis—Churchill made Colonel in the English Army.

CHAPTER
XX.
——
1675-7.

WE know little of Colonel Churchill's proceedings during the years 1675 to 1677, beyond the fact that he spent the summers with the French army on the Rhine, and shared in all its hard-fought victories. The following letter from a French lady at Metz, written to him in 1711, proves that he was also so employed during the summer of 1677:

'It would not be easy to forget a nobleman like you, and it is to me an indispensable duty to remember all my life the kindness you showed me at Metz thirty-four years ago. You were then very young, my lord, but you already gave hopes by your excellent qualities of that courage, refinement of manner, general bearing and conduct which have, with so much justice, qualified you to command all men. And what is still more to your honour, my lord, all the world, friends and enemies, bear witness to the truth of this which I have the honour to write to you. I make bold to tell you that your generosity in dealing with me made itself felt then, for those who came to burn and lay waste my lands of Mezeray, in the plain, spared them, alleging they had been ordered to do so by a great personage.'*

* Given in the original French, vol. i., p. 8, of Coxe. The writer was a Madame St. Just.

During Churchill's frequent winter and spring journeys backwards and forwards between Turenne's army on the Rhine and England, he usually stayed some days in Paris. We find repeated notices of these short visits in the correspondence of the time. His fluency in the French tongue secured him an entry into Parisian society, and enabled him to enjoy it in a way that was open to few contemporary Englishmen.

His winters at home were meanwhile spent at Court in attendance upon the Duke of York. In the winter of 1674-5 there were private plays at Court, in which all the actresses were ladies. The Princesses Mary and Anne, Lady Henrietta Wentworth—afterwards mistress to the Duke of Monmouth—Lady Mary Mordaunt, the virtuous Mistress Blague, and Mistress Sarah Jennings, who acted the part of 'Mercury,' all took part in them.* The Duke of Monmouth, Viscount Dunblane, and other noblemen, often danced at these performances. Mrs. Betterton, the best actress of the day, was employed to teach elocution to the Princesses and Sarah Jennings. She also superintended the 'business' of each piece. 'Mithridates,' and the 'Masque,' entitled 'Calisto, or, The Chaste Nymph,' by Crowne, for which Dryden wrote the epilogue, were amongst the plays acted this winter.

Besides attending at Court, Churchill was occasionally engaged during these winters in military duties. In the army records of the time we find him mentioned now and then as a member of courtsmartial assembled in London, and he frequently attended reviews of the troops held either on Putney Heath, at Hounslow, or in Hyde Park.†

---

* Evelyn's Diary, $\frac{15}{23}$ 12, 1674. The good Margaret Blague, afterwards married to Sidney Godolphin, was a strange phenomenon at this coarse and dissolute Court. It was not until the Restoration that female performers were introduced on the English stage, and until that epoch there was practically no scenery used in our playhouses. The play became a most popular amusement during the reigns of Charles II. and his brother.

† For one which took place in Hyde Park about this time, we find the Master-General of the Ordnance directed to produce '8 field

In April, 1675, the Commons—who sat that year in the Banqueting House, Whitehall—pressed the King to recall the British troops serving under Turenne, and had this demand been acceded to, Churchill would not have shared in the battle in which Marshal Turenne fell, and where the English regiments in the French service fought so hard to avenge his death.*   It was under this renowned Captain— the·greatest strategist of his age—that Churchill learnt the art of war.   No pupil could have had a more competent master, and no master could have had an apter pupil.   The French have well said that Marlborough learnt from a French General how to destroy French armies.   It was Turenne's pupil who inflicted upon France those crushing defeats from which she never recovered until the transcendent genius of Bonaparte brought back victory to her standards.

Marlborough's tutor in war will for ever be accorded a high place amongst the greatest soldiers of all time, and as long as nations have any feelings of gratitude, France will continue to cherish his memory.   A born leader of men, of ancient and princely lineage, nature had liberally endowed him with the qualities of the hero.   His was a grand and lofty character, and although not free from the frailties of ordinary men, he was in moral worth far

pieces, viz., foure demi-culverings, and foure saker brasse ordnance and two mortar pieces with all their carriages and furniture thereunto belonging, together with two waggons, two tumbrells, and four tents, attended with a competent number of gunners, fifty pioneers with their respective officers.'   Eight a.m. was the time fixed for the review.   In May, 1675, Churchill's regiment, in which his brother Charles was then a captain, was ordered to be incorporated in that of Monmouth's.   It is curious to find how often young gentlemen were then allowed to hold commissions in the army and in the navy at the same time.   George Churchill was a lieutenant and Jasper Churchill an ensign ' in His Royal High[ness] the Duke of York's regiment of Foot,' whilst they were both serving afloat as naval officers.   The Right Honourable Sir Thomas Chickeley, Knight, was then Master-General of the Ordnance.

* See note by transcriber on letter No. 345 of Venetian Transcripts, No. 30, 1674-5, in Rolls Office.

above all his contemporaries. He was killed near Sanspach, in the sixty-fourth year of his age, and it is much to his credit that he died poor, although he had numerous opportunities of becoming rich. His consummate strategy, brilliant tactics, extreme activity, and the mixture of daring and caution with which he compensated for inferiority in numbers, remind us of Wellington in the Peninsula. Strict integrity and lofty patriotism were common to both Turenne and Wellington; but whilst the Englishman's task was more difficult, he was also made of sterner stuff. If he could not claim to possess the affection of his soldiers, he would have scorned the man who, at fifty years of age, changed his religion to please his King. Turenne once aspired to be the leader of the Huguenots in France, but he seems to have changed his views when he found that the Protestants were subdued, dispersed, and incapable of concerted action. Upon his return to Paris in 1667, he realized that his religion was a serious, if not a fatal bar to his advancement. He accordingly resolved to turn Catholic, and it is even said that he made the bestowal of a Cardinal's hat upon his nephew one of the conditions upon which he agreed to renounce the faith in which he had been reared. Turenne, educated in the strictest form of Calvinism, and taught to hate the Church which had so cruelly persecuted his co-religionists, thus became a Catholic from interested motives. Yet no French historian points the finger of ridicule or reprobation at him for having done so. How differently would English party writers have treated Marlborough had he changed his religion to please his master, James II.!

In November, 1676, the French Ambassador in London wrote to Louvois that the Duke of Monmouth was anxious about the recruiting of his regiment in the French service. He was not satisfied with the Lieutenant-Colonel commanding it in the field, and wished, as James did also, to replace him by Colonel J. Churchill. Courtin said that a Mr. Macarthy, a nephew of the Duke of Ormond, was also anxious for the position, but he did not think him to be so well qualified as Churchill.

During all these years King Charles was at his old game, selling the interests of his country to his cousin of France. In the Archives of the French Foreign Office, there is a receipt, still preserved, for 'cent mille escus monnaie de France,' which was the second quarter of his salary. It is signed, 'Done at Whitehall the 25th September, 1676,' 'Charles R.'* Courtin informs Lewis in his letters, that the English members of Parliament are openly clamouring for French money. He assures his master, that the thousands so spent have been well employed, and that those who give nothing in England are badly served. Such was the morality of King, ministers, and courtiers, amongst whom Marlborough spent his younger days. Even the honoured name of Algernon Sidney figures on the list of those who took Lewis's money, but John Churchill's name is not there, and it is as certain as anything can well be, that at no time of his life did he ever take a bribe to the injury of England.

Charles at this time suffered most in public estimation on account of his brother's change of religion. He said himself that all his troubles might be traced to this cause, and added, that, 'all England has been in motion and apprehensive that I have other designs, or am taking measures for changing the Government and religion of my country. This is the rock against which I must guard myself: and, I assure you, I need everything to enable me to resist the continual efforts of the whole English nation; for, in fine, I am the only one of my party, except it be my brother.'†

In the winter of 1677-8 Charles made Churchill Colonel of a regiment of Foot in the English army. The date of his commission was altered so as to make him junior to Colonel Legge, James's prime favourite.

* French Archives of Foreign Affairs, vols. c., ci.
† Barillon's letter to Lewis XIV. of 1. 11, 1677.

CHAPTER XXI.

MARRIAGE OF WILLIAM AND MARY.

It was no love-match—Sir W. Temple—Mary's religious education—
Her personal charms—She is unwilling to marry William—The
marriage a serious blow to Lewis XIV.

The Princess Mary, eldest daughter of the Duke of York, was this year married to her first cousin, William of Orange. The event, though it did not at the moment seem to be one of unusual importance to England, had a profound influence not only upon the Duke of Marlborough's career and upon English history, but also upon the future of Protestantism and liberty throughout Europe. It was no love match on either side. Policy and personal ambition alone influenced the bridegroom, who thought it would help him in his struggle to defend Holland; while as for the poor, weeping bride, she was allowed no voice in the matter, but had to marry an ungainly little foreign Prince whom she did not like, and had not yet even learned to esteem.

There had been negotiations about this marriage as far back as 1674, and the King was then so anxious to bring it about, that he sent Lord Ossory to Holland to arrange it. William had also seemed inclined for it at first, but he afterwards drew back, thinking that the match was not a sufficiently good one.* When the matter was first mooted, Lewis XIV. did all he could through his paid agent, 'Madam Carwell,' to strengthen James's opposition to it on religious

* Lord Ossory's letter in Carte's 'Ormond,' vol. ii., p. 447.

grounds, and even went so far as to flatter him with the hope that his daughter might marry the Dauphin.

In 1674 the probability that Mary should ever be Queen of England was small indeed, but three years later matters wore a changed aspect. Protestant Britain from north to south had become alarmed at the bare possibility that James might succeed his brother as King, and the Test Act was the result. Its immediate effect was to give the Princess Mary a political importance she had never possessed before. Her father had no sons, and were he finally excluded from the succession, the crown would by right devolve upon her at the death of Charles II. She had, therefore, become an eligible match for an ambitious prince, and William showed how fully he understood this, by reopening the question of the alliance in conversation with his trusted friend Sir William Temple. That able diplomatist, who was one of the few Englishmen, if not the only one, whom William ever trusted implicitly, urged the match, and gave a reassuring and satisfactory account of the appearance, temper, and unaffected piety of the Princess.* She had been carefully trained in the Protestant faith by H. Compton, afterwards Bishop of London, who had instilled into the minds of both the princesses, Mary and Anne, an intense hatred of priestcraft, and was accordingly detested by the whole of the Roman Catholic party.

William was aware of Charles's antipathy to the Protestant party and of his leaning towards the Church of Rome.† He also knew how strongly his proposed marriage with Mary was opposed by his enemy Lewis XIV., and how deeply English Protestant sentiment had been wounded by the marriage of both Charles and James to Roman Catholic princesses. Thus he concluded that the marriage of James's eldest daughter to one who was already regarded as the champion of religious liberty, could not fail to prove acceptable to all classes in Great Britain.

* Sir William Temple's 'Memoirs.'   † Harris's 'Life of William.'

After much discussion with Temple, the Prince set out for England, landed at Harwich, proceeded at once to Newmarket, where the Court was then residing, and was well received by Charles in the palace which he had lately built.

William was most anxious to judge for himself if Mary really was all that his friend Temple had described her, and Charles, to please his nephew, curtailed his intended stay at Newmarket by several days, and went to London. There they met, and William found that Temple's description of the Princess was in no way exaggerated. He was extremely pleased with her, as, indeed, he had every reason to be. She was tall, handsome, graceful, and good. Her piety, deep and real, sprang from a sincere, honest heart, thoroughly imbued with the faith she professed. She was a sincere believer in the constant care of an ever-present God, whose hand she recognised in all the events of her life. It was her Maker, she felt, who directed all she did, and she bowed, therefore, to every duty imposed upon her as the result of His commands.

But this strange Prince was not a suitor at all calculated to attract a girl still under sixteen years of age. Taciturn and reserved to the verge of moroseness, sullen in expression, ungracious in conversation, he was essentially unlovable.* We know him now as one of the world's most remarkable men, but it is no wonder that the child about to become his wife, should have wept bitterly at the prospect before her. Queen Catherine, to console her, contrasted Mary's position with her own when she left Portugal to marry a prince she had never even seen. 'Yes, madam,' sobbed her niece; 'but, remember, *you* were coming *into* England, *I* am going *out* of it.'

Mary was James's favourite daughter, and he looked upon this match with peculiar abhorrence, but his objections were somewhat lessened by an increase of income for life which the King gave him from the profits of the Post-office. Charles hoped by this marriage to regain favour

* See Chapter XIV. for a description of his character and appearance.

with the people, who, he thought, would regard it as a pledge that both he and his brother meant to stand by the Protestant cause.* Moreover, Charles knew how thoroughly the sympathy of England was with the Dutch and against the French, for as Courtin told Lewis, 'the English hate us, and only desire a pretext to show openly their animosity.'

J, 11,'1677.   Churchill was present at William's marriage, which took place at eleven o'clock on the night of Sunday, the Prince's birthday, in Mary's bedroom in St. James's Palace, and Charles found scope for his coarse wit as he himself drew the curtains round the bride and bridegroom with the shout of 'St. George for England.'

No royal marriage has in a like degree influenced the whole current of English history, for the Revolution to which it led, ranks in our national annals with the Reformation and the Norman Conquest. The marriage was fraught with the deepest interest for all who loved freedom. Had it not taken place, it is difficult to see how the nation could have ever rid itself of James II., or how the Crown could have been settled on the Protestant princes of the House of Hanover. Charles little thought, when he ordered his brother to give the Princess Mary in marriage to William, that he was virtually placing the English crown upon William's head, to the exclusion of James, and of his male heirs for ever! It was a sad blow to Lewis XIV. All his scheming and bribery had ended in the marriage of the heiress-presumptive to the English Throne with his most deadly enemy. Lewis, said the English Ambassador in Paris, received the news, 'as he would have done the loss of an army.'

For the next eleven years, the palace of Loo was the common meeting-place of all Englishmen, who, dreading the re-establishment of Popery in England as fatal to liberty, had already begun to plot against James.

---

* Letter from Barillon to Lewis of ¹₁ 11, 1677. See Dalrymple, vol. i., p. 179.

Holwell House.

CHAPTER XXII.

The birth and birthplace of Sarah Jennings—Her forebears—Sarah's mother—Her sister Frances, Lady Tyrconnel.

In this year John Churchill married Sarah Jennings.[*] Marriage, always a momentous affair, affected the character and fortunes of Marlborough in a very special way. It was during one of his annual visits to England at the end of the year's campaign—probably in the winter of 1675-76 —that he met this extraordinary woman, then a girl of fifteen, and was fascinated by her wit and startling beauty. He was at the time still much under the Duchess of Cleveland's influence, and it was said that he was only able to free himself from her meshes by a stratagem, which supplied her with a new and handsome lover in his place.

The birth of Sarah Jennings is thus registered in the abbey church of St. Albans : ' 1660, June, Sarah dã of Richard Jennings, Esqr., by ffrances his wife, was borne the fifth day of June, and baptized the 17th of the same.'

Her exact birthplace has been variously stated by historians. She herself fixes it, by naming St. Albans as her ' native town.'[†] From the abbey churchwardens' book it

---

* Henry St. John, one of the chief conspirators in the plot which destroyed Marlborough's power, was born this year.

† In the deed by which she endowed the Marlborough Almshouses for old soldiers in that place. At p. 5, vol. i., of Mrs. Thomson's ' Memoirs of the Duchess,' there is the following note which corroborates this statement that she was born in St. Albans, and not in Holywell

appears, that when she was born her parents lived in a
house in the middle ward rated at £30 per annum, which
shows it to have been a house of some pretensions. They
also owned an old house at the end of the town, called
Holywell House, but they did not occupy it at the time of
her birth. When Churchill built new Holywell House in
1684-85, he pulled down the old one, which had stood on
the road, close to the bridge over the river Ver.* It had
been built in the sixteenth century by Sir Ralph Rowlat,
who had obtained possession of the Holywell property, and
also of the manor of Sandridge, upon the dissolution of
the monasteries.† His daughter Elizabeth married Bernard
Jenyns, of Fanne, Godalming, and of Braboeuf, Guildford,
both in the county of Surrey, and by this marriage the

House, outside that place : 'A member of the highly respectable family
of a former Rector of St. Albans distinctly recollects that it used to be
the boast of her aunt, an old lady of eighty, not many years deceased,
that she had herself been removed, when ill of the small-pox, to the
very room in the house where Sarah, Duchess of Marlborough, was
born. This was a small building, since pulled down, and its site is
now occupied by a summer-house between what is called Holywell
Street and Sopwell Lane, in St. Albans, and within the space afterwards occupied by the pleasure-grounds of the great house at Holywell.'

* The new house was surrounded by well-laid-out grounds and
gardens ; there was a fine pond, in which, Chauncy, who wrote in 1700,
tells us, were 'trout and other fish, for convenience of his table.' It was
finally sold in 1837, and was eventually pulled down in 1846. Some
remains of the stables still exist as out-houses to the cottages built
between the present restraightened road, and the old diverted one.
Some of the ornamental windows shown in the Gothic bay on our
left of the picture may still be seen in the neighbouring farm-houses,
having been sold when the house was pulled down in 1846. In the
grounds of this mansion was a holy well, from which the place
derived its name. In it, tradition alleges, the nuns of Sopwell used
to dip their hard bread to make it eatable.

† He was a Master of the Mint to Henry VIII., and died March, 1544,
and was succeeded by his son Ralph, who died 28, 4, 1571. Both were
buried in St. Albans.—Parish Register. It was upon the son's death,
without issue, that the property went to Elizabeth Rowlat, who had
married Bernard Jenyns.

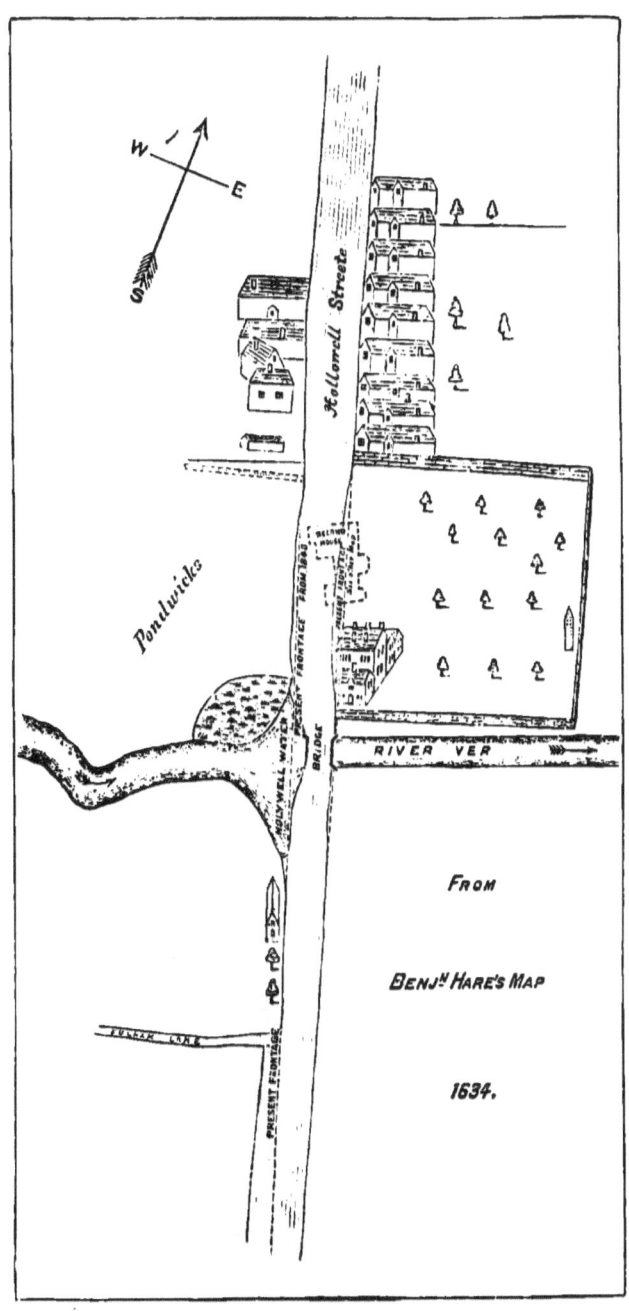

PLAN OF HOLYWELL STREET IN 1634.

To face p. 154, Vol. I.

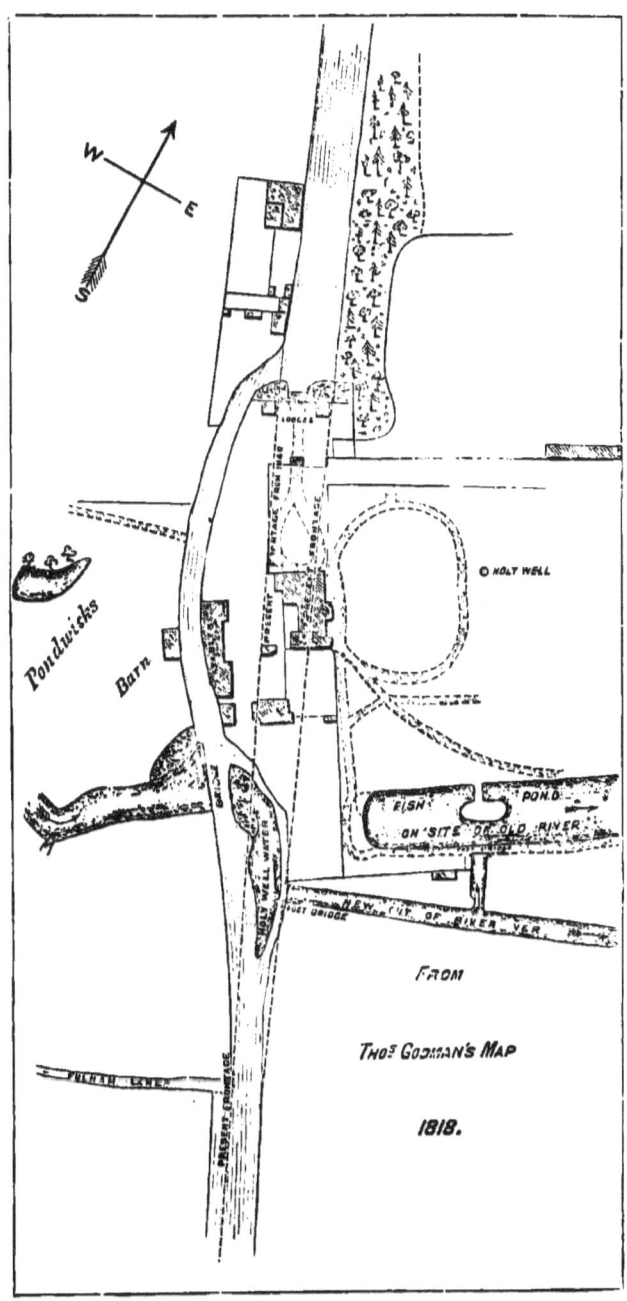

W E S

Pondwicks

Barn

LODGES

HOLT WELL

FISH POND
ON SITE OF OLD RIVER

NEW CUT OF RIVER VER
FOOT BRIDGE

FROM

THOS GODMAN'S MAP

1818.

PLAN OF HOLYWELL STREET IN 1818.
To face p. 154, Vol. I.

CHAPTER
XXII.

1678.
10, 4, 1572.

Holywell and Sandridge estates passed to the Jenyns family. By a strange coincidence their son, Ralph Jenyns, acquired the manor of Churchill, in Somersetshire, where he died in 1572.

Sir John Jenyns, Sarah's grandfather, was High Sheriff of Herts in 1625, and sat in two Parliaments for St. Albans.* About the year 1610 he built a fine brick mansion, Water End House, at Sandridge, on the north bank of the river Lee.† He was made a Knight of the Bath by James I. at the same time as his own son, afterwards Charles I. Sarah's father was Richard Jennings, Esq., of Sandridge, Herts, of Churchill, Somerset, and of Fann and Brabœuf, Surrey, and he was patron of the living of Sandridge.‡ He had been Member of Parliament for St. Albans in 1642, and again from 1661 to the time of his death, seven years afterwards. Sarah refers to him as owning 'property in Somersetshire, Kent, and St. Albans, of about four thousand pounds a year.'§ With that indifference to the spelling of family names which was common even down to the beginning of this century, we find the name spelled at various times 'Jennens,' 'Jenens,' 'Jenyns,' 'Jennyngs,' and 'Jennings.' The heads of the family had been squires for many generations, and had remained Royalists throughout the 'Great Rebellion.'

Born in 1619; died in 1668.

If a comparison were instituted between the families of the two lovers, it would be found that the lady came of the more ancient lineage. The Jennings were, without doubt,

* That of 1628 and of 1640—'the Long Parliament.'

† It was about one mile south-west of Ayot St. Peter.—' History of Hertfordshire,' by Cussans. There is a tablet in St. Peter's Church, at St. Albans, to the memory of his daughter Anne, who died 8, 12, 1656. On it he is described as of Holywell, in St. Albans. He had a very large family by his wife Alice. He died in 1642, and she in 1663.

‡ The Parliamentary Commission of 1650 reported this living to be worth £35 a year, and to be in the gift of R. Jennings, Esq.

§ ' Private Correspondence,' vol. ii., p. 112. As already stated, he had, before Sarah was born, sold his property in Somersetshire—the Manor of Churchill—in 1562, to Sir John Churchill, Master of the Rolls, and first cousin to Marlborough.

entitled to bear arms from an early period, but, as was
commonly the case, they possessed no crest until the reign
of Henry VIII., when one was granted to ' Sir John
Jennyns, Knt., of Churchill, Co. Somerset.' This 'crest
and helm ' was confirmed to him by deed of 1563.*

The mother of Sarah Jennings was Frances, daughter
of Sir Gifford Thornhurst, Bart., of Agnes Court, Old
Romney, Kent.+ Tory writers have asserted that she was
an infamous woman of mean origin. Like the mother
of Prince Eugène, she also was said to be a sorceress.
She is referred to by Mrs. Manley as 'The famous Mother
Shipton, who, by the power and influence of her magic art,
had placed a daughter in the same station (as Arabella
Churchill) at Court.'‡ These outrageous slanders, for which
Swift is mainly responsible, had their origin in party spite
alone.§ Mrs. Jennings was respected in her own county,
as may be seen by this extract from a letter written by a
neighbouring lady to Sarah in after-life: 'I must own
my affection to the memory of your noble mother, who
honoured me with her love, and bestowed upon me many

* This deed, dated 7, 5, 1563, is now at Blenheim Palace. Sir John
Jennings is recorded as a lunatic in the pedigree given in Mr. E.
Green's ' Manor of Churchill.'

+ Agnes or Aghne Court is now a farmhouse. Sir Gifford Thorn-
hurst had married Susanna, daughter of Sir A. Temple, Knight, of
Chadwell, Essex; he died in 1627 without male issue. His widow
married secondly, Sir Martin Lister, Knight. The marriage license of
Sarah's mother and father runs thus: ' 1643, Richard Jenyns, Esq., of
St. Albans, bach., 24.—Frances Thornhurst, of St. Martin's-in-Fields,
spinster, 18, her father dead, consent of mother, now wife of Sir Martin
Lister, Knight,' etc.

‡ 'The New Atalantis.' See also 'Oliver's Pocket Looking-glass, 1711.'
Sarah's mother was the Damereta of Mrs. Manley, and the 'Mother
Haggy' of 'The Story of the St. Albans Ghost.' There is a picture of
her at Althorp; the face and expression are most unpleasant.

§ 'The St. Albans Ghost,' published in 1712, is a coarse pamphlet,
devoid of wit, and is from beginning to end a scandalous libel on the
Duchess of Marlborough and her family. In Swift's journal it is thus
mentioned: 'I went to Lord Masham's to-night, and Lady Masham
made me read her a pretty twopenny pamphlet called "The St. Albans
Ghost." I thought I had writ it myself, so did they; but I did not.'

costly favours,' etc.[*]   She was an intimate friend of
Elizabeth, Lady Anglesey, and lived with her for years
in London after she left St. Albans.   A number of Lady
Anglesey's letters to her have been preserved, and they
show how highly she was esteemed by her friend.   The
following is a specimen :

'*Saterday. Novemb.* 19*th*, 1692.

'My dearest frances I hope y^u do not take it ill of me
y^t Mrs Midleton troubles y^u for it was never in my thought
nor had I seen her when she sent y^u her letter : nor can I
now se her I am so ill with a cold and nothing will cure or
make me happy but ye sight of y^u.   I am in new mourning
for a brother's widow of mine: So I canot be pleased but to
have y^r presence if y^u will save my life com to the greatfull
hart of her I acknowledg she is y^r most obliged true friend
.& servant   E. ANGLESEY.[+]

'Mrs. Midleton wod be at ye aldermans if she may.   My
Lord Marlbury has behaved himself so well he has y^e
praise of all ye world.'

This letter is addressed : 'These ffor the honb^{le} M^{rs}
Jennings at her house in St Albans hartford sheir.'

Like her famous daughter, the mother had a violent and
uncertain temper, as may be gathered from the following
correspondence.   In one of the letters, written during the
time Colonel Churchill was courting Sarah Jennings, we
read of a violent quarrel, apparently ending in blows,
between mother and daughter: 'Mrs. Jennings and her
daughter, Maid of Honour to the Dutchesse, have had

* The writer was Mary Wittewronge, daughter-in-law of a neighbouring knight of that name, who lived at Rothamsted Park, near St.
Albans.   Appendix, vol. i. of Mrs. Thompson's Life of Sarah.

† She was daughter of Sir James Altham, Knt.   Her husband was
Arthur Annesley, son of Viscount Valentia; born 1614, died 1686.   He
was created Earl of Anglesey.   He held many high offices in Ireland,
and afterwards in England.   He was a man of letters and a great
English historian.   He refused to go with Charles and James in their
violent measures against liberty, and was dismissed from the office of
Privy Seal in consequence.

so great a falling out that they fought: the young one complained to the Dutchesse that if her mother was not put out of St. James's, where she had lodgings to sanctuary her from debt, she would run away; so Sir Alleyn Apsley was sent to bid the mother remove, who answered, with all her heart : she should never dispute the Duke and Dutchesse's commands, but with the Grace of God she would take her daughter away with her . . . . . . so rather than part with her, the mother must stay, and all breaches are made up again.'

What a state of society ! A month later the feud between mother and daughter was renewed, with the result described in this further letter :

' M^{rs}. Sarah Jennings has got the better of her mother, who is commanded to leave the Court and her daughter in itt, notwithstanding the mother's petition that she might have her girle with her, the girle saying she is a mad woman.'*

The following letter from Sarah, written early in her married life, describes another serious altercation she had just had with her quarrelsome mother :

Saturday night.

' I have thought very often sence I left my deare Mother what was the reason of all that disorder and ill-humer the night and morning before I came away, and if I thought I had don any thing that you had reason to take ill, I should be very angery with my self, but I am very sure I did not intend any thing but to pay you the duty I ought and if against my will and knowledg I have committed any fault, I hope you will forgive it and I beg you will consider how often I stop'd the coach as wee came home and beg'd you to come in which I could doe for noe other reason but for feare you should get your death and what reason had you when you came home to say soe

---

* These two letters are from Lady Chaworth to her brother, Lord Roos. See Historical MSS. Commission, Twelfth Report, part v., 1889, pages 32 and 34.

many cruell things to me and bety Moody which I can't but take to my self, the post is going and I can say noc more but that I hope I shall see you or hearc from you very soone and I that I will ever bee your most duty full Daughter whatever you are to me. CHURCHILL.

'for Mrs. Jenyns at her hous in St Albans hartfordshire.'*

CHAPTER XXII.

1678.

Many of Sarah's letters to her mother are amongst the Blenheim Palace papers. They are couched in affectionate and respectful terms, and most arc addressed : ' For Mrs. Jenyns at the Countess of Anglesy's hous London.'

The mother left her manors, lands, and personal pro-perty to Sarah for her sole and separate use, so that her 'dear son-in-law, John Earl of Marlborough, tho' I love him with all my heart, shall not have any benefit,' etc.+ The expression in her will of a fervent faith in Christ proves how unfounded are all the calumnies about her scepticism and witchcraft, which Tory writers published to annoy the daughter whom they hated. But it must be admitted that, in the violence of her temper, in her cross-grained dis-position and erratic conduct, we find traces of that species of insanity which I believe to have been inherited by her daughter Sarah.

Sarah's grandfather, Sir John Jennings, had many children, most of whom died in infancy. He was suc-ceeded by his son Richard, Sarah's father. Her brother John, his heir, died in 1674, and was succeeded by her other brother Ralph, who also died without issue, when the property devolved upon his three surviving sisters,

Buried 27, 9, 1674.

Ralph, born $\frac{10}{20}$ 10, 1657 ; buried $\frac{13}{23}$ 7, 1677.

* The exact copy of this letter is given as a fair specimen of her spelling and mode of writing in early life.

† The will of Sarah's father was proved in 1668, and her mother's will, dated $\frac{12}{22}$ 2, 1691-2, in 1693-4. The father's burial in St. Albans Abbey is recorded in the parish register of 8, 5, 1668. He is there styled Esquire, and burgess of the Parliament for St. Albans. He was born 1619, and married 1643. The mother in her will desired she might be buried ' att the Aby Church att St. Albans as near as I can be conveniently laid by my first four children.' She did not mention her daughter, Lady Tyrconnel, in her will.—Spencer House Papers.

Chapter
XXII.

1678.

Frances,
born 1648 ;
died 1730-1.

Frances, Barbara, and Sarah. The year following Barbara died, and her only child dying in 1679, Frances and Sarah inherited the property, share and share alike.* In 1684, John Churchill bought up the share of his only surviving sister-in-law, and became sole proprietor of the Hertfordshire property of his father-in-law, Richard Jennings.† This Frances was twelve years older than Sarah, and had joined the household of Anne Hyde, Duchess of York, about 1663-4.

The Maids of Honour of that period were very wild, and the mad freaks of Frances Jennings, with Miss Price, another Maid of Honour, are duly recorded in the pleasant pages of De Grammont.‡ Frances Jennings married, in 1665, Count George, eldest son of Sir G. Hamilton, of Dunnalong, county Tyrone, and grandson of the second Earl of Abercorn.§ He was then Captain of

---

* On the wall of the north aisle of St. Albans Abbey Church is a tablet to the memory of Barbara, with a high-flown inscription, describing her many virtues. She had married Edward Griffith, Esq., of St. Albans, by whom she had one child, also called Barbara, who only outlived her mother one year, and was buried in the same grave. The mother died in London ²³-⁹ 1678-9, in the twenty-seventh year of her age ; the daughter died ²⁵-⁷ 1679. Griffith was subsequently secretary to Prince George of Denmark, and later on became a ' Clerk-Comptroller of the Green Cloth.' He died ¹¹ 2, 1710-11.

† The deed of sale, dated 1684, is by Dame Frances Hamilton, wife of Richard Talbot, Esq., 'one of the daughters and co-heirs of Richard Jenyns, late of St. Albans,' etc.—' The Manor of Churchill,' by E. Green, F.S.A., p. 5.

‡ See Pepys' ' Diary ' for 21, 2, 1664-5.

§ The Hamiltons were then Roman Catholics. It was Sir George's brother Anthony who wrote the De Grammont ' Memoirs ' in French. Count George did good service with the British troops in the French army. He was at the battles of Sintzheim, Entzheim, and Mulhausen in 1674. He distinguished himself at Einsheim, where he was severely wounded. He was with Turenne at the time of his death, and afterwards rose to be a major-general in the French army. He left three children (all daughters) by his wife Frances ; the first, Elizabeth, married, in 1685, Richard Parsons, first Viscount Rosse ; the second, Frances, married, in 1687, Henry Dillon, eighth Viscount Dillon ; and the third, Mary, married, in 1688, Nicholas Barnwell, third Viscount Kingsland. At the Irish Court they were known as the Three Viscountesses.

the King's Troop of Guards, and one of his sisters was a Maid of Honour. He was a Roman Catholic, and Frances Jennings upon her marriage conformed to his religion. In 1667, together with many other loyal Roman Catholics, he was compelled to resign his commission by the law which forbade all members of that faith from holding posts in the public service. Leaving England, he entered the French army, with a strong recommendation from King Charles to Lewis XIV. He was killed during the retreat of the French on Saverne, after the Battle of Zebernstieg in 1676.

Frances Jennings, 'la belle Jenyns' of De Grammont, was very beautiful, with a lovely pale complexion and brilliantly fair hair. 'Nature had given her charms which it is impossible to describe, and to which the Graces had given the finishing touches. Her face gave one the idea of Aurora, or the goddess of Spring.'* The amorous James, Duke of York, made serious love to her, but was repelled with that proud contempt which distinguished the conduct of both these sisters at Court. After three years of widowhood, she married in 1679 a lover of her girlhood, Colonel, or, as he was commonly called, 'Lying Dick' Talbot. A strong Roman Catholic, of an old English family long settled in Ireland, he had been a faithful attendant upon the Royal brothers when in exile during the Commonwealth. For years after the Restoration, he had been Gentleman of the Bedchamber to the Duke of York while Frances Jennings was one of the Duchess's ladies. A steadfast adherent to the House of Stewart, Richard Talbot had even proposed to Charles II. to assassinate Cromwell with his own hand, and had made a journey from Holland to England with that avowed object. He was subsequently committed to the Tower for a similar design upon the Duke of Ormond, whose administration of Ireland displeased him. His brother was made Roman Catholic Archbishop of Dublin, and he was created Earl—and after-

* The De Grammont 'Memoirs.'

wards, in 1689, Duke—of Tyrconnel by James II. He had
originally commended himself to James as a tall, handsome young fellow, ' who wore good clothes, and was of a
clear and ready courage.' If not famous, he is still remembered in Ireland as the brutal Lord-Lieutenant who,
during his three years of office, established the Government under which Protestants of every denomination were
robbed and cruelly ill-treated, many being put to death.*
His ambition was only equalled by his avarice, and as
Lord-Lieutenant he was able to indulge both those
passions. He was the originator of the ' Brass,' or, as it
was then commonly styled, ' Gun ' money, the remembrance of which is perpetuated in the well-known Orange
toast to ' the pious, glorious, and immortal memory of
King William III., who saved us from Popery, slavery
and knavery, *brass money* and wooden shoes.' Tyrconnel
died of apoplexy—some said of poison—during the siege
of Limerick, in 1691. His widow, Frances, lived for some
years at James II.'s Court in France, and then settled
in Ireland, where she made good her claim to part of the
Tyrconnel estate. She died in 1731, and was buried in St.
Patrick's Cathedral.

* The Parliament assembled in Dublin in May, 1689, disappeared
after the Battle of the Boyne the following year. Its proceedings, and
the policy pursued by those in power at the time, are worthy of a careful study. In the few weeks it sat it repealed the Acts of Settlement,
confiscated the property of 2,600 Protestants by name, and allowed
only two months to any of them who wished to do so, to come forward
and stand their trial.

CHAPTER XXIII.

As a child, Sarah Jennings had frequently resided at Court
when her elder sister Frances was in waiting upon the
Duchess of York.* During these visits to St. James's,
Sarah became the playmate of the Princess Anne, her junior
by nearly five years. An attachment soon sprang up between
the two girls, and Anne loved to have Sarah constantly with
her. Sarah also attracted the notice of Mary, the Duke of
York's second wife, who was only two years her senior, and
whilst still quite a child she became Maid of Honour to
that beautiful but unhappy Princess.

Though less lovely than her elder sister, Sarah was still
radiant with beauty, and possessed a graceful figure, and
great power of fascination. Numerous portraits enable us
to admire her distinguished but scornful style of beauty;
there was 'sweetness in her eyes, invitation in her looks,'
wrote Sarah's most scurrilous assailant when describing
her appearance.[†] Sir Godfrey Kneller has recorded for

* Anne Hyde died $\frac{31}{16}$·? 1671, and James married Mary of Modena
at Dover $\frac{29}{9}$-$\frac{11}{12}$, 1673.

† 'The New Atalantis.'

us her small regular features so full of life, her pretty mouth expressive of disdain, her slightly turned-up nose with its open, well-shaped nostril, her commanding air, the exquisite pose of her small head, always a little inclined to one side, her lovely neck and shoulders, and her rich, straw-coloured hair, which glistened in its profusion as if sprinkled with gold-dust. Colley Cibber, who as a servant, waited at table when the Princess Anne, with her attendant, Lady Churchill, dined at Nottingham in 1688, says: 'All his senses were collected in his eyes, which during the whole entertainment wanted no better amusement than of stealing now and then the delight of gazing on the fair object so near him.'* He goes on to say : 'If so clear an emanation of beauty, such a commanding grace of aspect, struck me into a regard that had something softer than the most profound respect in it, I cannot see why I may not without offence remember it.' And again : 'I remember above twenty years after, when the same lady had given the world four of the loveliest daughters that ever were gazed on, their still lovely mother had at the same time her votaries, and her health very often took the lead in those involuntary triumphs of beauty.' Over those with whom she talked she exercised a charm, a fascination, that held them enthralled as much by her graceful wit as by her seductive beauty. But the adorer who worshipped at her shrine, was, without quite knowing how, soon made aware of the imperious temper that smouldered within her, always ready, if stirred, to burst forth as if from a hidden volcano, and annihilate the offender. Her portraits, however, do not convey this idea, and no one could imagine from them that so stormy a spirit lay hidden beneath such a lovely exterior.

Her education had been much neglected, but like many clever people brought up at courts, where all that is wittiest as well as most learned is to be found, she had acquired more practical knowledge than was possessed by

* See his 'Apology.'

many classical and philosophical scholars. In conversation she was bright and quick, although on paper she expressed herself in long, involved, and often ungrammatical sentences. Her handwriting was bad and indistinct, and when an old woman she referred to it, as ' my ridiculous hand.'* She spelled as incorrectly as both the queens, Anne and Mary, as her husband, and as most of the exalted people of her time. She had never been taught arithmetic, but yet she contrived to master the most complicated accounts by some curious process of her own.†

To draw her character is no easy task. As she was when a girl, so she remained as a young mother, as Queen Anne's favourite, as wife to the greatest man of his day, and in old age as his widow. Neither time nor increased knowledge of the world ever changed or in any way softened her. She was essentially an unimaginative, un- impressionable woman, with no illusions about men or about events either human or Divine, and without senti- ment of any kind, except perhaps where her husband was concerned. His love for her was deep, pure, unselfish and passionate. All his letters, meant for no eye but hers, breathe the same loverlike devotion. They make the reader feel, that from first to last, his one great dread was, that she might cease to love him. She did love him sincerely, but in her own haughty and tigerlike fashion. There was nothing demonstrative about her affection, but such as it was, she gave him her whole heart. In most of the rela- tions of life both were egoistical and covetous, yet their marriage was absolutely uninfluenced by mercenary con- siderations. Their mutual attachment was stronger even than their undoubted worldliness.

Both were commonly charged with venality by numerous and powerful enemies. We are told that within the palace itself there was a busy market for Government offices; that Queen Anne's own relations were kept at a distance, whilst

* ' Marchmont Papers,' vol. ii., p. 79.
† Lady M. Wortley Montague, vol. i., p. 74.

patronage was monopolized by one woman to whom there
was no access but by the golden road, etc.* At that time
no person with places at his disposal, made any more
scruple of selling them than of receiving his settled salary
or the rents of his estate, and it was a matter of common
notoriety, that Secretaries of State as well as Cornets of
Dragoons, bought and sold their commissions. King
Charles himself had to buy from Lord Brandon the
command of the King's Troop of Life Guards, which he
wanted for his son Monmouth, and Prince Rupert paid
Lord Mordaunt £3,500 for his Company and the governor-
ship of Windsor Castle. But there is absolutely no proof
whatever that Marlborough or his wife ever sold any
employment or favour beyond the two trifling places of
which she herself tells.† On this subject she says: 'A
little before I succeeded Lady Clarendon in the post of
first lady of the bedchamber to the Princess of Denmark,
Her Highness wrote to me that she intended to take
two new pages of the back-stairs, but that she would
not do it till my Lady Clarendon was gone, that I might
have the advantage of selling those two places.'‡ She
gives the fullest particulars of this matter, and goes on to
say: 'I solemnly swear, as I hope for happiness here and
hereafter, that besides the case of the pages to the Princess
which I have told you of, I never did receive the value of
one shilling in money, jewels, or any such thing, either
directly or indirectly, for the disposing of any employment,
or doing any favour during my whole life, nor from any
person whatsoever, upon any such account, and that if
there is any man or woman upon earth that can give the
least proof to the contrary, I am contented for the future
to be looked upon both by friends and enemies as one of
the vilest of women, worse than Abigail herself, when I
consider her as instrumental in doing the greatest mischief

* Cunningham's 'History of England,' vol. i., p. 258.
† 'The Conduct,' p. 306.
‡ *Ibid.*, p. 306.

that a nation can suffer.' She adds : ' Soon after the Queen came to the crown, I was the cause of having the strictest orders made against taking of money for the disposing of places that were ever known at the Court, which, however consistent it was with having any designs of my own of making money that way, I leave anyone to judge.'*

We are bound to accept this solemn statement as absolutely and literally true, in the absence of evidence, still less of proof, of any sort or kind to the contrary. She published the ' Conduct,' from which much of this is extracted, in 1742, when, as she adds, most of those she had appointed to places were still alive. Had her statement been in any tittle untruthful, many would have been only too glad to expose her. That none ever did so, is strong negative evidence in support of her solemn statement, and as she very convincingly says, had there been any truth in these charges, her enemies, when they came into power, would most certainly have found someone, by the offer of substantial rewards, to inform against her. But ' they never pretended to name or to appeal to any one person for a proof of what they laid to my charge.'† Even her bitter enemy, Harley, bears witness to her unimpeachable integrity in the management of the Queen's money affairs, and when dismissed from office, Anne pronounced her honesty to be above suspicion. Nevertheless, her love of money is undoubted, a taste which she shared with her husband. To amass wealth was a pleasure that increased with her years ; and the mode in which she distributed it in her will, is well worth the consideration of those who wish to understand her curiously complex character. She left Lord Chesterfield a large sum of money to mark her approbation of the manner in which he opposed the Court. ' She was scarcely cold, however,' writes the cynical Horace

---

* Vol. xliv., p. 2, of Coxe's MS. in the British Museum. Also ' Conduct,' pp. 311, 312.

† ' The Conduct,' p. 311.

Walpole, ' before he returned to the King's service.'*   She also left William Pitt £10,000, to record her sense ' of his merit in the noble defence he made for the support of the laws of England and to prevent the ruin of his country.'

She did many kind acts in her old age, and helped friends with money whom she knew to be in difficulties. Hugh Earl of Marchmont, one of her executors, had been long distinguished with whatever affectionate esteem she was then capable of feeling, and when his father died, she wrote pressing him to accept £1,000, being, she said, the half of what she meant to leave him in her will. To make the arrangement more acceptable to him, she hoped that he would, if he preferred it, regard the money as a loan.† She helped Lord Stair with £5,000 to extricate him from debt, and desired in her will that he should not be asked or pressed for it.‡ She paid Dr. Hook £5,000 for being her amanuensis and editor in the publication of her 'Conduct.'§ She gave that vainest of avaricious men, Pope, £1,000 as ' a favour,' without doubt on the tacit understanding, if not upon some more formal agreement, that he was to suppress the lines in which he had scathed her as ' Atossa,' and vilified her husband. His lines on Marlborough are bad in every respect. They are slipshod, unmanly, unfeeling, untruthful, and unworthy of a great English poet. By his acceptance of this money Pope proved himself possessed of all the sordid qualities he so emphatically condemned in his inimitable ' Moral Essays.' In fact, he sold, for money, immunity from the blighting bitterness of his venomous pen. His subsequent intention to publish these lines, only frustrated by his death, furnishes a characteristic instance of that perfidious double-dealing in which he so often indulged. Such was this self-appointed censor, this preacher

---

* Horace Walpole's ' George II.'   Her will was dated 11th August, 1744.

  † ' Marchmont Papers,' vol. ii., p. 207.

  ‡ *Ibid.*, vol. ii., p. 108.

  § Hook was a Quietist, and when he endeavoured to win her over to Popery, she dismissed him summarily.

of a morality he did not practise—at least, when money was to be made by sinning against it.* The fact was, he loved money no less than Marlborough. Bolingbroke, one of the Duke's bitter political enemies, tells us that he intended, as executor to Pope, to burn all the poet's papers which reflected upon Marlborough or his wife.† But Bolingbroke was a magnanimous gentleman, and, alas! we cannot say the same of his friend the poet.

Sarah, both as spinster and wife, knew what poverty meant, and it should not be forgotten, that for the first five or six years of her married life her husband's means were small. Their Court salaries were insignificant, his army pay did not amount to much until he was given a regiment in 1685; and besides these sources of income, he had only the annuity of £500 which he had purchased from Lord Halifax. Indeed, he was far from being well off until he obtained command of the armies abroad in 1703. But he was always a frugal man. His wife wrote of him : 'From the very beginning of his life he never spent a shilling beyond what his income was.' 'He never squandered money.': In her will she left £10,000 to two literary men to write her husband's life, on the condition that they introduced no line of poetry into the work. Poetry was in her mind inseparably connected with Pope, whom she had every reason to detest, whilst in her curiously constituted and unlearned mind, she no doubt despised his calling also. She wished, moreover, to show that no imagination was needed to enhance Marlborough's fame, as truth and justice, unaided by fancy, were alone

---

* See ' Marchmont Papers,' vol. ii., p. 334, for letter from Bolingbroke on this subject. See also vol. iii., pp. 85-93, of Courthope's edition of Pope.

† ' Marchmont Papers,' vol. ii., p. 332. Pope's friends refer often to his habit of equivocation; his enemies called it by a harsher word. His apologist says : ' It is impossible to acquit him of equivocation and double-dealing amounting to perfidy.'—See Courthope's Pope, vol. iii., p. 85.

‡ From a paper by the Duchess of Marlborough in Spencer House.

necessary for the narration of deeds like his. In her later years, she was ever on the watch to guard his reputation, and she evinced the keenest anxiety that he should be handed down to posterity as the greatest man of his age. She prepared his voluminous papers with this object in view, and said, that were she a man, she could desire nothing better than to write his history herself.* 'Could you not,' she added, 'write from his correspondence the most interesting story in the world?' Her husband was bitterly and unjustly slandered, and the more aggressive his enemies and accusers became, the louder and more vindictive grew his wife's language. She just tolerated his friends, but she detested with diabolical intensity every living creature who thwarted him, maligned his character, or dared to belittle his achievements.

The following curious minute, though not in her hand-writing, was evidently written from her dictation.† It has no heading or date, but is docketed, 'Some instructions to the historian for beginning the Duke of Marlborough's history.' It commences thus: 'I have determined to give the materials in my possession to the gentlemen that are to write the Duke of Marlborough's history. They are Mr. Glover and Mr. Mallet.' She adds, they 'are to finish it as soon as they can, with the approbation of my executors and the Earl of Chesterfield.' 'I hope the history will be writ as soon as 'tis possible, for while I am living I shall be able to answer any questions that they may have occasion to ask, for I would have nothing in it but what is the real truth.' She then remarks upon the large sums England had at times to pay for wars that ended in failure, whereas those conducted by her husband were crowned with success.

When Sir Robert Walpole was poor and unknown, she helped him with money and obtained employment for him. He was grateful at the time, and thanked her in the most obsequious terms. Subsequently she learned to dislike and despise him for his hard drinking, debauched tastes,

* Lady M. W. Montague.   † Spencer House Papers.

coarse language, and ill-bred manners. His government
by corruption was odious to her, and she loved to contrast
him, his ways and his actions, with the stern patriotism
of her son-in-law Sunderland, with the integrity of her
devoted friend Godolphin, and with the polished address
and the pure married life of her great and gifted husband.
Horace Walpole in after-years revenged her abuse of his
father, by scattering broadcast every species of malicious
sarcasm and ill-natured story about her. Few study
Sarah's own version of her life, whilst his witty letters
are universally read : and as long as he could make a
telling hit, or clothe his animosity in a racy epigram, he
troubled himself little as to the accuracy of his details.

Late in life, when writing to a friend, she expresses a
hope that her strong Whiggism may not be objected to.
She could never, she says, change her principles on that
score, for as soon as she could understand anything at
Court, she perceived the good reasons there were for
holding them. 'I knew that King Charles and King
James were with remarcable titles taking money of the
King of France to betray their own honour and country,
and the last of these Kings sent a man into prison
for saying that he was a Roman Catholic, who I saw goe
twice a day to mass. And at the same time I saw that
neither of these Kings could indure a Whigg, and were
very fond of the Torys, which made me think with reason
that the first were very *rascalle* (?) men ; but I have learnt
that there is no great difference in partys, and I now have
very great abhorence for both. . . . But as to what is called
the Whigg notion, that I will never part with ; that Parliament should punish ill ministers, and by that means oblidge
weak or bad princes to keep their coronation oaths, and for
their rewards I think they should bestow them as they
please, without being imposed upon by the tenders of either
party.' *

Her feelings of like and dislike were always in the super-

* Historical MSS., Appendix, Ninth Report, p. 474.

lative, and she showed no indulgence towards the faults of those she hated. Her temper prevented her from calmly discussing any subject, for she could not brook contradiction. Like Swift, she rated those who did not agree with her as enemies, for, without knowing it, she divided the world into two camps of friends and foes. In dealing with those around her, she could not counterfeit indifference, nor would she even suffer it from others. She was too open and downright, and too violent a hater, to have any duplicity in her manner. She was free in conversation, and cared little for what others thought of her or her opinions, firmly believing that she herself was always in the right.

She may be said to have lived at Court from the age of twelve. She was educated in a society where almost all were debased and corrupt, and it was wittily said, that if men had gone into mourning for the immorality of their wives, sisters, and daughters, half the Court would have been continually in black. Yet her virtue was above suspicion, not because of any religious principle, or deep sense of right or wrong, but because she was too proud to sin against the laws of morality, and because she loved her husband with a fierce and exclusive earnestness all her own.* In the history of her long life, it is difficult to find many commendable acts which were due to consideration for others, or to any purely virtuous impulse. Her love for and marriage with a poor, and comparatively obscure officer, was the one unworldly step in her life. She never seems to have been influenced by virtue for its own sake, or by any lofty conception either of honour or of right. Capable

---

* Evelyn, lamenting over the depravity of the Restoration epoch, is able to point to one really good and religious woman about Court, his friend Miss Blagge, then Maid of Honour to the Queen. She afterwards married Godolphin, who subsequently became the well-known peer and Minister of Anne's reign. Miss Howard, also a Maid of Honour, who became Lady Silvius, was equally celebrated for her virtue and piety. The two sisters, Lady Ranelagh and Mary, Countess of Warwick, were also remarkable then as good and virtuous women in that depraved age.—Overton's ' Life of the English Church.'

of kindness, and even of generosity to those who for the time were her favourites, she was yet in all her instincts an essentially worldly and unlovable woman. To the pursuit of personal advantages, she brought a quick, active intelligence, and an amount of solid, stern resolve, seldom found in her sex. Hers was no meek heart, and she had little reverence for God or man. At Court she had seen much of the self-seeking Bishops and Deans of her day, and had learnt to view with contempt Churchmen like Swift, whose one aim was preferment. No belief in revealed religion, or dread of future punishment, restrained her will or influenced her conduct; she seldom mentioned religion except to scoff at it, and it was only from a contempt for Romanism, and from an intense hatred to priest-craft, that she spoke and wrote of herself as a Protestant. True, but not tender, she lived for forty-four years with her husband as happily as her domineering nature would have allowed her to live with anyone. But she never shared his strong faith, nor allowed him to exercise any influence over her mind in spiritual matters. She seems to have died as she had lived, ridiculing all belief in God and immortality. She was a sceptic in religion, but hers was the scepticism of indifference; and if she did not believe in the Divinity of Christ, she at least created none of the sham gods of modern philosophy. When eighty-two years of age, she wrote: 'Though the philosophers prove nothing, to my understanding, certain, yet I have a great mind to believe that kings and first ministers souls when they die go into chimney-sweepers. And their punishment is that they remember they were great monarchs, were complimented by Parliament upon their great abilities, and thanked for the great honour they did nations in accepting the Crown, at the same time that they endeavoured to starve them, and were not capable of doing them the least service, though they gave them all the money in the nation.'* In a letter to

* 'Marchmont Papers,' vol. ii. This letter is a very fair specimen of Sarah's involved style of writing.

the Princess of Orange written in March, 1688, Anne endeavours to defend her lady-in-waiting from the charge of irreligion. This letter is interesting also as Anne's estimate at that date of Lady Churchill's character: ' Sorry people have taken such pains to give so ill a character of Churchill. I believe there is nobody in the world has better notions of religion than she has. It is true she is not so strict as some are, nor does she keep such a bustle with religion ; which I confess I think is never the worse, for one sees so many saints mere devils, that if one be a good Christian, the less show one makes the better, in my opinion. Then, as for moral principles, 'tis impossible to have better ; and without that, all that lifting up of the hands and eyes, and often going to church, will prove but a very lame devotion. One thing more I must say of her, which is, that she has a true sense of the doctrine of our Church, and abhors all the principles of the Church of Rome ; so, as to this particular, I assure you she will never change.'

As years went by, and the husband of her choice grew famous—the central figure in Europe—Sarah's pride in his renown equalled in intensity the love she had always felt for him. The depth of that pride is exemplified in the answer she gave when, as a widow and still handsome, the ' proud Duke of Somerset ' asked her to marry him. ' Were I only thirty,' said she, ' I would not permit even the Emperor of the world to succeed in that heart which has been devoted to John, Duke of Marlborough.'

That at one time in her life at least she felt like other women, is evident from the tender satisfaction with which as an old woman she loved to dwell upon the remembrance of those young days before the pure, though even then, haughty love of the girl had been buried in the worldly aims of the callous society-woman. She destroyed most of her own letters to her husband, preserving only those from him, but in a bundle of his papers I found the following scrap in her handwriting : ' Wherever you are,

whilst I have life my soul shall follow you, my ever dear
Lord Marlborough; and wherever I am, I shall only kill
the time [until] night that I may sleep, and hope the next
day to hear from you.'* This bears neither date nor
address, but it was, I think, written in 1692, when he had
been committed by William to the Tower.

In the care with which, all through her stormy life, she
preserved the early letters of her lover, we find an evidence
that even in her cold capricious breast there ever burned
some spark of that romantic sentiment, of those true and
tender feelings which make the whole world kin. A bundle
of papers at Blenheim Palace is endorsed in her handwriting: 'Copies of my letters to Mr. Churchill before I
was married and not more than fifteen years old. There
is in this packet several letters of his, all read over in
1743.'† It is further endorsed thus by her: 'Letters from
Mr. Churchill before and after I was married, which I
desire Grace Ridley may have to burn without reading
them.—Read over in 1736, and again in 1743.' The
bundle is again endorsed in the same handwriting: 'Read
over in 1743, hoping to burn them, but I could not do it.'
These last six words go far towards redeeming her memory
from the sweeping condemnations of those who describe
her as absolutely without any soft, womanly corner in her
heart whatever.

She was a woman for whom book education would have
done much. It would doubtless have somewhat curbed her
impetuous temper, and taught her reason. But that she
could control herself when she fully realized that it was in
her own interest to do so, is fully proved by the power and
influence she obtained over the Princess of Denmark. It
was only when she foolishly imagined she was strong
enough to stand alone without the Queen's support, and
when, in consequence, she ceased to exercise that watchful
control over her mad temper which she had previously

* Blenheim Palace Papers.
† This was the year before she died.

maintained, that she lost her dominion over Anne. But though able to curb her temper when she would condescend to try, she was no match for such astute plotters as Abigail Hill and Harley. Strange to say, she never seems to have understood how hurtful to Marlborough's best interests were these defects in her, and she never sought to correct them from other motives, because she mistook her angry outspokenness for honesty of purpose. She could brook no delay in the fulfilment of a wish; whilst he, on the other hand, worked with extreme calmness and method towards the attainment of any object he had in view, believing, as he said, that 'patience will overcome all things.'* The scurrilous pamphlets which his political opponents put forth enraged her, but, as a rule, affected him so little, that, referring to one of them, he writes: 'The best way of putting an end to that villainy is not to appear concerned. The best of men and women in all ages have been abused. If we can be so happy as to believe ourselves, so as to have no reason to reproach ourselves, we may then despise what rage and faction do.'†

What a contrast was there between her temper and his! Few great men in history possessed his cool imperturbability and calculated self-command. No amount of provocation could ruffle that calm exterior, or, when he had become a great man, betray that cautious tongue into any rash or unguarded expression. His wife remarks upon it, as an extraordinary and unprecedented occurrence, that when he received the unworthy and ungrateful letter in which Queen Anne dismissed him from her service, he flung it 'in a passion' into the fire.

The stories of the Duchess's violence are numerous. Here is one: During an altercation with the Duke, which took place one day whilst she was at her toilet, she burst into an uncontrollable fit of passion. Beside herself with rage, she cared not what she said or did; and the more

---

* A letter from Marlborough to Godolphin.
† This letter refers to 'The Memorial of the Church of England.'

provoked by his imperturbable calmness, she was determined to make him feel where she knew he could be
most easily wounded. Now among her many charms, her
lovely hair was an especial object of his admiration. The
woman is rare indeed, in whom rage could so overcome
vanity as to cause her to injure permanently her own good
looks in order to spite a husband she loved. But Marlborough's wife was such a one, and when he left the room,
she cut off some of her long and beautiful tresses, and
placed them where he must see them. They disappeared,
and she never knew what had become of them until after
his death, when she found them in a cabinet where he
kept his most cherished treasures under lock and key. As
an old woman, she loved to repeat this anecdote against
herself, and always cried when relating it.*

Adversity exercised no chastening or softening influence
upon her temper, which became worse the older she grew.
During one of those outbursts of passion in which she was
wont to revile the Queen, the Duke told a person who was
present, not 'to mind what she said, for she was used to
talk at that rate when she was in a passion, which was a
thing she was very apt to fall into, and there was no help
for it.' Upon another occasion, when referring to his
wife's temper and strange behaviour to the Queen, he said:
'There was no help for that, and a man must bear with
a good deal to be quiet at home.'+

The Duke, however, when present, exercised some control over her, and it was not until he died that the violence
of her temper, as it is described by her contemporaries in
the reign of George II., assumed the character of madness.
One who knew her well describes her as deficient in wisdom
and greatness of mind.‡ In her extreme old age, the man
whose goodwill she thought to have secured by the round
sum she had paid him, said with more correctness than
generosity, that she found 'all her life one warfare upon

---

* Lady M. Wortley Montague's letters ; Horace Walpole.
  † Burnet, vol. vi., pp. 30, 31.   ‡ Speaker Onslow.

earth.'* She had no tact. Each fresh victory gained by her illustrious husband, served only to intensify her ferocity, and the higher the position he won for her, the more unbridled became the license of her bitter tongue. Prosperity and riches served but to accentuate her failings. The spoiled beauty of a Court, the petted favourite of her Sovereign, the wife of the foremost man of his day, she yet enjoyed no real happiness, and knew neither peace, nor repose. Feared and detested, she spent her life in quarrels, and Godolphin tells us, he rejoiced when she was long absent from Court, as he was thus spared the altercations which entered largely into her every-day life.† When at last she died at a great age, hated and hating, with no faith in God or man, she was tormented by the maddening reflection that the calumnies which had been maliciously heaped upon her and upon her husband, would be handed down as truths to future generations.

Prior to Queen Anne's accession she occupied the insignificant position of Bedchamber-Woman, but in one short day, from being a person who until recently had been forbidden the Court, she became its ruler, endowed with more power than any other subject in the kingdom. And how did she bear this access of good fortune? To her credit be it remembered, that she loved England and liberty, and if she used her opportunities to advance the interests of her family, no instances are recorded of unworthy men being preferred to office through her influence. Yet, at one time her authority was such, that she could make and unmake ministers, and all men bowed before her.

Sarah always spoke out what was in her mind at the moment, with a quick impetuosity more creditable to her honesty than to her worldly wisdom. As she said herself: 'You know my way is to tumble out the truth just as it comes in my head.'‡ But the result of this habit was disastrous to her, for it eventually so wrecked her

* Pope.   † Cunningham, p. 77.
‡ Letter in 1726 to Dr. Hare.

power and influence with the Queen, that she lived to see her husband degraded and held up to scorn by hired libellers; and after his demise to realize, that even her own children loathed her and desired her death. Well might she write in her old age, that men who wished to know the value of Court favour and the vanity of human ambitions, should read her history.

A careful study of her life shows plainly, that whilst many of her actions display a strong taint of the insanity she had inherited from her lunatic great-grandfather, her ability, on the whole, has been much overrated. For although the book in which she professed to describe her 'Conduct' at Court is cleverly put together, and there is a taking and defiant swing about its pages which is peculiarly her own, most of her utterances display more temper than wisdom.

Chance made her the early playmate of a weak-minded Princess, and the poor, unknown Colonel whom she married for love afterwards became the foremost man in Europe. Had she never known the Princess Anne, and had she accepted one of the rich courtiers who wished to marry her, Sarah Jennings would now be as little known to history as the other maids of honour, whose mad freaks scandalized the moral and dignified Evelyn, and at the same time, supplied Pepys with so much material for his incomparable 'Diary.'

It would be impossible to deal fully with Marlborough's history, if that of his wife were omitted. Her intimacy with Queen Anne, and the commanding influence it gave her after the death of King William, materially affected the greatest events of his life. The part she played, not only in his private life, but in his public career, cannot therefore be ignored.

Her temper and her doings often tried him sorely, but his devotion to her never wavered. All his letters to her breathe the passionate affection and admiration of the lover. In one he says: 'I do assure you, upon my soul, that I had much rather the whole world should go wrong than that you should be uneasy.' He then refers to her 'dear letters,' and adds, that she is 'dearer to him ten thousand times than ever she was before.'[*] Upon one occasion she went to Margate to see him off for Holland, and at the end of his voyage he wrote: 'It is impossible to express with what a heavy heart I parted with you when I was at the waterside. I could have given my life to have come back, though I knew my own weakness so much that I durst not, for I should have exposed myself to the company. I did for a great while with a perspective glass look upon the cliffs, in hopes I might have had one sight of you.'[†] When this letter was written, he had been married nearly a quarter of a century.

No two women could be more dissimilar in character and disposition, than Queen Anne and her imperious favourite. The Queen was a great stickler about all matters of etiquette, and had a Royal solicitude for trifles. The length of a tie or the cut of a wig was with her a question of importance which demanded serious discussion. Sarah cared nothing for these things. All she cared for was power, and she had it as long as she continued to be first favourite. Through her influence Marlborough virtually ruled England. But her influence did not last. She never accurately gauged Anne's disposition. Her peculiar temperament rendered it impossible for her to stoop to the flattery which is so dear to personages of Queen Anne's mental calibre; and, above all, she lacked the unflagging patience, self-abnegation, and self-restraint, which are indispensable qualifications in a Royal favourite. She fell from her high position through her own unfitness to retain it, and her husband fell with her. Not all the fame he had achieved, nor all the services he had rendered England, could secure him even command of the army when the Queen's favour had

---

[*] Correspondence of Sarah, vol. i., p. 2.
[†] Cox, vol. i., p. 158.

been transferred from his wife to the cunning and soft-tongued Abigail. In that age of Court intrigue, to stand well with the Sovereign was essential to success in public life. William certainly selected Marlborough for the command in Holland, although he did not like him; but he did so because he felt that he could not undertake it himself. Highly as he valued Marlborough as a soldier, it is probable that appreciation of his military capacity influenced William in this selection less than the conviction that Marlborough alone, through his influence with Anne, could effectually push the war which William had so much at heart. In other words, it was Sarah's influence over Anne which secured Marlborough this command, and it was consequently to his wife that he was indebted for his first great opportunity.

CHAPTER XXIV.

JOHN CHURCHILL'S COURTSHIP AND MARRIAGE.

Churchill's first meeting with Sarah — Their love affair encouraged
by Mary of Modena—Their love-letters—Their respective families
object to the match—Engagement broken off for a time—His
father urges him to marry Catherine Sedley—Sarah and he marry,
but there is no record of their marriage—Names of their children.

CHAPTER
XXIV.

1677.

JOHN CHURCHILL and Sarah Jennings met for the first time
in the Duchess of York's drawing-room in St. James's
Palace, and danced together upon that occasion—she being
then in her sixteenth year, and he twenty-five. We learn
her age from the following endorsement in her own handwriting on the back of one of his love-letters. 'I was
fifteen when this was written.' It has been generally
admitted that it was a case of 'love at first sight' on both
sides.

He was without doubt the most likely man then at Court
to captivate any woman, and especially to throw a spell
over the heart of a very young girl. He possessed every
quality, but riches, most calculated to endear him to the
opposite sex. Besides, she was flattered by her conquest
of the Duchess of Cleveland's handsome and fascinating
lover.

Sarah's love for him must have been intense, for in no
other way can we account for this wayward Court beauty
accepting the hand of a poor officer, a mere needy soldier
of fortune. But she was very young, and her imagination
as well as her heart was really touched.

The Duchess of York countenanced, if she did not

actually encourage, the love affair, though the two families concerned were bitterly opposed to so imprudent a marriage. The Jennings' property in Herts was settled upon Sarah's brother, and her parents could afford her no allowance or portion of any sort. They naturally expected their beautiful daughter to make a great match, and she had already had many suitors—amongst others, the Earl of Lindsey, afterwards Duke of Ancaster, who is referred to as 'Your Grace's lover' in a letter written to her long after.* Sir Winston Churchill's lands were small and much encumbered. He was in needy circumstances himself, and barely able to support his wife, still less to provide for his son.

There was certainly nothing prudish in the Court manners of the day; and lovers were allowed great freedom and were permitted to meet when and where they liked, without the restraint of a duenna or third party of any kind. In their daily intercourse, men and women used words and expressions which would now sound not only coarse, but indelicate. It was no unusual thing for a maid of honour to receive a lover in her bedroom; and we are told that during this courtship Colonel Churchill took especial pleasure in tying and untying the garters of Mistress Jennings.† The following letter from the French Ambassador gives an amusing account of English Court society of that period. Writing from London to the Minister Louvois, in September, 1676, ²⁴/₁⁹, 1676. Courtin refers to a little party he was about to give to four ladies of the Court, one of whom was Sarah Jennings. He says the ladies' lovers were also to be invited, in order to have plenty of dancing, whilst he played at ombre, and he thus describes the fashions of the day: 'There is nothing so dainty as the English woman's *chaussure;* their shoes fit them with great nicety; their skirts are short, and their silk stockings very clean and tidy. English ladies

* Letter of May, 1710, from Mrs. Maynwaring. See 'Private Correspondence of Duchess of Marlborough,' vol. i., p. 314.
† Bolingbroke.

do not mind showing a great deal of their legs, which are perfect pictures. Green stockings are most in vogue, with black velvet garters, fastened above the knee by diamond buckles. Where there is no silk stocking, the skin is very white and satiny.'*

Amongst the papers at Blenheim Palace is a bundle of Churchill's love-letters. Unfortunately only a few of Sarah's answers have been preserved; they are in a package endorsed by her, 'Some copies of my letters to Mr. Churchill.' Those given in this chapter are selected as most likely to interest the reader. As far as possible, they are given in their proper chronological order. They are all undated and unsigned, and begin abruptly without any conventional 'Dear' or 'Dearest heart,' etc. There is frequent allusion in them to the violent head-aches from which, like Cæsar, Marlborough suffered all through life. He sometimes refers to them as so bad that he was entirely prostrated and felt as if he were about to die. He frequently begs her to make appointments for meetings, and often asks that she will see him in her 'chamber.' In one of his earliest letters he writes: 'At night I shall have the happiness, I hope, to see you in the drawing-room. I cannot remember what it is that I said to you that you took so ill; but one thing I do assure you, that I will never say or do aught willing that I think you may take ill. Ah, my soul, did you love me so well as I, you could never have refused my letter so barbarously as you did; for, if reason had bade you do it, love would never have permitted it. But I will complain no more of it, but hope time and the truth of my love will make you love better.'

From Colonel Churchill to Mistress Jennings.

'If your happiness can depend upon the esteem and love I have for you, you ought to be the happiest thing breathing, for I have never anybody loved to that heat I do you. I

* Archives of French Foreign Office.

love you so well that your happiness I prefer much above my own; and if you think meeting me is what you ought not to do, or that it will disquiet you, I do promise you I will never press you more to do it. As I prefer your happiness above my own, so I hope you will sometimes think how well I love you; and what you can do without doing yourself an injury, I hope you will be so kind as to do it—I mean in letting me see that you wish me better than the rest of mankind; and in return I swear to you that I never will love anything but your dear self, which has made so sure a conquest of me that, had I the will, I had not the power ever to break my chains. Pray let me hear from you, and know if I shall be so happy as to see you to-night.'

From Colonel Churchill to Mistress Jennings.

'I was last night at the ball, in hopes to have seen what I love above my own soul; but I was not so happy, for I could see you nowhere, so that I did not stay above an hour. I would have writ sooner, but that I was afraid you went to bed so late that it would disturb you. Pray see which of these two puppies you like best, and that keep, for the bitch cannot let them suck any longer. They are above three weeks old, so that if you give it warm milk it will not die. Pray let me hear from you, and at what time you will be so kind as to let me come to you to-night. Pray, if you have nothing to do, let it be the latest, for I never am truly happy but when I am with you.'

From Colonel Churchill to Mistress Jennings.

'I have been so extreme ill with the headache all this morning that I have not had courage to write to know how you do; but your being well is what I prefer much above my own health. Therefore pray send me word, for if you are not in pain I cannot then be much troubled, for were it not for the joy I take in the thought that you love me, I should not care how soon I died; for by all that is good I love you so well that I wish from my soul that that minute

that you leave loving me, that I may die, for life after that
would be to me but one perpetual torment. If the Duchess
sees company, I hope you will be there; but if she does not,
I beg you will then let me see you in your chamber, if it be
but for one hour. If you are not in the drawing-room, you
must then send me word at what hour I shall come.'

From Mistress Jennings to Colonel Churchill.

' If your intentions are honourable, and what I have
reason to expect, you need not fear my sister's coming can
make any change in me, or that it is in the power of
anybody to alter me but yourself, and I am at this time
satisfied that you will never do anything out of reason,
which you must do if you ever are untrue to me.'

From Colonel Churchill to Mistress Jennings.

' You complain of my unkindness, but would not be kind
yourself in answering my letter, although I begged you to
do it. The Duchess goes to a new play to-day, and afterwards to the Duchess of Monmouth's, there to dance. I
desire that you will not go thither, but make an excuse, and
give me leave to come to you. Pray let me know what you
do intend, and if you go to the play, for if you do then
I will do what I can to go, if the Duke does not. Your not
writing to me made me very uneasy, for I was afraid it was
want of kindness in you, which I am sure I will never
deserve by any action of mine.'

From Mistress Jennings to Colonel Churchill.

' At four o'clock I would see you, but that would hinder
you from seeing the play, which I fear would be a great
affliction to you, and increase the pain in your head, which
would be out of anybody's power to ease until the next new
play. Therefore, pray consider, and without any compliment to me, send me word if you can come to me without
any prejudice to your health.'

Sir Winston and Lady Churchill were anxious that
their eldest son should marry a woman of fortune, and

fixed upon their kinswoman, Catherine Sedley, then about twenty-five years of age, as a suitable wife for him. She was not good-looking and she squinted, but her father, Sir Charles Sedley, was rich, and able to provide well for her. Colonel Churchill saw how useful her money would be to him, a fact which his parents made the most of in urging this match upon him. She is described by Barillon as clever, but very plain, and extremely thin. She inherited much of her father's wit, and was renowned at Court as the witty Maid of Honour. But the project came to nothing, and when the match was finally broken off, she became the acknowledged mistress of James, who made her Countess of Dorchester upon his accession to the throne. $\frac{30}{30}$ 1, 1686. She hated priests, and loved to turn them into ridicule, and they feared and hated her in return.* When at the Revolution Queen Mary turned her back upon her, the affronted but witty mistress exclaimed: 'I beg your Majesty to remember that if I broke one of the Commandments with your father, you broke another against him.'† Most of James's mistresses were so ugly, that his witty brother said they were prescribed by his confessor as a sort of penance for his sins. Catherine Sedley, in reference to herself, to Susan Lady Bellasis, and to Arabella Churchill, declared : 'I know not for what he chose us ; we were none of us handsome, and if any of us had had wit he was too dull to find it out.'

When this negotiation with Catherine Sedley reached the ears of Sarah, her anger knew no bounds, and the letters she wrote to her lover on the subject show what an adept she was even then in bitter invective. She upbraided him angrily for his alleged inconstancy, at once declared the engagement to be at an end, and loftily advised him 'to renounce an attachment which militated against his worldly prospects.' She announced her intention of going to Paris with her sister, Lady Hamilton.

* She eventually married Lord Portmore, and died 26, 10, 1717.
† Note by Lord Dartmouth.

There is in her letters no semblance of regret at what
she conceived to be his altered intentions. The following
is one of them : 'As for seeing you, I am resolved I
never will in private nor in public if I could help it ; and
as for the last, I fear it will be some time before I can order
so as to be out of your way of seeing me ; but surely you
must confess that you have been the falsest creature upon
earth to me. I must own that I believe I shall suffer a
great deal of trouble, but I will bear it, and give God
thanks, though too late I see my error.'

The continued objections of his family, seem at length to
have influenced him in favour of the Sedley marriage, and
for some time at least, the question of settlements was under
discussion. For the moment he apparently realized how
imprudent it would be for a man in his position to marry
a penniless girl, and the more completely to break off his
engagement with Sarah Jennings, his friends urged him to
go abroad for a time on the plea of ill-health. This is referred to as follows in a letter from Barillon to Louvois : ' I
assure you he (Churchill) pursues Sarah Jennings, Madam
Hamilton's sister, who is the prettiest of the Duchess
of York's Maids of Honour, and whom the Duke of York
is always ogling.   At a ball given by that Princess,
Sarah Jennings had a greater wish to cry than to dance.
Churchill, who is her lover, says he is in consumption, and
that he must have change of air in France. I wish notwithstanding, that I was as well as he is. The truth is, he
wishes to get out of this love affair. His father wants him
to marry a relation, very rich and very ugly, and will not
consent to his marriage to Mademoiselle Jennings. He is
believed to be also somewhat worldly himself.'

Such was, of course, the generally-accepted story at
Court, but we now know what his real feelings were in
this affair. He was fully aware that, from a worldly point
of view, his parents were right, and he was wrong ; but
his love was too strong for his wisdom, and he could
neither bring himself to marry the ugly Catherine Sedley

for her money, nor to give up the beautiful girl whose
affections he had won. Yet this is the man of whom
our great historical novelist writes : ' In the bloom of youth
he loved lucre more than wine and women.'*

The hasty, indignant and petulant letter in which Sarah
broke off the engagement was too much for him. It drew
from him an earnest appeal that she would forgive him,
believe in his constancy, and renew their plighted troth.

In one of the many letters in which, at this time, the
lover declares his undying devotion, he adds : ' Do but
have patience but for one week. You shall then see that
I will never do aught that shall look like a fault.' On this
she wrote in after-life : ' This letter was writ when I was
angry at something his father and mother had made a dis-
agreeable noise in the town about, when they had a mind
to have him marry a shocking creature for money.'†

Henry Savile, who was one of Churchill's intimate
friends, writes to his brother from Whitehall, where he was
in waiting : ‡ ' Mrs. Sedley's marriage with Jack Churchill ‖, 5, 1677.
neither is, nor I believe ever will be, any more talked of,
both the Knight§ and the Colonel being willing to break off
fairly, which important matter (betwixt you and I) is referred
to me by both partys, and for both their goods I think it is
best it should cease.'

Having finally broken off negotiations with Mistress
Sedley, he again writes to Sarah : ' As for the power you
say you have over yourself, I do no ways at all doubt
of it, for I swear to you I do not think you love me,
so that I am very easily persuaded that my letters has
no charms for you, since I am so much a slave to your
charms as to own to you that I love you above my

* Macaulay's ' History,' vol. iii., p. 438.
† Blenheim Papers. That ' shocking creature ' was his kinswoman,
Mistress Sedley.
‡ Savile was eight or nine years older than John Churchill.
§ Sir Winston Churchill.
‖ Copied from the Spencer House Papers. I have since found it
also in the Camden Society Papers of 1858.

own life, which by all that is holy I do. You must give me leave to beg that you will not condemn me for a vain fool that I did believe you did love me, since both you and your actions did oblige me to that belief, in which heaven knows I took so much joy that from henceforward my life must be a torment to me for it. You say I pretend a passion to you when I have other things in my head. I cannot imagine what you mean by it, for I vow to God you do so entirely possess my thoughts that I think of nothing else in this world but your dear self. I do not, by all that is good, say this that I think it will move you to pity me, for I do despair of your love; but it is to let you see how unjust you are, and that I must ever love you as long as I have breath, do what you will. I do not expect in return that you should either write or speak to me, since you think it is what may do you a prejudice; but I have a thing to beg which I hope you will not be so barbarous as to deny me. It is that you will give me leave to do what I cannot help, which is to adore you as long as I live, and in return I will study how I may deserve, although not have, your love. I am persuaded that I have said impertinent things enough to anger you, for which I do with all my heart beg your pardon, and do assure you that from henceforward I will approach and think of you with the same devotion as to my God.'

From Mistress Jennings.

' I am as little satisfied with this letter as I have been with many others, for I find all you will say is only to amuse me and make me think you have a passion for me, when in reality there is no such thing. You have reason to think it strange that I write to you after my last, where I protested that I would never write nor speak to you more; but as you know how much kindness I had for you, you can't wonder or blame me if I try you once more, to hear what you can say for your justification. But this I must warn you of,— that you don't hold disputes, as you have done always, and to keep me from answering of you, and yourself from saying what I expect from you, for if you go on in that manner I will leave you that moment, and never hear you speak more whilst I have life. Therefore pray consider if, with honour to me and satisfaction to yourself, I can see you; for if it be only to repeat those things which you said so often, I shall think you the worst of men, and the most ungrateful; and 'tis to no purpose to imagine that I will be made ridiculous in the world when it is in your power to make me otherwise.'

From Colonel Churchill to Mistress Jennings.

'It is not reasonable that you should have a doubt but that I love you above all expression, which by heaven I do. It is not possible to do anything to let you see your power more than my obedience to your commands of leaving you, when my tyrant heart rates me to make me disobey; but it were much better it should break than to displease you. I will not, dearest, ask or hope to hear from you unless your charity pities me and will so far plead for me as to tell you that a man dying for you may hope that you will be so kind to him as to make a distinction betwixt him and the rest of his sex. I do love and adore you with all my heart and soul—so much that by all that is good I do and ever will be better pleased with your happiness than my own; but oh, my soul, if we might be both happy, what inexpressible joy would that be! But I will not think of any content but what you shall think fit to give, for 'tis you alone I love, so that if you are kind but one minute, that will make me happier than all the world can besides. I will not dare to expect more favour than you shall think fit to give, but could you ever love me, I think the happiness would be so great that it would make me immortal.'

From Mistress Jennings to Colonel Churchill.

'If it were sure that you have that passion for me which you say you have, you would find out some way to make yourself happy—it is in your power. Therefore press me no more to see you, since it is what I cannot in honour approve of, and if I have done too much, be so good as to consider who was the cause of it.'

From Colonel Churchill to Mistress Sarah Jennings.

' When I left my father last night, and proposed to come and speak with you, I did not believe that you would have been so unkind as to have gone away the minute I came in, fearing that I might else have spoke to you, which indeed I should have been very glad to have done. I beg you will give me leave to see you this night, at what hour you please. Pray let me hear from you, and if you do not think me impertinent for asking, I should be glad to know what made you go away.'

From Mistress Jennings to Colonel Churchill.

' I am willing to satisfy the world and you that I am not now in the wrong, and therefore I give you leave to come to-night—not that I can be persuaded you can ever justify yourself, but I do it that I may be freed from the trouble of ever hearing from you more.'

From Colonel Churchill to Mistress Jennings.

' When I writ to you last night I thought I writ to one that loved me; but your unkind, indifferent letter this morning confirms me of what I have before been afraid of, which is that your sister can govern your passion as she pleases. My heart is ready to break. I wish 'twere over, for since you are grown so indifferent, death is the only thing that can ease me. If that the Duchess could not have effected this, I was resolved to have made another proposal to her, which I am confident she might have effected, but it would not have brought so much money as this. But now I must think no more on it, since you say we cannot be happy. If they should do the first, I wish with all my soul that my fortune had been so considerable as that it might have made you happier than your going out with your sister to France will do; for I know 'tis the joy you propose in that, that makes you think me faulty. I do, and must as long as I live, love you to distraction, but would not, to make myself the happiest of men breathing, press you to aught that you think will make you unhappy. Madame, methinks it is no unreasonable request to beg to see you in your chamber to-night. Pray let me hear presently two words, and say I shall ; and, in return, I swear to you if you command my death I will die.'

Endorsed in the Duchess's writing :

' A letter in which he says something of some proposals made to the Duchess.'

From Mistress Jennings to Colonel Churchill.

' I have made many reflections upon what you said to me last night, and I am of the opinion that could the Duchess obtain what you ask her, you might be more unhappy than if it cannot be had. Therefore, as I have always shown more kindness for you than perhaps I ought, I am resolved to give you one mark more—and that is, to desire you to say nothing of it to the Duchess upon my account ; and your own interest when I am not concerned in it, will probably compass what will make you much happier than this can ever do.'

From Colonel Churchill to Mistress Jennings' Waiting-woman.

' Your mistress's usage to me is so barbarous that sure she must be the worst woman in the world, or else she would not be thus ill-natured. I have sent a letter which I desire you will give her. It is very reasonable for her to take it, because it will be then in her own power never to be troubled with me more, if she pleases. I do love her with all my soul, but will not trouble her, for if I cannot have her love I shall despise her pity. For the sake of what she has already done, let her read my letter and answer it, and not use me thus like a footman.'

Addressed :

' For Mrs. Elizabeth Mowdie.'

From Mistress Jennings to Colonel Churchill.

'I have done nothing to deserve such a kind of letter as
you have writ to me, and therefore I don't know what
answer to give; but I find you have a very ill opinion of
me, and therefore I cannot help being angry with myself
for having had too good a one of you; for if I had as little
love as yourself, I have been told enough of you to make
me hate you, and then I believe I should have been more
happy than I am like to be now. However, if you can be
so well contented never to see me as I think you can by
what you say, I will believe you; though I have not other
people; and after you are satisfied that I have not broke
my word, you shall have it in your power to see me or not
—and if you are contented without it I shall be extremely
pleased.'

From Colonel Churchill to Mistress Jennings.

'To show you how unreasonable you are in accusing me,
I dare swear you yourself will own that your going from me
in the Duchess's drawing-room did show as much contempt
as was possible. I may grieve at it, but I will no more
complain when you do it, for I suppose it is what pleases
your humour. I cannot imagine what you meant by your
saying I laughed at you at the Duke's side, for I was so far
from that, that had it not been for shame I could have
cried. And for being in haste to go to the Park, after you
went I stood near a quarter of an hour, I believe, without
knowing what I did. Although at Whitehall you told me I
should not come, yet I walked twice to the Duke's back-
stairs, but there was no Mrs. Mowdie; and when I went to
my Lord Durass's, I would not go the same way they did,
but came again down the backstairs; and when I went
away, I did not go in my chair, but made it follow me, because I would see if there was any light in your chamber,
but I saw none. Could you see my heart you would not be
so cruel as to say I do not love you, for by all that is good
I love you and only you. If I may have the happiness of

seeing you to-night, pray let me know, and believe that I am never truly pleased but when I am with you.'

In a letter endorsed in Sarah's writing, ' This letter was when he was to settle the time of marrying me with the Duchess,' he evinces anxiety lest she should lose the good-will of Mary of Modena. He writes : 'I am sure if you love me you will not at this anger the Duchess.'

In another letter he says, with reference to a present he sent her : 'I hope you will like the waistcoat; I do assure you there is not such another to be had in England.' He says elsewhere : ' You complain of my unkindness, but would not be kind yourself in answering my letter, although I begged you to do it.' The wife of James II., must have been fond of early rising, for in another loving epistle he says : ' I hope you so wise as to value your own health before your duty to the Dutchess, so that you did not walk with her at five this morning.'

Strange to say, there is no actual record of their marriage, which was celebrated in secret, owing to the opposition of the two families, and was not announced till some months afterwards. The Duchess of York was alone cognizant of it at the time, and was possibly the only witness of the ceremony. She gave the bride valuable presents, and proposed some pecuniary arrangement— referred to in these letters—to enable her to marry, which was at first rejected by the haughty Maid of Honour. It is not possible to fix the exact date of the wedding, but it took place in the winter of 1677-78. This is borne out by the following endorsement in Sarah's handwriting on a letter addressed to her as M^{rs}. Jennings, by Churchill, on Friday, $\frac{14}{24}$ 4, 1678, from Brussels : ' I believe I was married when this letter was writ, but it was not known to anyone but the Duchess ' (of York). This letter begins : 'I writ to you from Antwerp, which I hope you have received before now; for I should be glad you should hear from me by every post.'*

* See next chapter for the whole text of this letter.

Eight children were born of this marriage, of whom two died in infancy. The following transcriptions of entries in the Duchess of Marlborough's Bible, now at Althorp, relate to the other six :*

'The 15th September 1712 at two in the morning the Earl of Godolphin dyed in the Duke of Marlborough's house in St. Albans, who was the best man that ever lived.'

'Henrietta was born the 19 July 1681 about ten in the morning her god mothers and god father was my mother, my sister Godfrey and Sir John Churchill.'†

'Anne was born the 27 day of Feb : her god mothers and god father were, the Princess of Denmark, Lady Sunderland and Lord Rochester.'‡

'Jack was born the 12 of January 1686 about six o'clock in the morning, his god mother and god fathers, Mrs. Strangeways, Lord Tyrconnell and Lord Godolphin.'

'Betty was born the 15 of March 1687, her god father and god mothers, Lord Renston, Lady Scarborough and Lady Freckwell.'

'Mary was born the 15 of July 1689, at 2 o'clock in the morning : her god father and god mothers The Prince and Queen and Lady Darby.'

'Charles was born the 19 of August, 1690, between six and seven o'clock in the morning, his god mother and god fathers, Lady Fitzharding, Lord Dorset, and Mr. Russell.'

No mention is made in this Bible of their first child 'Harriot,' who was born in 1679, and died before July, 1681, when the second Harriot, or Henrietta, was born.

For the first seven years of their married life her soldier-

---

* The Bible was printed at Oxford in 1685.

† Her 'sister Godfrey' was Arabella, Marlborough's sister, who had married Colonel Godfrey.

‡ The year was either 1683 or 1684, as she was nearly sixteen when married in January, 1700.

husband had no chance of displaying his genius for war, and even at the Battle of Sedgemoor he only held a subordinate position. For all these years he was little more than the favourite and confidant of James, Duke of York. When James came to the throne, Churchill proved himself to be a skilful negotiator in the service of a master whose missions, however, never rose above the level of intrigue. It was an age of intrigue, in which no man seemed capable of pursuing a straightforward line of action. 'I never knew a man lost on a straight road,' said the great Achar, but John Churchill, and all the Englishmen who played any considerable part in the events of the time, seem to have been incapable of taking a straight path in the conduct of public business.

CHAPTER XXV.

CHURCHILL AS A MARRIED MAN; HIS NEGOTIATIONS WITH
WILLIAM OF ORANGE.

Churchill in the confidence of the two Royal Brothers—Parliament meets in January, 1678—Charles threatens France with war, but Churchill does not believe in it—Churchill goes to Flanders to command a brigade — William discovers the ability of Churchill, and makes friends with him — Charles makes peace with Lewis for a consideration.

CHAPTER
XXV.

1678.

THE newly-married couple spent their first winter, and then the spring of 1678, at Mintern, in Dorsetshire, with Churchill's parents, who had bowed to the inevitable, and had become reconciled to the match which they had striven to prevent. It is evident from his letters that his mother's temper was occasionally sorely tried by the overbearing and insolent behaviour of her daughter-in-law; indeed, it was no easy task to keep the peace between these two quarrelsome women. But his poverty made him glad—even under such conditions—to secure a home for his wife, whom he had not then the means to establish in a house of his own. He appears to have contemplated hiring a house near London, because he was anxious to remove her from the Court and its temptations. But he abandoned this idea from want of means, and from the great horror which he had of spending more than he could afford. Sarah in one of her letters gives as the reason, that she was 'soon after made Lady of the Bedchamber to the Princess of Denmark.' But Anne was not married until 1683, so it is evident that his wish to withdraw his young wife from Court extended over the first five years of their married life.

Whilst staying with his father at Mintern, Churchill made frequent journeys to London for his turn of waiting upon the Duke of York. He left his wife behind upon these occasions, but always kept up a steady correspondence with her during his absence. The following letters, unsigned and undated, are some of those he then wrote to her :

'Here is no news to send you : however, I will not omit one post of writing to you ; for as you are always in my thoughts, I would when I am from you be perpetually conversing with you by letters, and repeat to you what I so often have sworn to you,—that you are dearer to me than my own life ; but I find you are not of the same mind, for when you write you are afraid to tell me that you love me. Waiting this week has tired me so, that to-morrow I do not intend to go abroad, but the next [day] I intend to go to see a house which, if I think you will like it, I shall see about taking it, for I never will willingly do anything that I think you will not approve of.

'My duty to my mother, and love and service, if you please, to everybody else.'

'Saturday.' Addressed : 'For Mrs. Churchill, at Sir Winston Churchill's house at Mintorne, to be left at the post-house at Dorchester, Dorsetshire.'

Endorsed in the Duchess's writing : 'When this letter was writ, Lord Marlborough intended that I should always live near London and never see the Court, but soon after made me lady of the bedchamber to the Princess of Denmark.'*

'These two last days I have been mightily afraid of having got an ague, but I hope it will prove to be nothing but a great cold, for it does now lie so extremely in my head that I can hardly look upon the paper to write ; but you are so dear to me that I will never omit writing, for fear you should think it proceed from unkindness, which I

* Blenheim Palace Papers.

can never be guilty of to you. I will not complain, but it is now three weeks and above since you writ to me. On Monday I come down in the coach with my sister, so that I desire that the coach may be on Tuesday at Salisbury, and if you are well I do not doubt but that you will be so kind as to meet me there. My duty, pray, to my father and mother. It will be absolutely necessary for you to be at St. Albans for a fortnight after you come from my father's. Therefore pray write to your mother to know if she approves of it. I have already spoken to your sister Hamilton about it, and she tells me that your mother will be overjoyed at it; but, however, it is fit you should write to her about it. So, my dearest dear, till Tuesday farewell.

'Saturday.' Addressed : 'For Mrs. Churchill, at Min- torne, to be left at the post-house at Dorchester, Dorset- shire.'*

From the time of his marriage until the accession of James, Colonel Churchill was much in the confidence of the two Royal brothers, but he was kept in ignorance of their designs against the liberties of the people and the Protestant religion.† They only divulged their plans for the re-establishment of the ancient faith to Roman Catholics, though they frequently employed him upon secret missions of importance, as the ease with which he spoke French and his natural ability fitted him for foreign negotiations. He thus had many opportunities for acquiring skill in diplomacy, and in the management of men, an experience which stood him in good stead in his later career. These foreign missions often brought him into contact with William of Orange, and an intimacy was established between them that proved of great advantage to both at the time of the Revolution.

The underhand proceedings of Charles in relation to

---

* Blenheim Palace Papers.

† Dalrymple, vol. i., p. 208 : Letters from James to William of $\frac{2}{12}$ 4, 1678, and $\frac{7}{17}$ 4, 1678. Also Lediard.

the marriage of the Princess Mary had so incensed Lewis,
that he at once stopped his pension, and ordered an army
to march into Flanders. Parliament had been prorogued
until April, 1678, as part of the consideration for the money
paid by Lewis to Charles; but now, as a counter-stroke to
the stoppage of his pension, Charles ordered Parliament to
reassemble for business in January, 1677-78.

When Parliament met, Charles announced that he had
made an alliance with Holland for the protection of
Flanders, and that it was his intention to help the Dutch
and their allies in their resistance to French aggression.
He had, he said, in accordance with the desire expressed by
both Houses, already ordered the English regiments then
in the pay of Lewis XIV. to quit the French army. This
policy required a strong fleet at sea, and an increase of
about 30,000 men to the land forces, and for these objects
a large money vote was necessary.* But Parliament was
not in a mood to grant this at once, as it was shrewdly
suspected that the King meant to use these troops and the
money for other purposes. The House of Commons would
only vote supplies on terms so humiliating to Charles that
he could not with any dignity accept them.

The utter rottenness of society and the internal demoralization of public life at this period are well illustrated by the
proceedings in this Session of Parliament. The French King
pulled the strings, and gave or promised bribes all round.
All through the winter and spring, Lewis was again engaged
in a very secret negotiation with Charles. The exact sum
which the latter was to receive for the sale of England's

---

* The army was to be raised to twenty-six battalions of Foot, of 1,000
men each, four regiments of Horse and two of Dragoons, each of 490
men. All the old companies were to be increased to 100 men each;
Lord Craven's (now the Coldstream Guards), the Lord High Admiral's,
and Lord Mulgrave's (now the Buffs) were to be raised from twelve to
twenty companies each. The Lord High Admiral's regiment was
originally raised for sea-service in 1664, and consisted of six companies
of 200 men each, all armed with muskets, which was unusual, as in
the ordinary Foot, one-third of the men were still armed with pikes.

honour and interests, was well haggled over.   Lewis thoroughly understood the distrust with which the English people regarded their King, and how much they dreaded the proposal to supply him with an army, lest it should be used against them.   Thus, while he was intriguing with Charles, his agents were bribing the leading members of both sides in English politics, to thwart Charles if he should manifest a serious intention to follow any course hostile to French interests.

At length, after much debate, and with undisguised misgivings, the House of Commons voted a million to enable 'his Majesty to enter into actual war against the French King.'   So far, all the threats of war by Charles, as well as his secret negotiations, had failed to make any impression upon Lewis.   French troops were still pressing forward in the Low Countries, where several strong places had already fallen.   War between England and France seemed now almost inevitable, but Churchill never believed in it.   He knew the minds of both the Royal brothers too well to accept their assurances on such a point.   In March he was recalled to London by the Duke of York, and upon his arrival, he wrote the following letter to his wife, whom he had left at Mintern : 'I hope from me you expect no news but what concerns myself.   I got to town by a little after three, very weary.   However, I drest myself, and went to the Duke for to know what he had to command me. He told me that the reason that he sent for me was that he did believe that there would be occasion to send into Holland and Flanders, and that he would have me here to be ready to go.   By the French letters on Saturday they expect to know whether we shall have peace or war ; but whatever happens I believe you may be satisfied that I shall not be in danger this year.   Mrs. Fortry tells me that she will write to you this night, and send you all the news she knows.   Your pendants are done, but the Duchess has not yet given order to Mr. Allen to pay for them.   I believe you will like them, for they are to my mind very fine for the price.* Mr. Villiers has not money to pay for my place, so that the Duke has consented to Mr. Fortry's buying, in case we agree. I have my ring from my Lord Ossory, which I will keep till I see you, hoping you will like it, it being, as all things that I have in this world, at your command. So assuring you that I do, and ever will as long as I live love you, and only you.

'My duty to my mother, with my love and service to everybody else. Thursday.' Addressed: 'For Mrs. Churchill, at Sir Winston Churchill's house at Mintorne, to be left at the post-house at Dorchester, Dorsetshire.'†

His orders came at last. He was to proceed to Flanders on the part of the King, with power to settle the strength of the land and sea forces to be maintained by each of the Powers who were allied against France.‡ Those Powers were also to state the lowest terms upon which they would make peace. In a letter to William, James describes the object of Churchill's mission as intended 'to adjust all things with you and the Spaniards concerning our troops.' He goes on to say, that Churchill was fully instructed on the subject of his mission. In company with a Colonel Duncan, he sailed from the Downs in the frigate *Solebay* on Friday morning, and reached Flushing that same night.§ He was $\frac{1}{6}$ 4, 1678. well received at Brussels, where rumour said that the Duke of York was expected to arrive shortly, to assume command of the English contingent.

Soon after his arrival in Holland, further orders from the King reached him. He was directed to arrange with William for the safety of the four British battalions that

* These were some of the presents the Duchess of York gave Mrs. Churchill on her marriage.

† Blenheim Palace Papers.

‡ Sir Jos. Williamson's notes in F. O. Papers in Rolls Office, No. 31 of 1676-78. This is taken from papers dated 7th and 8th April, 1678, and is apparently in Marlborough's handwriting.

§ Dom. Papers, Car. II., Rolls House.

‖ F. O. Papers in Rolls Office, No. 307 of 1678. The news-letter containing this is dated the Hague, $\frac{13}{4}$ 4, 1678.

Chapter XXV.

1678.

had been pushed forward, unsupported, to Bruges.* Being
seasoned troops they were especially valuable to an army
so largely composed of recruits, and it was feared that the
French, knowing this, might by a sudden forward movement, take the place before arrangements could be made for
its defence.† Monmouth, who had been appointed to command the English contingent, had landed at Ostend in
March. He reported to the King, that until the British
regiments arrived, the only garrison there was some 400
Spaniards, whom he described as 'miserable creatures.'‡

¼ 4, 1678.

In a letter to his wife from Brussels, Churchill says he
wrote to her 'from Antwerp, which I hope you have
received before now; for I should be glad you should hear
from me by every post. I met with some difficulties in my
business with the Prince of Orange, so that I was forced to
write to England, which will cause me to be two or three
days longer abroad than I should have been. But because
I would lose no time, I despatch all other things in the
meantime, for I do, with all my heart and soul, long to be
with you, you being dearer to me than my own life.' He

¼ 4, 1678.

goes on to say that he hoped to leave Brussels on Sunday,
and to reach Breda the day following for a conference with
William of Orange, who was then staying there. From
thence he would write again: 'Till when, my soul's soul,
farewell.'

William had already begun to realize the expediency of
cultivating the friendship and goodwill of leading Englishmen. It was, therefore, natural that he should wish to
make a favourable impression on Churchill, and to greet
him with all the cordiality of which his cold nature and
stiff manner made him capable. He was already in corre-

* The 1st Foot Guards—twelve companies—under Lord Howard,
had landed in March at Ostend, from whence they were pushed on to
Brussels in August. Our Minister at the Hague says in a letter of
¼ 3, 1678, '20 companies of 100 apiece are now passing over to
Flanders, beyond the 2,800 already there.'

† Dalrymple, vol. i., p. 208. James to William, ¼ 4, 1678.

‡ Fifth Report of Historical MSS., p. 17.

spondence with many of those who had most influence with Charles II., and had begun thus early to impress and influence the men who regarded a Protestant King as essential to the preservation of English liberty. It may even be said, that the general scheme of his plan for the Revolution ten years afterwards, was concocted at this time. It was doubtless during this mission that William became aware of Churchill's tact and talents, and also of the fact that he was a genuine soldier, a skilled diplomatist, and a sound man of business; that he was, in fine, a man who would be something more than a mere pawn in the great game which William already hoped to play in England, and therefore one whose goodwill was worth securing.

Many messengers passed between Whitehall and Churchill whilst he was employed on this mission. It ended in a Convention made by him on the part of the King with the Prince of Orange. In the following letter, William refers to the successful conclusion of the Convention :*

'A la Haye, ce 3 de May, 1678.

' Je ne vous dirai rien de la manière que nous avons adjusté les choses avec Mr. Churchill, puisqu'il vous en informera. Mr. de Godolphin est arrivé hier au soir, je suis bien marri de n'avoir peu effectuer si promptement ce que le Roy désiroit, et ce qui est si nécessaire. Mr. l'Ambassadeur Hyde et moy vous en informeront au long. Je n'ose pas vous en dire d'aventage. J'espère que de vostre costé vous faites ce que vous devez, pour moy je ne manquerai jamais du mien n'y d'estre toutte ma vie entière- ment à vous.'†

In his heart Charles neither wanted war, nor was he anxious to obtain more power than he possessed. It

---

* To Lord Danby, F. O. Papers in Rolls Office. State Papers: Holland, No. 307 of 1678.

† This letter is in Mr. A. Morrison's collection. It is endorsed:

' Prince of Orange, 78, 3 May.—Clerk's writing.
That he dares not say more.—Duke of Leed's or Danby's writing.'

was his brother who urged him ceaselessly to rule despotically without a Parliament; but his own love of ease and of a quiet life made him fear to embark upon measures which he felt must embroil him with his people, and give him trouble.* Whilst, therefore, every outward preparation was made for war with France, Charles was engaged in secret negotiations for peace, in the course of which Lewis worked so skilfully upon his customary impecuniosity, that a bargain was easily struck, and a secret treaty was concluded through the agency of the French Ambassador in London.† It thus came to pass, that whilst Temple was arranging in Flanders with the Dutch and Spaniards for the vigorous prosecution of a war against France, the two kings had concluded an arrangement, which, in spite of outward and visible hostility, bound them together as friends.

In accordance with the terms of this secret treaty, agreed upon as early as the month of March, Charles promised, for a consideration of 6,000,000 livres (£240,000 sterling), that if Holland, in the space of two months, failed to accept the terms offered at Nimeguen, he would disband his lately-raised army, and remain neutral during the war between France and the allies of Holland. He also promised not to call his Parliament together for the following six months. This treaty was only known in England to James and Lord Danby. It was in Charles's own handwriting, for, as Barillon wrote to his Court, 'none of his subjects are bold enough to sign it.'‡

17 5, 1678.

17 5, 1678.

* Dalrymple, vol. i. Barillon's letters to Lewis XIV. In one of 18, 4, 1678, he says: 'I do not believe he (Charles) cares much for being more absolute than he is ' (p. 194).

† Paul Barillon d'Anconcourt, Marquis de Branges, was the Ambassador of France in London at this time.

‡ Dalrymple, vol. i., p. 212. The original treaty is now in the Archives of the Foreign Office in Paris. It is given in full in Dalrymple. See also letter from the Lord Treasurer to our Ambassador in Paris, dated 25, 3, 1678, in Harris's Life of William, p. ii. of Appendix.

CHAPTER XXVI.

The Army largely augmented—Formation of grenadier companies—
The discipline of the troops—Feeding the Army in the field.

On Churchill's return home in May he found a considerable force under arms for service in Flanders. Several new regiments had been raised, and the popular feeling in favour of war with France had become very strong among all classes. Monmouth was already in the field at the head of the English troops in Holland, a position which the Duke of York coveted greatly. James's thoughts were constantly upon the succession in the event of his brother's death, and if, whenever that took place, he could only be in command of the army, he believed he could easily secure it.[*]

The British regiments in the French service were recalled, recruits came pouring in from all sides, and in six weeks about twenty thousand had been enlisted. But the pay of the private soldier, when compared with the wages of the labourer, was relatively much better then than it is now. 'We are beating up drums every day for new levies, and soldiers come in plentifully and cheerfully.'[†] The greater part of the new army was encamped on

* Dalrymple, vol. i., pp. 203, 204.

† Rawdon Papers; letter from Lord Conway to his brother of $\frac{13}{18}$
1, 167$\frac{7}{8}$.

Hounslow Heath, where many then saw for the first time the 'new sort of soldier called grenadiers, men dexterous in flinging hand "granados." * They wore furred caps with coped crowns like janizaries, which made them look very fierce, and some had long hoods hanging down behind, as we picture fools; their clothing being likewise pybald, yellow and red.'† There were at first only two or three grenadiers in each company, but in 1678 they were collected and formed into a separate company in each battalion. 'Horse grenadiers' were also formed at this time, the men being armed with muskets and bayonets. The peculiarity of their dress continued far down into the eighteenth century, even after the use of hand-grenades had been discontinued, and is referred to in the following verse of the well-known song, 'The British Grenadiers':‡

> ' Then let us crown a bumper,
> And drink a health to those
> Who carry caps and pouches,
> And who wear the looped clothes.
> We give it from our hearts, my boys,' etc.

Although recruits were easily obtained, it was not easy

---

* Each grenadier carried three grenades in a pouch, each grenade weighing 3 or 4 lbs.

† Evelyn, vol. i.. p. 497. The men wore 'ffox tails' at 3s. 6d. apiece in their hats. See Mackinnon's 'Coldstream Guards,' vol. ii., p. 280.

‡ By warrant of $\frac{13}{34}$ 4, 1678, the following arms were issued to the grenadier company of the Coldstream Guards (the company consisted of 1 captain, 2 lieutenants, 3 sergeants, 3 corporals, and 100 privates): 103 fusees, with slings to each; 103 cartridge boxes, with girdles; 103 grenadoe pouches; 103 bayonets; 103 hatchets, with girdles to them; 3 halberts and 2 partisans.—Mackinnon's 'Coldstream Guards,' vol. ii., p. 275. The clothing of each private of Foot cost £2 13s.; of Horse, £9; and of each Dragoon, £6 10s. The other companies of each battalion were, in 1678, armed thus: 60 men with muskets and dagger-shaped bayonets made to fit into the muzzles; 10 with light firelocks; and the remaining 30 with pikes sixteen feet long. The lieutenants carried partisans, the sergeants halberts. The pike, as an arm for the rank and file, was only laid aside in our army in Anne's reign. They were carried by captains and subalterns until about the end of the eighteenth century.

to maintain discipline, as Parliament was still extremely
jealous of the army. There had been several mutinies
amongst the troops encamped at Blackheath,* and although
many of the mutineers were sent to the Tower, numbers continued to desert. Even when the army was being organized
for service abroad, it was most difficult to check desertion.
We read of a man being tried by the civil power and
hanged ; yet when others were ordered to embark, they ran
away by scores.† From Lord Morpeth's regiment 200
deserted ; and a lieutenant, having surrendered his commission, warned his men to ponder over what they were
about to do, for they were being deceived as he had
been, into the idea that they were intended to fight the
French, whereas they were about to be used to enslave
their own country. They flung down their arms and
bolted to a man.‡

In the military correspondence of the time we read of
the difficulty there was in supplying food, especially bread,
for the army in Flanders. Supplies were then invariably
provided under contract by rich Jews or mercantile firms
abroad. In August Monmouth writes to the Lord Treasurer
from Brussels : 'To gitt all things necessary for the Foot
that is to march into the field, and that which is the most
necessary, I am afred I shall feal of which is the bred, for
I told the Prince if hee would have thess battalions that
ar wth mee come to the army hee, or the Duke of Ville- ¶ 8, 1678.
hermosa must give them bred.'§

* 'Hatton Correspondence,' vol. i., p. 111.
† He was hanged at Tyburn, 19 7, 1678.
‡ 'Hatton Correspondence,' vol. i., p. 166.
§ Mr. A. Morrison's collection of letters.

CHAPTER XXVII.

CHURCHILL EMBARKS FOR ACTIVE SERVICE IN HOLLAND.—THE
PEACE OF NIMEGUEN.

The French King's breach of faith—Charles again threatens war
Peace made and the Army largely reduced.

CHAPTER
XXVII.

1678.

MATTERS having been secretly arranged between Lewis
and Charles, the former made a separate peace with
Holland. But when the time arrived for carrying out its
provisions, he would not surrender the Spanish towns in
Flanders which he had stipulated to restore. Holland
was most indignant at this gross breach of faith; all
Europe sympathized with her, and war was again on
every tongue. In England public feeling ran so strongly
against France, that Charles had to bow before it. He
once more despatched Sir William Temple to the Hague,
with orders to make a new treaty of alliance with Holland
for an immediate war against Lewis XIV. It is, however, clear that he took this step in the hope of being
able to screw more money out of Lewis, and to obtain
further subsidies from Parliament. James knew and
approved of all Charles's negotiations with Lewis, yet
he wrote constantly to William of Orange to assure him
of his desire for a war with France. His letters display a
dissimulation quite in keeping with the opinion commonly
entertained of his character.* His real policy was the
closest possible alliance with Catholic France, but he hoped

* See vol. i., p. 284, etc., of Dalrymple, where these letters are given.

by a pretended zeal for war against her, to ingratiate himself with the English people, who, as he knew, hated the
French, and sympathized deeply with Protestant Holland.

Lewis had paid agents both in Holland and in England,
who kept him informed of all that went on in both
countries. He was furious with Charles for his double-
dealing. In order to estrange England and Holland, he
disclosed the fact of his secret treaty with Charles, and to
punish him he stopped his pension, rejected his overtures
for another secret treaty and refused his request for a fresh
gift of money. It was now Charles's turn to be angry.
He felt that he had overstrained the endurance of his
paymaster, and that he had been completely outwitted.
Enraged with Lewis and with himself, he entered warmly
into new plans against France. The enrolment of recruits
began afresh, and all England rang once more with the
sound of warlike preparations. Churchill, writing to Sir
C. Lyttelton in July, says there are 'no nuses, but now
we are again very furious upon the war: so that I hope it
will not be long before I have orders to come over.' A few
days later, to the same correspondent, he writes: 'It is
generally believed we shall have war.'*

That same week he was again sent to Holland to arrange
details with the Dutch, and William, writing from the
Hague to Lord Danby, says: 'I will tell you nothing of
how we have arranged matters with Mr. Churchill, as he
will tell you of it himself.' The agreement then drawn up,
was, amongst other things, to regulate the 'precedency' of
the superior officers in the allied army when it took the
field. In it Churchill is described as 'Lieutenant-Colonel
of the Regiment of the Duke of York,† Gentleman of
H.R. Highness's Bedchamber, and representing his Majesty
Charles II.'‡

The following letter from Churchill to his wife was

* Historical MSS., Second Report, p. 36.
† The Admiral's regiment.
‡ MS. in British Museum, 20,937, vol. i., f. 289.

evidently written upon his return to England, when awaiting in London orders for embarkation. Its date must have been about August, for that is the date of a letter from James to William in which he conveys the same news regarding the immediate embarkation of troops for Ostend.*

'Your enclosed for Mrs. Fortry I gave Joan (?) as soon as I had it, and she has sent it again to her. You are very unjust to me in making a doubt of my love, since there is nothing in this world I desire so much as to be able to give you proofs of how well I love you, for by all that is good and holy, you are dearer to me than my own life, for could I follow my own inclinations I would never be from you. On Tuesday Thursday is appointed by the King and my Lord Treasurer for renewing proposals for the bread for the army, and I hope that day it will be decided that I shall have it, so that I am resolved, God willing, to be at Salisbury on Wednesday night, where I desire the coach may be for me. Here is no talk now but of war, but I hope it will end in peace, so that I may have my desire of being with you. My duty and service to everybody.

'Saturday. Pray let my father know that if he has writ, his letters are miscarried, for I have not heard from him since he went. You may tell him that last night there was ordered **18** troops of Horse and 15 troops of Dragoons to go over with all expedition; and they say that three regiments of Foot more shall follow very speedily.' Addressed: 'For Mrs. Churchill, at Sir Winston Churchill's house at Mintorne, to be left at the post-house at Dorchester, Dorsetshire.'†

Affairs dragged on in an undecided way for some months, but at length Churchill, always ready to embark, received the following commission from his old comrade-in-arms, the Duke of Monmouth, who had been once more appointed to command the army in the Low Country:

'You are forthwith to repair to the Army in Flanders, to command there as eldist Brigadier of Foot, And your

* Dalrymple, vol. i., p. 246. † Blenheim Palace Papers.

Brigade is to consist of the two Battalions of Guards, one Battalion of the Holland Regiment, and the Regiments of Her Royal Highnesse and Colonel Legg.*

'Given under my hand at Whitehall this 3d day of Septembr, 1678.   'Monmouth.

'To Coll. Churchill.'†

Before embarking, Churchill wrote the following letter to his wife: 'Yours of the last of August I have received, and am extremely pleased with your kind expressions in it ; and I do assure you in return it shall be my study to take satisfaction only in what pleases you. You may rest satisfied that there will be a certain peace in very few days. This news I do assure you is true ; therefore be not concerned when I tell you that I am ordered over, and that to-morrow I go. You shall be sure by all opportunities to hear from me, for I do if possible love you better than I ever did. I believe it will be about the beginning of October before I shall get back, which time will appear an age to me, since in all that time I shall not be made happy with the sight of you. Pray write constantly to me. Send your letters, as you did before, to my house, and there I will take order how they shall be sent after me. So, dearest soul of my life, farewell.

'My duty to my father and mother, and remember me to everybody else.

'Tuesday Night. My will I have here sent you, for $\frac{n}{13}$ 9, 1678. fear of accidents.' [Unsigned.] Endorsed in the Duchess's writing: 'Lord Marlborough, to ease me when I might be frighted at his going into danger.'

The ship in which he and Brigadier-General Sir John Fenwick embarked for Holland was driven by head-winds into Margate, where he wrote again to his wife :‡ 'The

* This brigade was to be ' the first,' and the regiments of which it was to consist are now the Grenadier and Coldstream Guards, the 'Buffs,' or East Kent Regiment ; her Royal Highness' Regiment was a Dutch corps, and that commanded by Colonel Legge was the Duke of Ormond's Regiment, afterwards disbanded.

† Blenheim Palace Papers.   ‡ *Ibid.*

cross winds have forced us into this place, where we shall stay till to-morrow morning. I could have wished that I might have met with the same orders that Mr. Berkeley has, which is to come back. I have writ to the Duke to desire that I may not stay any longer than I needs must, so that I hope very quickly to have orders to come back, till when I am sure I shall not be happy, for nothing but the being with you can give me true comfort. You may be sure the minute I come for England you shall not only hear from me but see me. Pray remember to everybody. Margett, Sept. 8, 1678.' [Unsigned.] Addressed: 'For Mrs. Churchill at Mintorne, to be left at the post-house in Dorchester, Dorsetshire.'*

He thoroughly understood Charles's character, and his expectations, based on that knowledge, were quickly realized. He had been but a short time in Holland when preliminaries of peace were agreed upon by Lewis and William, and our young Brigadier-General was enabled to rejoin his wife at home.

The Conference which sat at Nimeguen ended in a general peace, called after that place.† The English troops returned home in March, 1679.‡ Most of the lately-raised regiments were disbanded, and the country was for a time flooded with idle and disorderly men. The system then pursued of suddenly raising, and as suddenly disbanding regiments, led to great abuses, misery and crime, so much so, that when any corps was to be disbanded, orders were usually sent to the nearest troops of Life Guards or Horse to patrol the roads in the neighbourhood for the protection of the inhabitants.

* Blenheim Palace Papers.

† The Peace of Nimeguen, between France and Spain, was signed 10, 8, 1678; between France and Holland and the Low Countries on 17, 9, 1678; and between France and the German Empire, as well as between the latter and Sweden, on 5, 2, 1678-9.

‡ Hamilton's 'Grenadier Guards.' They consisted of 16 battalions —about 10,500 men; 27 troops of Horse—about 1,600; and 12 troops of Dragoons—about 950. The total force was about 13,000 men.

CHAPTER XXVIII.

THE POPISH PLOT.

⅛ 8, 1678.

In the autumn of 1678 Titus Oates, a navy chaplain who had been dismissed for immoral conduct, divulged a conspiracy for the assassination of the King, which is known in history as the 'Popish Plot.' He communicated on oath all he knew about it to a justice of the peace, Sir Edmondbury Godfrey, and about a fortnight later, the dead body of that worthy knight was found on Primrose Hill. He had evidently been murdered, though not by footpads, for his pockets had not been rifled, and it was generally believed that he had met his death at the hands of the Catholics implicated in the plot. Throughout the country, and in London especially, the excitement was intense. The Protestant majority called aloud for vengeance, and a large reward was offered for the discovery of the murderers. The King in a speech to the House of Lords not only proclaimed his readiness to uphold the laws for the security of the Protestant religion, but undertook to arrange for its maintenance and protection under his successor, provided the right of succession according to English law and custom was rigidly safeguarded. But Parliament, though well packed with courtiers, showed an

CHAPTER XXVIII.

1678.

⁹ 11, 1678.

earnest desire to probe the Popish plot, and the prejudice
against the Duke of York was much increased by the trial
and conviction for high treason of Coleman, secretary to
the Duchess.   In the end a cruel law was passed by which
Papists were disqualified from sitting in either House of
Parliament, his Majesty's subjects, under severe penalties,
were forbidden to attend any church 'where the Romish
worship is celebrated,' and the year ended with a proclamation for the disarmament of all Roman Catholics.

Charles's second, or, as it was commonly called, the Long
or Pensioning Parliament, was now eighteen years old. The
Commons had been elected by the people in the exuberance
of enthusiastic loyalty upon the restoration of their King
by Divine right.   Parliament was, however, no longer the
tractable body it had been at first.   It was loyal, but
essentially Protestant, and it was determined that England
should never be ruled by a Roman Catholic.   It had just
impeached the Lord Treasurer, Danby, and it seemed resolved to have some victims for the past twelve years of
disgraceful misgovernment. Charles wishing to save Danby
and to rid himself of a Parliament that had become his
master, dissolved it, to the dismay of Shaftesbury and the
Protestant party. A new Parliament was called, but Charles
never afterwards obtained another so lenient to his crimes,
so blind to his social depravity, and so anxious to forgive
and to forget the past.

The hostility of the new Parliament to James soon
became apparent, and its tone was more defiant than
that of its predecessor.   The people had been worked
into a frenzy by rumours of plots against the Protestant
religion, and their representatives, though less violent,
were determined to have their way.   It is difficult now to
realize how intense was the hatred of Roman Catholics
which the murder of Sir E. Godfrey, together with the
discovery of the 'Popish Plot,' had aroused.   There can be
no doubt that there had been a serious conspiracy for the
complete extirpation of Protestantism in England, and that

some fanatics had plotted the assassination of Charles in order to put James on the throne. But the Protestant faction made the most of the perjuries of Oates and others in order to aggravate the popular feeling against Popery, the object being, by fair means or foul, to exclude James from succession to the throne. Parliament declared the King's life to be in danger from the Papists, and as a precautionary measure begged him to forbid his brother the kingdom. Much against his will, Charles felt it necessary to comply with this request, and banished James to Brussels in March, who went there accompanied by the Duchess, Lord Peterborough, Colonel and Mrs. Churchill, and some other attendants.* Anne was at first kept at home by order of the King, but was allowed to rejoin her father in the following August. The King soon found how great was his mistake in dissolving the Long Parliament, for that which replaced it was by no means inclined to grant him supplies unless he would entirely abandon his brother. He consequently dissolved it, and summoned another to meet in the following October. The elections went everywhere against him. The western counties, especially Somerset, Dorset, and Devon, were strong in their openly expressed opposition to James, to his religion, and to the arbitrary power which he was known to favour, while society and the country at large, were divided into two hostile factions, to whom the nick-names of Whig and Tory were now for the first time given.

James occupied the house in Brussels in which King Charles had lived before the Restoration. There the Princess Anne was allowed her own Protestant chaplain, and with the Churchills and her servants was permitted to have religious services according to the rites of the Church of England. To the credit of James, it must also be added that he had not up to this time attempted to induce her to change her religion.† Indeed, the advice of

*, 3, 1679.

²²⁄₇ 7, 1679.

---

* James and his household reached Brussels ⁵⁄₉ 1678-9.
† Life of Anne, London, 1721, vol. i., p. 12.

her Broad Church, if not free-thinking friend and companion, Sarah Churchill, who had already obtained a great influence over her mind, would have been of itself a powerful antidote to Roman Catholic tendencies.

James took a gloomy view of his position in Brussels. 1, 4, 1679. 'I see so little likelihood,' he writes to Legge, ' of things going well in England, or of my being sent for back, that I would have you think of getting my carriages sent to me, as it is very inconvenient being without them.'*

$\frac{4}{7}$ 8, 1679. In another letter, a few months later, he asks to have his fox-hounds and huntsman sent to Brussels, as there are plenty of stags about, and the country, he adds, 'looks as if the fox-hunting would be very good.' By degrees a little Court collected round him in his exile, and we read of Sarah's widowed sister Frances, of Lady Bellasis, Lady Wentworth and others being of his party.+

Whilst in Brussels, James kept up a constant correspondence with his brother, and with his friends in England. When ordered abroad he seems at once to have thrown himself into the arms of France, looking to Lewis for help whenever the English Throne should become vacant. Churchill did not, we are assured, mix himself up in the party intrigues of the day, though he was frequently sent to Paris and London by his royal master on secret missions. He was at home in May, 1679, and he carried back to James a very kind letter from the King.‡ He was again in London in August. James plied his brother with repeated applications for permission to return home. He knew that his banishment was due to the plots of Monmouth and the Protestant party, who wished him to be out of England whenever the King should die, and if this could be accomplished, he believed it to be their intention to pro-

* MSS. British Museum.

† Letter of $\frac{19}{5}$ 5, 79, from Sir R. Bulstrode at Brussels; F. O. Papers in Rolls Office, Flanders, No. 119.

‡ Dalrymple, i., p. 298. Churchill returned to Brussels, Tuesday night, 16, 5, 79. Historical MSS., Dartmouth Papers, p. 33.

claim Monmouth King, as the son and heir of Charles.
It was this which made absence from England so terrible to
James, for he well knew the strength of the Anti-Catholics,
and their determination to exclude him from the throne
if possible.   He found with dismay, that Monmouth was
steadily gaining in favour with the English people, and,
still worse, that it began to be reported, that he had been
born in wedlock, Charles having, it was said, married his
mother before the Restoration.   The leading people about
the Court, mostly Roman Catholics, loudly contested the
truth of this story, for, according to their views regarding
'Divine right,' to change the order of succession would be
nearly as great an act of sacrilege as Cromwell's murder
of Charles I.

In August the King was suddenly taken so seriously ill
that Sunderland, Halifax and Godolphin thought it necessary to confer with Hyde, Feversham and the King's
mistress, 'Madam Carwell,' as to what should be done.
They decided to ask Charles to allow them to send for his
brother.   His answer was, 'Yes.'*   James was accordingly
summoned home, and left Brussels in haste, taking with $\frac{29}{30}$-$\frac{8}{9}$, 1679.
him only Lord Peterborough, Churchill, Mr. Doyly, a barber,
and two footmen out of livery.   He was disguised in ' a
blacke peruque only, and a plaine stuffe suit, wth out his
starre and Garter, and rode post to Calais.'†   Upon reaching Dover, Churchill, wearing the scarf of a French officer,
pretended to be the chief person of the party.   The post-
master, however, recognised him and the Duke of York
also, though he pretended not to do so, seeing that they
were disguised.   James and Churchill outrode the others, and
reached the Barbican in Smithfield late on Sunday even- $\frac{1}{2}$, 9, 1679.
ing.   There they took a hackney coach, and drove to the
house of Sir Alleyn Apsley, the Treasurer of James's

* Ranke, vol. vi., p. 40.
† Carte MS., ccxxxii., fol. 23.   The description of this journey is
well told in a letter dated $\frac{6}{10}$ 9, 1679, from Lord Longford to the Earl
of Arran.

Household, where they slept." They reached Windsor
early the next morning, when James, on his knees, asked
his brother's forgiveness for his sudden arrival. He had
been previously warned to act as if he thought Charles
were entirely ignorant of the cause of his reappearance at
Court. His story was, that hearing of the King's illness,
he had come home forthwith, but now that his Majesty
was quite recovered, he was ready to go back at once to
Brussels if the King wished it. Charles received his
brother with every mark of affection, but soon realized
that he dared not retain him in England whilst popular
feeling was so strong against him. Nineteen-twentieths of
the people were ardent Protestants, and bitter haters of
Popery, while the great majority were strongly attached to
the English Church. The sudden reappearance of James
at Windsor revived amongst them the fear and hatred
with which they regarded him.

Whilst in England upon this occasion, Churchill wrote
the following letters to his wife:† 'I did not write to
you from St. Omer, having but just time to write what
the Duke commanded me to Worden. By this you will
find that we are landed in England, so that now we
shall not be long before we shall be at Windsor,
from whence you shall be sure to hear from me by
the first opportunity, for I hope I am not deceived in the
belief I have that you love me, which thought pleases me
more than all other things in this world, and I do assure
you that whilst I live I will never give you any reason to
do other than love me, for I had much rather lose my own
life than to lose you or your love. Pray do not fail of

---

* Sir A. Apsley lived in St. James's Square; he was a devoted
Royalist, who, after the Restoration, made large sums in handling
the money voted by Parliament for the navy. James, as Lord High
Admiral, confided this public money to his keeping. He was Falconer
to the King and M.P. for Thetford from 1661 to 1678, and died 1683,
aged 67.

† Blenheim Palace Papers. These letters are neither signed nor
dated.

writing every post to me. If you give them to Colonel Worden he will take care to send them safe to me. So, having no more at present, I rest, assuring you that you shall always find me what I now am, truly and wholly yours. My service, pray, to all my friends.' Addressed: ' For Mrs. Churchill, at Brussels.'

' I write this although I do not know when it will come to you, only to tell you that this morning I am a-going for France. As soon as I come for Paris you shall be sure to hear from me. When you write to me you have but to direct them to your sister, and she will give them me. Pray tell Colonel Worden that I do not write to him because there is yet no resolutions taken, but I believe they that bring this may bring news. You must be sure to come for England when Lady Anne comes. I am in haste, therefore excuse me that I say no more than that I am, what I desire to be as long as I live, only yours. Thursday morning.' Addressed: ' For Mrs. Churchill, at Brussels.'

During his short stay in England, as mentioned in this letter, James had sent Churchill to Paris on a secret mission to his patron, Lewis XIV. Churchill carried with him a letter in which James described him as ' master of my wardrobe, to whom you may give entire credit.'[*] The object of the mission was to forward the secret treaty already alluded to, upon which Charles was then engaged with Barillon.

Letter dated
9, 1679.

Charles would have liked to keep James in England, provided the arrangement in no way incommoded him, for self was always uppermost in his thoughts. But if James's presence were to cause him trouble by exciting popular clamour against the Court, then James and his interests must go by the board. He soon found that this would be the case, as his brother's reappearance had already brought upon him a very general suspicion of favouring Popery. James's idea of kingship was the same as

* Dalrymple, vol. i., p. 321.

that of his father: to secure to the people the full enjoyment of their property, but to allow them no share in the Government of the country or in the management of public affairs, which were, in his opinion, exclusively the province of the King.   Acting on these principles, James had never concerned himself with what the English people thought or wished, and he now urged his brother to disregard the popular feeling, and to let him live, if not in England, at least in Scotland.   This compromise was agreed to.   The King thought that at Edinburgh, whilst removed from sight, he would still be always at hand if required.   Much as Charles loved the handsome Monmouth whom he believed to be his son, it is doubtful whether he ever seriously contemplated setting aside his brother's rights in his favour.   It is, however, probable that, had Charles died before James had returned from Brussels, Monmouth — the Protestant Duke, as he was called by the people—would have been proclaimed King by the powerful ' Exclusionist ' party.   James, fully alive to this, had long urged the King to send Monmouth abroad, and at last he prevailed.   Monmouth was ordered to leave the kingdom at the same time that James left for Scotland.   Driven forth like Ishmael, and deprived of his command in the English army, he took up his residence in Holland, where he was cordially received by the Princess Mary and her shrewd, far-seeing husband.

It was about this time that Churchill was offered a seat in Parliament.   The question was duly weighed and considered, but he wisely determined to keep aloof from politics, and except as the agent of his Royal master, to take no part in the schemes or cabals of ministers and courtiers.

CHAPTER XXIX.

CHURCHILL GOES WITH JAMES TO SCOTLAND: THEY RETURN TO ENGLAND.

Churchill goes to Edinburgh with James—Sarah's first child born —
James returns to London.

SHORTLY after James's return to Brussels, where Churchill
rejoined him, his heart was gladdened by an order
from the King to return home.   To account for his
brother's reappearance in England, Charles announced in
the *Gazette* that James found it so inconvenient to reside
in the territory of a foreign Prince, that his Majesty had
given him leave to live in Scotland.   On his journey home,
James paid his daughter Mary a visit at the Hague, and
this was the last time he ever saw her.   His stay in London
was short, and leaving the Princesses Anne and Isabella
behind, by order of the King, he started by land, with all
his household, for Edinburgh.   The journey was made 27, 10, 1679.
with great pomp and ceremony, and he was entertained
by most of the large towns through which he passed.
Churchill accompanied him, but Sarah, who was expecting
her first confinement, was left in lodgings at the west end
of 'Germaine Street,' on the south side, some five doors
from St. James's Street, where she was joined by her
widowed sister, Lady Hamilton.   Her first child 'Harriot'
was born about the end of November, but did not live
long, and there is no mention of her in the Duchess's
Bible, nor in the paper at Blenheim wherein she records,

in her own handwriting, the births of her children who lived beyond babyhood. In a paper, however, marked 'Pedigree,' now in Spencer House, the births of Harriot and of a boy named Charles are recorded. No dates are given, but the girl was her first, the boy her last child, and both died in infancy. The following letters, written by Churchill to his wife during the journey to Edinburgh, allude to the birth of the child 'Harriot':

'I this day received a letter from you, which was the third I have had since I saw you, which is kinder than I could reasonably have expected from you, although I love you better than my own life. You tell me in your letter that you know not what to do, by reason that neither my father nor mother has writ. If the child is born before they write, you may take somebody else for godfather or godmother in the place of my father. I know my Lord . . . . .* will be very willing if you send to him. Pray in your next let me know if Mr. Griffith be as yet bought out. We leave this place on Monday next, so that in ten days after we expect to be at Edinburgh; but before I get thither I hope in God I shall hear you are safe and out of all danger, which news I long for most extremely, for believe me, upon my soul you are dearer to me than ever you were. I love you so well that I desire life no longer than you love me and I love you. Pray when you are not able to write to me yourself, make somebody or other write, so that I may constantly know how you do.

'York, November 3, 1679.' Addressed: 'For Mrs. Churchill, at her house in Jermaine Street, near St. James's, London. Free p. Mr. Frowde.'

'We expect every minute the post, for which I am very impatient, for I have now no satisfaction but that of hearing from you, and when you miss one post I shall be in great pain, for I shall then believe you are in labour. My eyes are not yet well, and the weather being so cold that I am afraid they will not be well until I get to Edinborough,

---

* Word illegible, but it looks like Feversham.

for there I intend to keep my chamber until they be well, for they are very troublesome to me. You may believe that I reckon every day of the month, for I long most extremely for the second of January, for I do still hold my resolution of coming from Scotland that day. As to Poidvine, I would have him to stay with you and not come to me, for although I shall want him yet I believe you would want him more; but pray tell him that at his leisure I should be glad to hear from him.* To-night we are to be at Newcastle, where we are to be very highly treated.

'Durham, November 14, 1679.' Addressed: 'For Mrs. Churchill, at her house in Jermaine Street, London.'

The journey to Scotland in those days of bad roads was usually made by sea, especially when ladies were of the party. But upon this occasion James, though a sailor, preferred the land route, as he wished to show himself to the people and, if possible, to regain their favour. He had once been popular — before he openly joined the Church of Rome, and when he was known as a successful Admiral. After his naval victory over the Dutch, in 1665, he had resided for some months at York, and was liked by the people of the city from which he took his title. He now visited it again, hoping to revive the feeling with which they had formerly regarded him, but was grievously disappointed by the coldness of his reception. He rested one or two days at all the important towns he passed through, and in some of them he was more cordially welcomed. After a wearisome journey of thirty-eight days he reached Edinburgh, where his arrival was announced by the ringing of bells, salutes, and bon- _{v. 12, 1679.} fires. A banquet was given in his honour by the Lord Provost, in the great Parliament House, at which he and Churchill were made burgesses of the city. James and his wife now began to keep Court there, and did their best to win popularity. Fond of the play, they

---

* Poidvine was evidently his valet; from his name it is probable he was a French Protestant refugee.

had taken a troop of actors with them, but their performances somewhat scandalized the strict Presbyterians of
the place. Churchill often refers to these plays in his
letters. He was always a good correspondent, and the
following letters to his wife are interesting :*

'I have received yours of the 10th, with a copy of the
letter you writ my mother, which if she takes anything ill
that is in that letter, you must attribute it to the peevish-
ness of old age, for really I think there is nothing in it that
she ought to take ill. I take it very kindly that you have
writ to her again, for she is my mother, and I hope at last
she will be sensible that she is to blame in being peevish.
I long extremely to have this month over, so that I may be
leaving this country, which is very uneasy since you are not
in it, for I do assure you that my thoughts are so fond of
you that I cannot be happy when I am from you, for I love
you so well that you cannot yourself wish to be loved better.
Pray present my service to the widow, and tell her that I
am very glad she is not married, and if she stays for my
consent she never will be.† Most of the Duke's and
Duchess's servants have parts given in "Aurenzebe," which
is to be acted by them before the Duke and Duchess. I am
with all my heart and soul yours.' 'Edinborough, January
15, 1679.' Addressed : 'For Mrs. Churchill, at her house,
Germaine Street, near St. James's, London.'

'January 17, 1679.

'Since my last to you we have had no letters, so that I
have not much more to say to you than that I do with all
my soul wish myself with you ; and now that I am from
you I do assure you I have no satisfaction but that of
receiving yours and writing to you, and flattering myself

note in left margin: ½ 1, 1679-80.

---

* They have been selected from the Blenheim Palace Papers.
† This refers to Lady Hamilton, Sarah's widowed sister. Frances,
whose husband had been killed in 1676 at the Battle of Zebernstieg.
Very shortly after this letter was written she married the notorious
Dick Talbot, afterwards Earl of Tyrconnel and Lord Lieutenant of
Ireland.

that it will not now be long before I shall be truly happy in being with you again. You are so well beloved by me that if that will make you happy you ought to be the happiest woman living, for none is so well beloved as you are by me. I hope by the first post in the next month to send you word what day I shall leave this country, which is very much desired by me—not for any dislike to the country, but from the great desire I have to be with you, for you are dearer to me than ever you were in your life.

'Pray bid Poidvine bespeak three or four pair of shoes for me against I come to town. My service to Harriot.' [Unsigned.] Addressed: 'For Mrs. Churchill, at her house in Germaine Street, near St. James's, London.'

'We have been all this day in expectation of an express, by which I was in hopes I might hear from you, which made me forbear writing till this minute; but it being now past, I did not dare expect any longer, for fear my letter might come too late to the post. We have had this afternoon a very ridiculous running match between Mr. Turner and Mr. Layborne, the latter being obliged to carry Mr. Vaghan all the way on his back, notwithstanding which he won the match. It was run about a mile from this town. The Duke and Duchess, and all the company of this place, were to see it. Although I believe you love me, yet you do not love so well as I, so that you cannot be truly sensible how much I desire to be with you. I swear to you the first night in which I was blessed in having you in my arms was not more earnestly wished for by me than now I do to be again with you, for if ever man loved woman truly well, I now do you, for I swear to you were we not married I would beg you on my knees to be my wife, which I could not do did I not esteem you as well as love you. If you please, my service to your sister.'[*]

Towards the end of January, 1679-80, Charles informed his council that he had ordered his brother James to return to England, 'not having found such an effect

* Frances, Lady Hamilton.

from his absence as should incline him to keep him longer from him.'* This was communicated by James to the Privy Council of Scotland in a speech which flattered all parties ; he expressed a feigned regret at leaving a country where he had, he said, so many good friends, and had received so many evidences of loyalty and affection for his person.†

Whilst waiting for a ship to take James and his household to London, Churchill wrote to his wife, begging of her to 'pray for fair winds, so that we may not stay here, nor be long at sea, for should we be long at sea, and very sick, I am afraid it would do me great hurt, for really I am not well, for in my whole lifetime I never had so long a fit of headacheing as now : I hope all the red spots of the child will be gone against I see her, and her nose straight, so that I may fancy it to be like the mother, for as she has your coloured hair, so I would have her be like you in all things else. Till next post-day, farewell. By that time I hope we shall hear of the yacht, for till I do I shall have no kind of happiness.'‡

The yacht *Mary*, under the command of Captain Gunman, with two other royal yachts, reached Leith at last, and in the former the Duke and Duchess of York with Colonel Churchill embarked for Deptford. They were received by the King with every mark of respect and affection. Mrs. Churchill resumed her waiting upon the Duchess of York, and her husband now saw their child ' Harriot ' for the first time.

* *London Gazette*, 29, 1, 1679-80.
† *Ibid.*, 9, 2, 1679-80.
‡ Coxe gives this letter in his first volume as dated the 3rd January. The original in Blenheim Palace, from which the above is copied, is dated 31st January.

CHAPTER XXX.

JAMES IS AGAIN SENT TO SCOTLAND, AND THE CHURCHILLS GO WITH HIM.

Court life at Newmarket—James anxious to provide well for Churchill
—Lewis bribes many English public men—James determines to
create a party in his favour in Scotland—The Exclusion Bill.

JAMES paid occasional visits to his brother at Newmarket,
where Charles had built a hideous residence. Life there
was entirely given up to amusement and revelry. 'The
mornings were spent on horseback, the afternoons at cock-
matches, the evenings taking the air, and the nights at
cards.'* But early hours were generally kept, and the
King sometimes went to bed at 9 p.m. The Churchills
often accompanied James upon these visits, but the
routine of Court life had become irksome to Churchill,
who longed for active work, responsible duties, and lucrative appointments. James was anxious to further his
favourite's wishes, and he had already importuned the
King more than once on this subject, but without result,
as there were many greedy courtiers to be provided for.
Soon after James's return to England, it was reported
that Churchill was to have the colonelcy of the 'Admiral's
Regiment,' the question of making him Governour of Sheerness, which had been raised the previous year, was revived,†
and later on the propriety of sending him as Ambassador to
either Paris or the Hague was discussed.

* 'Savile Correspondence,' Camden Society Papers.
† 'Hatton Correspondence,' vol. i., p. 226.

CHAPTER
XXX.

1680.

Henry Savile, the English representative in France, writing at this time to his brother, Lord Halifax, complains of Barillon's intrigues against him, and goes on to say : ' I am told that Mr. Churchill likes my station so well that he has a mind to it, and got his master to work for him, and by a very cunning artifice endeavours to make my friends willing to have me recalled upon pretence I live too high and shall ruin myself,' etc. In his answer, Halifax hopes that ' Churchill, whatever inclination he may have to be a Minister, will never give such a price for it as the supplanting of a friend.' A few days after this Savile again writes that he was unwilling to have uneasy thoughts of Churchill, who had been always his friend, but that it was from James the report first ' came which was improved into a story round the Town.'[*]

20, 5, 1680.

According to another rumour Churchill was to replace Sidney at the Hague. King Charles hoped by this arrangement to reassure his suspicious brother, who hated Sidney, and to prove to him that his interests at William's Court would be neither ignored nor neglected. Barillon writes, that ' the English Colonel is a man of no experience in public affairs, but that the Prince of Orange wishes to have him, and wants no other man as English Minister.'[†] This is a proof of how thoroughly Churchill had already ingratiated himself with William. Towards

22-3 1680.

the end of the year James recommended that Sidney should be removed from the Hague, and that Churchill should either replace him, or be sent to Paris, ' If Savil have a mind to come home.' ' You may remember,' he writes to Lawrence Hyde, ' this was once thought on, and let me know what your opinion is of it now : but this is only in case I should be with His Majesty again, for so long as I am from him I would not willingly have Churchill from me.'[‡] In other words, he was so essential

---

* These three letters are amongst the Spencer House Papers.
† ' Archives des affaires étrangères,' vol. 120, fol. 206.
‡ Singer's ' Clarendon Correspondence,' vol. i., p. 51.

to the Duke when in banishment for his negotiations with
the King, and also with the French Court, that, anxious as
James was to provide well for him, he had no intention of
parting with so useful a servant until he should once more
be established in England.

In May it was again reported that Churchill was to have
'the Duke's Regiment and the govt. of Sherenes.'* Sir
C. Lyttelton, writing from Sheerness in August, says:
'When I was at Windsor, I found by Churchill (who is ye
only favorite of his master) that his pretence to my command herre is not given over.'+ But notwithstanding all
these rumours, none of the proposed changes took place.

This year French gold was again liberally bestowed upon
the leading men in English public life. In a despatch
of July, Barillon mentions that he had bought Lady
Hervey, her brother Montague, Lord Holles, and two
useful Presbyterian ministers. He discusses the propriety
of buying Shaftesbury and Monmouth for 100,000 francs
apiece. He says that he has bought Hampden—the son
of the great Parliamentarian—for a thousand guineas, that
he has paid the Duke of Buckingham a similar amount,
whilst Algernon Sidney has taken five hundred guineas.
To others he had given smaller sums, to some as little as
one hundred and fifty guineas.

Parliament was to meet towards the end of October,
and, to avoid impeachment, James was ordered by his
brother to set out again for Scotland. Frightened by
Monmouth's rapid advance in public favour, he was at
the same time irritated by what he regarded as his brother's
cruel treatment; so much so, indeed, that before leaving
London, he told Barillon that he intended to stir up troubles
in Ireland and Scotland to avenge himself on the King,
his brother. But events proved that he reckoned without
his host, for when he endeavoured to intrigue with this
object, he found that he was too unpopular in Scotland

* 'Hatton Correspondence,' Camden Society, vol. i., p. 226.
† *Ibid.*, vol. i., p. 233.

to enlist any party in his interests. The truth was, that Charles was too worldly-wise to adopt the violent measures urged by James, and, remembering his father's fate, he felt that it would be madness at that juncture to attempt to rule without a Parliament.

Accompanied by his household, which included the Churchills, James embarked at Woolwich, and after a stormy passage of five days landed at Kirkaldy Roads in the last week of October. He was received with the usual honours, but when a salute was fired from Edinburgh Castle to announce his arrival, the only large piece of ordnance then in Scotland burst. It was a gun of some historical interest, commonly known as 'Mons Megg.' The superstitious regarded the occurrence as an evil omen foreboding no good to either Prince or nation.* Mary of Modena hated Scotland, though enforced absence from Court had the advantage of separating her unfaithful husband from Mrs. Catherine Sedley. For the next two years James resided in Edinburgh, where he took an active part in Scotch affairs, and strove to surround himself with a strong party that should be entirely devoted to his cause. His wife helped him to popularity by making her Court a pleasant one,+ but the Edinburgh people were never able to forget or to forgive the religion which this Royal couple openly professed, and James's cruel treatment of the Dissenters made him especially odious to a large and influential section of the people.

The great object which James always had in view was, that he might be allowed to reside, if not at Court, at least in England. Monmouth, idolized by the Protestant party, had become for the hour the hero and favourite of the English people, to whom circumstances, both at home and abroad, had conspired to make Popery

---

* Fountainhall's Notes, p. 3.

+ Tea had come into vogue in England at the Restoration, but was practically unknown in Scotland until Mary of Modena introduced its use at her receptions in Edinburgh.

more than ever hateful. Amongst other things, Lewis XIV. had recently decreed, that anyone who met the Host, and did not kneel before it, should be whipped through the streets by the hangman ; and although an exception was subsequently made in favour of English subjects, the circumstance tended to render priestcraft more than ever detestable to the freedom-loving people of England.

The year 1680 was pregnant with events affecting Churchill's Royal master. Parliament was determined to exclude him from the throne, and every effort was made by Sunderland, Shaftesbury, and Godolphin to secure this object. One of the clauses in the proposed Exclusion Bill, contained the proviso, that should James ever claim or endeavour to secure the Crown, he should be deemed a traitor, and suffer as such ; and that should he be found within the English dominions at any time after 1680, he and those who aided him were to be held guilty of high treason.

Although Churchill was admitted to James's political secrets, and had gained his confidence during many secret missions, he took no personal part in the intrigues and crooked politics of this time. Believing, as he evidently did, in his master's oft-repeated promises that he would not interfere with any man's religion, and that he only sought to secure for himself the liberty of conscience which he was anxious to see extended to every Englishman, Churchill sided with James in his antagonism to the 'Exclusion Bill.' A trusted friend has left the following on record : ' For though he had an aversion to Popery, yet he was always against the persecution for conscience sake, and at that time told me he thought it the highest act of injustice for anyone to be set aside from his inheritance upon bare suppositions of intentional evils, when nothing that was actual yet appeared to hinder him from the exercise of his just rights.'*

* ' The Lives of the Two Illustrious Generals,' etc., published 1713, p. 13. The author does not give his name, but his editor claims for him an intimate personal knowledge with Marlborough, which, published in 1713, was never contradicted by the Duke.

Charles opened Parliament the day after James had left for Scotland, and in his speech from the throne he expressed his readiness to concur in every measure necessary for the preservation of the Protestant religion, though he refused positively to deal with the question of the succession. But he soon found that he could do no more with this Parliament than with the last. To his horror, it was resolved that means must be adopted to destroy Popery and to banish a Prince who professed a religion incompatible with the welfare of the State. In order to stop further measures against his brother, Charles prorogued Parliament, a pro-

ceeding which aroused intense anger in all who loved liberty.

CHAPTER XXXI.

CHURCHILL EMPLOYED ON MANY MISSIONS TO THE KING.—HIS SECOND CHILD BORN.

Friendship between Churchill and George Legge—Parliament assembled
at Oxford—James sends Churchill on a mission to the King—The
last Parliament of Charles II. dissolved—William visits England.

TOWARDS the end of 1680 Mrs. Churchill returned to
London, leaving her husband in Edinburgh with the Duke
of York. During this temporary separation she received
the following letters from him :

'I hope that which I writ on Wednesday next day you
have received, it being writ with all my heart and soul, by
which I hope you will see that I desire nothing more in
this world than your love, and that it is, if you please,
absolutely in your power to make me love you as long as I
live. We have here the finest weather, they say, that ever
was known in this country at this time of the year. However, I have not my health as I could wish, for my eyes are
not yet well. All my misfortunes I attribute to my being
from you, which after this time I hope never to be so long
absent as long as I live. Pray let Harriot know by some
very intelligible figure that I am very well pleased with
her hair, and that I long to see her, hoping that since she
has her mother's coloured hair that she may be also like
her. When you see next your mother present my duty to
her.

'January 3rd, 1680. My brother [illegible] presents his

service to you.' Addressed: ' For Mrs. Churchill, at her house in Jermayne Street, near St. James's, London.'*

' I have received yours of the 6th, and I think you are unjust to me in saying that you do not think I would forbear doing aught when you desire me, when I vow to Almighty God I have not a greater pleasure in the world than in doing what I think would be agreeable to you, for on my faith you are dearer to me than all the rest of the world together. You say I ought not to judge you by myself, because you love better than I. Were that so, then were I happier than any man breathing, for 'tis you alone I only think kindly of, so that I should never be unhappy were I assured you loved me so truly well as I do you. I am not so unreasonable as to expect you should be kind if I were coquet, and made love to any other woman ; but since I do not, and love only you above my own life, I cannot but think but you are both unjust and unkind in having a suspicion of me, after so many assurances as I have given you to the contrary. In short, you are the only thing on earth I do love or ever can, which I beg you will believe. The bearer hereof, Mr. Ashton, says he will be in town as soon as the post, so that I would not let him go without a letter for you. It is post day, so that at night I will write to you again.'†

Another letter written about this time, shows the good fellowship existing between Churchill and his cousin George Legge,‡ who had been with him a long time in the household of the Duke of York. Legge had contrived to leave Churchill far behind in the race of life, and had become, through Court favouritism, Master of the Ordnance. Although styled Colonel, he had spent most of his time, from the age of seventeen, at sea. He had commanded several ships, and had done good service in both the Dutch

---

* Blenheim Palace Papers.

† *Ibid.*

‡ Churchill's great-grandmother, Elizabeth Villiers, and Legge's grandmother, Anne Villiers, were sisters.

wars of Charles II.'s reign. But Churchill was the more business-like of the two, and it will be seen from the following letter, that he did not scruple to give his cousin good advice upon money matters.*

'DEAR COUSEN,   'Jan. $\frac{5}{15}$ 1680-81 (Edinburgh?).

'I did 2 postes agoe recive yours of the 27th of the last month, but as yett I have not recived anny from my Lord Feavershame. I see by yours to the duke that came this day, that you are now Master of the Ordinance; I doe not doute but you are satisfied that I am glade of itt, and I doe ashure you that I wish that you may live long to enjoye itt, and as I wish you as well as any friend you have, soe I will take the liberty to tell you that you will not be just to your familly, if you doe not now order your affairs soe as that you may, by living within yourselfe, be able in time to clear your estaites. I will say no more on this subject att present, but when we mett you must expect me to be troblesome if I find you prefer your owne living before your children's good.' He goes on to remark upon the escape of Argyle from prison, and ends his letter: 'I am your affectionate kinsman and faithful frend and sarvant—J. CHURCHILL.'†

These two friends helped one another upon all occasions, and when at the Revolution Dartmouth fell into disgrace, Marlborough did all he could to procure his pardon and release from the Tower.

Charles again dissolved Parliament in January, because ₓₓ 1, 1680-81. the House of Commons had passed the Exclusion Bill, and had made demands, which if granted, would have seriously restricted the royal authority. Another Parliament was summoned to meet at Oxford. He avoided London because

---

* Eldest son of Colonel William Legge, an Irish adventurer and soldier of fortune, who was a loyal and faithful servant to Charles I. George Legge was born about 1647, was Groom of the Bedchamber and afterwards Master of the Horse to James, Duke of York; Master of the Ordnance in 1678, and created Baron Dartmouth in 1682.

† Historical MSS. : Lord Dartmouth's Papers, p. 55.

of its strong Protestant feeling, and dreading the support it would probably give the House of Commons should that House resolve to sit on and do the nation's business whether he liked it or not.* This change of venue increased the angry feeling, already general in the country, against Charles. There were many overt signs of discontent in the city, and the people showed their feelings by the enthusiasm with which they everywhere greeted Monmouth. James realized that he could have no chance of sympathy from any Parliament whilst popular sentiment was so strongly against him. He therefore sent Churchill on a secret mission to the King in January, charging him to let no one know the object of his journey. His instructions were that he was to see the King in private, and to entreat him not to assemble another Parliament whilst the public mind remained so agitated. He was to impress upon him that if he followed this advice it would show the world that he meant to be King in deed as well as in name. Churchill was also to persuade Charles to ally himself still more closely with Lewis XIV., as the only means by which he could maintain himself without the aid of Parliament. James added, that 'matters were come to such a head, that the monarchy must either be more absolute or quite abolished.' Above all things, Churchill was to urge the King to allow James to return to Court, if only for a few days. If not allowed to live in London, it was suggested that Audley End would be a suitable place of residence for him, being secluded in the country. The King's wishes would, however, be his law in this, as in all other matters. Churchill also carried a letter from the Duchess of York to Charles, in which she pressed upon him the unsuitableness of the Northern climate to her Southern constitution. Her health had already suffered, and she begged permission to visit either Bath or Tunbridge, whose waters were then held in high repute.

* 'Où il ne craindra pas que la séance se continuera malgré lui.'— Barillon au Roi.

Churchill was personally a favourite with Charles, who liked his polished manners, his gentle demeanour and persuasive address, whilst his devotion to the interests of the Crown made him valued by both the Royal brothers. The fact that he had remained a Protestant in the service of James gave him also a strong position in the country, and a claim to press his arguments upon the King. Upon reaching London, Charles accorded him an immediate interview, and he also visited the French Ambassador to deliver James's message as to his position in Scotland and the support he had secured there. Cross-examined by Barillon, Churchill frankly admitted that he did not think James could hold his own in that country without the open goodwill and help of his brother the King. Indeed, there is every reason to believe that it was the sound common-sense of Churchill, and his natural caution at this juncture, that saved James from being taken in by the wiles of Lewis, who was most anxious, by fomenting internal dissensions, to render England weak and powerless abroad.* Notwithstanding Churchill's persuasive powers, he was not able to change the King's resolution. Charles was unwilling to defy the country, and though he wished to serve his brother and to have him at Court, he felt bound to follow the advice of his Council on this point. He was warned, that to bring James back whilst the country was so much incensed against Catholics, would be to incur the risk of civil war, and as Charles would risk anything but that, his answer was distinctly unfavourable to his brother's petition.

The elections for the new House of Commons went everywhere against the interests of the Royal brothers, and when Parliament met at Oxford it was found, that a hundred of those who had sat in the last House were again returned, and that the new members were most hostile to Roman Catholics in general, and to James in particular. All were in an angry, dogged mood, determined

CHAPTER XXXI.

1681.

¹ 2, 1680-81.

¹ 3, 1680-81.

* Dalrymple, vol. i., p. 276.

to grant no supplies until the King should give his assent to the 'Exclusion Bill,' for the country was resolved that James should never wear the Crown.   Shaftesbury went so far as to propose to Charles that he should proclaim Monmouth as his legitimate heir.

Charles was furious at being thus thwarted, and seven days afterwards, stalking abruptly into the House of Lords, he, without further ado, dissolved Parliament, and quitted Oxford.   He felt strong enough to do this, for he had shortly before concluded a secret treaty with Lewis XIV., by which, for the term of three years, he was to receive a large subsidy that would render him, for the time at least, independent of his detested Parliament. The country was dumfounded at this proceeding, for this was the fourth Parliament that Charles had dissolved in anger within the space of two years.   It was the last Parliament of his reign, and he resolved to rule henceforth without one.   Civil war seemed imminent, and James looked forward to it with complacency, for by no other means, as it seemed to him, was there any chance of his succession being secured, or of the royal authority being re-established.*

It may be truly said that all the difficulties at this time between Charles and his Parliament had their origin in his brother's change of religion : but James began to suspect the King's good faith, and his mind was kept on the rack by every favour shown to his handsome and popular nephew, and by every fresh move of his wily Dutch son-in-law, in whom he also foresaw a rival for the Crown.   The possibility of being able to raise the standard of rebellion in either Scotland or Ireland had been for some time contemplated by James, and, as might be expected, Barillon was ordered to assure him of French support should he succeed in accomplishing his desires.+   But whilst Lewis

---

* Barillon to Lewis, 19, 8, 1680 ; Dalrymple, vol. i., p. 843 ; Hallam's 'Constitutional History of England,' vol. ii., p. 432.

+ Barillon's despatches of 18th and 31st October, 1681 ; Dalrymple, vol. ii., p. 331.

thus secretly promised him supplies, he took care to encourage Monmouth also with hopes of French assistance, and at the same time, paid large sums to secure the goodwill of the party which, thoroughly disgusted with monarchy under the Stewart dynasty, longed for the re-establishment of a republic in any form.

When the Princess Isabella died in London, her father pressed the King to allow his only other unmarried daughter, the Princess Anne, to join him at Edinburgh. This request was granted, and Anne set out for Scotland, leaving her friend Mrs. Churchill in London for her second confinement, an event which took place six days after Anne's departure. The child was christened Henrietta; its kinsman, Sir John Churchill, then Master of the Rolls, was godfather, and the godmothers were Sarah's mother, Mrs. Jennings, and Churchill's sister, Mrs. Arabella Godfrey.*

Churchill now spent much of his time in missions between James and the King. He was in London in May and June, and again in August for a short time, and was doubtless willing enough to undertake these journeys as long as his wife remained in England. But as soon as she was well enough to travel, she started to join him at Edinburgh. While expecting her arrival, he wrote to her as follows :

'I would not omit writing, although I am confident you must be come away before these can get [to] London. If you are not, pray then let some coffee be bought for Colonel Worden. I do not doubt but you will bring wax-lights, and all such things as you cannot get here. I am impatient to have you with me, so that if I should be so unhappy as that you are still at London, do not lose a minute in coming away to him that loves you above his own soul.'†

Soon after this letter was written, Mrs. Churchill resumed her duties in the Duchess of York's household at Edinburgh. her husband having gone as far as Berwick to meet her.

---

* Blenheim Palace Papers ; also Sarah's Bible, now at Althorp.
† Blenheim Palace Papers.

CHAPTER
XXXI.

1681.

p. 3, 1680-81.

p. 7, 1681.

p. 7, 1681.

p. 8, 1681.

p. 9, 1681.

Much to the annoyance of the two Royal brothers, Prince William of Orange visited England in June, and did his utmost to induce Charles to throw James over and to show his sympathy with the popular cause by assembling Parliament. In this advice William was an interested party, for he knew that his wife, the Princess Royal, would succeed at the King's death, if James were excluded by Act of Parliament; and he further knew that this was the avowed policy of the Protestant faction. He clearly saw the direction towards which the spirit of the age was tending, and deep in his subtle soul lay the determination to avail himself of every opportunity which this tendency afforded him. He had already begun to form a party in England and to curry favour with the leaders of those opposed to the Court, especially with Lord Russell. Gaining confidence as he proceeded, he even went so far as to dine with the Corporation of London in direct opposition to the King's wishes, and though he was well aware that both Charles and James clearly discerned his aims and deeply resented his conduct.

CHAPTER XXXII.

CHURCHILL WRECKED IN H.M.S. 'GLOUCESTER.'

Charles settles a large pension on the Duchess of Portsmouth, and sends for James—James and Churchill wrecked when returning to Scotland—James and his Household return to England.

EARLY in 1681-82 Charles became anxious to secure a permanent pension for his French mistress, the Duchess of Portsmouth, and for their illegitimate son, the first Duke of Richmond. He wished to settle five thousand a year upon her, and the crafty ' *Miss*, as they call these unhappy creatures,' wished the income secured upon the Post-office revenues.* But the whole of that revenue had been assigned to the Duke of York for his life, and the proposed arrangement could therefore only be effected with his consent, which was not easy to obtain, as James hated the pretty Frenchwoman for the favour she extended to Monmouth. To effect a settlement of this matter the King sent for James, who, leaving his family in Edinburgh, forthwith embarked at Leith, and accompanied by Churchill and Lord Peterborough, landed at Yarmouth, and immediately joined the King at Newmarket. From there Churchill wrote the following letter to his wife: the Henrietta mentioned in it was their second child, whom he had not yet seen : ' I have received yours by Hopton, which is the only letter I have had. I did in my last send you a letter from the child, and I did yesterday receive another from thence, which I do not send you, there being nothing in it but that

CHAPTER XXXII.

1682.

¹⁰⁄₃ 3, 1681-82.

* Evelyn's Diary.

she is very well. The beginning of next week I shall be there myself, so that by Tuesday's post you shall know how I like her. Everybody seems to be very kind to the Duke, so that we are in great hopes that your stay will not be very long in Scotland. I do assure you I do with all my soul wish you here, or myself with you, for I find absence from you is what I cannot bear but with great trouble. I will say no more but assure you that you are as dear to me as ever you were in your life. My service to Colonel Worden. By the next post I will write to him.' Addressed: 'For Mrs. Churchill, at Edinburgh, in Scotland.'*

There was no little difficulty in effecting the settlement of 'Madam Carwell's' pension, for James felt he had now something to barter in exchange for permission to re-establish himself at Court, and he therefore made the most of what he was asked to surrender. Only Hyde and Churchill were taken into the secret, and of course the latter worked exclusively in his master's interests. The bargain was, however, eventually struck, James consenting, or professing to consent, to the proposed arrangement, and the King allowing him to return and live in England.

Thenceforward, until the death of Charles, no post was filled nor was any important measure adopted without the knowledge and advice of James, who used all his influence in the cause of despotism, and to make English interests on every point subservient to those of France.

The King was anxious that the expected confinement of the Duchess of York should take place in England, and James was only too glad to go back to Edinburgh to bring
her to London. He embarked at Margate with Churchill, Legge and Mr. Griffin as his gentlemen-in-waiting, in the *Gloucester* frigate, which, in company with a small squadron, got under weigh by noon.† Sir John Berry commanded the

---

* Blenheim Palace Papers.

† This Mr. Edward Griffin was a Gentleman of his Bedchamber, and was to his death a stanch Jacobite. James created him Baron Griffin of Braybrook when with his army at Salisbury in 1688. He

Gloucester, and Captain Ayres was the pilot. There were about three hundred souls on board, for the Duke of York's party was a large one. Pepys, who has left a good account of the voyage, sailed with the squadron in an Admiralty yacht.

The weather was what sailors call dirty, so they anchored in the evening, but were again under weigh early the next morning. The pace was slow, and it was not until noon on Friday that the landmark of Dunwich Steeple on the Suffolk coast was sighted. During that night, or rather early on Saturday morning, the *Gloucester* grounded on the west point of the dangerous sand-bank known as ' The Lemon and Ore,' about sixteen leagues from the mouth of the Humber. To the consternation of her passengers, she bumped violently along the bank for some time, and broke her rudder, killing the man at the helm. James and his party were asleep when she struck, and by the time they had dressed there were some seven feet of water in her, and the sea was already breaking in through the gun-ports. The discipline on board was apparently bad, and the confusion was consequently great, each and all thinking only of their own safety. Through Legge's care a small boat was manned and brought round to James's cabin, from the window of which he stepped into it. This was done to prevent the crowd at the usual gangway from thronging in also. He took with him the Earls of Winton, Perth, and Middleton, the President of the Sessions, some of his pet priests, and Churchill, who was the last to enter the boat.* A few others flung themselves into her regardless of threats, and had it not been for Churchill, who, with his sword drawn, kept back the crowd, the boat must inevitably have been swamped. The Duke of York's party reached the

kissed William's hand after the Revolution, but was mixed up in all the plots against him. For these conspiracies he was sent to the Tower, where he died in 1710. The squadron consisted of the *Dartmouth, Ruby, Happy Return, Pearl,* and the yacht *Mary.*

* ' Lives of the Two Illustrious Generals,' etc., 1713.

CHAPTER
XXXII.
———
1682.

yacht *Mary* in safety, but several men of distinction were drowned in the *Gloucester*, besides some 130 sailors and many of James's servants.* The Captain, who stayed by the ship to the last, finally escaped by a rope over the stern into a boat. He was tried, and honourably acquitted of all blame.†

Sunday,
5, 1682.

The Duke of York and his sadly diminished party landed at Leith the following evening. Writing to Lord Treasurer Hyde a couple of days afterwards, James says, that he has not time to describe the wreck by the 'flying packet,' but that he has 'charged Churchill to do it.'‡ On the following

5, 1682.

Friday, James, with his family and little Court, embarked in the *Happy Return*, and after a long voyage anchored in the Thames. He at once proceeded to St. James's Palace, where he continued to live until his accession to the throne.

Whilst in Scotland, Churchill had exercised a most beneficial influence over James, and had been the means of saving 'from ruin and destruction' many persons 'whose scruples of conscience had rendered them obnoxious to the laws then in force and severely administered by the Episcopal party.'§ Upon his return to England, he carefully abstained from taking any share in the violent measures inaugurated by the Royal brothers, and was very chary of expressing opinions or of offering them advice.

---

* Hyde, James's brother-in-law, the Earl of Roxborough, Lord O'Brien, the Laird of Hopetoun, and Sir Joseph Douglas were amongst those who perished. Pepys, who was close by the *Gloucester* when she sunk, gives a good account of the whole affair. Sir John Scarborough, the Court doctor, was on board when she went down.

† His father was a loyal clergyman who had been deprived of his living by the rebel party in the Civil Wars. Sir John, who had been in the merchant service, had entered the navy as boatswain to the *Swallow* ketch in the West Indies in 1663. He was every inch a sailor, and died an Admiral. He lies in Stepney Church, where there is a monument to his memory.

‡ 'Clarendon Correspondence,' vol. i., p. 57.

§ 'The Lives of Two Illustrious Generals,' London, 1713.

CHAPTER XXXIII.

ANNE'S MARRIAGE. — PRINCE GEORGE'S CHARACTER. — MRS.
MORLEY AND MRS. FREEMAN. — CHURCHILL RAISED TO THE
PEERAGE.

Great friendship grown up between the Princess Anne and Sarah
Anne and her disposition — Her first suitor— Sarah made Bedchamber
Woman.

AT the beginning of the year it was rumoured that Churchill was to be made Secretary of State. The report was apparently based only on the fact that he had lately taken lessons in writing, which at least proves that he was conscious of his defects, and determined to rectify them as far as possible. When the rumour reached the king's ears, he said laughingly he was determined not to have two idle Secretaries.[*]

Charles was fond of tennis, and played frequently with Churchill, Godolphin, or Lord Feversham, all excellent players, so 'that if one beat the other, 'tis alternately.'[†]

In May Churchill accompanied the Duke and Duchess of York, the Princess Anne, and a large suite to Oxford, where they were sumptuously entertained. The University proposed to confer the honorary degree of D.C.L. upon James and upon several members of his Household. Churchill was amongst those selected, but being unable to attend on the appointed day, he missed that distinction.[‡]

* Historical MSS.: Appendix to Seventh Report, p. 368.
† Lady Chaworth to her brother, the Earl of Rutland, March 11, 1688. Historical MSS., Twelfth Report, vol. ii., p. 81.
‡ This information has been kindly supplied by the Librarian of the Bodleian Library.

During the early years of her married life, Mrs. Churchill was much thrown into the society of the Princess Anne, and their old intimacy, thus renewed, soon ripened into that strange friendship which, years afterwards, exercised so great an influence over both their lives, and over the destinies not only of England, but of Europe. The lady whom Sarah supplanted in Anne's warm heart was Mrs. Cicely Cornwallis — a kinswoman of the Hydes, and a Roman Catholic, so it is not difficult to account for this transfer of the Princess's affections.* Anne was now eighteen years of age, and, although she had had the small-pox in 1677, she was fair, of middle height, comely and graceful, with a good figure, good hands, rather high colour, regular features, and dark-brown hair. She possessed that great charm in a woman—a sweet, musical voice, with a clear and distinct utterance. She inherited her mother's genial disposition, and was charitable, and entirely devoid of ambition. She was shy and silent, and her ability, like her conversational power, was poor. Her education had been much neglected, though her memory was good. She shared her father's love of hunting, and took a great interest in 'dress.' But she had neither taste nor culture, and was capricious and vehement in her likes and dislikes. Though fond of flattery, she was kind, considerate, and courteous to all about her of every degree. Obstinate, as small-minded people usually are, she was like most of the Stewarts, idle and indolent, and always anxious to postpone the consideration of tiresome and difficult subjects. She was extravagant and fond of cards, at which she spent much of her time, and lost heavily. Those who were jealous of the Churchills insinuated that most of what she lost, found its way into the pocket of her favourite Sarah. In any case it is certain that her indulgent father

* Lord Dartmouth's notes to Burnet, vol. ii., p. 89; Strickland, vol. v., p. 398. Mrs. Cornwallis afterwards became Lady Superior of the Benedictine Convent at Hammersmith, then under the protection of Queen Catherine.

paid her debts more than once. All through life she was
a staunch upholder of the Church of England, which she
failed to see had become a political organization as much
as a sacred institution intended for the spiritual benefit
of the people. ' The Church's wet-nurse, Goody Anne,'*
was a sincerely religious woman. She strongly opposed
the appointment of any but devout and devoted clergymen
to the Episcopate. As Queen, she would never consent to
make Swift a Bishop, though pressed to do so by Harley
and St. John, who owed him so much. The people clung
to her and to her sister Mary with deep affection as Protestants who might yet save them from their Roman
Catholic father.

Her first suitor, Prince George of Hanover, had been
recalled from England by an ambitious father, who wished
him to marry a more richly endowed princess. Anne was only
fifteen then, but she never forgave the insult, and for ever
afterwards entertained the strongest antipathy for her rude,
ill-mannered, and uncouth little suitor, who afterwards
succeeded her as King George I. When she returned to
St. James's with her father in 1682, she was attracted by
the attentions of Sheffield, Earl of Mulgrave, who wrote
her verses and love-letters. The King, upon hearing of
this, immediately sent him to Tangier, and although the
Princess was married soon afterwards to a husband she
loved, she continued all through her after-life to take an
interest in the poetical lover of her girlhood.†

Charles was at this time anxious to allay the com-
motion caused by his brother's open practice of Popery and
his own suspected leanings towards it. He thought he could
not do this more effectually than by marrying his young

---

* Horace Walpole thus styles her in one of his letters, vol. vii., p. 55.
Cunningham's edition.
† He afterwards became Duke of Buckingham, and married Anne's
illegitimate half-sister, Catherine, the curious daughter of James by
Catherine Sedley, whose house has now been converted into Buckingham
Palace.

niece to a Protestant prince. The marriage of Mary to William of Orange, although it was in opposition to her father's wishes, had been most popular, and the King now thought of a Protestant husband for the Princess Anne. His choice fell upon Prince George, the youngest son of Frederick III. of Denmark, and the brother of the reigning King, Christian V.[*] Prince George of Denmark was just thirty, very tall, with light hair and fair complexion, and on the whole, good-looking, although somewhat marked with small-pox, and inclined to be fat. In disposition he was good-natured; he had a mild, gentle temper, but he was lazy, apathetic, dull of intellect, hated business, and was too fond of the bottle.[†] Charles said of him : ' I've tried him drunk, and I've tried him sober, but there's nothing in him.' In fact, he was a heavy, shallow fellow, who was no companion for either man or woman. He spoke French indifferently, and English not at all, but he had fought valiantly at the Battle of Landen, where he saved his brother from being taken prisoner. William of Orange was furious when he heard of this proposed marriage. He did all in his power to prevent it, and seems never to have forgiven the bridegroom, whom he hated ever afterwards.

1677.

The arrangements for the wedding were soon completed, and Churchill was ordered to Denmark to conduct the Prince in state to his new home. The royal yachts anchored at Gluckstadt, near the mouth of the Elbe, where the bridegroom-elect embarked. During his stay in Holstein, Churchill took part in several councils of war which Christian V. held to consider the disturbed state of the Continent near the Danish frontier, and upon taking leave, the King presented him with a sword set with diamonds and a ring worth five or six hundred pounds.[‡] After a

* Christian V. died 4, 9, 1699.

† Evelyn.

‡ The Danish army was then said to consist of from twenty to twenty-five thousand very good troops. Historical MSS., Appendix to Seventh Report, p. 365.

somewhat stormy passage, Prince George reached London, bringing with him Charles, Colonel Churchill's younger brother, who had accompanied the Prince in his previous visit to England in 1679. Ten years before that visit he had entered King Christian's household as a page.

CHAPTER
XXXIII.
—
1683.
½ 7, 1683.

The marriage took place in St. James's Chapel, at ⅞-¾, 1683. 10 o'clock p.m. on St. Anne's Day, and was celebrated with great pomp and festivities. The King settled £20,000 a year on the bride, and purchased the 'Cockpit' for her as a residence.* That old house stood on the site now occupied by the Treasury Offices in Downing Street, and opened into St. James's Park. Oliver Cromwell had lived there for some time, and not long before the Restoration Parliament had presented it to General Monk for his life.†

Before her marriage, when the establishment of her household was under discussion, she begged her father to make Sarah Churchill one of her Bedchamber Ladies. He consented, although there is reason to believe that his brother-in-law, Lord Rochester—who, with all his family, hated the Churchills—endeavoured to persuade him not to accede to this request. The result was communicated to Sarah by the Princess in the following note:

' The Duke has just come in as you were gone, and made no difficulties, but has promised me that I shall have you, which I assure you is a great joy to me : I should say a great deal for your kindness in offering it, but I am not good at compliments.'

From this it is evident that Sarah had herself in the first instance proposed the arrangement.

The salary attached to this position was only £200 per annum, but at that time even this small addition to their

---

* When James became King he increased her allowance to £30,000 a year, a sum larger than the income of the richest English noble of that time. The total revenue of England was then only about two and a half millions sterling per annum.

† It had been built by Henry VIII. as a cockpit, outside the Holbein Gate, and was afterwards converted into a place for dramatic entertainments, for which purpose it was used to the time of the Civil War.

income was most acceptable. This appointment had a considerable bearing upon the Churchills' future career, for it
apparently induced them to abandon finally their renewed
intention of retiring from Court altogether and settling
down into a country life at St. Albans.

When Lady Clarendon went with her husband to Ireland
in 1685, Sarah Churchill took her place as first Lady of the
Bedchamber to the Princess Anne, a promotion which
doubled her salary.

Anne preferred Sarah Churchill to all the other ladies of
her household, who, it must be admitted, were very unin-
teresting. She had long entertained a particular dislike
for Lady Clarendon, whom Sarah describes as one who
' looked like a madwoman and talked like a scholar ';* and
Sarah herself both hated and feared the whole Clarendon
family.

In recognition of his consent to Anne's marriage, James
was now once more appointed Lord High Admiral and a
Privy Councillor. He took Anne with him to Portsmouth
when he went to inspect the fleet, and on their return
journey they stayed at the Palace of Winchester, where
Anne wrote the following letters to her beloved Lady
Churchill : ' Winchester, September 20.—I writ to you last
Wednesday from on board the yacht, and left my letter on
Thursday morning at Portsmouth to go by the post, to be as
good as my word in writing to my dear Lady Churchill by
the first opportunity. I was in so great haste when I writ,
that I fear what I said was nonsense, but I hope you will
have so much kindness for me as to forgive it. If you will
not let me have the satisfaction of hearing from you again
before I see you, let me beg of you not to call me " your
Highness " at every word, but be as free with me as one
friend ought to be with another. And you can never give
me any greater proof of your friendship than in telling me
your mind freely in all things, which I do beg you to do ;
and if it were in my power to serve you nobody would be

* ' The Conduct.'

more ready than myself. I am all impatience for Wednesday; till when, farewell.'

A little later on Anne arranged that in future they should address one another under feigned names, so that all difference of rank might be suppressed in their correspondence. Sarah writes : ' She grew uneasy to be treated by me with the form and ceremony due to her rank : nor could she bear from me the sound of words which implied in them distance and superiority. It was this turn of mind which made her one day propose to me that whenever I should happen to be absent from her we might in all our letters write ourselves by feigned names, such as would import nothing of distinction of rank between us. Morley and Freeman were the names her fancy hit upon : and she left me to choose by which of them I would be called. My frank, open temper naturally led me to pitch upon Freeman, and so the Princess took the other ; and from this time Mrs. Morley and Mrs. Freeman began to converse as equals, made so by affection and friendship.'*

In course of time Anne grew to think that she could not live without the society of her dearly loved companion, who, unknown to her, had already obtained complete dominion over her mind. The very obstinacy of Anne's character rendered her more completely subservient to whomsoever happened at the moment to be her favourite, while at the same time she became less liable to fall under the influence of others. At this early period of their friendship Sarah could not have been influenced by any hope that the Princess Anne might become Queen ; and, besides, the insatiable ambition with which she is so commonly charged had certainly no existence in the early days of her married life. She may have been able to perceive in her husband many of those qualities which lead to success, but as yet she could have had no expectation of the greatness in store for him.

Her extreme frankness seems to have been her greatest

* 'The Conduct,' p. 14.

charm in the eyes of Anne, who, above all things, craved for the close intimacy of a true friend. Anne was one of those women who cannot stand alone. Like ivy, she required something strong to cling to, and the force of will possessed by Sarah marked her out as the friend and companion she needed. She had many friends amongst the Ministers and courtiers by whom she was habitually surrounded; but the reasoning of a clever man who tried persuasion could exercise no influence over her, though to the personal control of the woman upon whom she leaned for the time being, her warm and emotional heart was always open. But if that woman was to maintain her influence she must never leave her, and it was here that Sarah Churchill made her great mistake. Shrewd as she was in most things, she did not perceive this peculiarity of temperament in the mistress whom she first led gently and subsequently bullied, and she foolishly allowed another, who never left the Queen for a day, to usurp the power over her which had once been exclusively her own. Sarah's children and her domestic duties made frequent calls upon her time, and often required her to be long away from Court. Had she remained there constantly, not all the waiting women in England, or even any display of temper on her part, could have destroyed the paramount influence she so long exercised over the Queen. Sarah herself described Anne's friendship as the flame of an extravagant passion that extinguished itself either in indifference or aversion.

The contrast between the characters of the Queen and Sarah doubtless contributed to cement their friendship and lend it an intensity rare indeed in the intimacy of women. But there was no real equality in their partnership. Anne might imagine that she had placed their social relations upon a level, but she could not make herself the intellectual match of her lady-in-waiting. Although Mrs. Morley and Mrs. Freeman might converse and correspond with all the familiarity of social equals, Sarah's strong will and force of

character gave her complete mastery over the mediocre
intelligence of the Princess whom she served. Anne enjoyed this feeling of dependence; she allowed herself to
be not only led, but governed, and even kissed the hand
that ruled her. In their earliest intimacy, when they
played together as children of six and eleven years old
respectively, it was not so much the difference of age that
gave Sarah sway over her young companion—although a
difference of five years means much in the nursery and
schoolroom—it was the quick decision and energy of the
elder which enabled her to exert such unquestioned
authority over the dull-witted Princess. Sarah tells us how
from the first Anne had singled her out as the favourite
companion of her infancy. The bluntness of Sarah, who
prided herself that she never flattered either man or
woman, seems to have acted like magic upon the weakness of Anne's character. The Princess required a ruler,
and she found one for the time in her beloved Sarah
Churchill.

Restored once more to his former offices under the Crown
and to his Royal brother's favour, James wished to reward
the skilful negotiator who had largely contributed to bring
about this happy change in his position. He knew from
the King how strenuously Churchill had ever pleaded
his cause, and that he had done so without boring that
easily-wearied voluptuary. James pressed to have him
made a peer, and Charles consented—the more readily that
he liked him personally, and appreciated his diplomatic
skill and tactful address. Churchill was accordingly 31 12, 1683.
created Baron Aymouth in the kingdom of Scotland, and
as a further reward he was given command of the Third
Troop of Horse Guards.

Whilst the Princess Anne and her dear Mrs. Freeman
were at Tunbridge, Churchill sent the following letter to his
wife. It was written from his house at St. Albans, where
Sarah had left their children, and illustrates the domestic
side of his character, which we are too apt to overlook :

'Friday.—I received yesterday a letter which I did not expect, for I did not think that you would have complained this time of my want of writing, for I have not failed one day since I came. My Lady Sunderland's housekeeper by her lady's order brought a bottle of [illegible] for the children to drink, but I think it is too hot for their stomachs, so that I keep it for my own drinking, unless you send me word that they may drink it. You cannot imagine how I am pleased with the children, for they having nobody but their maid, they are so fond of me that when I am at home they will be always with me, and kissing and hugging me. Their heats are quite gone, so that against you come home they will be in beauty. If there be room I will come on Monday, so that you need not write on Sunday. Miss is pulling me by the arm that she may write to her dear mama, so that I will say no more, only beg that you will love me always so well as I love you, and then we cannot but be happy. [The following words apparently written by a child, its hand being guided.] I kiss your hands, my dear mama. Harriot.'—Addressed: ' For my Lady Churchill, at the Princess's at Tunbridge.'

Charles now governed without a Parliament, and, having deprived London and the other cities of their charters, he was master of the position. Thenceforward he virtually appointed the Lord Mayor and Aldermen of London, and the municipal authorities in all the large towns of the kingdom, and being able to pack the juries in trials where the Crown or its authority was concerned, he could ensure the conviction of all whom he wished to punish. Herein he was greatly assisted by unworthy judges, who, being dependent upon his goodwill, were but too ready to do his bidding. In fact, the Crown, which brooked no opposition, seemed for the time to have crushed the spirit of the people, while the cruel violation of their liberties drove many of England's noblest sons to conspire against the Royal brothers. In this eventful year, Lord Russell, Algernon Sidney, and some other leading men died at the hands of the executioner for their complicity in what is commonly known as the Rye House Plot. Lord Essex also, whilst a prisoner in the Tower, died under what were considered suspicious circumstances. The King and the Duke of York were actually in the Tower at the time, having gone there to visit that ancient royal fortress and palace.*

Throughout this year, whilst James was inciting the King to despotic measures, William was untiring in urging him to call Parliament together, knowing that the final exclusion of James from the succession would be one of its first measures. It was not love for England or liberty that prompted this advice, but rather anxiety to see his wife declared heir to the Crown, for William, like most men of the time, was a self-seeker.

* It was publicly announced that Essex had committed suicide, but it was generally thought he had been murdered.

CHAPTER XXXIV.

DEATH OF KING CHARLES, AND SUCCESSION OF JAMES II.

James's speech in Council well received—His determination to have his
own way—Wants money—Sends Churchill to Paris on a mission to
Lewis—Coronation of James—Churchill made an English Peer—
James attends Mass openly—Churchill's house at St. Alban's—Is
made Governour of the Hudson Bay Company.

ON Friday, the festival of St. Anne, 1685, died the witty
and worthless Charles II. His stupid brother, equally
ignoble and far less amiable and agreeable as a companion,
succeeded him as James II. Some years before one of the
ablest and most upright of contemporary Englishmen had
predicted that his accession would mean the end of the
world.*

The exertions of Shaftesbury and the party led by him
before his imprisonment had been all in vain. In spite of
the most earnest efforts, they had failed to accomplish the
exclusion of James from the throne, either by law or by
force. The baffled and embarrassed exclusionists now
flocked to Whitehall, and endeavoured by obsequiousness
to make the new King forget their former hostility. Their
reception was not cordial, and they were made to feel that
the King would not forget their behaviour to the Duke of
York.

It is difficult to say what were the real feelings of the
nation at the King's death. The dread of having a Roman
Catholic King was so great that even those who denounced

---

* Sir William Temple.

Charles for his private immorality and public crimes received the news with sorrow and dismay.

James's speech to his council on the afternoon of his brother's death was a solemn lie, inasmuch as he promised to stand by the liberties of his people and to protect their established religion. But the impression it made every-where was good. Who would doubt the word of an English King?—'which' (with all reverence be it spoken) 'is as sacred as my text,' said Dr. Sharp in his sermon upon the occasion.*

His subserviency to the priests was so well known abroad that the Spanish Ambassador at his first audience warned him to beware of them as counsellors in matters of State. James, in a fury, asked him 'if in Spain men sought advice from their confessors.' 'Yes, we do,' was the reply, 'and that is why our affairs go so ill.'† The Ambas-sador went on to advise moderation, but James answered: 'I will lose all or win all,' and that resolve cost him his crown. Charles was wiser, for when on his death-bed he gave James the key of his strong-box, he warned him 'not to think of introducing the Romish faith into England, it being a thing that was most dangerous and impracticable.'‡

For a time James thought it advisable to retain his brother's Ministers in office, but as all of them, with the exception of Rochester, had been more or less hostile to his succession, it was not long before changes were announced. The two objects he was determined to accomplish were bound, sooner or later, to bring him into collision with his people: the first was to re-establish the Romish faith, and the second to rule absolutely without a Parliament. He was cunning enough to avoid frightening his Protestant Ministers at first. Except Halifax, none of them had anything to urge against his ruling despotically, and he felt that if he were allowed to rule England without a Parliament, he would soon

* Caldmay's 'Autobiography.'
† Harris's 'William III.,' vol. i., p. 171.
‡ Sir G. Rose's 'Commentaries on Fox,' a note to page 88.

achieve the other object, which was the paramount aim of his life.* But the Ministers, one and all, insisted that Parliament should be called together, and, much as he hated the idea, he felt bound to comply. At the same time he sent for the French Ambassador, and begged him to explain to his master that this compliance meant no hostility to France. He had been compelled to it, he said, because certain revenues granted by the House of Commons had lapsed at the King's death, and could only be reimposed by a similar authority. He took occasion to assure Barillon that he would always look to Lewis for advice in every matter of importance, and would never cease to act in his interests.

James was in sore want of money, but even he felt shy in asking for it personally. To beg through a third party was, however, less unpleasant, so his brother-in-law, Rochester, was told to inform the French Ambassador that unless Lewis supplied him with funds he would be at the mercy of his Parliament. Barillon was aware that all English Parliaments, whether Whig or Tory, High or Low Church, were opposed to France and in favour of Holland. It was, therefore, to the interest of Lewis XIV. that the King of England should be as far as possible independent of his Parliament, and dependent upon French gold. During the long years in which Charles continued to be a pensioner of the King of France many secret treaties were made between the two Sovereigns. James knew them well, and he knew also that Charles had sold England's goodwill for money, and that Lewis had bought it to secure himself a free hand in his designs upon Holland and in his dealings with William.† For some time before the death of

---

* It was James who had persuaded Charles to make Sir George Savile Viscount Halifax after the first Dutch war. He subsequently threw himself entirely into the popular party with Shaftesbury, and was accordingly hated by James. He and his brother were great friends of John Churchill. He was one of those who went bail for Marlborough when sent to the Tower in 1692.

† Mackintosh, p. 336.

Charles II. the French King had become somewhat remiss
in his payments, but upon this important occasion he
hastened to send James a dole of £20,000.* It was very
acceptable, though by no means as much as was expected.
James, however, thought it politic to express his gratitude
in tearful thanks to the French Ambassador. but he hinted
at the same time that the amount was not large enough,
and Barillon so informed his master. To thank Lewis
personally for this welcome present, James sent Churchill
to Paris, his ostensible mission being to notify officially to
the French Court the death of Charles and the accession
of James.† The French Ambassador informed his master
that Churchill was selected for this duty because he was
in possession of all particulars bearing upon the secret
understanding between the two Courts, and because he was
so highly esteemed by James. He could therefore, he
said, better explain many particulars by word of mouth
than could be done by letter. Barillon ended by warning his
master that the Envoy had been told to ask for considerable help in money. But, as a matter of fact, Churchill's
orders were partly cancelled before his departure, and
James desired that money should not be directly asked for.

Lord Churchill was received and lodged at Versailles
with all the honour due to an 'Envoy Extraordinary from
his Majesty of Great Britain.'‡ He had audience of the
'most Christian King,' and was attended by most of the
English gentlemen in Paris, clad in the deepest mourning.§
He was officially received by the Dauphin, and by the
Dukes of Burgundy, Anjou, and Orleans. Three days

* The exact sum was 500,000 livres, which is about the equivalent
of £20,000.

† Barillon to Lewis, $\frac{19}{2}$ 2. 1685 and 26, 2, 1685. See Fox's
'James II.'

‡ In a letter from R. Tempest, dated Paris, $\frac{3}{13}$ 3, 1685, it is stated
that, 'Milor Schurchil a este bien regale ici de plusieurs seigneurs de la
Cour.' F. O. Papers, Rolls Office, France, No. 307 of 1685.

§ F. O. Papers of 1685, bundle 307 in Rolls Office.

¦ London Gazette.

afterwards he formally took leave of these august personages, and quitting Paris, set out for England with a letter to his master, in which Lewis thus referred to him : ' As I cannot doubt you will give to his report the same credence that I have given to what he communicated to me from you, I refer you to him for the rest, and particularly for the confidence which you may place in my friendship.' *

Churchill was directed by James to observe every ceremony used at his official reception, as it was his intention to receive the French Ambassador in England with exactly similar formality. This plan was punctiliously carried out upon the arrival of Marshal de Lorge, who came to England in the same yacht with Churchill to congratulate James upon his accession.† Referring to James's proceedings at this period, the French King said that, notwithstanding all the fine things given out in his name, ' he was as willing to take French gold as his brother had been.'

It was upon this occasion that Churchill, in a conversation with Lord Galway upon James's attitude towards the Church of Rome, said : ' If the King should attempt to change our religion I will instantly quit his service.'‡ In this notable and solemn declaration is to be found the keynote of all his subsequent conduct to James II., and of his action at the Revolution.

As Gentleman of the Bedchamber, Churchill assisted at James's coronation. The ceremony took place on St. George's Day with great pomp ; but when the crown was placed on the King's head it tottered and nearly tumbled off, to the dismay of the Queen and other superstitious persons present.§ Amongst the many ill-omens which are

* Translation given by Coxe from the original in the Mallet Papers.
† Lediard, vol. i., p. 36; F. O. Papers in Rolls Court, France. No. 307 of 1685.
‡ Burnet, vol. iii., p. 216.
§ In the *London Gazette* the following advertisement appeared immediately after the Coronation : ' Lost, at their Majesties Coronation, the button of his Majesty's Sceptre set about with twenty-four small diamonds, three rubies and three emeralds ; a pendant pearl from his Majesty's Crown,' etc.—*London Gazette*, No. 2,030.

said to have marked the day's proceedings, it was discovered that the wind had rent the flag on the White Tower when it was hoisted to announce that James had been crowned.*

In the following month, to reward Churchill for all his faithful services, James made him an English peer. Introduced to the House of Peers by Lords Maynard and Butler of Weston, he took his seat as Baron Churchill of Sandridge, in the county of Herts. Sir Winston Churchill was at the same time appointed Deputy-Lieutenant for Dorsetshire.

James having mounted the throne without open opposition from any quarter, now thought himself strong enough to throw off the mask in the matter of his religion. The celebration of the Mass was forbidden by law, yet the very Sunday after his accession he attended Mass in state. He now addressed himself to the abrogation of the Test Act. The steps which he took with this object are described in a subsequent chapter.

James's first, and indeed his only, Parliament met in May. It was loyal and profoundly obsequious, for he had taken every precaution to have it packed with his friends, including four of the Churchill family—Sir Winston and his son George, Sir John, and William Churchill. The King's speech from the throne was dictatorial, and almost threatening in tone, though he assured his hearers that he possessed 'a true English heart.' The nationality of his heart apparently varied according to the audience whose local pride he wished to flatter. Barillon, a month later, reports to his master that James had said to him : 'He had eaten King Lewis's bread, that he had been brought up in France, and that his heart was French.' Charles II. used to read his speech ; this was an innovation on an old custom, but he excused himself by saying that he could not

P. 6, 1685.

P. 7, 1685.

* Dr. Geo. Hicks, in a letter to Dr. Charlett, dated $\frac{23}{9}-\frac{1}{3}$, 171$\frac{9}{?}$. The canopy carried over the King's head broke, and his son by his mistress Sedley died that day.

look in the face those from whom he had so frequently to beg large sums of money. James had no such qualms, and he now openly demanded to have settled on him for life the revenues that his brother had enjoyed, and he concluded by informing Parliament that the Duke of Argyle had landed in the Highlands with an armed following.

The House of Commons, though it would not tolerate rebellion, hesitated to make a settlement for life upon a Roman Catholic Sovereign. But in the end its servility overcame its caution, and the demand was granted without conditions. It was unanimously voted that the House relied with confidence on the King's royal word to rule by law, and to support the Church of England, for, they said, the Protestant religion was dearer to them than their lives.

When not in attendance at Court, Lord and Lady Churchill now passed their time in Holywell House, their newly-built home at St. Albans.* Here Churchill thoroughly enjoyed a domestic country life, and found unqualified pleasure in his wife's society and in the companionship of his children, with whom he dearly loved to romp and play. Like a good country gentleman, he began to take a useful part in local business, especially in the municipal affairs of St. Albans. Soon after his return from France, James, at his request, granted a new charter for that ancient town, and Lord Churchill was appointed High Steward in room of Sir Harbottle Grimston.† In the Corporation Minute Book Churchill's name is signed to the 'Declaration against the Solemn League and Covenant'—an oath that all who accepted office were obliged to take in accordance with an Act of Parliament passed soon after the Restora-

---

* This new house was rated in the Corporation books at £50, the highest rated house in the parish. He paid £11 5s. per annum as rates for it.—A. E. Gibbs, Esq.

† The Corporation Records of St. Albans. The fee of this office was one 'broad gold piece, worth £1 3s. 6d.' It had at various times been held by remarkable men: the Lord High Treasurer Burghley, Lord Ellesmere, when Lord Chancellor, the great Sir Francis Bacon, William, Earl of Salisbury, etc.

tion. Through Lord Churchill's interest his sailor brother George was returned as member for the town, and retained the seat until 1708.

Churchill had always been in the habit of speculating in shares, and generally with considerable success. He at this time had 'an adventure '—or, as we should now say, bought £1,200 worth of shares in the Hudson's Bay Trading Company, which had been incorporated by royal charter in 1670. The company was paying from 10 to 50 per cent. per annum.* James, and later on William III., owned stock in it, and various people about the Court followed their example. Churchill's ability and great business capacity soon won for him the position of Governour of the company, in succession to Prince Rupert, who had occupied the chair since its incorporation, and, doubtless, the experience which he thus obtained was of great use to him subsequently. Those who are accustomed to the practice of war fully understand that no one can conduct a campaign or administer an army successfully who is not a thoroughly good man of business.

* Sir Donald Smith, now the Governor of the Hudson Bay Company, has kindly furnished me with this information.

CHAPTER XXXV.

EARL OF ARGYLE LANDS IN SCOTLAND.—IS TAKEN AND BEHEADED.

Monmouth in Holland, under the influence of Argyle.

To please his brother, Charles had banished Monmouth early in the previous year. The exile took up his abode in Holland, where, in company with his mistress, Lady Wentworth, he stayed until the death of Charles in the following winter.* He was now thirty-six years of age, and, after a dissipated youth, was settling down to domestic life. Spoilt and petted by an indulgent father, he had sown his wild oats surrounded by servile courtiers. Though a man of no real worth, his genial disposition and fondness for hounds, horses, and all kinds of English sport had won for him the love and good wishes of the English people, who saw in their 'Protestant Duke' a possible King, who might save them from the Duke of York and his priests. As the Protestants outnumbered the Roman Catholics in Great Britain by about fifty to one, Monmouth was naturally regarded by James as a dangerous rival. Throughout life it was his fate to be alternately the plaything of cruel fortune, the dupe of flatterers, and the idol of dissolute

* Lady Harriet Wentworth was Baroness Nettlestead in her own right and heiress of her grandfather, the Earl of Wentworth, who died in 1667, her father having died before that year. She was also heiress to her other grandfather, the Earl of Cleveland. She died of a broken heart nine months after her lover's execution. Barillon says she had a child by Monmouth.

JAMES, DUKE OF [...]

ladies, as well as the tool of religious zealots and designing politicians. Shortly after the Restoration he and James had, it was said, both aspired to the favours of the same lady, who naturally preferred the young and fascinating nephew to the ogling, middle-aged uncle. This circumstance may have served to embitter their personal relations, but the real cause of their hostility was the fact that both aspired to the Crown.

In Holland Monmouth was thrown much into the society of the unfortunate Earl of Argyle, who had fled thither to escape the death to which he had been condemned by James in Scotland after an infamously unjust trial. Argyle, who thirsted for revenge, found himself in Holland the centre of a crowd of discontented Protestant plotters. He soon obtained complete influence over the confiding Monmouth, and it was agreed between them that if both should still be in banishment when the King died, Argyle should raise the standard of revolt in Scotland, and Monmouth should do the same in England. Accordingly, upon the unexpected death of Charles II., and the unopposed accession of James, the two conspirators determined to carry out their agreement without delay.

Argyle started for Scotland early in May, and before 2, 5, 1685. setting out extracted a promise from Monmouth that he would sail for England in a few days to carry out his share in the plot. But Monmouth was not in a position to do this, for he wanted everything requisite for a serious enterprise. He had neither arms, military stores, ships, nor money wherewith to buy them. Had it not been for his promise, he would certainly have postponed the attempt, as his friends in England had not as yet been made fully aware of his plans, nor were any adequate preparations for a rising completed.

Argyle's following was small, and the chiefs who did rally to his standard soon quarrelled amongst themselves. His attempt was an utter failure. He was taken prisoner, and beheaded at Edinburgh in June. 30-6, 1685.

Lord Churchill took so leading a part in the suppression of Monmouth's rebellion, that it is desirable I should enter somewhat fully into its history. The ease with which these risings in favour of Protestantism were put down had a baneful influence upon James's policy, and led him on to those acts of tyrannous folly which directly brought about the Revolution.

CHAPTER XXXVI.

Ferguson the Plotter—Monmouth has a party at home—His want of money—He embarks—His unfitness for the command of such an expedition.

WILLIAM, as soon as he heard that James had been proclaimed King without opposition, ordered Monmouth to quit Holland. He knew that this step would be highly appreciated by his father-in-law, with whom it was then his interest to stand well. In the far future he still saw the possibility of the crown of England devolving upon his wife, the Princess Royal. He had already schemed to bring this about, and he meant to continue his efforts upon every favourable opportunity. But the fulfilment of his hopes depended upon many changes and chances in the whirligig of time, whereas at the moment it was of the first importance that he should deal with the facts which immediately confronted him. His political existence, and that of his beloved country, were seriously threatened by Lewis XIV., and his most urgent need at this juncture was material help in troops and ships. Although the Protestant ruler of a Protestant State, it was just possible, he thought, that a King who was at once his uncle and his father-in-law might be disposed to afford him help, Catholic though James was.

It has been repeatedly denied by William's admirers that he was cognizant of Monmouth's aims or intentions; but it is tolerably certain that he, as well as James, was quite aware that Argyle and Monmouth had arranged for a simultaneous rising in Scotland and in England.* However, that he had not shared their secrets or countenanced their plans, is proved by Monmouth's own dying declaration. On the other hand it is certain, that up to the accession of James, William had evinced no disposition to further his father-in-law's interests by arresting the conspirators. He had not even told James what he knew of their plans and proceedings, and had steadily refused to expel Monmouth from Dutch territory. Even now, whilst assuring James of his wish to serve him, he allowed Argyle and Monmouth to start from a Dutch port with an interval of three weeks between their respective departures, well knowing their destinations and intentions. Common-sense told the astute William that the crazy plans of Argyle and Monmouth must end in failure — a failure which would be to his advantage. It would remove from his path a rival for the English crown who was the favourite Protestant candidate; it would keep alive and strengthen the Protestant sentiment, already strong in England; it could not fail to intensify the wide-spread abhorrence of Popery; and, above all, it would give James an opportunity, of which he would be quick to avail himself, of putting the insurrection down with a cruel severity that could not fail to make him and his religion still more odious to all classes of his subjects. There can be no doubt that William did not wish Monmouth success. Had it been otherwise, he would certainly have delayed the despatch from Holland of the six British regiments for which James applied as soon as he heard that Argyle had reached Scotland. William sent them to England without demur; he even offered to send

* Echard, Hallam and others hold William to have known nothing of Argyle's and Monmouth's intentions, but James asserts that he did, and 'had promised to send some supply of arms, etc., after him.' Clarke's 'Life of James II.,' vol. ii., p. 24.

some good Dutch troops also, and to take command himself
of the army that was to operate against Monmouth. He
was evidently sincere ; and in making these offers he could
not have been influenced, as it is sometimes said that he
was, by Monmouth's assumption of the royal title contrary
to the terms of some supposed agreement between them.
When Bentinck made these proposals in William's name
to King James, Monmouth had not yet proclaimed himself
King.

Compelled by William to leave Holland, Monmouth took
up his abode at Brussels. Hunted from that city by the
Spanish authorities, who were moved by his uncle James,
he hid himself in Amsterdam. It was there that he
arranged with Argyle and the other conspirators the details
of the plot for the simultaneous invasion of England and
Scotland.* One of the chief movers in this undertaking
was the notorious Scotch minister, Robert Ferguson,
commonly known as 'The Plotter.' He had been chaplain
and factotum to Lord Shaftesbury ; and, deeply implicated
in the Rye House Plot, he had fled to Holland, where he
lived in an atmosphere of conspiracy. He was the Judas
in Dryden's 'Absalom and Achitophel,' but he finally
changed sides, and ended his days as a scheming Jacobite.
Being at this time, however, a Protestant enthusiast, he
obtained a considerable influence over Monmouth, and
used it to incite him to rebellion. God, he said, would
never forsake those who fought in His sacred cause and in
that of liberty. Though full of subtlety, he lacked wisdom
and common-sense, and a more dangerous adviser for a man
of Monmouth's calibre it would be difficult to imagine.†

---

* The English refugees who took the lead in all these schemes were
Lord Grey of Werke, Sir J. Cockran. Colonel Holins. Captain Mathews,
Mr. Wade of Bristol, Rimbolt, Daw and Ferguson ('The Plotter').

† He belonged to an old Scottish family. His father had been
M.P. for Inverary in the first Scotch Parliament of the Restoration.
It was he who composed that long, badly-worded proclamation which
Monmouth published upon landing, in which he accused James of
having murdered his own brother the King.

At the end of April William wrote to Rochester, assuring him on his word of honour that he did not know if Monmouth were still in Holland. Should he find him, he would, he said, at once order him to quit the country. Three weeks afterwards, by James's directions, a circular was sent to all the county authorities of England and Scotland enjoining vigilance, as it was known that Argyle had sailed for Scotland, and it was thought that a descent upon some part of the North of England might be attempted by Monmouth with a view to join him. There is no doubt that Monmouth's intention to raise the standard of rebellion was known in the West at least two or three weeks before he landed at Lyme Regis. On June 1 the Mayor of Taunton wrote to warn the Mayor of Exeter that he had ascertained from intercepted letters that an immediate rising in the West was in contemplation.* Up to the last, so well was Monmouth's secret kept by his followers, that it was generally believed his attempt at insurrection would be made in the northern counties, where he was popular and possessed many friends.

Monmouth wanted arms, but, above all, he needed money. Had William favoured his enterprise, he could, at least in secret, have helped him financially. To raise money, Monmouth pawned his own jewels and those of his mistress for 32,000 guilders (£2,733). The English refugees subscribed what they could, and, amongst others, the great Locke gave £400. But the total amount collected was ridiculously small when compared with the magnitude of the undertaking and the issues involved. With the money so obtained, Monmouth purchased what arms and military equipment he could, including four small field-pieces, which constituted all his artillery.† He

* Historical MSS., Fifth Report, p. 371.

† He paid £3,000 for these four field-guns, 1,500 cuirasses, 1,500 swords, pikes and muskets, a small number of carbines and pistols, and some 200 barrels of powder. His advisers persuaded him that those who were to join him on landing would all come well armed.

foolishly bought 1,500 breastpieces, which were of no use to him. They were left at Lyme Regis when he marched for Taunton. Muskets or matchlocks would have served his purpose better than armour, for which his peasant followers did not care. For the hire of the 32-gun frigate in which he himself sailed he paid £5,500. Had William given him arms and accoutrements for, say, 20,000 men, the rebellion might have had a very different ending.

About 2 o'clock on Sunday morning, May 24, Monmouth and his friends left Amsterdam in a lighter for the three ships which he had previously sent on to the Texel. His party numbered about seventy persons, including his private chaplain, Mr. Hooke, an Independent preacher, who subsequently became a Roman Catholic, and a devoted adherent of James II., whom he followed into exile.* Head-winds retarded the lighter, and it was not until Saturday that she reached the ships. After some difficulties with the Dutch authorities, who, instigated by the English Ambassador, wished to detain the ships, they weighed anchor at daybreak on the following morning, and sailed for the English coast.† The wind and weather were unfavourable, and no fewer than twelve days were spent at sea before they anchored in the bay off the little village of Lyme Regis, only a few miles distant from John Churchill's birthplace. James had given his fleet strict orders to keep the sharpest possible look-out for Monmouth's little squadron; yet for twelve days it beat about the Channel without being discovered, and finally reached a port where its men and military stores were landed, not only without interruption, but without the fact being even discovered by any one of James's numerous ships of war.

The day after Monmouth quitted Amsterdam, William

---

* He entered the French army, and rose to be a Lieutenant-General.

† Colonel Bevis Skelton was then our Ambassador at the Hague. In the previous reign he had been compelled to leave the army because he was a Roman Catholic.

sent to Rochester a full detail of the plan for the intended risings in Scotland and England, and Bentinck on the same day reported to him that Monmouth's destination was the West of England. William added most solemnly that neither he nor the Princess Mary had been in any way privy to the schemes.

Although William offered to help James in the suppression of the rebellion, there was a strong feeling in Holland in its favour. Prayers were offered up in many churches asking God to bless an undertaking which thousands of pious people believed to be conceived in the interests of true religion.

Though personally brave and a favourite with his men, Monmouth lacked the qualities of a leader. He was wanting in firmness and decision, and especially in that force of character which inspires others with confidence in their leader's views. He had seen but little of war; he had served exclusively with regular troops; and from the first he had evinced a want of confidence in the raw levies who rallied to his standard. He was one of that sort of cut-and-dried, old-fashioned officers, who could not believe it possible that badly-armed, slovenly-looking regiments, untrained in the formal evolutions of a regular army, could be of any real military value. To officers of his class it was, and still is, heresy to hold that a man can be capable of doing a soldier's work unless he is dressed like a cockatoo, and drilled to stand like a ramrod, with his nose in the air. Monmouth was not the man to lead a desperate enterprise, in which success depended upon the rapid conversion into soldiers of dull West-Country peasants. No one knew this better than the astute Prince of Orange, who had lately had ample opportunities of gauging his character and capacity.

From the first Monmouth seems to have been fully conscious of the difficulties and dangers of the enterprise into which he had been driven by the importunity of Argyle, by the fiery preaching of Ferguson, and by the

pleadings of the numerous British exiles in Holland.
Dangerous and desperate ventures call for a leader endowed
with natural genius for war, and with inborn qualifications,
of which Monmouth possessed none.

The only man of any note who landed with him was
Forde, Lord Grey of Werke.* He had long been one of
Monmouth's supporters, though he had good reason to
believe that the 'Protestant Duke' had been his wife's
lover.+ To him Monmouth, unfortunately for his cause,
gave the command of all his mounted men, for his conduct
in action affords good grounds for the accusation of cowardice
so freely alleged against him. After his capture he was
despicable enough to buy his unworthy life by giving
evidence to secure the conviction of brave men who had
believed in and followed him.

* He was born 1654, and died $\frac{25}{5}\cdot\frac{6}{9}$, 1701. He was a coward, and
a bad man all round. In 1682 he seduced his sister-in-law, Lady
Henrietta, daughter of George, Earl of Berkeley, and on $\frac{20}{30}$ 8, 1682,
had carried her off—she was only eighteen years of age—from her
father's house, the Durdans, at Epsom. Pardoned by James for the
part he took in Monmouth's rebellion, he was created Earl of Tankerville, in 1695, by William III., who also made him a Privy Councillor
and afterwards Lord Privy Seal. His only child—a daughter—married
Charles Bennet, Lord Ossulston, who in 1714 was created Earl of
Tankerville. He was the 'cold Caleb' of 'Absalom and Achitophel.'
He was a zealous Exclusionist, and had been concerned in the Rye
House Plot.

† Henry Sidney's Diary, by Blencowe, vol. i., pp. 287, 263.

CHAPTER XXXVII.

Churchill's activity — Encounter with the rebels — The Militia disaffected — Feversham supersedes Churchill in command — Feversham's character — He reaches Bristol.

AT 4 a.m. of Saturday, June 13, an express reached London to announce that Monmouth had landed at Lyme Regis two days before.* It came from the Mayor of that little Dorsetshire seaport, and was dated June 11, 'near twelve at night.' from Honiton, to which place he had ridden on his way to Exeter to inform the Duke of Albemarle, the Lord-Lieutenant of Devon, of Monmouth's landing. Two other loyal burgesses of Lyme had also set out late the same evening to carry the news to London. They rode hard throughout the night, and, upon reaching the City, went straight to the house of Sir Winston Churchill, who represented their borough in Parliament. He and his son, Lord Churchill, carried them to Whitehall, where they were questioned, on oath, by the King in Council.

Their news was that Monmouth had arrived on the previous Thursday at Lyme with a frigate, one small vessel, and a dogger,† and had occupied the town with about 300

---

* Lyme Regis is 143 miles by road from London, and is 22 miles west of Dorchester.

† A 'dogger' was a small craft—sometimes merely a fishing-boat—with one mast.

armed men; that he had landed; and, lastly, that he had
set up his standard, and had issued a proclamation in
which he denounced James 'as a usurper, a murderer, a
traitor, and a tyrant.' This intelligence was at once communicated to Parliament, and a Council was forthwith
called by which measures were taken with the utmost
promptitude. A Bill of Attainder against Monmouth was
passed through both Houses of Parliament, £400,000 was
voted to enable the King to put down the rebellion,* and a
reward of £5,000 was offered for Monmouth's body, dead or
alive.† Immediate orders were sent to call out the militia
of the West, and officers of the regular army were
despatched to advise the lieutenants of counties upon all
military matters. The six British regiments in the Dutch
service were recalled from Holland, and four companies of
the Irish Guards were ordered to England.‡ All 'commission officers' were directed to join their regiments
forthwith.

Monmouth's friends were known to be numerous in
London, where an outbreak was expected: James committed many of them to prison. All the troops that could
be spared from the capital, and those collected from other
towns, were ordered to march for Salisbury without delay.
James selected Lord Churchill to command them, and
conferred upon him the rank of Brigadier.§ He set out ¹⁹⁄₂₉ 6, 1685.

* The Bill of Attainder passed the House of Commons in two days
and the House of Lords in one.

† Parliament, having voted supply and passed Monmouth's Bill of
Attainder, was adjourned from ²⁶⁄₇ 7 to ¹⁴⁄₄ 8, and subsequently to
¹⁸⁄₁₁ 11, 1685. It met then for a few days, and was prorogued to ¹²⁄₆ 2,
168⅚.

‡ Three of these British regiments were Scotch, and had long been
in the Dutch service; three were English, and had been raised in
1674 from the regiments which Charles had been compelled to disband when peace was made with Holland in that year.

§ A fortnight later he was promoted to be Major-General 'over all
forces, horse and foot,' ²³⁄₃ 7, 1685. Both Kirke and Trelawney were
commanded to take their orders from him. The troops with which
Churchill set out were: Four troops of the Earl of Oxford's Horse,

from London on Saturday, June 15, and on the 17th reached Bridport, where he found some of the Militia already collected. On the following day he pushed on to Winsham, and on the 19th established his headquarters at Chard, eighteen miles south of Bridgewater, and one hundred and forty miles from London. Here he found himself in the familiar scenes of his early boyhood, for Ash House was only about eight miles to the south-west of his headquarters. He at once set to work with that earnest activity which distinguished him all through life. The day after his arrival he wrote as follows from Chard to the Duke of Somerset: 'This morning I received yours. I am now in Somersetshire, and shall join you by following the Duke of Monmouth so close as I can on his marches, which I think is the only way for me to join you or to do the King's service; but I think you should force the Duke of Albemarle to join you, for he has a good force of men, and is not so well able to attend the Duke of Monmouth's march as I am, by reason of the King's Horse which I have with me.' *

He scoured the country in all directions with his mounted troops, and, hearing of some rebels in the neighbourhood of Taunton, he sent a small party of Oxford's Regiment to look them up.[†] The result was a skirmish in the forest of Ashill, about half-way between Chard and Taunton, and to this day the spot is known as the 'Fight Ground.' Lieutenant Moneux, in command of the King's party, was mortally wounded, and a few were killed on both sides.[‡] Churchill reported that he found

now the Royal Horse Guards Blue; four troops of the King's Dragoons, now the Royal Dragoons, of which Churchill was Colonel; five companies of the Queen Dowager's Regiment, now the Queen's or West Surrey. A few days later five more troops joined the Royal Dragoons. More troops were to follow as soon as possible (Dom. Papers, British Museum).

  * Historical MSS., Duke of Northumberland's Papers, p. 97.

  † The Blues.

  ‡ 'History of Chard.' by E. Green, p. 51.

the rebels in force at Taunton, well armed and daily increasing in numbers. From this date until the final struggle at Sedgemoor he never lost touch of them, and followed close upon Monmouth's footsteps wherever he went. By his energy, and the continual movement of his mounted troops, he prevented many from joining the rebels, who would otherwise have gone to swell Monmouth's army. At this work his local knowledge was of great use to him. As is always the case with our rapidly-improvised armies, transport was the first serious difficulty, increased by the fact of the whole country being in sympathy with Monmouth. But Churchill drew what supplies he could from the neighbouring villages, and pressed the available horses and waggons for the King's service. The Axminster parish books contain several entries of expenses incurred by his orders: 'Paid for four carts to go to Chard to attend on the Lord Churchill, and guides, and other expenses, £1 11s. 0d.'; 'For one cart and five pack horses, to convey Captain Churchill's Troop of Dragoons to Crewkern, £1 2s. 0d.,' etc.*

On Friday, the 21st, Churchill wrote as follows to the Duke of Somerset, who was still at Bristol: 'Chard.—I received you letter this morning, and will certainly be on tuesday at 11 in the morning at Bridgewater, where I hope you will meet me with what Militia you have. I have forces enough not to apprehend the Duke of Monmouth; but quite contrary should be glad to meet with him and my men are in so good heart. This afternoon Colonel Kirke's regiment joins me, which will be an addition to your strength.'† Later on in the day he had another letter from the Duke of Somerset, which made him somewhat change his plans, for in reply he wrote that he intended to 'march to-morrow to Langport, so that I will follow him' (Monmouth) 'as close as ever I can. I intend to be at

---

* 'Book of the Axe,' p. 347.
† Historical MSS., Duke of Northumberland's Papers, p. 98.

Wells on tuesday, where I hope I shall find you, and that will be much better than to send a troop of Horse.'*

The Militia had no sympathy with the Royal cause, and fully shared the Western sentiment for Protestantism and Monmouth. The Duke of Albemarle was so fully alive to this fact that as early as June 12 he had asked officially for the aid of regular troops. In answer to this request, Sunderland informed him that Churchill, with some detachments, was to start at once for the West, and that the Governour of Portsmouth had been ordered to send some field-guns also, under an escort of five companies of the Queen's Regiment.† These guns, sixteen in number, started accordingly under the command of Lord Churchill's brother Charles, who was Lieutenant-Colonel of that regiment. The original intention had been that Lord Churchill should command all the troops to be employed against Monmouth, for James had confidence in his ability, and had not as yet taken any strong religious prejudice against him. But he had not been many hours on his road to the West before the King seems suddenly to have remembered the obligations he was under to Turenne for effective help and many acts of kindness received from him when in exile before the Restoration. He could now in a measure repay that generous soldier by giving the command in the field to his nephew, Lord Feversham, in whose loyalty and courage he implicitly believed. It would be a cruel blow to his faithful servant Churchill, but that must be ignored. Feversham was accordingly made General-in-Chief of the Forces in the West, with Churchill under him as second in command.

Lewis Duras, a French Protestant noble, had come to England to escape persecution on account of his religion.‡

---

* Historical MSS., Duke of Northumberland's Papers, p. 98.

† This regiment is now the King's Own or Royal Lancaster Regiment.

‡ Though a Protestant, he never swerved from his allegiance to James. Born in 1638, he died $\frac{8}{10}$, 4, 1709.

His father was the Marquis de Blanquefort ; his mother was
Turenne's sister. He had been naturalized as an Englishman in 1665, and succeeded his father-in-law as Earl of
Feversham twelve years afterwards. Dark-complexioned
and of middle height, he was just twelve years older than
Churchill. A man of affable and polished manners, he was
honest and well-meaning, but slow and infirm of purpose.*
He is said to have been a suitor for the hand of Monmouth's
mistress, Lady Henrietta Wentworth, and now, by a strange
coincidence, he was about to command in the field against
his successful rival.† He was not accounted a strong
Protestant in England, though, when in France, he would
not, like his two brothers and his uncle Turenne, change
his religion to please Lewis XIV. This campaign in the
West proved him to be no General ; and it showed that,
in common with many of the French nobles of that time,
he had no regard whatever for the lives of the peasantry.
He gained no respect from his officers, who pronounced
him heavy and indolent from over-eating. A serious injury
in the head some five or six years before had necessitated
the operation of trepanning, and it is possible that his lazi-
ness and addiction to sleep may have been the result of
this accident.‡ In spite of his being a Protestant, he was
so much disliked as a foreigner by the faction opposed to
James, that as early as 1680 it had been resolved in the
House of Commons 'to present an address to his Majesty , 1, 1680.
to remove Lewis, Earl of Feversham, from all military
offices and commands, as a promoter of Popery and of
the Popish interests.' This feeling was doubtless due to
his being James's close friend and supporter.

The change of command was not a happy move for
James, and no man who understood war would have made
it. Foreigners never have been popular in England, and
British troops were not likely to do well under Lord

* John Macky, Reresby, Burnet.
† Roberts' 'Monmouth,' vol. ii., p. 85.
‡ Hatton, 'Correspondence,' vol. i., p. 171.

Feversham, even had he been an able soldier, which he
certainly was not.

In Sunderland's early letters to Churchill no mention is
made of Feversham's appointment. He tells him that the
King had received his letter of the 17th, and that he
(Sunderland) had also received his two letters of the same
date. Even then Churchill was a good correspondent,
keeping his Government well informed upon all such
military proceedings as he considered it advisable that they
should know. Sunderland goes on to say that, according
to the information obtained by the King, it was believed
that the rebels were making for Bristol, and it was therefore
desirable that Churchill should place himself somewhere
between them and that city. James thought that Bridgewater would best answer the purpose, and the Excise
officers there were accordingly ordered to place £4,000 at
his disposal, but the selection was entirely left to him.
Sunderland told him, further, where the several regiments
of militia had been ordered to assemble, and named some
regular officers who had been selected to accompany those
regiments for the purpose of dry-nursing their inexperienced
colonels.

On June 17 Sunderland wrote to tell Churchill
that the Duke of Beaufort had been ordered to secure Bristol
with any militia he could collect from the counties under his
jurisdiction.* The Hampshire, Berkshire, Surrey and Sussex
militia had been called out, he added, and sent respectively
to Salisbury, Reading, Farnham, and the New Forest.

Colonel Kirke reached Salisbury from Andover† on the
18th, on which day, although Lord Sunderland wrote to
tell the Duke of Somerset that the King had 'appointed
my Lord Churchill to command his forces which are
marched down into the West, and would therefore have
your Grace constantly correspond with him,' there is not a
word about Feversham. He adds in a postscript : ' I believe

* The Duke of Beaufort had reached Bristol, of which he was
Governor, on June 16.

† A distance of 17½ miles.

my Lord Churchill is now with ye Duke of Albemarle.'* It is therefore evident that on Thursday, June 18, this change of commanders had not been finally determined upon. Indeed, it would appear from Sunderland's letter to Churchill of Friday, the 19th, in which there is no mention of Feversham, that when it was written the change had not even then been made. Later on in that day, however, Sunderland wrote to tell Churchill of his supersession. He says that the King has 'given the Earl of Feversham a commission to be Lieutenant-General,' and that he was to command all the Lieutenants of the Western Counties. Churchill was ordered to send back by bearer all the news to Feversham, who was then on the march for Bath, that would be useful to him as Commander-in-Chief.+ He adds 'that three battalions of the Foot Guards, 150 of the Horse Guards, two troops of the Earl of Oxford's, and two troops of Dragoons,' were to march for Bath as soon as possible. His next letter would, he said, contain a commission giving him the rank of Brigadier-General. In a letter of the same date he tells the Duke of Somerset that the King had made Feversham Lieutenant-General, and that the latter was to march for the West on June 20 'with a considerable body of Horse and Foot, and that the train of artillery is to follow on Monday' (June 24).‡

The promised reinforcements§ left London for Bath on Saturday, June 20, and, in four marches, reached Marlborough, where they halted for orders. Feversham set out for Bristol on the same day, and the artillery train of sixteen brass pieces, from the Tower, followed. He reached Bristol about noon on June 23, and spent the

June 6, 1685.

June 6, 1685.

* Historical MSS., Duke of Northumberland's Papers, p. 97.
§ State Papers, James II., Domestic, bundle 2.
‡ Historical MSS., Duke of Northumberland's Papers, p. 97.
§ Two troops of Oxford's Horse, under Sir Thomas Compton, and two troops of the Royal Dragoons, two battalions of the 1st Guards, one battalion of the Coldstream, and five companies of Dumbarton's Foot.
   Feversham's guard consisted of ' 150 Horse Guards and 60 Horse Grenadiers.'

remainder of the day with the Dukes of Beaufort and Somerset in sight-seeing. Two days before, he had ordered the latter to destroy the bridge at Keynsham, near Bristol, and had recommended that the bridge at Bath should be similarly dealt with.

We have every reason to believe, from Churchill's letters, that he felt his supersession most deeply. He knew Feversham to be an indolent glutton of no military reputation. At the age of thirty-five he had at last, as he thought, been given an opportunity of showing what he could do as a General commanding in the field. If he succeeded, as he would most surely have done, he knew that honours and lucrative appointments would be his reward. And now that fame and fortune seemed to be within his grasp, to have them snatched from him in favour of an unknown and incompetent Frenchman was hard indeed. Had he been the scion of a noble house, no such slight would, he knew, have been put upon him; but as a poor soldier of fortune, the son of a ruined Cavalier of humble position, he had to accept the inevitable, and bear the injustice with what grace he might. Sufficiently philosophical to be resigned, he was yet too ambitious to be contented.

James was alarmed for the safety of Bristol, and from the first expected that Monmouth would try to obtain possession of so important a seaport. It was known to contain a large number of people hostile to the King, and therefore friendly to his popular nephew. The Duke of Beaufort, Governour of Bristol, had been ordered to occupy the city with the militia of Gloucester, Monmouth, and Herefordshire. Lord Abingdon with the militia of Oxford, and the Duke of Norfolk with that of Berks, were to march on Reading. The Surrey militia was ordered to Farnham, and that of Hampshire to Salisbury. The Earl of Dorset was to occupy the New Forest with the Sussex Militia Horse under Lord Lumley.* Bath was held by the Somersetshire

---

* Although he had left the Church of Rome and become a Protestant, he was loyal to James as his lawful King.

militia, under the Duke of Somerset; and the Wiltshire, under Lord Pembroke, were marching upon Chippenham. Colonel Oglethorpe, with a party of the Life Guards, had been sent forward to Warminster to obtain information, and met Feversham at Bath on June 24 with the news that on the evening before Monmouth had been at Shepton-Mallet.

On June 24 it was known in London that Monmouth was near Glastonbury, closely watched by Churchill, who on the 22nd had sent a party of forty Horse from Langport to look the rebels up. A slight skirmish had ensued, and Monmouth's squadron, said to be double the Royalists in number, had been driven back to the rebel camp.*

Feversham had ordered the Royal forces to concentrate at Bath, where he found them collected, including Churchill's troops, when he arrived on June 26. He had found it necessary to leave his guns and impedimenta for the moment at Devizes under a guard. Owing to the wetness of the season, the roads were in a deplorable state, and, as the country was much enclosed, the guns would seriously hamper his movements.†

We must now go back a little, and describe Monmouth's movements previous to the date at which the Royal forces sent to oppose him had been thus concentrated at Bath.

---

* *London Gazette* of 24, 6, 1685.

† Historical MSS., Dartmouth Papers, p. 126. He had sixteen guns in all; nine left London on June 24, escorted by five companies of Dumbarton's Regiment (the Royal Scots).

CHAPTER XXXVIII.

MOVEMENTS OF THE REBELS AND OF THE ROYAL FORCES PRIOR TO THE BATTLE OF SEDGEMOOR.

Lord Grey runs away during the attack on Bridport—Fletcher goes
back to Holland—Skirmish near Axminster—Monmouth writes to
Churchill—He reaches Taunton, then Keynsham—Is repulsed at
Bath—Tents supplied to the Royal Army—Wells : Complaints of the
Artillery—Marlborough's power of foresight.

CHAPTER
XXXVIII.

1685.

11 6, 1685.

MONMOUTH commanded silence upon landing with his little
band of followers at Lyme Regis, and, falling on his knees,
thanked God for a safe voyage, and implored His blessing
on the enterprise thus begun.   The village was in a
ferment, and before the Duke had left his ship the leading
inhabitants had discussed the propriety of firing their big
gun at it.   Want of powder brought the debate to an
abrupt end, but, as the next best thing, the town drums
were beaten to call the borough militia to arms.   One man
answered the summons, and he, finding himself alone,
thought it better to join Monmouth, a proceeding for which
he was hanged after the battle of Sedgemoor.

The news of Monmouth's landing spread rapidly through
all the Western country where he had many adherents.
About a week before, the militia had been embodied as a
precautionary measure against any possible rising in consequence of Argyle's attempt in Scotland.   But it was soon
discovered that the loyalty of this force could not be
depended upon.   The agricultural labourers, tradesmen,
and mechanics were on the side of the Protestant Duke.

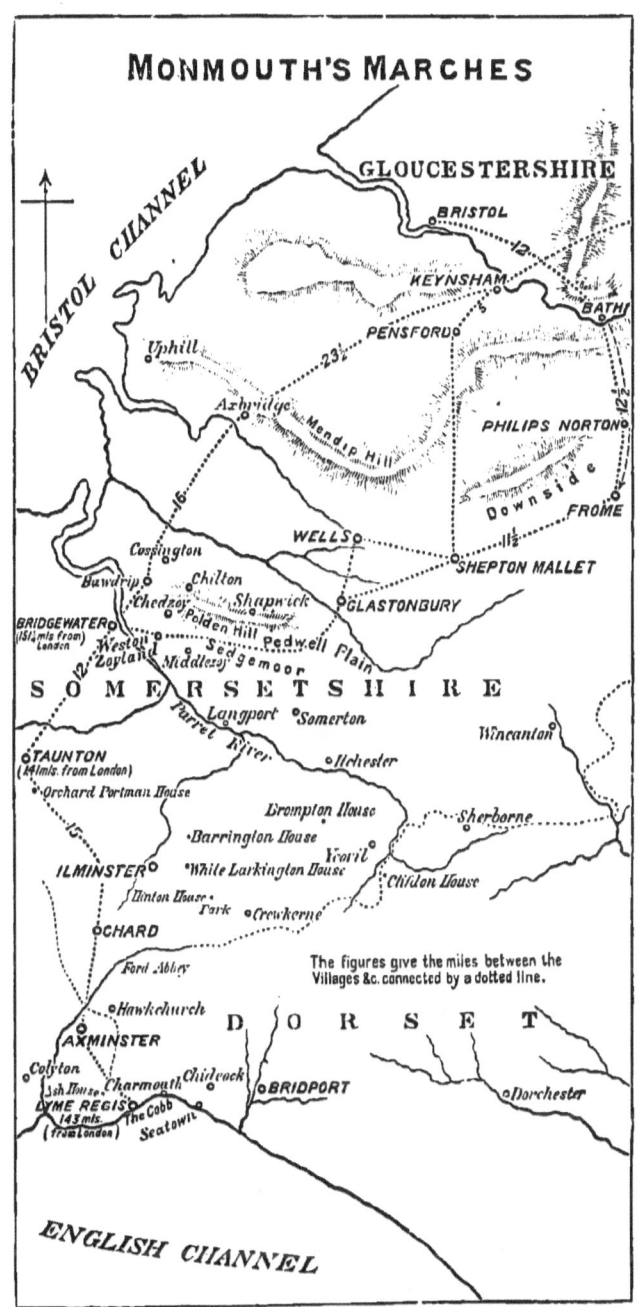

PLAN OF MONMOUTH'S MARCHES IN 1685.
To face p. 286, Vol. I.

There were no regular troops at hand, and before they could arrive from London, much might be done by an active, intelligent leader. But Monmouth was not the man for this work. It was of the utmost consequence that he should inspire his followers with confidence in his courage, determination and ability. This is the first step towards success in all rebellions, and it requires resolution in council, as well as vigorous action in the field. But where prompt decision was necessary Monmouth hesitated, and, by vacillation and half-hearted measures, he lost the opportunities presented to him by favouring fortune. It is curious to note how often the leader has been afforded such opportunities at the beginning of a rebellion, opportunities which history tells us are always as fleeting as they are precious. Unless seized at the moment they are lost for ever, and their loss means death to the rebel's hopes, if not to himself. Monmouth does not seem to have realized this, or to have appreciated the critical nature of an undertaking in which he must either ride on the crest of the wave of triumph or be hopelessly engulfed. Two such opportunities soon offered themselves to him, but of neither was he capable of availing himself.

Friday, Saturday, and Sunday were spent in landing stores, guns, arms, etc., from the ships, and in distributing them amongst the peasants and mechanics who flocked to join him. The country gentry held aloof, and few even of the middle class or small yeomen enrolled themselves under his standard; but amongst those who did join him was Joshua Churchill, commonly known as Colonel Churchill. He was not a near relative of Sir Winton's, but he came from the same stock; indeed, several families of the name were then living in Dorsetshire.* Daniel De Foe, the author, was one of Monmouth's recruits.

* There is a portrait of Colonel J. Churchill in Collinton House, Dorchester, and it is tolerably certain that he belonged to that branch of the family. He was a younger brother of William Churchill, the London printer, who had made money at his trade. His elder brother,

Large numbers were anxious to throw in their lot with him, but he could not accept their services, as he had no arms to give them. Every effort was made to improvise weapons, and many of the men had nothing better than scythes fastened lengthways to long poles. Want of ready money was a great hindrance, but the smiths in all the neighbouring villages were hard at work, night and day, converting scythes and forks into pikes, and it was boastfully announced that with these they would 'easily mow down the Popish army, and make new-fashioned Protestant hay.'* Never before, or since, was a rebellion undertaken with such scanty means. †

The two opportunities referred to now presented themselves, and both were lost through mismanagement. The first was at Bridport—only eight miles from Lyme Regis—where the Dorset militia had been ordered to assemble. They had not as yet all turned out, and those who had assembled had taken no precautions against attack or surprise. The regiment was known to be Protestant in feeling, and therefore not likely to fight with much heart for their bigoted Catholic King. What more easy than to attack them

Awnsham, was the well-known bookseller and publisher who carried on business at the sign of the Black Swan, Paternoster Row. When this branch of the family became rich, they purchased many manors in Dorsetshire. Another brother, John, was the printer who received £1,000 for printing the manifesto of William III. In the War Office Commission Books there is an entry of 'Joshua Churchill, Gent.,' who was made Ensign in the Earl of Monmouth's Regiment, ¹⁄₁ 7, 1689, and became a Lieutenant ¹⁄₁ 4, 1692. I think this is the man who in 1710-11 was appointed to command the Marines, then ordered to Canada. See Luttrell.

* 'A complete collection of all the Reports, lyes and stories which were the forerunners of the Great Revolution of 1688,' p. 51. Some of these rude scythe weapons may be seen in the Tower.

† His paymaster was Mr. Heywood Dare, who had been one of his leading councillors in Holland. He was an earnest man, well known amongst the Nonconformists of the West. The Commissary-General was Mr. Sam Story. His surgeons were Drs. Temple, Gayland and Oliver.

vigorously by night? Such a blow, if struck home at this early period of the rebellion, could not fail to be of incalculable advantage to the rebel cause. 'First blood,' especially where raw levies are concerned, gives a confidence to irregular troops out of all proportion to the amount of success obtained. Monmouth seems to have understood this, but he had not the military skill or experience to give effect to it with the undisciplined men at his disposal; and, though he wisely resolved to attack before the whole of this militia regiment had assembled, he unfortunately gave command of the operation to Lord Grey. With 400 men Grey started for Bridport on Saturday night, intending to make his attack at daybreak on the following morning. He marched in silence all through the dark, and at the first streak of dawn, under cover of a heavy mist, he fell upon the unsuspecting enemy, who had no guards or outlying piquets to warn them of their danger. The surprise was complete, and success seemed assured, when Lord Grey, in a panic, ran away at the head of his mounted men. Colonel Venner, the second in command, drew off his Foot in tolerable order, and reached Lyme Regis without molestation from the astonished militia. Had Grey behaved with even ordinary courage the affair must have been a brilliant success, and would have obtained for Monmouth the militia arms and accoutrements, of which he stood so much in need. There is little doubt also that many of the militiamen would have openly joined him, and the moral effect of this would have been great in London, as well as in the locality.

Monmouth was at his wits' end how to act. The only gentleman with him had turned out a coward, and yet he did not dare to dismiss him, although urged to do so by Fletcher, who was next in importance to Grey. Fletcher had been of Monmouth's council in Holland, and was invaluable from his social standing, military knowledge, and general ability. But it would seem that from the first an unlucky fatality pursued Monmouth, for by another most untoward accident he was now to lose Fletcher, the ablest of his followers. During the preparation for the attack on Bridport Fletcher had a dispute about a horse with Mr. Dare, a Taunton goldsmith, whom he shot in an outburst of anger, and had to fly the country in consequence.*

The Reverend R. Ferguson accompanied the expedition as chaplain. He was a genuine demagogue, who thoroughly understood his trade, and was animated by the demagogue's habitual disregard for truth. Before leaving Holland he had drawn up a 'declaration' for the English people, setting forth their grievances. It was a long rambling indictment against James, who, it was asserted, had poisoned King Charles II. This 'declaration' was made public at Lyme Regis, and was well received by the ignorant people whose passions it was intended to arouse.

After a stay of four days at Lyme Regis, Monmouth moved on Monday to Axminster—a distance of only five and a half miles—with a force of about 3,000 men. Every man wore in his hat a green bough, which thenceforward became the distinguishing mark of the rebels. As he neared Axminster he discovered the Duke of Albemarle, with the Devon militia, approaching from Exeter, to form a junction with the Somerset militia, under Colonel Luttrell. Here was his second great opportunity. There was some little skirmishing, in which Albemarle soon discovered, to his cost, that his men would not fight in earnest against Monmouth. Both militia regiments retreated in considerable disorder, many men throwing away both arms and accoutrements to facilitate their flight ; one battalion fell back as far as Wellington, a distance of twenty-two miles. Lord Churchill describes this affair in the following letter to James : ' I am sorry to send your Majesty this ill news : which is unless speedy course be taken, we are like to lose this country to the rebels : for we have those two regiments run away a second time, that are

---

* Dare had been convicted in 1680 of using seditious language, was fined and imprisoned, but eventually escaped to Holland, where he joined in Monmouth's plot, and came to England in his ship.

mentioned in a letter directed to my Lord Sunderland from
their colours, and it happened thus : The Duke of Albemarle
sends to Sir E. Phellipps and Colonel Luttrell, that he would
be at Axeminster on such a day with some forces, and would
have them meet him there : so away marched those two
regiments, one out of Chard and the other out of Crewkern :
and when they came to the top of the hill within half a
quarter of a mile of the town, there came out some country
people, and said the Duke of Monmouth was in the town :
at that, one Captain Littleton cried out, We are all betrayed ! so the soldiers immediately look one upon another,
and threw down their arms and fled, leaving their Officers
and Colours behind : half, if not the greatest part, are gone
to the rebels. I do humbly submit this to your Majesty's
commands in what I shall do in it, for there is not any
relying on these regiments that are left unless we had some
of your Majesty's standing forces to lead them on and
encourage them : for at this unfortunate news I never saw
people so much daunted in my life . . . I have sent away
just now to the Duke of Arl. to send 4,000 men to Crewkern
and Chard, and that I will be there as soon as I hear they
are arrived. I shall wait for your Majesty's commands
here if there be not occasion any where else of my appear-
ing.'* This letter has no date or address, but it was
probably written at Bridport on June 17. Here, again, it
was of the highest importance that Monmouth should
attack the militia vigorously. To wait, as he did, until the
arrival of regular troops had given confidence to the militia,
was the height of folly. All the standing army that could
be spared was, he knew, on the march to crush him. To
neglect, therefore, to attack was to show his ignorance of
the game on which he had so inconsiderately staked all.
The arrival of Lord Churchill at Chard, coming immediately
after these two failures, may be said to have sealed the fate
of this ill-planned and feebly-conducted rebellion. From
the first Monmouth seems to have been impressed with the

June 6, 1685.

* Historical MSS., Duke of Northumberland's Papers, p. 99.

conviction that it would be folly to risk any serious engagement until he had had time to drill his raw levies; but he
forgot that an active opponent like Churchill was not likely
to allow him the time he wanted.

His landing had been a success: no regular troops were
at hand to meet him, and the undisciplined militia were at
heart in his favour. Had he boldly attacked them, and
pushed forward to Exeter, there can be little doubt that a
considerable number of them would have joined him—a proceeding which would have supplied him with money, arms
and ammunition, all of which he sorely needed. He might
then have marched rapidly upon Bristol with at least
10,000 fairly armed adherents, and the possession of that
important seaport, with its supplies of men, arms, provisions and money, would have given him a real chance
of success. He failed to understand that loss of time was
absolutely fatal to his cause, for every day brought the
regular forces nearer to him. As long as Bristol was safe,
and the rebellion was confined to the country south of the
Severn, James could afford to wait, as indeed he did, until
he had collected a sufficient force to crush Monmouth's
badly-armed levies at a blow. There was no military reason
why the militia should run away from Monmouth's raw
levies; but they really only wanted a pretext to desert.
Monmouth's miners and weavers were their friends, whose
cause they believed to be their own. They had none of that
professional military spirit, the outcome of discipline, which
causes regular soldiers to fight as they are ordered, no
matter against whom; and in the course of duty even to
fire upon those to whom they are bound by ties of kindred
and affection.

There is little doubt that Monmouth, who was fully
aware of Churchill's strong Protestant sentiments, expected
him, his old lieutenant and former comrade, to make
common cause with him. When the newly-appointed
Brigadier-General reached Chard in hot haste from London,
he received a letter from Monmouth, in which, as King of

England, he claimed Churchill's allegiance. Churchill, still firmly believing in his master's promises and good intentions, dismissed the trumpeter who brought him the letter, telling him that he knew no other King than James, the brother of his late Majesty Charles II.; at the same time he forwarded Monmouth's letter to the King.

The rebel plan of campaign was to march upon Taunton, the stronghold of dissent, then to make for Bridgewater, and thence on to Bristol, where Monmouth expected to obtain a large accession of numbers and ample supplies of money and arms. From Bristol he meant to push into Gloucestershire, where he hoped his friends from Cheshire would join him, and so reinforced he would march upon London. It was a daring project that could only be accomplished by great rapidity of movement, promptitude, energy, and determination, and it required much tact in dealing with the people on whose assistance he depended. His first objective point was Bristol, which by the route indicated was only about seventy miles, or say four or five days' march, from Lyme Regis, and he ought to have been there by June $\frac{28}{30}$, that is to say, three days before Fever-sham arrived.

As he advanced large numbers flocked to join him, but finding that he had no arms to give away, most of them returned home again. He was sorely disappointed that no gentlemen of any note joined him. His old friend, ' Tom of Ten Thousand, or ye Protestant Squire,' Thynn, of Longleat, had been murdered ; but many others, who had also made much of him during his previous visit to the West, during what was locally known as ' The Dakeing Days,' were conspicuously absent. On the other hand, as the militia could not be trusted to act against him, the Lieutenants of the counties were powerless, and were well satisfied if they could prevent the people generally from joining him. Disinclination to help the King's troops with supplies or transport was everywhere apparent. There was a sturdy feeling of independence in those western counties,

$\frac{28}{30}$, 1685.

Chapter
XXXVIII.

1685.

where Protestantism had taken a firm root, and where the inhabitants loved liberty more than loyalty. These poor mechanics, weavers, and miners were, however, unaccustomed to the use of arms, nor had they any idea of what war was like. But cruelly, indeed, were they subsequently made to feel its dread realities.

May 6, 1685. On Thursday, after a sort of triumphal march, Monmouth entered the ' very factious town ' of Taunton.* The people had turned out everywhere on the road to greet him with acclamations and good wishes, and the inhabitants of the surrounding country poured into Taunton to do him honour. The Corporation and citizens—mostly Dissenters—had been ardent Parliamentarians during the Civil War, and at one time had held the town against Goring and 10,000 Royalists. This episode was not forgotten at the Restoration, when to punish the city its charter was annulled, and the walls and defensive works of the place were demolished.† But the townspeople were now in a frenzy of delight, and hailed this poor, ill-born Duke as their deliverer, and as the protector of their religion, which they believed it was the intention of King James to destroy. The young girls strewed his way with flowers, and presented him with a Bible. He accepted the present amidst the wildest enthusiasm, and kissing it, assured his hearers that ' he came with a design to defend the truths contained in it, or to seal them with his blood, if there should be occasion for it.'‡ How heartlessly and shamelessly he afterwards broke this solemn and self-imposed oath !

> ' Thee saviour, thee the nation's vows confess,
> And never satisfied with seeing bless;
> Swift, unbespoken pomps thy steps proclaim,
> And stammering babes are taught to lisp thy name.'

These lines, applied to Monmouth in the previous

---

* King James so refers to Taunton in his Memoirs, Dalrymple, ii., Appendix, p. 23.

† Toulmin's ' History of Taunton.'

‡ Echard, Dalrymle.

reign, read like a prophecy of the reception he was to meet
with at Taunton.   On June 20 he was proclaimed King, as
James II., in a public document full of falsehood.   He
presumed even to touch for the king's evil.   By this
assumption of the kingly title he hoped to obtain adherents
from amongst the upper classes, who, he was told, only
hung back because they did not know at what he was
aiming.   He knew England well enough to feel that he
could achieve no great success unless he had at least some
proportion of the landed gentry on his side.   But until he
made them understand that he had no intention of re-
establishing a republic, few gentlemen cared, it was said, to
throw in their lot with a movement which might mean
nothing more than a repetition of Cromwell's military
despotism.   The arguments of those who urged him to proclaim himself King fell upon willing ears.   But the result
was far from what had been anticipated.   No gentleman of
consequence was won over, although about 4,000 of the
peasant class joined Monmouth at Taunton.   In the Royal
army he and his men were laughed at as ' Gaffer Scott
and his vagabonds,' and his proclamation was turned into
contemptuous ridicule.

In pursuance of his original plan of campaign, he now
moved to Bridgewater, twelve miles further on, and from
there he sent Danvers and his private chaplain, Hooke, to
London to direct the projected rising in the city.*   This
had been arranged for as part of the programme, and, notwithstanding the precautions taken by the King, there is little
doubt that it would have taken place had the rebels won
at Sedgemoor.†   On the following day Sunderland wrote to
Feversham that Churchill had reported ' that the fourteen

---

* Hardwick State Papers, 1778, vol. ii., p. 332.   Hooke was born in
Dublin, 1664, and, from having been a fiery Protestant, ended his days
as a Jacobite.   In 1702 he was employed in communications between
Marlborough and the French Court, and also at the Pretender's Court
at St. Germains.

† James states this in his memoirs ; Macpherson, vol. i., p. 143.

CHAPTER
XXXVIII.

June 6, 1685.

July 2, 1685.

July 2, 1685.

days for keeping the militia of Devon do expire three days
hence.' This difficulty was met by an order to Feversham
and to Churchill also—when he was detached from Feversham's headquarters—to offer to all the Western militiamen, willing to serve on beyond the fortnight, the same pay
that was given to the regular army.*

Monmouth was enthusiastically received at Bridgewater,
where he lodged in the old castle which had surrendered to
Fairfax after the battle of Langport in 1645. But wet
weather now set in, and the rain fell in torrents, as if to
atone for the two previous years of excessive drought.
On Monday the rebel column continued its march under
the depressing influence of this heavy downpour, and,
wading through deep mud, it reached Wells by way of
Glastonbury. During this march Monmouth was closely
followed and watched by Churchill's mounted troops, both
Horse and Dragoons. A party of forty troopers, sent out from
Langport, encountered a squadron of rebel Horse and drove
it back upon the main body. Monmouth's infantry had
also been attacked on the march by some of the Foot
Guards under his half-brother, the Duke of Grafton. The
day's skirmishing convinced him of the unfitness of his
raw, improvised levies for any serious engagement with
regular troops, and the conviction so depressed him that he
bitterly reproached himself for his rashness in undertaking
so arduous a task. He began to realize how much it was
beyond, not only his resources and the power of his untrained followers, but also beyond his own ability to conduct
or control. Like his reputed father, he loved ease, and
lacked the dogged perseverance and reckless courage which
such an enterprise demanded. Ever since his landing he
had suffered from fits of depression, during which his one
thought was to get back to Lady Wentworth. So great was
this infatuation, and so feeble his sense of personal honour,
that, to escape to her arms from his then difficult position,
he would not have scrupled, had retreat been possible, to

* State Papers, Domestic, James II., bundle 2.

have left in the lurch this crowd of peasants who had
taken up arms in his cause.

At Wells, Wade and Roe, two Bristol men who had come
with him from Holland, urged him to push boldly on at
once, and take Bristol by a sudden assault.* They assured
him that, although the walls were strong on the Somersetshire or southern side, they were weak on the Gloucestershire side, and that if he crossed the Avon at Keynsham
Bridge the place might be easily stormed and captured.
They dwelt upon the money and arms which the city would
furnish. Large numbers of men, they said, only awaited
his arrival in that stronghold of dissent to declare in his
favour. The militia garrison was small, and it was well
known that the Duke of Beaufort, the Governour, who had
marched in only a week before, had good reason to doubt 1? 6, 1685.
their loyalty. The advice was sound: but, irresolute and
half-hearted, Monmouth hesitated for several days and was
lost, as many other weak Generals have been lost before and
since. He distrusted his men, and he distrusted himself;
but at last he gave way, and, marching by Shepton Mallet 2?-?, 1685.
and Pensford, reached Keynsham Bridge. The bridge had
been broken to stop his progress, but having repaired it, he ??-?, 1685.
moved across to the northern bank. After much discussion,
it was at last resolved to await the cover of night, and then
to attack Bristol. In the meantime, anxious to provide his
jaded followers with comfortable quarters until dark, he
moved them back across the river to find food and shelter
in Keynsham. He hoped that this move would also tend
to deceive the enemy into the belief that he had abandoned
all intention of an assault upon the city. He had, however,
scarcely established his men in billets, when two tired
troops of Royal Horse, under Colonel Oglethorpe, came
blundering into Keynsham, not knowing that it was occupied
by the rebels. The Colonel, thus surprised, did the wise
thing: he boldly charged, routing Monmouth's mounted ??-?, 1685.

---

* These two men, implicated in the Rye House Plot, had fled to
Holland for safety.

troops, and killing some of his Foot. In the end, however, he was driven off, leaving some prisoners in the rebels' hands, but Monmouth might easily have destroyed him, had he attacked with vigour and surrounded him in Keynsham.* From his prisoners Monmouth learnt that the Royal army was close at hand, and scouts sent forward to Bristol brought him word in the evening that Feversham had re-entered the city. Completely surprised by Oglethorpe's appearance, he took that officer's detachment to be the head of Churchill's column, by which his footsteps had been so persistently dogged, and he became apprehensive of being hemmed in between that force and the main body of Feversham's army in front. Indecision, and the despondency which so often follows upon it in war, again took possession of his mind, and he could not be induced to attack. All arguments were unavailing, even though he was assured of a plot amongst his friends in the city to open the gates if he would but attack it boldly.+ He could only think of retreat, and would only discuss what point he should make for.

The real position was this. Feversham had reached Bath from Bristol about 6 a.m. on June 24, and had there learned that Monmouth was at Shepton Mallet on the previous evening. To ascertain for certain the rebels' whereabouts, he sent Oglethorpe's party forward, and learned from it at midnight that Monmouth was at Pensfold, only six miles from Bristol, and evidently bent upon the capture of the city. He knew that the militia garrison was not to be depended on, and, becoming anxious for its safety, he at once despatched all his mounted troops to its assistance. Ordered to push on with all speed through the night, they

---

* Oglethorpe's detachment had in fact fallen into a trap by marching without any precautions into Keynsham, where the rebels, equally careless, had neither guards nor piquets to protect them from surprise. His detachment consisted of only one troop of the Blues and Captain Talbot's troop of Militia Horse. Historical MSS., Ninth Report, p. 2, Mrs. Stopford Sackville's Papers.

† Oldmixon, Ralph, vol. i., p. 879.

reached Bristol before daybreak on June 25, about the time
that Monmouth reached Keynsham Bridge. Feversham
followed with all his Foot as quickly as he could.

When Monmouth decided not to attack Bristol, it must
have been clear to his followers that the game was up. He
felt this himself, and more than ever his thoughts were
now turned to retreat, and how he could best effect his own
escape. He was in favour of moving upon Gloucester,
crossing the river Severn, breaking down the bridge behind
him, and marching up the right or western bank through
Shropshire into Cheshire, where he counted upon help from
many powerful friends. He consulted his officers, but they
preferred a move into Wiltshire, where it was reported that
a large number of armed men awaited his arrival. Bad
weather and worse roads had destroyed the men's shoes,
and the four days' march to Gloucester would be trying to
them. The Royal cavalry, now close by, would, it was
feared, hang upon their rear during those marches, and,
retarding their progress, would give Feversham's Foot time
to come up. Bristol had escaped them, but why not attack
Bath ? It was only six miles off, and might, they urged,
be taken by a rapid march before Feversham could double
back to its assistance. This was a foolish plan, and could
lead to little, even if successful. If Monmouth dared not
meet the Royal army in the field, to shut himself up in
Bath and allow himself to be surrounded there would bring
his cause to swift and certain destruction. But it was
decided to make the attempt, and Monmouth accordingly,
setting out at dark, reached Bath at daybreak on the
following morning. He seems to have relied much upon $\frac{26 \cdot 7}{6 \cdot 5}$, 1685.
night operations when in presence of the enemy, and he
always succeeded in effecting them without molestation, so
ignorant of their business were the officers opposed to him.
Indeed, the study of this campaign makes it evident that
Churchill was the only officer on either side who displayed
activity, vigilance, or any knowledge of war.

The capture of Bristol was the last chance upon which

Monmouth had any right to calculate, and although Feversham's want of military skill gave him another at Sedgemoor, he certainly did not deserve it. Fortune seldom so favours the unwise, the feeble, or the unenterprising leader.

The citizens of Bath, then a small walled town, shut their gates, killed the bearer of the flag of truce sent to summon the place, and refused to surrender. Churchill's horsemen dogged Monmouth's footsteps, pressed upon his column, and slew his stragglers. His undrilled cavalry, with their ill-broken horses, could not stand against the Royal troopers, and after leaving Bath he did not venture to halt until he had reached Phillips Norton, about seven miles south of that city. Feversham's army reoccupied Bath on the same day, and was there joined by the infantry from Portsmouth and London, and by all Lord Churchill's forces. The Royal army was now concentrated for the first time during the campaign. Monmouth had been led to hope that many officers of the regular army would have joined him on the borders of Wiltshire, but none came, and his heart fainted within him. He was in despair, and haunted with a dread of assassination, which the offer of £5,000 for his body, dead or alive, caused him to anticipate.

His intention had been to start early on Saturday morning for Frome, only five miles off; but before he could get clear of Phillips Norton he was attacked by the Royal troops under his half-brother the Duke of Grafton. Feversham had sent the Duke forward at the head of some Life Guards, Dragoons, and 500 Foot, with orders to attack the rebels as soon as he came up with them. Feversham ordered his guns and the rest of the troops to follow as best they could.* This was the first day on which the Royal army marched as one body strong enough to assume the offensive. Hitherto the operations had been directed by Churchill, who had never been strong enough to go straight for Monmouth and force him to a decisive action. He had

* *London Gazette.*

been obliged to act with great caution, and could only afford to hang upon the rebel rear and attack his weak detachments. But the Royal army being now concentrated, Feversham was sufficiently strong to bring matters to an issue, and it was his policy to do so as quickly as possible. As soon as the Duke of Grafton reached Phillips Norton and found the rebels still there, he attacked it. Some hours of skirmishing, with varying success, ensued ; on the whole, Monmouth's men fought well and stoutly behind the hedges which lined the lanes leading into the village. In this encounter the rebels had certainly the best of it ; they only lost eighteen men, whilst the loss in the Royal army amounted to eighty.* Darkness at last put an end to the affair, and Monmouth, anxious to get away from the regular infantry, marched to Frome that night in a heavy downpour of rain. The roads had been reduced to such a deplorable condition by the wet weather that all movements were difficult. He entered the town at 8 a.m. on 28.5, 1685. Sunday, after a most fatiguing march, his infantry much exhausted and in need of rest. Feversham made no attempt to pursue, his excuse being that he did not wish to expose his men to the discomfort of marching in heavy rain. As he could not force his way into Phillips Norton, he retired to Bradford to obtain shelter for them and for his overworked horses. This retrograde movement on his part was, however, a tacit admission that his attack had been a failure.

In Frome Monmouth expected to receive a convoy of arms and stores, but great was his disappointment to find that it had been captured a few days before his arrival by some militia under the Earl of Pembroke. His anxiety was further increased by hearing as he did for the first time of Argyle's defeat and capture, and by learning for a certainty that Feversham had been largely reinforced with the best of James's regular troops and a number of guns.

* The 1st Foot Guards (now the Grenadier Guards) alone lost 8 men killed, 30 wounded, and 8 taken prisoners.

Want of arms prevented him from adding to his own army, and want of money increased the difficulty of feeding the men he had already.* Although well received by the people of Frome, a heavy gloom settled upon him, which quickly turned into despair. The bad news from Scotland struck terror into his followers, of whom it is said that 2,000 deserted him here. Like most weak men in difficulties, he asked everybody's advice. He was pusillanimous enough to propose that with the Horse he and his friends should make with all speed for Poole, in the hope of finding shipping there, whilst the Foot should disperse and shift for themselves as best they might. He may possibly have thought that the pardon promised by James to those who should lay down their arms would secure from harm all whom he thus proposed to desert. But he really had no settled plan ; for whilst this proposal was under consideration he wrote to Danvers in London, urging him to hasten the projected rising there, from which all along he had expected much.

A council of war was called on Sunday afternoon at Frome, to discuss the propriety of the proposed flight to Holland. Strange to say that, in contrast to the usual practice of such councils, opinion was in favour of a more manly policy, but it was felt that, the enemy being too strong to encounter in the open, an immediate retreat to Bridgewater could not be avoided.

The rebel leaders, notwithstanding the fate of Argyle in Scotland, still clung to the hope that Protestant London would rise, and create a powerful diversion in their favour. They believed that the absence of all James's best troops would greatly increase the chances of a successful insurrection in the City. As a matter of fact, the capture and execution of Argyle had already made James confident of success. He was in high spirits, and felt strong enough to stifle any attempt at insurrection in the capital, whilst he

---

* It is said that when he landed, he had only £300 in his military chest. Clarke's 'James II.,' vol. ii., p. 51.

knew that Feversham's army was amply sufficient to meet and destroy Monmouth in the field. So assured was he, that he sent orders to the Irish troops which had just landed in England to re-embark and return home.

The movements of the army in the West were so seriously hampered by want of tents that Feversham asked for camp equipment, and tents for three thousand men were accordingly despatched with the guns then leaving London for his army.* When informing Feversham of this, Sunderland wrote that the King was of opinion that he and Churchill should keep henceforward together. He evidently doubted Feversham's military skill, and wished him to have Churchill at his side as an adviser. The King, he added, did not think that the rebels had now any design upon Bristol, but, nevertheless, he was preparing more troops which could be sent forward if required.

Up to the arrival of these tents the Royal army had been accommodated in farm buildings and villages—a system open to many abuses. We are told that the people suffered more from the violence and exactions of the Royal soldiers billeted upon them than they did from the undisciplined rebels. Mr. Henry Shere, who commanded the Royal Artillery, says in one of his letters: 'In plain English, I have seen too much violence and wickedness practised to be fond of this trade, and trust we may soon put a period to the business, for what we every day practise amongst the poor people cannot be supported by anyone of the least morality.'† Feversham's cavalry having reported that the rebels were about to move from Frome to Warminster, the Royal army marched south to Westbury to attack them. There it was joined by the guns and mortars which had been ordered to halt at Devizes, with their escort of five

----

* Historical MSS., Dartmouth Papers, p. 126; and State Papers, James II., Domestic, bundle No. 2. Upon the march at home, and even sometimes abroad, the horses were sheltered at night in tents specially made for the purpose, four horses being allotted to each tent.

† Historical MSS., Dartmouth Papers, p. 126.

companies of Dumbarton's Regiment.* The next day
Feversham marched to Frome, from which place Churchill
sent the following letter to his wife, deploring the slowness
of their movements :

'30th June.—I have received your picture which you
sent by my Lord Colchester. I do assure you that it was
very welcome to me, and will be when I am alone a great
satisfaction to me, for the whole world put together I do
not love so well as I do you, for I swear to you I had much
rather lose my own life than lose you. Therefore for my
sake I recommend to you to have a care of yourself. We
have had abundance of rain, which has very much tired
our soldiers, which I think is ill, because it makes us not
press the Duke of Monmouth so much as I think he
should be, and that it will make me the longer from
you, for I suppose until he be routed I shall not have
the happiness of being with you, which is most earnestly
desired by me.' (Unsigned.) Addressed: 'For my Lady
Churchill.' †

Monmouth now marched by way of Shepton Mallet to
Wells. Here his men not only lived at free quarters, as
they had done throughout, but they plundered the well-to-do
townspeople. The cathedral clergy were avowedly hostile,
and were known to have lent the Duke of Somerset £100
towards his military preparations.‡ This accounts for the
difference between the behaviour of the rebels at Wells and
their conduct elsewhere. Whilst the rank and file stole the
lead from the cathedral roof to cast into bullets, Monmouth's
Commissary-General, Sam Story, compelled the wives of
the canons who had fled to pay ransom for their houses.§ In
the papers of the cathedral we read of £4 'paid away for a

---

* Historical MSS., Ninth Report, p. 3, Mrs. Stopford Sackville's
Papers.

† Blenheim Palace Papers.

‡ Historical MSS., Wells. Cathedral Papers, p. 264.

§ Story, though a fiery rebel, was pardoned by Jeffreys for helping
to extract £15,000 from the rich lawyer Prideux, who had not taken
any active part in the rebellion.

new silver verge to replace one stolen by the rebels ';* and,
again, ' this Cathedral Church has suffered very grievously
from the rebel fanaticks, who have this morning laid hands
upon the furniture thereof, have almost utterly destroyed
the organ, and turned the sacred building into a stable for
horses.'†

A waggon of Kirke's Regiment, laden with arms, ammunition, and money, here fell into Monmouth's hands. It
had been left behind in Wells from want of horses, all
those with Kirke's troops being required to drag the guns
over the deep country roads. From Wells, Monmouth
marched through classic Glastonbury to Pedwell Plain,
east of Sedgemoor, and, bivouacking for the night, pushed
forward to Bridgewater the following morning. In these
movements the rebels were not molested by the Royal
horse, for since Feversham assumed the personal direction
of the concentrated army, Monmouth was not worried night
and day as he had been previously by the energetic
Churchill. Feversham followed slowly, and encamped on
Saturday, July 4, at Somerton, the ancient capital of
Somersetshire, with his Foot, train, and artillery, whilst
the Horse and Dragoons were billeted in the neighbouring
villages and farm buildings. The Militia regiments were
in rear in the villages of Middlezoy and Othery. A patrol
pushed forward close to Bridgewater, was nearly taken by the
rebels, but it brought back word that they had broken the
bridges, and were engaged in fortifying the town. Feversham now issued an order prohibiting all persons from
giving the rebels help or succour, on pain of being dealt
with as rebels themselves.‡

The following letter from Churchill to the Earl of
Clarendon is interesting, as an expression of his feelings
at being obliged to serve under a General for whom he had
no respect. He evidently wished to stand well with

---

* Historical MSS., Wells Cathedral Papers, p. 264.
† Historical MSS., Dartmouth Papers. p. 127.
‡ ' Clarendon and Rochester Correspondence,' vol. i., p. 141.

Feversham, the Court favourite, who had begun to appreciate his diligence and activity, but every line of the letter evinces impatience at his subordinate position :

' Somerton, Jully 4th, 1685.—My Lord, I have recived your Lordshipe's kind letter, and doe ashure you that you waire very Just to me in the opinion you had of me, for nobody living can have bene more obsarvant then I have bene to my Lord feaversham, ever since I have bene with him, in soe much that he did tell me that he would writt to the King, to lett him know how diligent I was, and I should be glade if you could know whether he has done me that Justice. I find by the enimes warant to the constables, that they have more mind to gett horses and sadells, then anny thing else which lookes as if he had a mind to break away with his Horse to som other place and leave his Foot entrenched att Bridgwater, but of this and all other things you will have itt more att large from my Lord feaversham, who has the sole command here, soe that I know nothing but what is his pleasure to tell me, soe that I am afraid of giving my opinion freely, for feare that itt should not agree with what is the King's intentions, and soe only expose myselfe ; but as to the taking caire of the men and all other things that is my duty, I am shure nobody can be more carefull then I am ; and as for my obedience, I am sure Mr. Oglethorpe is not more dutyfull then I am ; when you are att leasure, ten lins from you will be a greatt pleasure to me, who have not many things to please me here, for I see plainly that the troble is mine, and that the honor will be another's ; however, my life shall be freely exposed for the King's service.—I am, with all truth, my Lord, your Lordshipe's humble servant, CHURCHILL.'

On the following day, Sunday, Feversham moved his camp to Sedgemoor, and took up a position behind the Bussex Rhine, facing Bridgewater, in front of, and to the west of, the little village of Weston-Zoyland. The position was a good one, and had been occupied in July, 1645, by

Lord Fairfax, when he besieged Bridgewater after his victory over Goring at Langport. The tents were pitched on a spot then known as Brinse Moor. Thus, after some twelve days of marches, countermarches, and insignificant skirmishes during very bad weather, in a land of hedges and green meadows and fruitful orchards, the Royal army, under Feversham and Churchill, found itself at last face to face with Monmouth's ill-armed mob, there being only about three miles' distance between the two forces.

Throughout this short campaign there were frequent complaints of the guns hampering the army's movements. There seems to have been no good feeling between the artillery and the other arms of the service. The guns in those days moved with the baggage in rear of the army; this fact, added to the difficulty of the roads, caused them to reach their quarters at the end of each day's march, about three hours later than the other troops. This gave rise to grumbling on the part of the gunners, who complained bitterly that their wants and interests were neglected. Mr. Henry Shere, the Master-Gunner —knighted for his services during this short campaign—in his letters to the Master-General of the Ordnance, is very angry because 'no deference for the artillery, as was practised in other armies and was their due,' had been paid him and his gunners. He accused Kirke of ill-treating him, and enlarged upon the indignities to which he was subjected, and upon the great amount of work thrown upon him. He had, he said, to perform other duties besides his own, having been 'made a Secretary of War, Governour of Carriages, of sick and wounded, and a Commissary of provisions.'

Feversham's movements were slow from first to last, even when full allowance is made for the bad weather and the absence of good roads. He showed no strategic skill, and allowed Monmouth the initiative throughout; but, fortunately for him, his opponent was incapable of turning it to any useful purpose. To say that his tactics were bad is lenient criticism of a soldier who, in the action which ended the rebellion, allowed himself to be surprised by an undisciplined mob. Every day that a rebel force like that of Monmouth is suffered to rest in peace is a tacit recognition of its power, and so raises it in public estimation, and helps to swell its numbers. Men begin to believe in a rebel army which Government troops hesitate to attack.

Churchill, always a man of insight, was right in the conclusion which he had drawn from Monmouth's eagerness to obtain horses and saddlery, and conjectured truly that his great wish now was to get away north to his friends in Cheshire. It was characteristic of Marlborough that from apparently small indications he possessed the power of divining his enemies' plans, and was thus enabled to forestall them. From the experience of the recent past, he foresaw with admirable clearness the immediate future, and was able, as it were, to map out coming events from a study of the position at the moment. He could balance future probabilities with strange accuracy, and could fill in with living figures the sketchy outline furnished by the spy. Without this peculiar gift—one of the instincts that mark the born General — no campaign can be directed with success. To realize what is going on beyond a range of hills, or any other natural barrier to human vision, and out of the reach of reconnoitring parties, is one of the problems which perpetually confronts the military commander. On the correct solution of that problem depends greatly the success of all military operations. Throughout all his campaigns, Marlborough understood, by instinct, as it were, what his enemy was about, what his aims were, and how he hoped to accomplish them. From a close and minute study of the possible, he was able to calculate the probable, and from a knowledge of his opponent's character, ability, and his way of looking at things—the result of his own Argus-like observation—to determine with almost prophetic accuracy the general course of events. No book-learned rules of analogy or reasoned-out deductions helped

him to his conclusions. They were, like his wife's arith- Chapter XXXVIII.
metical calculations, arrived at by some unconscious mental
process all his own. The General who has the misfortune 1685.
to be unread in the science of war, but who is able by
inference, or a sympathetic imagination, to form a true
conception of his enemy's plans and intentions, will generally
do far better in the field than one who has not these gifts,
though his head be crammed with military history, the
theory of strategy, and the rules of tactics. Those who,
like Jomini, have written the best text-books upon war
have seldom been leaders of armies, whereas others, born
to command and endowed with the unerring military instinct which prompts them to do the right thing at the
right moment, have frequently been unable to express a
reason for the faith that was in them, or to explain how
it was they reconciled their practice with accepted principles.

CHAPTER XXXIX.

THE BATTLE OF SEDGEMOOR.

CHAPTER
XXXIX.

1685.

J. 7, 1685.

ON the evening of Saturday, Monmouth was told of Feversham's arrival at Somerton, and the next day he could see his tents spread out upon the heath in front of Weston-Zoyland, not four miles distant. The time had come when he must decide finally whether he would or would not fight a battle. Three courses, of which he must now choose one, were open to him; either to advance upon Feversham's position and fight him in the open, to await his attack in Bridgewater—having done all he could to put that place in a state of defence—or, lastly, to avoid fighting by an immediate retreat.

Were his enthusiastic but ill-armed and untrained levies fit to cope in the open with the regular troops before him? Did their zeal for the Protestant cause compensate for their want of military training? It was the old, old question between the relative value of enthusiasm and discipline. Destitute himself of any real heartiness in the cause of Protestantism, he spurned the very notion of such a comparison or calculation. He wisely rejected the idea of a battle in the open as ridiculous, while the second course found favour with few of his followers, and would not bear examination. To shut himself up in Bridgewater would mean certain, though not perhaps immediate, death to him

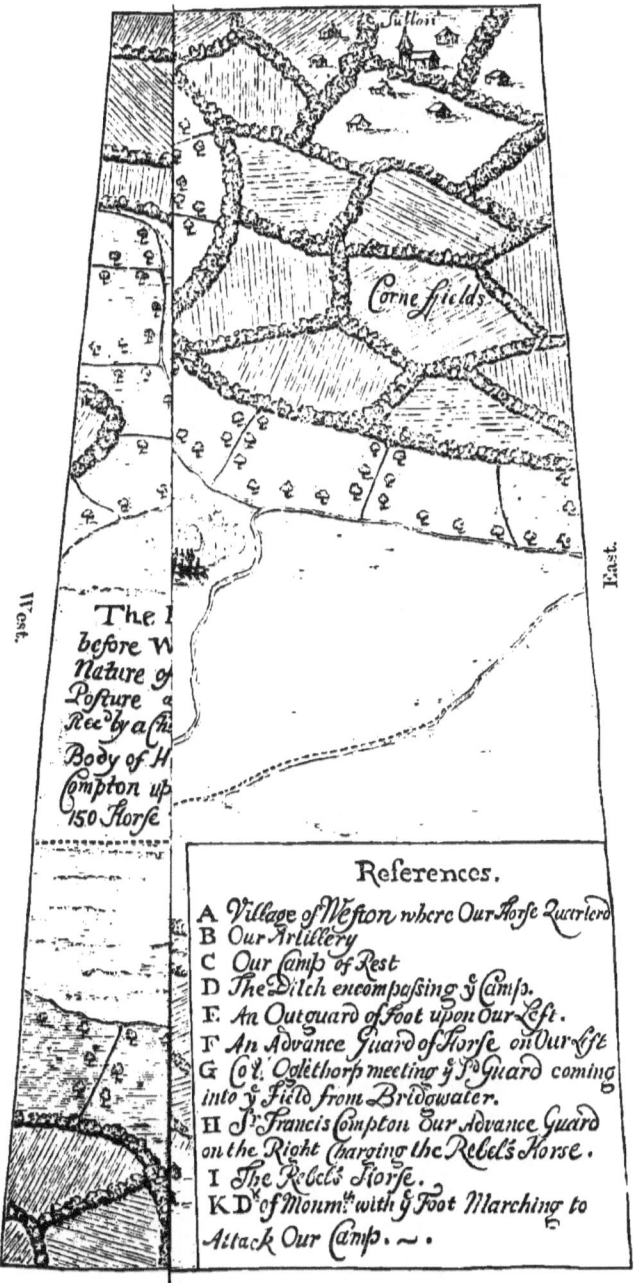

Sutton

Corne fields

West.

East.

The
before W
Nature of
Posture a
Rec^d by a
Body of H
ompton up
150 Horse

References.

A *Village of Wefton where Our Horfe Quartered*
B *Our Artillery*
C *Our Camp of Reft*
D *The Ditch encompafsing ye Camps.*
E *An Outguard of Foot upon Our Left.*
F *An Advance Guard of Horfe on Our Left*
G *Col. Oglethorp meeting y^e J^ts Guard coming into y^e Field from Bridgwater.*
H *Sr Francis Compton Our Advance Guard on the Right Charging the Rebel's Horfe.*
I *The Rebel's Horfe.*
K *D of Monm^th with y^e Foot Marching to Attack Our Camp.*

North.

The Plann of the Moore before Weston shewing the Nature of Our Encamping and Posture at the instant of Action, the 6 of July, upon the Rebels Body of Horse; by S. Francis Compton upon Our Right with his Horse & Dragoons.

SEDGE MOORE

References.
A Village of Weston where Our Colt. Retired
B Our Artillery.
C Our Body of Foot.
D The Ditch encompassing y Camp.
E An Outguard of Foot upon Our Ft.
F An Advance Guard of Horse on Our ft.
G Col. Oglethorp meeting y Guard coming out y Fuld from Bridgwater.
H S. Francis Compton Our Advance Guard on the Right Charging the Rebels Horse.
I The Rebels Horse.
K D. of Monm. with y Foot Marching to Attack Our Camp.

PLAN OF SEDGEMOOR.

Copied from Mr. E. Dummer's map in Pepysian Library, Cambridge.

and his followers, for he must in time be surrounded and cut off from help and from all supplies by an army already well provided with guns and ammunition, and receiving daily accessions of strength. He rejected that course, therefore, without further argument. The third alternative, a rapid flight, only remained for consideration, and this he determined upon. In no other way could he escape the battle he was now so anxious to avoid.

The question then was, in what direction could he most easily and profitably escape? He ultimately resolved to make for Cheshire, by way of Axbridge, Keynsham, and Gloucester. In fact, he would now carry out the project which he had already formed when he made his half-hearted and futile attempt upon Bristol. To keep his plan secret, he made believe to hold Bridgewater, openly announced his intention of fortifying it, and in order to impress the idea upon the inhabitants, made a general requisition throughout the neighbourhood for the necessary implements. He did not, however, deceive Churchill, who had long felt sure that he meant to get away into Cheshire, a belief which was now shared by the Royal army at large. On Sunday morning, with a view to put his enemy off the scent, Monmouth issued orders for a retreat upon Taunton. But when he moved his men to the Castle Field on the eastern bank of the river, and posted his waggons and guns on the Keynsham road, it was evident that Taunton was not his real object.* His secret intention was to start just after dark for Keynsham, and his waggons being in their natural position in the column of route, would facilitate the operation.

As he was crossing the town bridge to join his men in the Castle Field, he was met by a farmer named Godfrey, who had just arrived from the neighbourhood of Feversham's camp.† He came to give Monmouth information

---

* The Castle, which had been taken and destroyed by Fairfax, stood 25·7, 1645. in the town on the left or western bank of the Parret.

† The place where his father lived, near Sutton Malet, two miles north-east from Weston-Zoyland, is still called 'Godfrey's Farm.'

as to the Royalist army, and the exact position it occupied. Godfrey assured him that no efficient watch had been kept the previous night in Feversham's camp and billets, where all was drunken revelry; that no preparation was made for defence, because no one dreamed of the possibility of attack, and that even the sentries went to sleep, so universal was the belief that Monmouth's sole aim was to get away into Gloucestershire without further fighting.

Here was an opportunity for a bold night attack, the most deadly, but the most difficult of military operations. To be successful, it requires not only skilful combinations arranged beforehand, but the bravest, most confident, and best disciplined troops, directed by the most experienced staff, and led by well-trained officers. It was natural, therefore, that Monmouth should hesitate to decide upon such an operation, considering the character of the levies which he had at his disposal. They had rallied round his standard to fight 'for religion and for liberty,' but in his heart he felt that they lacked the discipline and cohesion essential for an enterprise of this sort. On the other hand, it presented the only possible way to victory. There is a strong element of chance in every battle, but it enters most largely into those fought in the dark; and this fact often commends a night attack to the commander of the weaker army, especially in circumstances so desperate as those in which Monmouth now found himself. But his resolve to adopt this course was not the result of any close or calm calculation of chances. It was rather the despair of the ruined gambler, who, worn out with a continued run of ill-luck, stakes in desperation all that remains to him upon one last throw of the dice. If he meant to fight at all, the sooner the better, for delay meant the arrival of reinforcements for the Royal army. He knew that the three English and the three Scotch regiments of Foot in the Dutch service had been recalled, and were to take the field against him.

Farmer Godfrey, anxious to make Monmouth understand thoroughly the position occupied by Feversham's army, took him up the high tower of Bridgewater Church. From that point of vantage, with the aid of a telescope, Monmouth was able to make out clearly the plan of the Royal camp. He even recognised Dumbarton's Regiment,* and a battalion of the Foot Guards in which he had formerly served, and as he laid down his glass, he said with a sigh, 'I know those regiments, and they will fight ; if I only had them I should not doubt of success.'

From the information supplied by Godfrey, and from his inspection of Feversham's position, it seemed clear to Monmouth that the Royal army lay open to a night attack. He could see that the camp faced two ways : the infantry towards the north, and the artillery towards the west, with a considerable interval between them.† The militia, he ascertained, occupied villages in the rear, beyond immediate supporting distance of the regulars in front. Feversham was so convinced of Monmouth's intention to retreat as quickly as he could, that he had evidently thought it unnecessary to entrench his well-chosen and already strong position. It was clear to him that assault upon it by day could only end in defeat, while a night attack by the rebels was a contingency that did not even occur to him. How many an army has been surprised or has suffered disaster from similar causes !

Weak men are given to oscillate between the two extremes of utter despair and absolute confidence, and Monmouth, who an hour before had been in a condition of hopeless despondency, was now in the highest spirits, carried away by Farmer Godfrey's assurance that the Royal camp could be easily surprised. Upon quitting the church tower, he exclaimed exultingly that Lord Grey's cavalry would have little difficulty in surprising the Royal Horse and the Headquarters in Weston-Zoyland. 'We shall have no more to do,' he said, 'than to lock up the stable-doors, and seize

---

* Now the Royal Scots, the oldest regiment in the army.

† This was the position General Fairfax occupied on July 7, 1645, the day after he had driven the Royal troops over Sedgemoor with great loss.

the troopers in their beds.'* He had sufficient military instinct to feel that one last great opportunity was now open to him, thanks to the carelessness and folly of his French antagonist. He summoned a council of his officers and put the question, 'Shall we attack the Royal army to-night, if we can surprise it?' All agreed, provided the enemy's Foot were not entrenched. Godfrey was accordingly sent back to Weston-Zoyland to obtain positive information on this point. He returned saying that there were no works of any description in front of the Royal camp, and upon being further questioned by Monmouth, he gave a detailed account of the disposition of the Royal army. He said that the guns, under a guard of Churchill's Dragoons,† occupied the left of the line facing west and commanding the road from Bridgewater, whilst the Infantry camp on their right, and about a quarter of a mile to the north-west of the village church, was thrown back at a right angle and faced north towards the moor. There was an interval of about 150 yards between the Infantry and Artillery camps. The road ran practically parallel to the river Parret, which protected Feversham's left. Feversham's Horse and Dragoons were, he said, billeted in Weston-Zoyland. He omitted, however, to mention the important fact, that sweeping round the northern and western sides of the position was a deep wide drain, or canal, called the 'Bussex Rhine.' Great ditches, of which this was one, traversed the moor in many directions. They had been dug in ancient times to drain the low-lying districts, and in some places, as at Weston-Zoyland, to protect the village gardens and cornfields from floods. They were locally known as 'rhines' or 'rhoynes,' and were at all seasons formidable obstacles, owing to their immense size, to their unsound banks, and deep muddy bottoms. They could only be crossed, even by single horsemen, at fords, called by the peasantry 'plungeons' or 'steanings,' and their passage by troops at night was a difficult and

* Oldmixon.   † Now the Royal Dragoons.

dangerous operation. Owing to the late heavy rains, there were several feet of water in the Bussex Rhine, which ran at a distance of about a hundred yards in front of the infantry camp. To the left of the infantry this great ditch bent back abruptly at right angles in front of the guns, and flowed close by into the river Parret.

Godfrey's omission to report the existence of the Bussex Rhine in front of the Royal army was fatal to Monmouth. To come as he did, unawares and at night, upon such a formidable obstacle with undisciplined troops, was certain to occasion confusion, if not panic. History tells us of many military operations which, though apparently well planned, have failed entirely because the scheme of attack was based upon imperfect information. The civilian spy often does not understand the relative importance of obstacles. He gets over them himself with the greatest ease, and it does not occur to him that an army will have greater difficulty. The tactical importance of a wet ditch even as big as the Bussex Rhine is incomprehensible to the peasant or farmer who has been accustomed to cross it daily at a ford or by a single plank.

In Saxon times Sedgemoor was a vast marsh, but in 1685 it was a low-lying peat moor that extended for about twelve miles in a north-westerly and south-easterly direction between the high ground near Somerton and Langport and the estuary of the river Parret, near Bridgewater. It was often flooded after heavy rains, when the river overflowed its banks. The villages stood upon small elevations some few feet above the surrounding moor, and in times of inundation looked like little crowded islands in what might then pass for an inlet of the sea. Hemmed in between the river and the Polden Hills, Sedgemoor is from four to five miles in width. A great part of it was below sea-level at high tides, and in many places it was so marshy as to be quite impassable for troops; but at the present day drainage works have converted much of this peat country into rich meadows and farm land.

Godfrey's second report overcame any opposition there may have been to the proposed night attack. The plan decided upon was to make, under the cover of darkness, a wide detour to the north-east, round Feversham's right flank, so as to avoid Chedzoy, where there was a detachment of Horse, and round any other outposts there might be in that direction, and to fall in the dark upon Feversham's right flank and rear. It was hoped that the mounted troops would be able in this way to reach and set fire to the village of Weston before any alarm could be given in the Royalist camp. Feversham's cavalry were billeted in the village, and in the confusion that such an attack was certain to cause amongst them, Monmouth's Horse were to push through it and fall upon the infantry camp in rear, whilst the rebel Foot assailed it in front. An attack if so delivered could not fail to spread panic and confusion amongst troops suddenly roused from sleep, all the deeper in their case from the heavy potations in which they were known to indulge every evening. It was assumed that the guns, which were separated from the Horse in the village, and from the Foot encamped outside it, would not be able to come into action; whilst it was hoped that Monmouth's four little field-pieces would materially help in the attack upon the camp. The plan was well conceived, and it nearly succeeded. In fact, so complete was the surprise that, had Monmouth known in advance of the Bussex Rhine and arranged accordingly, the battle of Sedgemoor might easily have had a different ending, and we might now remember as the preserver of our liberties and of Protestantism, not William of Orange, but the illegitimate son of poor Lucy Walters.

The thriving little town of Bridgewater presented an animated, picturesque scene on that Sunday afternoon. The diminutive harbour, filled with coasting craft, told of unusual commercial activity; and the narrow streets and lanes, crowded with red-coated deserters from the militia, and with rough scythemen in the homespun of the neighbouring hills, proclaimed an unwonted excitement. The clank of swords and spurs upon the rough cobble pavement, the beating of drums, and the noisy revelry of soldiers living at free quarters, resounded on all sides. The day was long remembered there for its stirring events.

During the forenoon Monmouth's move across the river to the Castle Field had caused a great stir in the town. There had been many solemn leave-takings in anticipation of the march into Cheshire ; but as soon as it was rumoured that an attack upon the enemy's camp was intended, the excitement knew no bounds. It was felt that, whatever might be each man's individual fate, the coming battle must make or mar the cause for which they had taken up arms. Hundreds of women bid good-bye to husbands, brothers, and sweethearts, and many a sobbing mother kissed for the last time her stout-limbed son. The 'God speed' spoken then was no mere conventional farewell ; it was a solemn prayer, a heartfelt aspiration for the success of what was believed to be a holy cause.

The church was thronged with earnest worshippers imploring God to bless them with victory in the coming battle. Ferguson, the chaplain to the army, preached at the castle to a huge gathering upon the text : 'The Lord God of gods, the Lord God of gods, He knoweth, and Israel he shall know ; if it be in rebellion, or if in transgression against the Lord, (save us not this day).'* Everything conspired to heighten the effect of the stream of fiery eloquence which this fanatic poured forth to a listening and excited crowd of armed enthusiasts. His burning words inflamed their earnest hearts, and they firmly believed that their God would fight for them.

In the town itself almost every coign of vantage was occupied by some Puritan preacher, who used all his oratorical power to excite his hearers, and to urge them to fight manfully for what was pronounced to be the cause of God and of the Covenant ; but these preachers made no

* Joshua xxii. 22.

allusion to the fact that all were expected to fight for King
Monmouth, who claimed to reign as the grandson of him
whom they had beheaded. They only called upon the
people to be stout of heart, and to fight for the Lord of
Hosts and for the Protestant cause.

Monmouth's force, consisting of Lord Grey's Horse and
five battalions of Foot, numbered 3,500 men in all.* They
were undrilled to the use of arms, badly officered, and
entirely undisciplined. Grey's troopers were mounted upon
young unbroken horses, which had recently been taken from
the marsh lands, where they were reared. The four small
field-pieces were in charge of a Dutch gunner. Attached
to each battalion were about a hundred scythemen, who
acted as a sort of specially favoured company. Unfortunately for Monmouth, the day before, when he had no
intention to fight, he had sent two of his best troops of
Horse to Minehead, about twenty-six miles west of Bridgewater, to collect horses, and to bring in some six guns
known to be there. It is difficult to state the number
who actually took part in the battle, for many had deserted
at Frome and during the retreat from that place to Bridgewater. Besides, owing to the difficulty of night movements
in confined lanes and over roadless moors, many of those
who marched that evening from Bridgewater lost their way
in the dark, and took no part in the battle. Lord Grey's
lack of courage was so notorious that Monmouth was urged
to divide his horse into two bodies, so that, if one ran away,

---

* Wade's confession in Harl. MSS. in Hardwick Papers. The detail
was as follows :   MEN.

A small mounted body-guard of about		-	-	-	40
Lord Grey's Horse	-	-	-	-	600
Monmouth's, or the Red Regt., commanded by Col. Wade	-	800
Monmouth's White Regt., commanded by Col. Foulkes		-	400
Monmouth's Blue Regiment, commanded by Colonel Basset	-	600
Monmouth's Yellow Regt., commanded by Col. Matthews	-	500
Monmouth's Green Regt., commanded by Col. Holmes		-	600
A company of Foot from Lyme Regis	-	-	-	80
	Total	-	-	-	3,620

the other might still accomplish the important part which
the mounted men were expected to play in the attack; but
he did not dare to act on this sensible advice through dread
of offending his solitary well-born follower.

Feversham's army consisted of some troops of Household Cavalry, one regiment of Dragoons, six battalions of
Foot, and sixteen guns, about 2,800 men in all, not
counting officers, or the men who served the guns, or the
1,500 militia, which took no part in the battle.*

* The detail of the Royal army is as follows: 150 men selected from
the three troops of Life Guards and 60 Horse Grenadiers under Lord
Churchill's friend and connection, Lieut.-Colonel the Hon. F. Villiers;
seven troops (about 400 men) of the King's Regiment of Horse, now
the Royal Horse Guards Blue, under Sir Francis Compton, who was
also as senior cavalry officer in command of the Horse; three troops
of Churchill's Dragoons, now the Royal Dragoons, under Lord Cornbury (about 150 men): the fourth troop of this regiment was eight
miles off at Langport, watching that passage over the Parret which
was unfordable between it and Bridgewater. The Foot consisted of
six battalions encamped in the following order from right to left: Five
companies of the Royal Regiment, then known as Dumbarton's,
now the Royal Scots, under Lieut.-Colonel Douglas: one of these
was a grenadier company; seven companies, of which one was the
grenadier company, of the first battalion of the King's Guards, now
the Grenadier Guards, under the Duke of Grafton; six companies of
the second battalion of the same regiment under Major Eaton; six
companies of the 2nd Regiment of Guards, now the Coldstream
Guards, under Lieut.-Colonel Sackville; five companies of the Queen
Dowager's Regiment, now the Queen's or West Surrey Regiment,
under Colonel Kirke: it was on the extreme left, and rested on the
road from Bridgewater, which crossed the Bussex Rhine close by;
five companies, of which one was the grenadier company, of the
Queen's, previously known as the Duchess of York and Albany's
Regiment, now the King's Own or Royal Lancaster Regiment:
it was then commonly known as Trelawney's Regiment, and was
commanded by Lieut.-Colonel Charles Churchill. There were besides
several militia regiments (about 1,500 in all) distributed in the villages
of Middlezoy and Othery, two or three miles behind the position on
the moor. They could not, however, be trusted in action, as by the
number who had deserted to Monmouth and other signs they showed
an unmistakable sympathy with the rebel cause. The total strength
of the Royal army was fourteen troops of Horse and Dragoons, or
about 700 men, and thirty-four companies of Foot, or about 2,100

The Castle Field, where Monmouth's little army mustered, was three miles by the direct road, or, for so small a column moving at night, say an hour and a quarter's march from Feversham's position. But by the circuitous route actually followed, the distance was over five and a half miles, and the last two led over the roadless and difficult moor. In point of time, the march occupied about two and a half hours. Before starting, Monmouth received information that many of the Royal troopers in the village had already gone to bed drunk, and that in the camp the Foot soldiers had had more than enough of the country cider.

men. The artillery consisted of sixteen guns, each piece manned by one gunner and one matross, and supplied with forty round shot and fifteen case. It was under the immediate command of Mr. Shere, who was helped during the battle by Dr. Mews, the soldier Bishop of Winchester, commonly called 'Old Patch.' His portrait hangs in Farnham Castle, and shows the patch on his cheek from which he gained his nickname. A Fellow of St. John's, Oxford, in 1637, he was ejected by the Roundheads, and became a soldier in Holland, where he received the wound in his cheek, over which he always wore a patch. Returning to England at the Restoration, he was made Bishop of Bath and Wells, 1672, and translated to Winchester, 1684. This is very much the history of Henry Compton, Bishop of London; of Dolben, Archbishop of York; of W. Bew, Bishop of Llandaff; of J. Lake, Bishop of Chichester; of Crighton, Bishop of Bath and Wells; of John Fell, Bishop of Oxford; and of some others who sheathed their swords to enter the Church. Under the engraved portrait of Dr. Mews is printed, ' P. Mews, qui pugnavit et oravit pro pace regni et ecclesiæ.' I conclude the verbs are placed in this order as an insinuation that he esteemed fighting above devotion. It was said of him that he was ' fitter for a Bombardier than a Bishop.' For his services at Sedgemoor he received from the King a medal, which is represented in the above-mentioned picture. He once came near being hanged by the Cromwellians. This was the last occasion upon which a prelate took the field in England, though Bishop Walker was killed in Ireland five years later, and Bishop Polk fell in 1864 in command of a Confederate Army Corps. Shere was a man of science, and well skilled in gunnery. He had translated Polybius into English. King James knighted him for his services upon this occasion. The sixteen guns were made up of two 12-pounders, nine demi-culverins, four 6-pounders, four sakers and two minions. See letter from Duke of Somerset. p. 6 of Ninth Report of Historical MSS.

His spirits rose on hearing this, and he began to imagine that the enemy were already at his mercy. The circumstances were most favourable, and he naturally felt that, if his soldiers did not fail him, he had a good chance of success.

Monmouth's own regiment, under Wade, formed the advanced guard of the daring little army as it moved off from the Castle Field at 11 p.m., closely followed by the other regiments of Foot, the Horse under Lord Grey coming next, and the four small field-guns bringing up the rear. The strictest silence was enjoined, and peremptory orders were issued that no shot should be fired until they were actually in the enemy's camp. The 'countersign,' by means of which they were to recognise one another in the dark, was 'Monmouth, and God with us.' *

The full July moon had risen shortly after eight o'clock, and was near the meridian as the rebel army filed silently along the Eastern Causeway, as that part of the Bristol road was then called. The direction of the march was north-easterly for about two miles to the junction of Bradley Lane with the Bristol road. There Monmouth halted to allow the Horse to get to the front before entering on the open moor. The track followed under the guidance of Farmer Godfrey is still known as 'War Lane.' †

In the narrow lanes, before the column emerged upon the open moor, the movements were much retarded through the difficulty of keeping the undrilled troops in anything like military order. Before turning from these lanes to cross North Moor, Monmouth parked his forty-two baggage-waggons, under a small guard, at Peasy Farm. The tracks over the moor would certainly be impassable for

---

* In Clarke's 'Life of James II.' it is stated that Monmouth's 'countersign' was 'Soho.' He quotes 'Pennant's London' as his authority for the statement that 'Soho Square' had been previously known as 'Monmouth Square,' and that the new title was adopted because it had been the rebel countersign that night. Monmouth lived in the centre house of the Square, which faces the statue.

† Roberts' 'History of Monmouth.'

laden carriages by night, and besides, this arrangement rendered his column more easy to handle. For some unknown reason, he also left one of his four field-guns there. The night was still, but a heavy mist had risen, which, hanging over the low-lying moorlands round Chedzoy and Sutton, and between those villages and Weston-Zoyland, made it difficult for sentries and vedettes to see any distance. Lord Feversham had ascertained from spies that Monmouth had moved his men in the course of the afternoon from their billets in Bridgewater to the Castle Field, and that arrangements had been made for a march to Bristol that night. It was desirable to ascertain what road Monmouth should take, although there was no intention of pursuing him until next morning. Late in the evening, Feversham accordingly sent out Colonel Oglethorpe in command of the third troop of Life Guards, with orders to watch Monmouth's movements.* He was to push forward to the north-east of Bridgewater, and to cross the two roads leading from it to Bristol and Keynsham.

Feversham's men and horses were tired and somewhat used up by their recent marches and counter-marches over bad roads in most inclement weather. He consequently wished to spare them a night pursuit of what he believed to be a flying enemy, thinking that his troops, after a good night's rest, would next day be in a better condition to overtake them. His other dispositions for the protection of the camp were; a detachment of the Royal Dragoons at the bridge over the Parret in Langport; another of one hundred Horse and fifty Dragoons under Sir Francis Compton in Chedzoy, to watch the right front,

---

* Oglethorpe was one of James's most faithful followers. Colonel of the Holland Regiment at the Revolution, he resigned, and the regiment was given to Charles Churchill, Marlborough's brother, who retained it until 1707, when he was transferred to the Coldstream Guards. After Oglethorpe's death, it was sought by Mrs. F. Shaftoe to prove that the Pretender was the child of Sir Theophilus and Lady Oglethorpe.

the path which led by that village into Bridgewater, and the one to the east of it along which the rebel column eventually advanced; an outpost of forty Horse on the direct road to Bridgewater, with orders to patrol to its front and to watch the left flank of the Royal position; and still further towards that flank and about 350 yards to the west of Feversham's guns there was a piquet of fifty musketeers in a sort of walled sheepfold known as Penzoy Pound, upon which the cavalry posts and detachments protecting the left were to retire if attacked.* One hundred of Dumbarton's regiment were kept under arms all night as an inlying piquet.† Feversham himself remained at Chedzoy until late waiting for Oglethorpe's return, and in the belief that, if the enemy moved, he should be able to hear them from that village, as the night was still. A messenger from Oglethorpe's party reached him about midnight with a report that nothing had been seen of the enemy. As quiet seemed to reign on all sides, Feversham returned to his quarters, undressed, and went to bed. He has been commonly blamed for allowing himself to be surprised that night, and the commander is very properly always held responsible for any such disaster. But it must be admitted that the dispositions he made would have protected him against surprise had Compton and Oglethorpe known their work and done it properly. Feversham's fault was not, I think, so much an unskilful disposition of his piquets and outposts as the fact that he went to bed in ignorance of his enemy's doings and intentions. All through this short campaign there were traitors in both camps who supplied the opposite side with information. Yet Feversham never seems to have known what his enemy was doing, or where he was going, a fact which of itself proves that he did not know his business. Had he

* Mrs. Stopford Sackville's Papers, Ninth Report, p. 4, Historical MSS. The sheepfold is marked E on the accompanying sketch of the position.

† Cannon's 'History of the Royal Scots.'

been a competent commander, Monmouth could not have moved from Bridgewater that night without his knowledge. Before he assumed command, Churchill, with only a small body of cavalry at his disposal, had hung upon the rebel army so closely that it could go nowhere, and neither do nor plan anything of which he was not fully aware. He harassed it night and day, cutting off stragglers, and preventing many from joining Monmouth who would otherwise have done so. But Feversham, with a stronger and much better army than the rebels could muster, always suffered Monmouth to take the initiative, and to do and go where he pleased, whilst the Royal army merely blundered after them.* For the disgraceful condition of things in the Royal camp Feversham must also be held responsible, and consequently for the fact that he was taken unawares. Upon the night in question there would seem to have been but few sentries or vedettes posted anywhere, and report says that most of those few had fallen into a drunken sleep.

Oglethorpe carried out his orders most negligently. Instead of being rewarded as he was for his services at Sedgemoor, he ought to have been dismissed the army for incompetence and carelessness. Although he crossed both the roads he was ordered to examine, he could not have pushed the smallest patrol along either in the direction of Bridgewater, for had he done this he could easily have ascertained what Monmouth was about. With the most culpable neglect of duty, he returned to Chedzoy without having seen or heard anything of an enemy at that moment on the march and close to him. Passing through Chedzoy, he made for the Weston and Bridgewater road or track, and upon reaching it turned westward towards the enemy, until within half a mile of Bridgewater. Sending forward a patrol of four men to the gates of the place, he ascertained what he might have discovered long before—that Monmouth had left the town by the Bristol Road. This news startled

---

* Including the militia, the Royal army was much stronger than the rebels.

him somewhat, and he hastened off to inform Feversham, but he was too late; Monmouth had begun the attack before he reached even the cavalry piquet on the Bridgewater-Weston track. As he approached that outpost the firing had already begun on Feversham's right, and all was confusion in the Royal camp, especially in the village of Weston, where the Horse were billeted.

In the meantime, whilst Oglethorpe was careering uselessly over the country in search of the rebel army, Monmouth, after a short halt at Peasy Farm to park his waggons and reform the column of route, struck out into the thick mist in a south-easterly direction by a track which led to Weston-Zoyland across the bleak North Moor. He purposely made a wide sweep eastward to avoid the enemy's cavalry outpost in Chedzoy. The track he followed passed about midway between it and the high ground on which Sutton Mallet stands. Anyone who has led a column into action by night over a flat, roadless country along a track which can only be followed with difficulty in the dark, will understand the trying nature of the task imposed upon Farmer Godfrey. Some of the accounts dwell upon his confusion, but it was most natural that he should be perplexed under the circumstances, although he knew the locality thoroughly well by daylight.

The track crossed two great ditches before reaching the Bussex Rhine. Over the first, known as the Black Ditch, which traversed the North Moor, Godfrey led the column successfully by the ford, or steaning, near Parchy. The troops reformed in two columns to the south of the ditch, the Horse on the left, the Foot on the right, and advanced in that formation to the next great ditch, called the Langmoor Rhine. In his anxiety to give a wide berth to the Royal Horse in Chedzoy, Godfrey had led somewhat too much to the eastward, and, puzzled by the fog, he missed the ford. There was consequently much delay and difficulty in getting over this second rhine, deep as it was with mud and water. Many horses were bogged, and a number of men, in their endeavours to find a crossing-place, strayed far from the beaten track, lost their way, and were seen no more. The passage was at last effected about a mile north of the Royal camp, and the clock in Chedzoy steeple struck one as the rebels began to reform south of this second ditch. A short halt was made to enable the Foot to form up whilst the Horse pushed well ahead. Up to this moment Feversham and all his host lay fast asleep, ignorant of the storm which was about to burst upon them. Feversham's dispositions upon this occasion afford a good illustration of how it is that disasters are brought about, whilst those of Monmouth show how great is the advantage gained by cleverly-spread false information as to your intentions. The General who has thoroughly deceived his enemy has already half beaten him.

After a short halt, Monmouth again put his column in motion, no orders being given in tones above a whisper. Anyone making a noise was to be at once stabbed by his nearest comrade, a necessary precaution upon such an occasion.* The solemn silence of a night-march near the enemy is awe-inspiring in itself, but in the weirdness of that lonely moor every circumstance contributed to make it exceptionally impressive.

As soon as Lord Grey's Horse began to advance south of the Langmoor Rhine, it was discovered by a vedette of the Life Guards, who, firing his pistol, galloped towards the infantry camp, calling upon everyone to turn out, as the rebels were upon them.† Monmouth, finding his presence

---

* Historical MSS., Rutland Papers, vol. ii., p. 90. This is stated on good authority by Charles Bertie in a letter to his niece, Lady Rutland.

† The Rev. Robert Ferguson (the 'Plotter') was with the Horse at this moment, and asserts that the alarm was given by a traitor, Captain Hucker, of Lord Grey's Horse. But his narrative is untrustworthy, and I think the version given here is more correct, although Dalrymple asserts that when Hucker was tried by Jeffreys he pleaded his treachery to Monmouth upon this occasion in mitigation of his crime. Dalrymple, vol. i., Part I., Book II., p. 200.

thus discovered, ordered Grey to push forward as quickly as possible into Weston, and set fire to it as originally intended. This, it was anticipated, would throw the Royal Horse into utter confusion, in the midst of which Grey might take the Foot in rear, whilst Monmouth attacked it in front.

As the shouts of alarm rose over the dreary waste of fog-covered moor, all was soon confusion in the village and in the adjoining camp. Troopers, half asleep and still stupid from the previous night's debauch, mounted in hot haste, or rushed noisily about their billets in search of horse, arms, or breastplate. Though the full moon was still high, the thick mist rendered it difficult to distinguish objects only a few yards distant. Saddles could not be found, bridles were missing, and turmoil and disorder reigned supreme. The surprise was complete; but an immediate attack, boldly delivered and pushed home, could alone convert it into a victory, and Lord Grey was not the man to make it. All the advantages upon which Monmouth had justly calculated from an unexpected attack were thrown away and lost through the cowardice of this man. There is a critical moment in every surprise, which, if seized upon and properly utilized by the attacking party, leads almost certainly to victory; whereas, if neglected, another chance seldom presents itself. When Grey had crossed the Langmoor Rhine, he dismissed Godfrey, not knowing that there was still one more great ditch, the Bussex Rhine, between him and Weston. The Horse unluckily made for the camp rather than for the village, and so missed the usual crossing-place. It may have been that Grey mistook the lighted matches of Dumbarton's regiment, which shone feebly through the mist in front of him, for the lights of the village. Finding himself thus brought to a standstill by this unexpected obstacle, he unfortunately turned to his right—westwards—instead of to his left. The result was that he soon found himself opposite the infantry camp, alive with men 'falling in' for a night alarm.

Had Grey been a true soldier, he would certainly have turned up, not down, the canal-like ditch to look for a ford, especially as the more he worked to his left the more he would have turned his enemy's flank. Meanwhile, some of the rebel Horse that had strayed away to the eastward, under Lieutenant Jones, had a little skirmishing with Compton's Life Guards, who now came trooping in from Chedzoy to defend the village ford across the Bussex Rhine.

Lord Grey found himself facing Dumbarton's regiment, which was on the extreme right of the line. The officers of this battalion, of greater experience in war than those of the other regiments, were somewhat more on the alert. As it was the only regiment present which still retained the matchlock, the others being armed with the newly introduced snaphaunce or flint musket, Grey was able to mark its position by the burning matches.*

Whilst he was trying to cross the Bussex Rhine, Monmouth, close behind, was pressing forward with the Foot, his three little iron field-guns being at the head of the column. It is not known at what point in his advance Monmouth became aware of the formidable ditch which protected the front and right flank of Feversham's position. King James states, in his account of the battle, that Monmouth knew nothing of the Bussex Rhine until he came upon it with his Foot. Godfrey accompanied the Horse, and there may not have been anyone with Monmouth who knew the locality well. Besides, a guide taken from the local peasantry might not have thought it worth while to mention such a ditch, through ignorance of its military importance and of its bearing upon the approaching battle.

Monmouth, pike in hand, began to form for attack when within about eighty paces of the Rhine, his men much out

---

* Whilst matchlocks were in use it was no uncommon ruse at night to impress your enemy with an exaggerated notion of your strength by placing lines of sticks, with burning slow matches attached to them, in front of a position to be defended.

of breath from the quickness of the pace at which he had led them forward. The strictest injunctions were given against firing without orders, and the five little battalions had just begun to advance when their panic-stricken Horse came flying back past them. It would seem, that when trying to cross the ditch in front of them, they were challenged by Dumbarton's regiment and a battalion of the Foot Guards from the opposite side. 'Who are you for?' 'The King.' 'What King?' 'Monmouth, and God with us,' was the prompt answer. 'Take this with you, then,' was the reply, as the battalions poured a volley upon the startled troopers. Several saddles were emptied, and the untrained marsh mares upon which the rebels were almost exclusively mounted, taking fright, rushed madly to the rear. This incident had an extremely unfortunate effect upon the courage and confidence of the Foot, and rendered them unsteady at the very moment when they needed all their nerve and spirit. It demoralized them in an instant, and the alarm extended quickly on all sides. In the rear, numbers of stragglers, who had lost their way in the dark and were now pressing eagerly forward upon meeting the flying cavalry, joined in the stampede under the impression that all was lost. The panic was thus communicated to the drivers of the baggage and ammunition waggons left at Peasy Farm, and they at once made off for their homes at Ware and Axbridge.* Such is the infectious nature of a scare, especially at night. Lord Grey seems to have joined in the flight, and to have done nothing to stay it. Monmouth's servant, Williams, who was taken prisoner, stated that he had heard his master say, whilst the fighting was going on, that it was Grey's cowardice which had lost the battle.

The General in command was comfortably in bed when

---

* Mrs. Stopford Sackville's Papers, Ninth Report, Historical MSS., p. 5. These drivers, the one gun left behind by Monmouth, and all his baggage and ammunition, were captured at Axbridge the following day.

the alarm sounded.   Not so Churchill, who ever since Feversham had joined hands with him had striven by his own vigilance and energy to neutralize the Commander-in-Chief's military incapacity and want of forethought. The instant the alarm was given, Churchill ran to the camp, and putting himself at the head of Dumbarton's regiment, formed it to the front along the southern bank of the Bussex Rhine, where it opened fire upon Grey's cavalry, as already described, checked the advancing rebel infantry and gave time to the rest of Feversham's army to assume a fighting formation.

It had been Monmouth's intention to wait for the firing of the village by the Horse, before he finally advanced with his infantry upon the Royal camp.   But when, during the cruel moments of waiting and expectancy, he saw, to his horror and dismay, Grey's troopers gallop wildly past him in hopeless flight, he felt that the original plan was no longer practicable.   A daring, determined and rapid advance with his Foot upon the camp might yet have won the day.   The Royal army was in confusion and still under the influence of that panic and demoralization which invariably seizes upon soldiers when attacked without warning in the dead of night.   The best troops often waver under such conditions, and if the assailant has but the heart and the necessary cohesion to drive home his attack—being near enough to do so—before the enemy has time to recover from his first surprise, he can generally count on victory.   Monmouth felt this, and hurried forward his Foot, directing his advance upon the burning matches of Dumbarton's regiment.   But untrained rustics, whose nerves were already shaken by the flying cavalry, could not be induced to keep their ranks or maintain order ; the battalions soon became mixed and then unmanageable. Wade's regiment was the first to reach the ditch and to reform preparatory to crossing.   It had not fired a shot as yet, but the next battalion, commanded by Colonel Matthews, at once opened fire.   That strange, heart-beating sensation,

that hush of expectancy which precedes the first outburst of infantry fire in many actions, especially at night,
was now over. But in this instance the firing put an end
to all order and obedience in Monmouth's ranks. Even
with regular troops it is most difficult to stop firing begun
at night under such circumstances; and the worst of it
is, that it generally spreads with a lightning rapidity that
taxes the powers of even the most experienced officers to
restrain. In this instance the bad example was followed by
the other regiments, and the fusillade so opened was the
beginning of the end, the death-knell in fact of Monmouth's
rebellion. The aim was wild, and far too high to harm the
Royal troops.* Regiments which have made a bad beginning
of this kind can seldom be induced to charge, and after about
an hour and a half of heavy but useless fire, a cry arose
for more ammunition. There was none to be had, the only
reserve having been left with the baggage at Peasy Farm,
some two and a half miles off. The three rebel guns had
come into action on the left of their Foot, and, directed by
the Dutch gunner in charge of them, did considerable execution in the closed ranks of Dumbarton's and the Guards'
regiments. But it soon became evident that it was a lost
battle for the rebels, and that all the advantages which a
night surprise gives the assailant were lost, owing to the
untimely fire of the Foot. The untrained levies were not
equal to the task which Monmouth had laid upon them.

On the Royalist side Dumbarton's regiment alone fired ;
the other regiments received the enemy's fire with great
steadiness without replying.† During the anxious hour and

---

* Letter from Phineas Pett, Carte MS. 72, folio 611, Bodleian Library.

† I have mainly followed the details given of this action by King
James, by Wade, and by Ferguson. James's account is clear, because
he learned all the occurrences from the chief actors, and visited the
scene of the battle in August the following year, as appears from the
churchwardens' accounts at Weston-Zoyland. 'The great Duke of
Wellington told Sir Walter Scott that "the most distinct writer on
military affairs he had ever read was James II."'—Sir W. Scott's
Letters, vol. ii., p. 77.

a half which followed upon the first alarm, and while the dandy Feversham was making his toilet before a tiny looking-glass, Churchill made his presence felt throughout the Royal army.* He perceived at a glance how necessary it was to have guns in action on the right, where the enemy was pressing most seriously. But the artillery had been placed in a position where they were now of no use, for they had no enemy in front of them, and they could not be brought to bear upon the rebel flank attack. He ordered some guns to be moved into line with the infantry, but this was not easily done. The recent rains had made the marshy soil deep and heavy, and darkness added to the difficulty of the operation. At this critical time the Bishop of Winchester, 'Old Patch,' came to the Master-Gunner's rescue with his carriage horses and helped to bring the guns into action.† They opened at a critical moment, when the three little field-pieces of the rebels were making havoc at short range in the Royal ranks. To support his artillery and to reinforce the right of the Royal army, now heavily engaged, Churchill next brought the Queen's and the Queen Dowager's regiments‡ from the left of the line along the rear of the four battalions already in action, and deployed them on the right of the line. It was now about 3 o'clock a.m., and the first glimmer of dawn began to show itself in the dull and blotted sky, heavy with the wetting mist which still hung over the moorland.

Seeing how steady the Royalist regiments of Foot had become, and perceiving that the enemy's fire had somewhat slackened, Churchill led a troop of his own Dragoons across the Bussex Rhine. The first thing he saw in the gray dawn was a wounded officer, whom he hailed with, ' Who art thou?' It was Holmes, the rebel Colonel, whose

---

* Oldmixon.

† A royal warrant of 26, 2, 1685, directs the payment of £40 to a Sergeant Weems · for good service in the action of Sedgemoor in firing the great guns against the rebels.'

‡ We find that four men of the latter received ten marks (£6 13s. 4d.) each as compensation for wounds received in this battle.

regiment had, early in the action, fired into the Royal
Dragoons when Churchill had formed them up on the right
of the Foot. To save them from this fire, an officer called
out in the dark, 'Don't fire, we are friends.' Holmes,
believing this, rode forward to the edge of the ditch, and
being challenged as to whom 'he was for,' answered,
'Monmouth.' The immediate reply was a volley which
wounded him badly and killed his horse. Happy had it
been for him had it killed him also, and so saved him from
the gallows.*

Churchill, having formed up his Dragoons beyond the
Rhine, charged the rebel guns, and killed or drove off those
who served them. Most of the Royal cavalry were still
behind the Bussex Ditch on the right of the Foot. But as
it grew lighter they also crossed and had some partial
encounters with the rebels. Oglethorpe ventured a charge
upon one of Monmouth's battalions, but was repulsed with
loss, and Sarsfield, who also charged with like result, was
unhorsed and left for dead on the field. Feversham would
not allow the main body of his cavalry to pass the Rhine
until it was light enough to clearly distinguish friend from
foe, but some of the Foot, seeing Churchill drive off the
rebel gunners, crossed and took possession of Monmouth's
three field-pieces.

Slowly the stars died out in the cold flush of dawn, and
still the battle raged, but in the growing light both sides
began to realize that Monmouth was defeated. When at
last day broke with that cold, pitiless light which
immediately precedes sunrise, crowds of the poor beaten
rebels could be seen streaming back towards Bridgewater.
Lord Grey's cavalry had disappeared, but a fierce fight still
raged on the fatal banks of the Bussex Rhine. There the
bulk of Wade's and of another rebel battalion still clung
undaunted, and, using their scythes and mining tools,

---

* Colonel Abraham Holmes was a religious zealot, and had been a
hard-fighting Cromwellian officer. He lost his arm in this battle, and
before even the stump was healed Jeffreys hanged him.

fought as only desperate men will fight in a religious cause.* They found themselves deserted by their comrades and by the Horse that should have protected their flanks, hard pressed as they were by the Life Guards and Churchill's Dragoons. This hopeless but gallant struggle was brought to an end at last by a determined attack of the grenadier companies of the Guards and Dumbarton's regiment. About three hundred of Monmouth's bravest followers fell in that charge, dying for an unworthy leader in what they believed to be a holy cause.†

Colonel Wade, with some two hundred of his men, now made for the fence behind him which divided the tillage from the moorland, and there about a hundred and fifty found temporary shelter. Most of these subsequently escaped to Bridgewater, where a few hundred other fugitives had already collected, together with three troops of the rebel Horse who had run away early in the battle without striking a blow. The moon set that morning at about 4 o'clock, and the sun rose upon a horrible scene where Englishmen met Englishmen in internecine strife.

Lord Grey had accompanied his Horse in their flight for some time, but eventually rejoined Monmouth about daybreak. Churchill and the Royal Horse had already crossed the Bussex Rhine, and it was evident that as soon as the light should enable the Royal cavalry to move freely over the moor, all chance of escape for the rebel leaders would be at an end. Grey, loath to die, urged this upon Monmouth. The day, he said, was irretrievably lost, and it was high time for them to think of their own safety. What a heart-breaking moment for the commander of men whom he had led to destruction! In the gray light of early dawn, Monmouth could see his gallant followers

---

* Evelyn's Diary of 8, 7, 1685.

† The French Ambassador, Barillon, in his despatch describing Sedgemoor, writes in high terms of the manner in which Monmouth's Foot had fought, and of the difficulty with which it was eventually broken by the Royal troops.

being hacked to pieces, slain in a struggle to place the crown upon his head. The proud gentleman, the brave high-mettled soldier, would have spurned Grey's craven advice, and would have elected to fall amidst those who were dying for him. But Monmouth was moved by no such manly impulse. In defeat, as in all moments of gloom, he evinced a contemptible lack of courage. It was not so much a fear of death as an unworthy love of life that moved him. For life he was prepared to sacrifice honour and all that makes life worth living. His decision, therefore, was quickly arrived at. Divesting himself of breast and back pieces, he galloped from the field with Grey and about fifty mounted men. He halted for a moment on the top of the Polden Range, and looked back. The firing still continued, and he could hear the loud turmoil of the battle, and amidst the smoke and purple mist of morning could even see the poor but stout-hearted peasants still fighting for the leader who had ignominiously deserted them.

The battle of Sedgemoor was lost chiefly through the bad handling and the misconduct of Grey's untrained Horse and the cowardice of its leader. Bold in council, he lacked the nerve to execute what his reason told him he ought to do. In safety he made skilful plans, but he had not the nerve to carry them out in the midst of danger. The din of battle seemed to paralyze his reasoning powers. He possessed the will, but lacked the resolute heart which can alone enable a man to reason and think when the very air seems filled with bullets and the busy sound of death. Had Grey pushed boldly forward into Weston-Zoyland at first, and set fire to the village as it was settled he should do, the Royal Horse would, I believe, have dispersed in panic. They could not have been collected again that day for any effective work; and there can be little doubt that the scare would have spread amongst the Foot with lightning rapidity. Darkness carries with it an undefinable terror, and most men, when suddenly roused from sleep, are strangely subject to a wild and unreasoning fright, which runs like an electric current through the ranks of a surprised army, and there is no predicting where it will stop. In the twinkling of an eye, a division may thus become a mad mob, dangerous only to itself, and an easy prey to any enemy who charges home. The appalling hum of alarm, the first symptom of panic, amongst troops at night, once heard, can never be forgotten; it haunts you always. It is the crisis of an instant, and the manner in which it is dealt with is a high test of the leader's nerve and force of character. Had Lord Grey known what a night panic meant, he would, the moment the alarm was given, have crossed the Bussex Rhine with all haste and boldly charged. Throughout this short campaign Grey had persisted in dealing with his raw levies, as if they had been regular troops. He checked and restrained their undisciplined ardour, and so robbed them of their best characteristic—their one good fighting quality—without being able to give them as a substitute any of the useful attributes of regular soldiers.

A merciless pursuit of the broken rebels now began, in which Dumbarton's regiment led the way, capturing Monmouth's standard with its gold-embroidered motto of 'Fear none but God.' Pressed by Lyttelton's troop of Horse, many of the fugitives made for the cornfields and inclosed ground which stretched away behind them. In this flight they lost about a thousand men. 'Our men are still killing them in yᵉ corne and hedges and ditches whither they are crept,' wrote a correspondent on the spot.*

The traveller can obtain a good view of the field of Sedgemoor if he mounts the high and fine old square tower of St. Mary's Church in Weston-Zoyland. The mower now whets his scythe where all was marsh and moorland in 1685. The rushes and the heather have

---

* This is said in the P.S. to a letter from Phineas Pett to the Duke of Ormond's secretary. It is dated Weston-Zoyland, July 6, 1685, seven in the morning. Carte MS. 72. folio 611, Bodleian Library.

disappeared, and a splendid pasturage, divided into wide rectangular fields, has taken their place. As the eye wanders over the pretty gardens which now surround the village and the well-stocked grass-land beyond, it is difficult to picture this quiet English landscape as it was two centuries ago, the scene of bloodshed, and filled with the din of contending armies. The jackdaw from the church tower close by now seeks its food on the gentle undulations, once big mounds, the guide says, where the dead were buried near that old Bussex Rhine which saved the Royal army from destruction. Glastonbury seems near at hand, and to the north are the Polden Hills, from which Monmouth, in his ignoble flight, caught a last glimpse of the battle. Chedzoy village, clustering round its church, is to the right as you look towards Bridgewater and over the intervening green meadows; the stillness of peace is broken only by the tinkling of cow-bells. The old, irregular ditches have given place to straight, wide drains, whose sedgy margins are here and there lined with pollarded willows, or withies, as they are locally called. There is only one old house remaining in Zoyland, but the church stands there, the monument of many centuries, the record of many changes, and the silent witness of many stirring events. On no Sunday, however, has its finely carved oak roof ever sheltered such a crowd of men as on the afternoon of the battle. It was no congregation met to honour God or to pray for mercy. It consisted of about 500 peasants who had been taken prisoners while fighting for their religion, and for him whom they regarded as its representative. Many were wounded, some were dying. There were no surgeons to dress their wounds, no friends to comfort them, and nothing to alleviate their suffering. The surrounding farmers, now only bent on propitiating the victors, brought barrels of ale and cider to the King's soldiers, but sent nothing to their imprisoned friends. The wounded and the dying of the defeated side are apt to fare badly; but here, though in the midst of sympathizing friends and countrymen, no man dared to give them even water or show them pity, lest he too should be included in the general condemnation.

As the setting sun that evening threw lengthened shadows from bush and mound across the dreary moorland, nearly every tree by the roadside had swinging from its branches the body of some poor weaver or Mendip miner. Happy, indeed, were those who had died like men that morning, fighting hard upon the banks of the fatal Bussex Rhine. The sun had never shone throughout a day of more wicked, more cruel butchery.

And so ended this battle in which well-armed British regulars, led by English gentlemen, slaughtered a mob of stout English peasants led by tradesmen and commanded by the illegitimate son of a King. It was the end of a rebellion in which some thousands of good West-Country folk were either killed in action or butchered by order of the King with all the apparent formality of the law, or sent to die as slaves in a deadly climate, contrary to the recognised customs of war and to the established rights of English freemen.

This, the last battle fought in England, was fought to secure James his crown. If through the folly and parsimony of our people we should ever see another, it will be fought in defence of London. The struggle will be, not for a dynasty, but for our own very existence as an independent nation. Are we prepared to meet it? The politician says Yes; the soldier and the sailor say No.

CHAPTER XL.

THE BLOODY ASSIZE.

Churchill's pursuit of the rebels—Monmouth captured—Marlborough returns to London—Judge Jeffreys—James's hardness of heart.

THE battle over, to push forward into Bridgewater with some 500 Horse and as many Foot was Lord Churchill's first care. He found the place deserted. To announce their 'nocturnal victory'[*] to the King, he sent an express which apparently reached Whitehall before any despatch from Feversham.

All next day the King's troops searched the neighbourhood and butchered the helpless fugitives, whom they found hiding in swamps and woods and ditches. Lord Feversham himself set an example of barbarity by causing many of the prisoners to be ruthlessly hanged without any form of trial—a proceeding opposed to all the laws of war. The day after the battle he marched into Bridgewater with a crowd of prisoners tied together like negroes in an African slave-dealer's caravan.[†] He hanged some twenty-two at once, and several more the next day. He was only prevented from committing further atrocities by the urgent representations of the Bishop of Winchester, who warned him that he might be called to account for murder. There was, however, little risk of this, for only a few days before James had expressed regret in a message to Feversham that when he entered Frome he had not hanged

[*] Dryden's 'Hind and Panther,' Part II.
[†] Kennett, vol. iii., p. 432; Oldmixon, i., p. 704.

' any persons found deserving, as he would have you do at other places if you shall see cause.' In all, some 2,000 poor peasants were killed in these two days of slaughter. The Royal army lost about 400 men killed and wounded, Dumbarton's regiment suffering the most.*

The following letters from Lady Sunderland conveyed to her ' very dear friend ' Lady Churchill the first news of the victory :+ ' I hope this will comfort your heart, my dear, and make you think at least of poor me, who can never be a moment pleased without you. My Lord Churchill is very well. Colonel Oglethorpe has come to-day, and says that the Duke of Monmouth is routed, 1,500 of his men killed, of which Ferguson is one. Lord Grey and he ran away, one at the head of the Foot, and the other of the Horse. Lord Churchill is sent at the head of 500 Foot and 300 Horse to summon Bridgewater to surrender. You may imagine this summons will easily be obeyed after this defeat. To-night we expect an express from your lord, and I would fain keep this till I have your lord's letter for you. My lord says Oglethorpe, he thinks, has one. I have sent to seek him. I can say no more.—I am yours, A. S.'

7, 1685. ' Tuesday,‡ nine and a half at night.—There is just now an express come from my Lord Churchill, which brings us the good news of the total rout of the rebels, and that the King's forces are in Bridgewater, and all the enemies scattered like dust. My Lord Churchill very well, and Captain Berkeley. There are three of the King's officers [illegible] for one mortally wounded, and about sixty Foot,

---

* Hamilton's ' History of Grenadier Guards.' Several of the wounded were received into Chelsea Hospital, and were given small bounties, rising to £9 each as a maximum. The wounded officers received from £15 to £100, according to their rank and the gravity of their injuries. £1,994 13s. 4d. was paid in compensation for the most serious wounds to 218 of all ranks.

† The date is evidently Tuesday, 7, 1685. It is in the Blenheim Palace Papers.

‡ This Tuesday was the 7 July. The letter is from the Blenheim Palace Papers.

but not three Horse killed of the King's. Everybody of the King's party has done bravely, but I'll say no more now; but a word for myself—how glad, how wondrous glad, am I to have this good news to send my dearest! Oh, that you would be so good as to come and revive me, which nothing else can! Good-night. . . . I am for ever yours.'

On July 8, two days after Monmouth had fled from Sedgemoor, he was captured, and on the 13th he and Lord Grey reached London. Crowds went out to meet him, and strove to take summary vengeance on Lord Grey.* He was in a coach with his hands tied behind him, and his guards had some trouble to save him from the people, who regarded him as Monmouth's betrayer. Monmouth, notwithstanding his abject and craven appeals for mercy, was beheaded on Tower Hill two days after. *J. 7, 1685.* *J. 7, 1685.*

Lord Feversham returned to London with the household troops, and the army was broken up. Lord Churchill went home, but wrote the following letter to his wife the day before he set out: 'Wells, July 9.—I have received three of yours this night by an express, all which I read with great joy. If you are not already come to town, I desire you will, for I hope it will not now be long before I shall be there, and I shall be at no ease till I am in your arms, whom I love above my own life. I intend on Saturday to send the coach forwards to lie on the road for me. To-morrow we march to Warminster, and there we resolve to stay till we receive the King's commands, which I expect with great impatiency, since they are to bring me to my dear soul.' Addressed: 'For my Lady Churchill, at the Cockpit, Whitehall.'† *J. 7, 1685.*

He returned to London with a greatly-increased military reputation, for it was well known that the successful issue of the campaign was owing to him, and not to Feversham. Amongst others who greeted him were the Deputy-

---

* 'A Compleat Collection of the Reports, Lyes and Stories, etc. etc..' p. 58.

† Blenheim Papers. Lady Churchill was then in waiting on the Princess Anne, who lived with her husband in the Cockpit, Whitehall.

Governour and committee of the Hudson Bay Company, who waited upon him with congratulations on his safe return. So ended the rebellion, which, with everything against it, was nevertheless not far from being successful. An army of undisciplined, badly-armed weavers and peasants under a weak and unwise leader, with a coward as second in command, and with no officers of any war experience, had come so near winning at Sedgemoor that the result of the battle was for some time doubtful.* Many well acquainted with the circumstances of the action, including Defoe, who served with Monmouth, maintained that, notwithstanding Churchill's exertions, it was the great wet ditch alone which saved the Royal army from the destruction it merited. Contemporary writers assert, that James was most indebted for this victory to the unwearied vigilance of Churchill before the battle, and to his skilful dispositions during its progress. In the official despatches he is said to have ' performed his part with all the courage and gallantry imaginable.'✝ And yet, three years afterwards, it was mainly through his assistance and influence with the army that William of Orange was enabled to march from Torbay to London without a life being taken.

To those who are inexperienced in war, though alive to the difference in military efficiency between the regular soldier and the untrained recruit, it is startling to find an army of regular soldiers so nearly defeated by little more than an equal number of undrilled peasants. But there is a most important element in war which is too frequently overlooked by writers who have never themselves felt the human pulse in action: you cannot drill even a savage into a mere machine for the destruction of your enemies. The old school in our army tried it for over half a century, to the destruction of all healthy and ennobling military spirit. Our army, too long ruled by those who looked upon the

---

* Many who took part in the battle always asserted that it was very near being a victory for Monmouth.

✝ *London Gazette* of 8, 7. 1685.

British soldier as a piece of mechanism, not even of a high order, and who stigmatized him as the ' scum of the earth,' has with difficulty shaken off this practice and the false theories upon which it was based. Sir Charles Napier, *the* soldier's friend of this century, revolted against the system, and was accordingly denounced by his contemporaries as a madman and a Radical. It is the spirit in an army that must be gauged if its fighting power is to be duly measured. How came it that General Lee was able to hold his own so long against armies enormously superior in number to his ill-clad, badly-fed warriors? It was the difference in the spirit animating the two contending sides which enabled him to do so. To get the most out of men, you must work them up into a kind of fanaticism, the outcome either of strong religious enthusiasm, of patriotism, or of revenge. Monmouth's miners and weavers were convinced that they were fighting for God's truth, and that God would be on their side as He had been of old with His chosen people in Egypt. It was this spirit which enabled them to face and nearly defeat the regular troops, who fought to order just as they would have drilled on Hounslow Heath.

A small force of Horse and Foot was left at Bridgewater and Taunton under the command of Colonel Piercy Kirke, a man of doubtful reputation, but an able soldier.* He was, however, soon ordered to London, and so did not take part in what James with grim humour referred to, as ' Jeffreys' campaign.' For now began that ' Bloody Assize,' the very mention of which, even after the lapse of two centuries, sends a thrill of horror through every Englishman. The pride which deters from the commission of shameful actions found no place in Judge Jeffreys' character. Born about 1648, he was educated at St. Paul's and then at Westminster School. His parents intended him for some trading occupation, but he took to the law instead. He had long been a favourite at Court, and had

* Kirke was the son of a Groom of the Bedchamber to Charles I. He was well born and well connected. He died at Brussels 31. 10. 1691.

CHAPTER
XI.

1685.

proved a willing instrument in the hand of Charles in the work of depriving the cities of their charters. He had presided at the trial of Algernon Sidney, and had procured his condemnation on inadmissible evidence and by misrepresenting the law to the jury. But although Charles made use of him, he had long refused to promote him. He had, however, at the urgent request of the Duchess of Portsmouth, made this villainous lawyer Chief Justice of Chester, turning out a loyal and faithful public servant in order to create the vacancy.* His taste for debauchery and his immoral habits were not kept within bounds by regard for even the most ordinary decency. The innate cruelty of this fiend found full scope during these assizes. He gloated over the misery of his victims, joked to their faces upon their misfortunes, mocked their mental anguish, and was hilarious when he saw their ghastly heads and quartered bodies on every highway and in every hamlet through which he passed. He hated Dissenters, and he wreaked his hatred upon them without mercy. To kill the body did not satisfy his craving for human suffering; his victims must be tormented by his outrageous but fluent buffoonery. His was the swaggering bravado of the true bully and coward, who stamps and swears when on the winning side, and when his own worthless carcase is secure from harm. On his return from the West, he boasted that he had hanged more men than all the judges put together since the Conquest.+ When taken prisoner in 1688, disguised as a merchant sailor, he was with difficulty saved from the mob, who would have torn him to pieces. Brought before the Lord Mayor, so great was his terror that he knelt and kissed the Lord Mayor's hand, to the intense astonishment of that civic dignitary.‡ He was

12, 1688.

* Luttrell, March 16, 16⅞⅝.   † Calamy, vol. i., p. 138.

† Sir John Chapman was Lord Mayor. He had a stroke a few days afterwards, it was said from the shock he had had at seeing the Lord Chancellor kneeling as a prisoner before him; from that shock he never recovered, and died ¹¹⁄ 3, 16⅞⅝.—See Historical MSS., Dartmouth Papers, p. 235.

a sycophant to his superiors, and fawned upon Sunderland, calling him in his letters ' dearest, dearest Lord,' whilst he was insolent and brutal to those in his power. In prison, and shortly before his death, he complained to the chaplain of his hard fate, saying, ' Whatever I did then, I did by express orders ; and I have this further to say for myself, that I was not half bloody enough for him who sent me thither.'* He drank himself to death in the Tower, and died a few days after the landing at Kinsale of the Sovereign whom he had served so obsequiously, but who did not hesitate, when it served his purpose, to accuse him of cruelty and venality. No tyrant has ever been deterred from cruelty for want of a fitting agent. Some wretch like Jeffreys is always to be found ready and willing to do the bidding of kings like James II. Let loose upon the peaceable Dissenters of the West, this monster turned their country into a charnel-house.✝ We shudder as we read of the more than bodily tortures inflicted upon the unhappy people of Somerset by order of a King who impiously claimed to rule by Divine right and the grace of God. The rich escaped execution by the payment of large fines and bribes to Jeffreys. The friends of many went to London to plead for mercy from the King who knew no mercy, and among them was one Hannah Hewling, whose two brothers were about

---

* This is on the authority of Speaker Onslow. The chaplain, the Rev. Dr. Scott, told this to Lord Somers, who told it to Sir Joseph Jekyll, who told it to Onslow. Woolrych's ' Life of Jeffreys.' See also Mackintosh, chap. i., p. 29. James wrote to the Prince of Orange as follows : ' Windsor, September 24, 1685. As for news there is little stirring, but that Lord Chief Justice has almost done his campaign ; he has already condemned several hundreds, some of which are already executed and the others sent to the plantations.' - Dalrymple, vol. ii., Book II., p. 53.

✝ ' He (Jeffreys) made all the West an aceldama. Some places were quite depopulated, and nothing to be seen in them but forsaken walls, unlucky gibbets, and ghastly carkasses (*sic*). The trees were laden almost as thick with quarters as with leaves. The houses and steeples covered almost as close with heads as at other times in that county with crows or ravens.'—'A new Martyrology : or the Bloody Assizes.'

to be tried by Jeffreys. At Whitehall she saw Lord Churchill, whose soft heart was deeply touched by her story. He said: 'I wish well to your suit with all my heart, but dare not flatter you with any such hopes, for that marble' (pointing to the chimney-piece near them) 'is as capable of feeling compassion as the King's heart.' She pleaded in vain.*

About 330 people were executed and 855 transported, against whom there was no evidence whatever, besides many who were left to linger in gaol. Free-born Englishmen were condemned to slavery by an English judge, and sent by an English King to die under a tropical sun. Some were sold, or ransomed at high charges, to enrich the King's wife and the ladies of her Court.† Churchill's name has never been connected in any way with this hideous traffic in the bodies of his own countrymen, though he might easily have availed himself of this opportunity to become rich.

When driven from England to live on the bounty of Lewis XIV., James endeavoured to explain away the guilt of these proceedings, and to throw the blame upon the judge.‡ But his letters to the Prince of Orange, and other contemporary documents which bear upon these judicial murders, rob his statements of all value. It does not come within the scope of this work to describe in detail these horrible events, but they cannot be passed over if the reader is to learn how brutal was the master whom

---

* A tombstone in Lyme Church has this inscription : 'Here lieth the body of William Hewling, son of William Hewling of London, and grandson of William Kyffin, Esq., Alderman of London, who suffered martyrdom before he was full twenty years of age, engaging with the Duke of Monmouth for the Protestant religion and English liberty against Popery and slavery, September 12th, 1685.'

† The Queen's share was ninety-eight prisoners from Taunton, who brought her from £1,000 to £1,500 ; her Maids of Honour were given the children who had been condemned for presenting flowers to Monmouth. These children brought in £2,000 to these ladies.—' Side-Lights on the Stuarts,' by Inderwick, p. 393, 1888.

‡ Clarke's ' James,' vol. i., p. 43.

Churchill deserted three years afterwards, and how much they influenced him in his reluctant determination. They startled him, and made him reflect upon his position, and upon what they meant in the nation's future, both as regarded its religion and its liberties.

These West-Country Dissenters were put to death because it was alleged that they were traitors. But traitors against whom? Traitors against a tyrant who was himself the worst of traitors to his country and to his people. A traitor who broke his coronation oath, who violated the laws he had sworn to maintain, and who was at all times a sworn enemy to the religion he had promised in the name of God to support. Had James possessed any magnanimity or kindness of heart, it would have shown itself in at least a discriminating leniency to the poor deluded followers of Monmouth, whom religious zeal had driven into rebellion.

It is easy to understand how such wanton punishments were regarded by a man of Churchill's humane disposition, and with what loathing he turned from the master whom he had served so long, and hitherto so faithfully, when his true character revealed itself in this 'bloody assize.' No act of cruelty or inhumanity has ever been alleged against Marlborough even by his most bitter detractors. A great lover of dogs, he naturally turned with loathing from the sight of pain or torture inflicted in any form, mental or bodily, upon any animal, man included. When the necessity of war compelled him to lay waste the Bavarian dominions, we know how repugnant that necessity was to him, how sincerely he deplored having thus to punish unoffending subjects in order to make their Prince suffer in pocket and reputation. We are asked to find fault with him for his desertion of the King, though it was in fulfilment of his announced determination to quit the Royal service if James ever attempted 'to change our religion and constitution.' He might with greater reason be condemned for remaining so long in his service after these proceedings in the West, and for having allowed his

feeling of loyalty to an old master to outweigh for so long the
duty he owed to his country. James was kind and amiable
to his children, to his friends, and to his servants, but he
would at any moment turn and rend the dearest friend who
presumed to thwart the great aims of his life, namely, the
possession of arbitrary power and the re-establishment of
Popery. He showed his hand plainly after Sedgemoor,
and one so gifted as Churchill, and so well acquainted with
James's character, could not fail to suspect what was now
in store for him and for the nation. The punishments
inflicted upon Protestants, and the partiality openly shown
to Roman Catholics, warned him that the day could not be
far distant when he should feel constrained to carry out his
avowed resolution.

All the judges who had taken part in the Bloody Assize
were received at Windsor and thanked for their services,
and Jeffreys was made Lord Chancellor.* Lord Feversham,
whom James admitted, ' few people allowed any great share
in the merit,' was given the Garter, ostensibly in recognition
of his victory, but in reality rather as a compliment to
his uncle, Turenne, than as a reward for any military
services he had rendered.† But as he donned the insignia
of this ancient Order, deep must have been his sense of
that internal humiliation which the weak and unstable at
heart must always feel when rewarded for a victory won by
the initiative of another. The King was fully aware how
much he was indebted to Churchill for the victory, and as
a reward he made him Colonel of the third troop of Life
Guards.

Churchill was one of the thirty peers selected by Jeffreys
to try Lord Delamere for high treason in connection with

---

* Autobiography of Sir John Bramston, p. 207.

† 　　　' Feversham in his Sedgemoor star and glory,
　　　　Proud as the Treasurer and pettish as Lory.'
James admits this : see Clarke's ' Life of James II.,' vol. ii., p. 42.
The witty Villiers, Duke of Buckingham, who hated Feversham, lam-
pooned him in an amusing squib called ' The Battle,' which was much
read at the time and from which these lines are taken.

Monmouth's rebellion. As junior Baron he gave his vote first. 'How say you, my Lord Churchill,' said Jeffreys, then Lord High Steward : ' is Henry, Baron of Delamere, guilty of the high treason where of he stands indicted and hath been arraigned, or not guilty ?' Churchill, according to custom, stood up uncovered, and with his hand on his breast answered, 'Not guilty, upon my honour.'* The other peers, perhaps encouraged by this fearless answer of the King's favourite, gave a similar verdict, to the disgust and fury of the King, who was present. Lord Delamere was one of the few tried by Jeffreys who were acquitted, a result entirely due to the fact that a jury of peers was not to be bullied into voting as the judge wished. This little incident warned James that, whilst his Gentleman of the Bedchamber was prepared to fight for him, he was not one who would vote against his conscience to please his master.

* Domestic Papers, Jac. II., 1686. Rolls House.

CHAPTER XLI.

James tries to fill the Army with Roman Catholics—His dislike to the Militia—His new Army establishment—His camp at Hounslow—His 'Articles of War'—The Portsmouth captains.

CHAPTER XLI.

1685.

THE battle of Sedgemoor impressed James with an undue sense of the power which the possession of a regular army would give him. If the popular Monmouth, with a practically unlimited following, could be destroyed by a handful of regular soldiers, a standing army would, he thought, enable him not only to put down rebellion, but to overcome all resistance to his will. With such an instrument at his disposal, who would dare to oppose his wishes? With its aid, he could afford to laugh at what we now understand by public opinion.

The large measure of support accorded to the rebellions of Argyle and Monmouth pointed to the existence of widely spread discontent, and gave James a plausible excuse for keeping permanently on foot a considerable body of regular troops. His attention therefore was unceasingly directed to this object, and he spared no effort to fill his regiments with Roman Catholics, upon whom alone he could confidently rely. His views on this point are summed up in his dying injunction to his son: 'Be never without a considerable body of Catholic troops, without which you cannot be safe.'* A standing army would, he thought,

---

* Clarke's 'Life of James II.,' vol. ii., p. 621. In 1680 the standing army was about 20,000 strong (3,000 were in Tangier, 7,800 in Ireland,

make him indeed a King according to his notions of kingship, for it would enable him to rule without a Parliament ;
and supported by a good Catholic army he believed that he
would be able to force his will upon the people without
danger to his Crown. 'The King of England told me,'
wrote Barillon, 'that, let what would happen, he would keep
the troops on foot, even though the Parliament should not
give him anything towards their maintenance.'

When Parliament met in November, the King, in his
opening speech said, that the duration of the rebellion
was owing to the inefficiency of the militia. 'There is
nothing,' he added, 'but a good force of well disciplined
troops in constant pay that can defend us from such as
either at home or abroad are disposed to disturb us ; and in
truth my concern for the peace and quiet of my subjects,
as well as for the safety of the Government, made me
think it necessary to increase their number to the proportion I have done.'* From time immemorial the militia
had been the only military force known to the Constitution. But James feared it, because it largely shared the
feelings of the people, and the recent events in the West
of England proved that he could not depend upon it to
carry out his aims. A standing army, on the contrary,
would be a thing apart. The army is a profession, a
guild, with its own peculiar standards of honour, and of
personal loyalty to the Sovereign, its acknowledged head.
In order to give effect to his intention to rule without a
Parliament, James felt it was necessary to get rid of the
militia, and to replace it by a standing army personally
devoted to himself. He did not disband the militia ; his
policy was to let it die gradually, and in pursuance of this
settled purpose he so neglected it that when William landed
it was almost useless. It had not been trained for a couple

2,800 in Scotland, and about 6,900 in England), and in January, 1685,
its strength was about the same.

  * Clarke's ' Life of James II.,' vol. ii., p. 48.

of years : it lacked arms, equipment and clothing, and large numbers of its Protestant officers had been either dismissed or had resigned in disgust at the King's treatment of the force.

James also stated in this speech, that he meant to employ Roman Catholic officers in the army. A serious discussion arose in the House of Commons both on this account and as to the amount which should be voted for the army. James asked for £1,200,000, but some wished to grant only £200,000. Lord Churchill's father spoke on the King's side, both as to the necessity of maintaining a standing army and of granting the larger amount. The smaller sum was, he said, ' much too little; soldiers move not without pay—no penny, no paternoster.'* In the end the Commons voted £700,000, but in the House of Lords the proposed standing army was denounced as illegal, because, among other reasons, it was commanded chiefly by men who, owing to their religion, could not by law hold commissions in the public service. This rebuff was too much for James, so he stopped further discussion on the subject by immediately proroguing Parliament to the 10th of the following February. As a matter of fact, no Parliament met again in his reign. He tells us in his memoirs that, as he was determined to keep on foot a standing army, and to employ Roman Catholic officers in it, he resolved not to again assemble a Parliament which had criticised both his proceedings and his policy.†

In February, 1686, he fixed the army establishment for England as follows [the troops raised in Ireland and Scotland were distinct, and were paid exclusively from the revenues of those countries]: three troops of Life Guards,‡ ten regiments of Horse, three of Dragoons, two of Foot

---

* See Parliamentary debate of $\frac{14}{11}$ 11, 1685.

† Clarke's ' Life of James II.,' vol. ii., p. 69.

‡ The total strength of the Life Guards, including the Scotch troop, on 1, 7, 1686, was 58 officers and 1,052 of all other ranks. In 1688 the strength was increased to 1,286 of all ranks. James looked upon this body guard as one of the mainstays of his throne.—Cannon's ' History of the Life Guards.'

Guards and fourteen of the line, besides sixteen 'independent companies' for garrisons. Of these, six regiments of Horse, two of Dragoons, and nine of Foot were formed from the troops raised by loyal country gentlemen in various localities during Monmouth's rebellion. Charles II.'s army of about 8,000 men of all ranks cost £280,000; that of his brother £600,000 per annum.

It will interest the military reader to know that in 1683 a regiment of Dragoons, or, as we should now call them, of Mounted Infantry, was for the first time added to our army. In raising this corps of men, mounted on small galloways but intended to fight on foot with musket and bayonet, Charles II. had followed the example of foreign Powers. Henceforth the expression of 'Horse, Foot and Dragoons' became common, and it is curious to note that the sequence in which these three arms are named corresponds with their priority in date of creation. The same thing may be remarked in these days, when, the mounted Foot soldier having been generally abolished, we refer to an army as consisting of 'cavalry, infantry and artillery,' the last-named arm being that most recently adopted.

Of 'the Royal Dragoons' Churchill was the first Colonel, ₁₂ 11, 1683. with Viscount Cornbury as his Lieutenant-Colonel.* Some troops were specially raised for it, and the four troops of the 'Tangier Horse,' then under orders to be disbanded, were added to them.+ The regiment was thus up to an establish- ₁₁ 4, 1684. ment of 350 men, divided into two squadrons of three troops each. In the following contemporary lampoon it is maintained that Court favour alone could account for an infantry officer being made Colonel of a mounted regiment :

> ' Let's cut our meat with spoons ;
> The sense is as good
> As that Churchill should
> Be put to command the Dragoons.'

* Churchill's commission is dated 12 11, 1683, and is now amongst the papers at Blenheim. The final warrant for raising the Royal Dragoons is dated ⁄₁ 2, 1684; Lord Cornbury was Lord Clarendon's eldest son.

† This order is dated 'Windsor, ⁄⁄ 4, 1684.'

Ireland was to James an inexhaustible recruiting-ground; not that he loved Ireland or Irishmen, but because he could always obtain there any number of Catholic soldiers, upon whom he could rely under all circumstances.

Throughout James's reign a camp was annually formed at Hounslow, where he assembled all the available troops not on garrison duty or required to overawe London. It was the Aldershot of the day, where he trained his men as soldiers. A free market was held there daily for the sale of provisions and necessaries for man and horse, no sellers to be charged 'anything for their standing, or on any account whatsoever.'* Soldiers injuring, molesting, or exacting money from those who sold were to be punished. ' A council, or general court-martial,' met at the Horse Guards every Friday morning, ' to hear all complaints between soldiers, or of civilians against the military.' The ' misdemeanours of officers and soldiers ' were to be punished by this court. Sergeants were forbidden to keep victualling houses, and privates were not allowed to marry without leave obtained from their captains.+

In August, 1685, King James reviewed at Hounslow twenty squadrons of Horse, one of Horse Grenadiers, one regiment of Dragoons, and ten battalions of Foot, a force numbering about 3,500 mounted men and six or seven thousand Foot.‡ In the summer of 1686 about 15,000 men and 28 guns were encamped there under Lord Feversham, and at a review the following year there were present three troops of Life Guards and one of Horse Grenadier Guards, nine regiments of Horse, three of Dragoons, four battalions of Foot Guards, and nine regiments of Foot. James attended frequently at the camp, and generally stayed to dine with Lord Feversham or some other superior officer.

---

* *London Gazette.*

† Domestic Papers, Rolls House. The order establishing this court is dated $\frac{11}{21}$ 3, 1687.

‡ Cannon's ' History of Regiments.' The squadron was then of three troops, with a total strength of about 150 rank and file.

He hoped thus to establish intimate relations with his officers, and also to make himself generally popular with the troops.* He dined in Lord Churchill's tent when the camp was formed in 1688, and he went there for the last time in August, when it was being broken up, and the troops dispersed to their quarters for the winter. He had a wooden chapel made on wheels, which stood 'in the middle of the camp between the Horse and Foot.'† Here Mass was said daily in the most ostentatious manner, to the scandal of the Protestants—who formed the great majority —whilst priests were employed to go amongst the soldiers, with the object of bringing them over to the Catholic faith. Just before William landed there were eight regiments of Horse and nine battalions of Foot encamped at Hounslow.

The discipline of the army under James was lax and bad. He made so much of his army that after a time all ranks assumed a somewhat arrogant air in their dealings with the people. The officers upon many occasions pretended to be above the civil power, and their insolence was often intolerable. From time immemorial it had been the practice for the General commanding an army in the field to frame a code of laws for the punishment of mutiny, desertion, and all crimes committed on active service. Articles of war had been published by Charles II. in 1673, but the lawyers of the day would not listen to proposals for the recognition of military laws that dispensed with the action of those civil courts in which they earned their livelihood. The judges declared that to hang a man for mutiny or desertion in England would be contrary to the law of the land. Indeed, the maintenance during peace of an army such as that kept up by James at Hounslow was unknown to the law. Consequently, when men deserted there was no law to which they were amenable, and in order to deal with them advantage was taken of an obsolete Act of Parliament,

* Ellis, vol. iv.

† 'A Compleat Collection of all the Reports, Lyes and Stories which were the forerunners of the Great Revolution of 1688,' p. 40.

which prescribed death as the punishment for those who
deserted the King during his wars in Scotland and on the
'high seas.' Judges who would not convict deserters
under this old law were removed from the Bench. We
frequently read of deserters being hanged in this reign by
order of the civil courts, whereas after the passing of the
Mutiny Act of William III. deserters were tried by court-
martial and shot instead of being hanged. The common
practice was to advertise deserters in the *London Gazette*,
and one or two guineas were generally offered as a reward
for their apprehension. The cavalry deserter seems usually
to have carried off his horse with him.*

James had yet to learn that even a standing army might
prove but a weak support for the Throne, and that there
was no security for it except in the affections and good-will
of his freedom-loving people. He was too dull to realize
that the thousands who had flocked to Monmouth's
standard fought not for the man, but for the cause which
he represented. This lesson was to be taught to James
by a people banded together with the one object of
ridding themselves of a King who refused to govern
according to their laws. When we recall the events of his
reign, and realize how nearly he succeeded in his attempt
to impose his will upon the country by means of a standing
army, the dread and jealousy with which our forefathers
regarded such an establishment are easily intelligible.

James had hoped to prevail upon all in the army,
Protestants as well as Roman Catholics, to help him in
procuring the repeal of the Penal Acts directed against his
religion. Wishing to try by experiment how far he could
rely upon the soldiers in this matter, he ordered the Major
of Lord Lichfield's, now the Suffolk Regiment, to tell his

---

* The Dragoon horses were generally mentioned in these advertisements as being 14½ hands. The price paid for the Dragoon's horse was
about one-third of that paid for the trooper in a regiment of Horse. In
1686 a contradiction was given in the *London Gazette* to the rumour
that there was much sickness and mortality in the camp.

men on parade that those who would not forthwith obey the King in the matter of the Test were to lay down their arms. To the dismay and disgust of James, who was present, the whole regiment grounded their arms with the exception of two captains and a few Roman Catholic privates. He turned away, muttering 'that for the future he would not do them the honour to ask their advice.' This incident was followed by another. The Duke of Berwick, Colonel of the Princess Anne's Regiment, and also Governour of Portsmouth, where it was stationed, issued an order that a number of Irish Catholics were to be enlisted in each company.* Several of the captains refused to receive them, and were supported in their refusal by the Lieutenant-Colonel. The captains memorialized the King, respectfully pointing out that they were not in want of recruits and could not be expected to discharge good English soldiers to make room for 'foreigners,' as they were pleased to style the men from Ireland.† They claimed the right to select their own recruits, or, if that were denied them, to resign their commissions. James, in a fury, ordered them to Windsor as prisoners under a guard, the order being addressed to 'Our dearly beloved natural son, James, Duke of Berwick,' etc.

These five 'Portsmouth captains,' as they were thenceforward called, and their commanding officer, were tried at Windsor by court-martial, and found guilty of disobedience. Churchill was a member of the court, and it is said voted for their being shot in the hope, as James asserts, of thereby increasing the King's unpopularity.‡ They were sentenced to be cashiered, but were only dismissed the army.§ The garrison of Portsmouth was naturally

* The Princess Anne's Regiment was called the ' Queen's ' in Anne's reign, by which title it is still generally known.

† The song of ' Lillibulero' was a scurrilous attack upon the Irish recruits of this time, and was very commonly sung about England during the trial of the ' Portsmouth captains.'

‡ Clarke's ' Life of James II.,' vol. ii., p. 169.

§ Colonel Beaumont, who commanded the regiment, was reinstated

affected by these proceedings. Many officers resigned, many privates deserted, and so unsatisfactory was the condition of affairs that the King ordered a regiment to proceed there from London.   James also strove to force his religion upon the navy by the appointment of a Roman Catholic chaplain to each ship.   He fondly hoped that his reputation as an Admiral would weigh with the sailors. But when the priests attempted to say Mass the officers had much difficulty in saving them from being thrown into the sea.*

by William III.   In 1688 an engraving was published, headed ' The Portsmouth Captains,' giving their likenesses with the following names : Lieut.-Colonel Hon. John Beaumont, Captains Hon. Thos. Paston, Simon Packe, Thos. Orme, John Port, and William Cook. Underneath was the motto ' Pro Latria, Patria, Atria.'

   * Harris's ' William III.'

CHAPTER XLII.

THE CHURCH OF ENGLAND AND JAMES.—HE TRIES TO RE-ESTABLISH POPERY.

Revocation of Edict of Nantes—Sam Johnson placed in the pillory—James's Declaration for Liberty of Conscience—James attacks the English Church—He dismisses many Protestants from the Public Service—He attacks the Universities.

THE overthrow of Monmouth led to the Revolution of 1688 by steps which it is easy to follow. A victory for James's army, it was yet the herald of James's downfall. Whilst Monmouth lived, there were two competitors for the Crown, who, as it were, divided the King's enemies into two factions, looking for a deliverer respectively to William and to Monmouth; but when the head of that ill-fated man rolled upon the scaffold, all hopes were concentrated on the Prince of Orange. James was, therefore, a loser by the death of Monmouth, inasmuch as it fixed the hopes of the disaffected exclusively upon the more dangerous of his two rivals. It was William who really gained, for whilst the hatred felt for James by a large section of the people was appreciably intensified, William was relieved of a British rival, highly favoured by Englishmen, and better known than himself. The cold, rude, and ungainly Dutchman could not hope to compete successfully with Monmouth, whose courtly manners and fine presence had made him the delight of his father's people.* William,

* James asserts that William sent Monmouth to his destruction in order to be rid of a dangerous rival for the Crown of England. Clarke's 'Life of James II.,' vol. i., p. 25.

the most astute of princes, a Stewart by his mother's side, and married to the Princess Royal, heiress presumptive to the throne, was now more than ever an enemy whom James had reason to fear.

The cruelties of Jeffreys after the rebellion had made James odious to his people. He believed at first that the execution of Argyle and Monmouth had inaugurated a new era for the ancient faith in England. In imagination he already heard the solemn music of the Mass, and saw the smoke of incense rise before the restored altars of every English parish church. The battle of Sedgemoor was something more than the overthrow of a rebellion ; it was, in James's eyes, a victory of the Roman religion over that of the Reformation. It made him so inordinately confident of his power that he threw off all disguise as to his intentions. 'It would give him,' he said, 'an opportunity of making himself master of his country.'* After the battle he believed himself to be far more of a king than his brother had ever been. Charles had never dared to attack Protestantism openly, though both brothers equally regarded it as equivalent to republicanism. But James had measured swords with the demon of liberty, had utterly worsted it, and had strewn the earth with the mangled bodies of its champions. With these sights before them, who would dare to babble more of liberty ? Who would venture to bandy words about religion with a King who could command the services of a judge like Jeffreys ?

In the first blush of his triumph James felt so strong that he even ventured to make a treaty with Holland against the interests of his paymaster, Lewis of France, but the temporary withdrawal of his pension may possibly have inspired this short and passing display of independence.

In the previous reign all the old charters possessed by the towns and boroughs had been annulled, so James was

---

* He said this in a conversation with the French Ambassador.

now fairly able to have whom he would elected to Parliament. To find willing tools who would do his bidding, he was constrained, however, to select in the counties men of inferior standing and doubtful reputation. He had a splendid position after Sedgemoor, and had he been a William of Orange or a Cromwell he might have accomplished great things. The country was prosperous, his revenue was ample, and, as his army and navy were strong and efficient, his alliance was courted by the two great Powers which divided civilized Europe between them. These advantages, however, did not satisfy the cravings of his narrow mind.

It was gall and wormwood to him to remember that he alone among kings was hampered by the interference of a Parliament. Every little German prince ruled despotically, and it was monstrous, he thought, that he, the descendant and heir of a long and glorious line of kings, should not be allowed to do so too. Lewis encouraged him in these notions, and promised his help to enable him to dispense with Parliaments, and to re-establish the spiritual power of the Pope in his dominions. This was no easy matter, for the people looked upon Parliament and Protestantism as the foundation of their liberties, whilst they regarded Popery as the religion of slaves. James never could grasp the change which the Reformation had brought about in the commonly accepted ideas of civil government, nor would he recognise the permanency of the authority which the struggle between his father and the people had conferred upon the House of Commons. He foolishly believed it possible to revive the power exercised by his vigorous Tudor ancestors. The fact was always present to his thoughts, that, by what might be almost termed an edict, Henry VIII. had changed the established form of religion, and he could not understand why he should not, in a similar way, force the people back to their ancient faith. To anyone holding his views of the kingly office, this was a natural reflection. In his own blind belief in the hereditary principle and the Divine right of kings, he failed to see that the people could have rights beyond those which had been freely given them by their Sovereign, or that privileges conceded could not be revoked whenever it should please the Sovereign to withdraw them. He fully understood the meaning of high treason as against the King, but he could not understand that treason of the King against his country was equally recognised as a crime by the English people. No private property was sacred in his eyes when the King required it for any purpose, however ignoble that purpose might be. The love of freedom, which for centuries had underlain all other sentiments in the English character, amounted in his eyes to rank rebellion.

The Church of England was powerful all through his short reign; more so, indeed, than it was under William and Mary, when the Non-juror party weakened it considerably. Mary always had a sincere affection for it, but that feeling was not shared by her Calvinist husband. Upon the accession of James, its ministers certainly entertained a deep attachment to their lawful Sovereign, the son of 'Charles the Martyr.' The Church taught that monarchy was a Divine institution, and James foolishly mistook this teaching for determination to support the King in all that he might do.*

But the anti-Popery feeling amongst the people was very strong at this time. The Edict of Nantes, which had secured the French Protestants the right to live and carry on business in their own country, was revoked by Lewis XIV.† Barillon describes to his master the intense satisfaction its repeal had afforded James, and how much

²⁴·¹⁷, 1685.

---

* The High Church Sacheverell thus referred in a sermon to Charles I.: 'Whose death, had it preceded that of Jesus Christ, would have seemed a true type of it, as it was the exact transcript and representation of it afterwards.'

† It had been granted to the Protestants of France in 1598 by Henry IV. His son Lewis XIII. and his grandson Lewis XIV. had both sworn to maintain it.

he approved of the successful fashion in which the system of 'dragonades' had been used to put down Protestantism. A close connection had long been maintained between the Protestant party in France and the English people,* and although James rejoiced that 'his most Christian Majesty' had revoked that memorable edict, the English people regarded the event with entirely opposite feelings. It had driven thousands of Protestant families from France to England and Ireland.+ The refugees spread abroad heartrending stories of the massacres, tortures, and cruel injustice inflicted upon Protestants by Lewis XIV., who, the people remembered, was the close friend and ally of King James. Lovers of liberty, who still held the days of the Commonwealth in regretful remembrance, were worked up to fever-pitch by these stories, which lost nothing of their horror by repetition. The French King thus came to be commonly regarded in England as a tyrant, who not only trampled freedom under foot, but ruthlessly handed over the followers of Luther and Calvin to the cruelties of a pitiless priesthood. As the popular detestation of Lewis and of Popery grew deeper and more intense, Englishmen turned all the more to William, the recognised champion of freedom and of Protestantism in Europe.

The Church of England had no real hatred of that absolute power which James claimed. As long as he respected her rights and left her property alone, as his brother Charles had done, she was little concerned whether James ruled with or without a Parliament.: According to the Church's doctrine, the people were

* Calamy, vol. i.

† Over 50,000 most industrious people were thus added to our population, and established silk and other industries here, which largely augmented our manufacturing wealth. The French nation, it is often said, never recovered the loss in intellect and honesty which this exodus entailed upon it.

‡ In the seventeenth century 'Divine right' had an extensive literature of its own, which may still be found cumbering the shelves of book-rooms in English country houses.

born his subjects, and he was born their King, and, as it were, elected by God Himself. Between James and the English Church there was, moreover, a great bond of union in their common loathing of Dissenters. The Court party had long accused the latter of being republicans, and, remembering the treatment which all Nonconformists had received since the Restoration, it would have been no wonder had they really sought to rid England of monarchy for ever. The High Churchmen were as anxious to persecute them as James could be. For years the Tory parsons had supported James's claim to the throne from conscientious motives, and they now fondly hoped that Sedgemoor would settle the question of the succession. Had not James promised them the free exercise of their religion and their liberties? A time-serving Dean preached 'that his Majesty's promises were free donatives, and ought not to be strictly examined or urged, and that they must leave him to explain his own meaning in them.'* Poor deluded people! they had still to learn how little reliance was to be placed on the word of a Stewart. Although the High Church party denied the King's authority in matters ecclesiastical, one of its leading principles was unquestioning obedience to the royal will in secular affairs. The Church had long held up to contempt the principle of a 'limited monarchy,' pronouncing it to be opposed to ancient custom and the Bible, and injurious to the welfare of the nation. Her ambition was to secure for herself the position which the Catholic Church enjoyed in France and in Spain; she claimed to dictate what the people should and should not believe, and to visit with condign punishment those who would not accept the 'Thirty-nine Articles.' To accomplish this end, the Church had preached the doctrine of 'passive obedience,' and by so doing had forged an instrument of torture for James's use against her. For every breach of that doctrine he re-

* James made him a Bishop for this sermon. Echard's 'History of the Revolution,' p. 70.

morselessly punished its inventors in person and in purse.
Charles II. had contented himself with striking at the civil
liberties of his people ; he had fined the rich and the great,
had robbed cities of their charters, and would fain have
made the people forget the very name of Parliament.*
But James would go further, and strike at their religion
also. 'I have heard it publicly preached,' wrote Defoe,
'that if the King commanded my head, and sent his
messenger to fetch it, I was bound to submit, and stand
still while it was cut off.' Such was the doctrine which,
preached by the Church, helped James in his endeavours
to re-establish by his own authority the religion and influence of Rome. 'Passive obedience' to the King—a
doctrine imported from Scotland with the House of Stewart
—was preached at this time from every English pulpit,
whilst all schismatics were denounced as the enemies of
God, of the Church, and of monarchy. James, hating both
Churchmen and Dissenters, felt that his true policy was to
use the former to destroy the latter, and then to turn
upon the Established Church and crush it. In order to
give effect to this policy in England, he strove to gain over
the Bishops and the parish clergy by the persecution of the
Nonconformists, whilst in Scotland he sought to force
Episcopalianism upon a people who loathed it.

As long as the King confined his illegal action to attacks
upon Dissenters and public liberty, the ministers of the
Established Church were content to serve him. But as
soon as he presumed to tamper with what they conceived to
be their privileges, with their property and their Universities, they turned upon him, resisted his action, and denied
his authority. When he showed himself determined at all
hazards to make his own religion paramount, he was
deserted even by Tories like Churchill, because they loved
the Protestant faith with a fervour which few in this free-
thinking age can comprehend. They not only deserted

* 'Secret History of the Reigns of Charles II. and James II.,'
p. 117.

him, but began to plot his destruction, and those who had believed most strongly in his coronation promises turned upon him with the resentment with which the deceived always regard the deceiver. It is a curious fact that throughout his short and ignoble reign James seems to have sought out the line of most resistance, the path along which he would be certain to encounter the maximum of difficulty and opposition. His folly in this respect was a combination of blindness and obstinacy rarely to be found in the ruler of a civilized state.

The Tory or High Church party persecuted the Dissenters. The Whigs, when in power, persecuted the Roman Catholics, and their penal laws were long a disgrace to the statute-book. But the objects of the two parties were different. The Tories sought to destroy the Dissenters in what they conceived to be the interests of the Church, and because of their opposition to absolute government. The Whigs, on the other hand, were more influenced by zeal for Parliamentary government. In their opinion the Romanists favoured the despotic sway of the King; and it was rather from a love of free institutions than from any undue hatred of Popery that they framed the penal laws.

During the reign of Charles II. the Roman Catholics had been hunted down mainly through the Protestant bigotry of Shaftesbury and his colleagues, whom the King was not able to withstand. The Protestant party had made a foolish and a cruel use of their power in punishing both Catholics and Dissenters; and now, fortune's wheel having turned, the ill-used Catholics avenged themselves upon the Episcopalians for the indignities and wrongs which they had received at their hands. One of the first to suffer was the Rev. Samuel Johnson. He had made himself obnoxious by his writings against Popery, and was prosecuted for libel, as well as for his work on 'Julian the Apostate.' He contended that resistance to the King would be justifiable if 'our religion or our civil rights were invaded.' For this doctrine he was sentenced to stand in the pillory, to be

degraded, and then to be whipped from Newgate to Tyburn.*
This cruel sentence was carried out to the horror of the
whole Established Church.

James felt that one of the first measures required for the
re-establishment of the Papal power in England was the
repeal of the Test Act, for as long as this law was in force
no Roman Catholic could legally hold any public position.
James told the French Ambassador ' that he meant to have
the Test and the Habeas Corpus Acts repealed by Parliament, as the former was destructive of the Catholic religion,
and the other of the royal prerogative.' The Ambassador
added that both Charles and James had often told him that
no government could exist with such a law as the Habeas
Corpus.† The Test Act once repealed, he could at pleasure
fill the army and navy with Roman Catholic officers, and
by degrees place the whole government of the kingdom in
Roman Catholic hands. At first the English Church took no
exception to the King's religion, and had he acted with
ordinary caution, it is doubtful if it would have openly
opposed the repeal of the Act. But under the influence of
the hurry which usually accompanies the excessive zeal of
small-minded men engaged in public affairs, he did not
know how to bide his time.

To get rid of the objectionable law, he angled for the
support of the Dissenters, and babbled to them of toleration and liberty of conscience. If he could but obtain
toleration for their sects, a similar privilege could not
reasonably be denied to his own faith. It has been pleaded
by some of his apologists that he aimed at general religious
toleration, but his whole history goes to prove that freedom
of conscience and religious liberty were equally hateful to
him. No Spanish Inquisitor ever detested religious liberty
more than he did, and it was not equality, but supremacy,
that he wanted for his own faith. In a letter to the Pope,

* Born in 1649, he had been a schoolfellow of Marlborough's at St.
Paul's. He had been private chaplain to Lord Russell.
† Dalrymple, vol. ii., p. 171.

he admits that he meant to destroy all forms of Protestantism in his kingdom, and that it was ' our determination
to spread the true faith over all our dominions.'*

The French archives give us a list, in which Lord
Churchill's name is included, of the peers who supported
James in his desire to abolish the Test Act. But it may be
taken for granted that his name was inserted because he
had long been known as one of the Duke of York's most
intimate friends. It was evidently assumed that, as a
member of James's household, he would support his old
master. He did not, however, act according to the hopes
of those who compiled the list ; and a contemporary writes
of him : ' Lord Churchill swears he will not do what the
King requires from him.'+ James felt that the time had
come when he must adopt strong measures if the Act
were ever to be repealed. He was fond of repeating the
old French maxim, that great evils require strong remedies,
and as if to prove its truth, he now resolved to nullify
the Test Act by a simple edict, and accordingly published
his celebrated ' Declaration for liberty of conscience.'

Ap. 4, 1687.

No more absolutely illegal act was ever done by an English
King. Its ostensible object was to remove the disabilities
from which Dissenters suffered, but its real aim was to
obtain for Roman Catholics equal rights with the Church of
England. That position once secured, it was hoped that
the time would soon come when the Roman Catholic
hierarchy should again occupy its old position of supremacy.
By this bid for the favour of the Dissenters James hoped to
sow disunion amongst Protestants, setting the whole body of
Nonconformists—then probably about one-sixteenth of the
population of Great Britain—in antagonism to the Established Church.‡ A few sects were at first taken in, but

* He said, in a Latin letter he wrote in 1689 from Dublin to the
Pope: 'Catholicam fidem reducere in tria regna statuisse.' Lord
Melfort, who, to please James, became a Catholic, carried this letter to
Rome. See Lord Somers' Tracts, No. x., p. 552.

† Johnston's Letters ; Mackintosh, p. 198.

‡ Mackintosh. p. 193.

the leading Dissenters saw through the cleverly-devised snare. They had never accepted the theory of passive obedience, and were wise enough to foresee that if the King could destroy the great edifice of the Established Church, with all its wealth, power, and popularity, they, the poor and despised Independents, could have little to expect at his hands. Baxter and Howe would have nothing to do with the trap which James had set for them. Their conduct did them the highest credit, for ever since the Restoration they had suffered cruel persecution at the hands of the Established Church. There were many also who, like Churchill, remembered that this pretended movement in favour of liberty of conscience was wholly at variance with James's conduct when Lord High Commissioner in Scotland. There he had exhorted the Council to suppress the conventicles, or, in other words, to put an end to the religious services of the vast majority of the Scottish people.* That James in his heart loathed the principle he pretended to uphold is evident from the congratulations which he bestowed on Lewis XIV. for his barbarous treatment of French Protestants; and there can be no doubt that he would have liked to deal similarly with his own heretics had he possessed the power. All tests, oaths, and restrictions upon conscience are opposed to the spirit of the present age, but it was not so in the seventeenth century. Full liberty of conscience for all persons as well as for yourself, was an idea not then in harmony with the views of any party in England, or, indeed, in Europe. The common people neither understood nor sympathized with it, whilst the educated perceived the ulterior motive with which it had been offered to them.

The Church soon found to her cost that her former subserviency was of no avail to secure the King's good-will. His public acts had already left her but a precarious right to be regarded as the National Church. To control her more effectually, James now created an illegal court, under the

* 'Life of James II.,' vol. i., p. 694.

presidency of Jeffreys, to try ecclesiastical cases.* This
was in direct violation of an express Act of Parliament,†
but James declared himself to be above the law, and
claimed the right to exempt his Roman Catholic subjects
from the operation of any objectionable Act, simply by the
issue of a dispensation under the sign-manual. This
assumption of authority struck at the root of all law and
liberty. He maintained that the laws of England were the
King's laws, and that consequently the King could grant
dispensations from them. He dismissed four judges who
refused to acknowledge this power, but he found others
ready to maintain this monstrous doctrine, as illogical as it
was historically false. Men whose duty it was to support
the laws of the land now trampled upon them 'under
colour of law,' simply to please a tyrannical King.‡ The
boldness with which James pursued his illegal aims at first
secured their success—and success, as usual, soon won him
adherents amongst the waverers, who began to range themselves freely on his side.

One of the first to feel the power of the new tribunal was
Henry Compton, Bishop of London.§ He was removed
from the Privy Council, and suspended from his bishopric
during the King's pleasure for refusing to punish Dr.
Sharp, a parish rector, for some anti-Popery sermons
which had offended the Jesuits. Compton, who subsequently took an active part in the Revolution, was then
one of the few prelates of noble blood. He had begun life

* It was styled 'A Commission for Ecclesiastical Causes.'
† Welwood's Memoirs.
‡ Welwood's Memoirs. Welwood was physician to William III.
His book was written at Queen Mary's desire.
§ He was fourth son of the Earl of Northampton, who was killed
fighting for the King at Hopton Heath, near Stafford. An elder
brother of the Bishop, Sir Francis Compton, had commanded the
Royal Horse Guards (Blues) at Sedgemoor. He was a Whig in all his
principles, and was one of the only two Bishops who voted for a King
when Parliament declared the throne vacant in 1688. He was an
eminent botanist. Born 1632, died √. 7, 1713.

as a cornet in the Blues, and only entered the Church at the age of thirty. His avowed hatred of Popery had made him a great favourite with the people, by whom he was nicknamed 'the Protestant Bishop.' He was a Broad Churchman of enlightened views, and by his earnest endeavours to bring the Dissenters within the pale of the Established Church he showed himself far in advance of his narrow-minded High Church brother prelates.

In defiance of the statute law, James now began to fill the Privy Council with men of his own creed. The Jesuit Father Petre was so appointed, and to him the King transferred the confidence which he had previously reposed in Churchill. Another of the many Roman Catholics whom James promoted to high position was the coarse-minded and unscrupulous Lord Tyrconnel, the fifth of that faith appointed to the Privy Council.

The Pope's Nuncio was received in state at Windsor, the Chapel Royal in St. James's was converted into a Roman Catholic church, and London was soon filled with priests, who paraded their monkish dress, to the horror of the people, and even began to rebuild their convents. Jesuits set up schools and seminaries in most of the chief towns. Roman Catholic bishops, consecrated in the Chapel Royal, were appointed to dioceses openly allotted to them, and their pastoral letters were published with royal license by the King's printer.*

The Roman Catholics in England were at this time divided into three parties; the first consisted of a few peers and gentlemen who were in favour of mild measures: the second followed the policy of the Pope, who, working through his Nuncio, wished to moderate James's ardour lest the people should be driven into open rebellion.† The

---

* Welwood's Memoirs.

† Letter from Innocent XI., in which he warned James not to push his anti-Protestant zeal too far. 'History of William III..' vol. i., pp. 173, 174. This Pope's name was Odescalchi. He was commonly called the 'Protestant Pope,' from his hatred of the cruelty imposed upon the

third party was known as the French or Jesuit party, of which Father Petre was the recognised head. Its main strength and hope were in the religious fanaticism of the Irish people. The uncompromising zeal of the King caused him to hold by this third party, whilst the Queen leaned towards the second, or Papal, faction.

James asserts that it was by Sunderland's advice that he introduced Roman Catholics into the public service. A small council of Catholic lords, with Father Petre, used certainly to meet at this time in Mr. Chiffinch's apartments under the presidency of Sunderland, and advise the King as to his policy.* Sunderland took care that they should all be men whom he could influence as he wished, and in this way he obtained complete power in the country.

James soon got rid of those who, like Lord Montague, had supported the Exclusion Bill in Parliament during the previous reign.† In fact, all lovers of liberty and of the reformed faith were one by one dismissed from office. The Dukes of Norfolk and Ormond, and a host of others, were deprived of their places because they opposed his measures. His zealous friend, Admiral Herbert, was removed from all his offices. The liberal-minded Halifax was dismissed because he would not help to repeal the Test and Habeas Corpus Acts.‡ James told him 'that though he would not forget past services, yet, since he would not consent to the repeal of the Tests, he was resolved to have all of a

---

Reformers. He was one of the greatest men who ever wore the triple crown.

* This secret Junto was a sort of inner committee of the Privy Council. It consisted of Father Petre and the Catholic Lords Sunderland, Powis, Bellasis, Dover and Castlemain.

† He was Ralph, third Lord Montague of Boughton, and Ambassador at Paris in 1669. He was dismissed by James from the position of Master of the Wardrobe, and replaced by Lord Preston, a Roman Catholic. He joined William in 1689, and was created first Earl, and then Duke of Montague. He died in 1709.

‡ Barillon to Lewis, $\frac{29}{11} \cdot \frac{10}{11}$. 1685. Appendix cxxviii. to Fox's history.

piece.'* Orders were issued to all Lieutenants of counties, to have none returned as members of Parliament who were not in favour of the King's high-handed proceedings. Sixteen refused to comply, and were at once arbitrarily removed. Many colonels—amongst them Lord Oxford, of the Royal Horse Guards—were removed from the command of their regiments because the King believed them to be opposed to his illegal acts.+ Seven members of Parliament were removed for voting contrary to the King's pleasure, and he discharged all the deputy-lieutenants and magistrates of counties whose answers to questions put to them about the Test Act were on the side of liberty and Protestantism. They were mostly replaced by Catholics, or by Dissenters in the few instances in which no Catholics were available.‡ In December, 1686, Lord Rochester, James's brother-in-law, was deprived of his post as Lord-Treasurer because he refused to be converted by certain Roman Catholic divines whom the King had ordered to lecture him on religious subjects. His other brother-in-law, Clarendon, was removed in February, 1687, from the position of Lord-Lieutenant of Ireland, and the post was given to the bigoted Tyrconnel. To the clergy who turned Catholic the King, in flagrant violation of the law, granted dispensations to enable them to retain their livings. Roman Catholic Governours were appointed to Portsmouth, Hull, and the other chief fortresses of the kingdom. When the Duke of Somerset refused, as Lord Chamberlain, to introduce the Papal Nuncio at Windsor, pleading that it would be illegal for him to do so, James said, ' But I am above the law !' ' That may be so, but I am not,' was the prompt reply.

The Universities were still anti-Catholic, but James was determined to convert them into Papal institutions. He

---

* Echard's ' History of the Revolution,' p. 77.

† Sir J. Reresby's diary, January, 1688.

‡ See ' Penal Laws and Test Act,' by Sir George Duckett, Bart., in which are given these questions and the answers to them.

began with Oxford, by an attack upon the rights and
privileges of Christ Church, University and Exeter Colleges.
The great Locke—Shaftesbury's friend—had been already
deprived of his studentship by King Charles to please his
brother, and James now proceeded to deal in the same
manner with nearly all the Fellows of Magdalen College,
and to dispose illegally of its revenues.* Cambridge also
was soon made to feel his displeasure. This was but a just
retribution for the previous servility of the Universities.
The day Lord Russell was beheaded a decree was published
by the University of Oxford declaring all restrictions upon
the King's authority criminal in the sight of God and
man.† The proposition that a free people should make
their own laws was condemned, and Passive Obedience was
enjoined as a guiding principle of our Constitution, and as a
religious doctrine.

But things had changed now, for the King presumed to
lay hands on Church property. The Anglican clergy rose
as one man to defend these nurseries of learning and
religious teaching. James might do as he pleased in civil
and military matters, but he must not tamper with the Act
of Uniformity. The Church had so long preached the
doctrine of Passive Obedience, and had submitted so completely to the King's wishes upon all other matters, that he
never expected open resistance to his authority from such a
quarter. The view of the Constitution held by the clergy
was 'Church and State,' which James construed into 'the
King and the Church,' and he had counted upon the
support of the Church until the time should come when he
might be strong enough to destroy it. The Bishops were
indifferent whilst James robbed the towns of their charters
and the people of their liberties, but when he began to

---

* James tried to force upon them, as President, a disreputable man
named Farmer, whom even Jeffreys considered too bad for the place.
His recommendation in James's eyes was that he had turned Roman
Catholic.

† The execution of Russell and Sidney had been, at the time, a
great triumph for James's party.

meddle with the Church's property and with its educational establishments, to suspend Bishops and to degrade parish rectors, they turned upon him and upon his co-religionists. Thenceforward the pulpits throughout the country rang, as in the days of the Commonwealth, with denunciations of Popery, and nothing more was heard of royal prerogative as a 'Divine right.' The storm thus raised opened James's eyes for the moment, but did not prevent him from taking further violent measures.

Elated by his easy victory over Dissent in the West, James was not the man to brook this defiance of his authority by the Established Church, and this attack upon his cherished religion. Urged on by the priests, he foolishly prohibited the clergy from preaching on controversial subjects—a measure copied from the days of 'Bloody Mary,' every remembrance of whom was hateful to the nation. He ordered the Bishops to enforce this unlawful decree, and sent those who were contumacious before his illegally constituted Ecclesiastical High Court. The English country gentleman has always been a man of strong prejudices, and at this period he had an intense detestation of priests, Popery, Dissenters and of foreigners, Frenchmen especially. The great bulk of the English people hated Popery more than they loved liberty, and resented James's attacks upon the English Church more than those directed against their free institutions.

P. 3, 1686.

This may sound strange to the present generation, but it was in accord with the spirit of the age. Religion then meant everything, and it was political even more than spiritual. A Dissenter was one who looked back with fond affection to the Commonwealth, and forward in hope of the advent of a second Cromwell. A Low Churchman necessarily held Whig principles, and looked for liberty under a limited monarchy and Parliamentary institutions. The High Churchman was a Tory who believed in the Divine right of kings and in Passive Obedience. When it is said that the people hated Popery, it does not imply that they did so exclusively on spiritual grounds, or that they were morally better than those who believed in transubstantiation; it means rather that they hated it as a political system based on priestly despotism and upheld by the authority and weight of an alien Church.

In this chapter I have dwelt at some length on King James's treasons against his people; on the measures which he adopted to deprive Englishmen of their liberties and to destroy the Protestant faith to which, under various forms of Church government, they were devoted. I have done so because a knowledge of these facts is essential to a clear understanding of the influences which worked upon the mind and conscience of Marlborough at this great epoch of his life, and drove him, much against his inclination and his interests, to desert his old master and throw himself heart and soul into the Revolution conspiracy.

CHAPTER XLIII.

CHURCHILL BEGINS TO INTRIGUE WITH WILLIAM OF ORANGE.

The Princess Mary forms an ill opinion of Sarah Churchill—The conspiracy against James—Dykvelt's mission to London—Sunderland's want of principle.

THROUGHOUT these years Lord and Lady Churchill lived much at St. Albans, but always spent part of each season at Court. When Sarah was in 'waiting,' both she and her husband lived with her Royal Highness the Princess Anne at the Cockpit, Whitehall.* In May, 1686, they were with the Princess during her lying-in at Windsor, and Sarah was godmother to the child then born. It died in the following November, being one of Anne's many children who seemed to come into the world only to disappoint the people's hope of a Protestant heir to the Crown. During the years immediately preceding the Revolution, Anne maintained a regular correspondence with her sister in Holland. Their letters are interesting, though often coarse in some details, and we gather from them that about this period Princess Mary conceived a rooted dislike for Sarah. Interested motives compelled her to suppress it for a time, but it burst forth unchecked,

* Although this cockpit had been diverted from its original purpose, we read of cockfights being carried on at this time in the King's cockpit at Windsor for a week together. Indeed, we have never had a King more devoted to sport of all sorts than James II. In the *London Gazette* of his reign will be found numerous laws and regulations made by him for the preservation of game.

later on, when the Churchills' services were no more required. Busybodies about the Court had poisoned Princess Mary's mind against her sister's favourite, and in writing to Anne she stated what she had heard against her. In the following letter Anne endeavours to remove this unfavourable opinion : 'Sorry people have taken such pains to give so ill a character of Lady Churchill. . . . I believe there is nobody has better notions of religion than she has. It is true she is not so strict as some are, nor does not keep such a bustle about religion, which I confess I think is never the worse, for one sees so many saints mere devils that if one be a good Christian the less show one makes it is the better in my opinion. Then as for moral principles, it is impossible to have better ; and without that all the lifting up of hands and eyes and going often to church will prove but very lame devotion. One thing more I must say for her, which is that she has a true sense of the doctrine of our Church, and abhors all the principles of the Church of Rome; so that as to this particular I assure you she will never change. The same thing I will venture, now I am on this subject, to say for her Lord ; for though he is a very faithful servant to the King, and that the King is very kind to him, and, I believe, he will always obey the King in all things that are consistent with religion—yet, rather than change that, I dare say he will lose all his places and all that he has.'* From this we may infer, that Churchill had repeated to the Princess what he had told Lord Galway in Paris after the death of Charles II., namely, that if James attacked the Church, or attempted to change the Constitution, he would quit his service. In the following year Anne again wrote to her sister about him, saying, ' He was one of those whom I can always trust, and whom I am certain is a very honourable man and a good Protestant.' She adds 'that if things continued as they were then going, no Protestant would be able to live here soon.'

From information obtained through the Churchills,

* Dalrymple, vol. ii., p. 167, Appendix to Book V.

Anne must have been fully aware of the conspiracy to dethrone her father. Indeed, there can be no doubt that she cordially sympathized with the designs of those who felt that, if their religion and liberties were to be preserved, James must be deprived of his crown. Her letters written at this time show the horror with which she regarded her father's treasonable dealings with the people, especially his violation of law in the retention of Roman Catholics in office, and his refusal to nominate English Churchmen to the Privy Council. Writing in 1686 to Lady Churchill about the Catholic Lords Powis, Arundel, Bellasis, and Dover, she says : ' I was very much surprised when I heard of the four new privy councillors, and I am very sorry for it, for it will give great countenance to those sort of people, and methinks it has a very dismal prospect. Whatever changes there are in the world, I hope you will never forsake me, and I shall be happy.' Since the notable occasion to which Anne had referred in one of her letters to Mary, the King had never spoken to her about religion, but she daily expected him to renew the subject. Should he do so, she was resolved, she said, to submit to everything rather than change her faith. Lady Churchill contrived by means of visits to Bath and Tunbridge, on the plea of Anne's health, to keep the Princess as much as possible away from Court at this time, and thus to prevent any pressure from her father on the subject of religion.*

In February, 1686-7, William sent Herr Van Dykvelt to London to ascertain the true state of political feeling.† He was to note who were in favour of, and who were against, Dutch intervention in English affairs. He carried back to Holland the written assurances of the best men in the country that the Prince's advent was eagerly looked for by a vast majority of the nation. Danby, Nottingham,

---

* Vol. 164. folio 217, Archives des Affaires Étrangères.

† He had his first audience with James at Whitehall 21. 2. 168⁹⁄₁ (*London Gazette*), having reached London three days before. He returned to the Hague the beginning of May, 1687.

Halifax, Rochester, Devonshire, Churchill, and a host of others, both Tories and Whigs, had already entered into correspondence with Prince William. Some desired his coming from strong Protestant sympathies; others from political hatred of Popery; and others, again, from a love of liberty, and of that Constitution which was believed to ensure it. Throughout the reign of easy-going Charles II., there was no great cause to be won; but as soon as the Crown had passed to his bigoted brother, all England rallied to the cause of Protestantism, and it stirred a larger proportion of the people than the cause of liberty had done under the despotic rule of Charles I. Many wished for a new King because they found that there was no public career open to them under James, unless they abandoned a faith they held dear, a faith which was closely associated in their minds with their conception of freedom. The strong men were for strong measures, but the weak gave Dykvelt shifty answers. 'Lord Halifax, with that undetermination of spirit which commonly makes literary men of no use in the world' of action, was amongst the half-hearted and wavering.* Compton, Bishop of London, undertook to manage the Church in William's interests, Churchill was to do the same with the Army, and Admiral Russell with the Navy.

Sunderland, being then Principal Secretary of State, was the most important actor in the Revolution conspiracy. He was poor, shamelessly avaricious, and accepted pensions simultaneously from the King of France and from the Prince of Orange.† Devoid alike of religious convictions and of the moral sense of right and wrong, he had become a Roman Catholic so that James might retain him in office. But he certainly loved England, and wished to see

* Dalrymple, p. 17, Part I. of Book V.

† In a letter of 6, 12, 1685, Lewis XIV. ordered Barillon to allow Sunderland a pension of 20,000 or even as much as 24,000 crowns, 'as long as he shall contribute whatever depends upon him to maintain a good correspondence between me and the King his master, and to remove every engagement which can be contrary to my interests.' Dalrymple, Appendix to Book V., p. 141.

her people enjoy the benefits of civil and religious liberty.
He was absolutely unscrupulous as to the means he
employed to secure those rights; and feeling that they
could never be safe as long as James was King, he set
himself to destroy James and bring in Protestant William
in his stead. Besides, he so clearly foresaw that James
must ruin himself by the policy he was pursuing, that had
he nothing but self-interest to urge him, he would have
sought—like the unjust steward—to make a friend of the
Prince who was James's inevitable successor. He also
loved power, and being the most artful of trimmers, he was
determined, whatever might happen, to hold on to office
and its emoluments, though the game was no easy one to
play. The way in which he conducted it showed that his
nerve equalled his cunning and sagacity. Until William
should land, it was essential to the success of the plot
that James should have complete confidence in his First
Minister's loyalty, and this Sunderland accomplished with
the most refined subtlety, in the end delivering James over,
shorn of all power, into the hands of his enemy.

It must be remembered that Churchill held no military
post at this time; Lord Feversham commanded the troops
upon all occasions when they were brought together—as,
for instance, at the annual camps on Hounslow Heath—
Lord Dumbarton, a Catholic, being second in command
there. Indeed, James while King never gave his former page
any high position, either in the army, at Court, or in the
government of the country. He liked and valued Churchill,
but owing to his strong Protestantism he never promoted
him beyond the position of Gentleman of his Bedchamber.
Dykvelt had been especially ordered by William to com-
municate with Lord Churchill, because of his influence
with the Princess of Denmark and with the army. This is
the letter he carried back from him to the Prince of Orange:
' Sir,—The Princess of Denmark having ordered me to $\frac{17}{27}$ 5, 1687.
discourse with Mons. Dykvelt, and to let him know her
resolutions, so that he might let your Highness and the

Princess, her sister, know that she was resolved by the assistance of God to suffer all extremities, even unto death itself, rather than be brought to change her religion, I thought it my duty to your Highness and the Princess Royal, by this opportunity of Mons. Dykvelt, to give you assurances under my own hand that my places and the King's favour I set at naught, in comparison of the being true to my religion. In all things but this the King may command me; and I call God to witness that even with joy I should expose my life for his service, so sensible am I of his favours. I know the troubling you, sir, with thus much of myself, I being of so little use to your Highness, is very impertinent; but that I think it may be a great ease to your Highness and the Princess to be satisfied that the Princess of Denmark is safe in the trusting of me, I being resolved, although I cannot live the life of a saint, if there be ever occasion for it, to show the resolution of a martyr.—I am with all respects, sir,' etc.*

This was a treasonable letter, but so also were the letters written to the Prince of Orange at this time by the Lords Halifax, Shrewsbury, Nottingham, Clarendon, Rochester, Pembroke, Latimer, Danby, Lumley, Bath, by the Bishop of London, by Admirals Herbert and Russell, by Mr. Sidney, and a host of other leading men. The English Ambassador at the Hague was at this time in the receipt of pay both from Lewis XIV. and from William of Orange, and plotting all the while to allay his own King's suspicions regarding the impending invasion.†

It was but natural that those Englishmen who felt as Churchill did about Protestantism, and as Lords Devonshire, Halifax, and others did about constitutional liberty, should turn to the Prince of Orange to save their country.

---

* Dalrymple, vol. ii., Appendix to Book V., p. 62.

† The English Ambassador was an Irish adventurer named White, who called himself the Marquis d'Albeville. He was a man of a very disreputable character, who, having long served Lewis XIV. as a spy, was made a Marquis in France.

The result was that a close correspondence soon grew up between William and those who were conspiring against James.* In July, 1687, Bonrepos informed the French Court that Sunderland, Godolphin, and Churchill were already working in secret to merit the Prince of Orange's favour, and that of all James's Council he was only served faithfully by Lord Jeffreys, whom he described as ' un-extravagant.'

Dykvelt's conduct in England was displeasing to James, who thought him too intimate with those whom he knew to be opposed to his measures. The more astute and abler Count Zulestein, William's illegitimate cousin, was consequently sent to replace him in London.†

* Dalrymple and Fox give some of this interesting correspondence.

† Zulestein was son of the General of that name, who was the illegitimate brother of William's father. He was a soldier, and endowed with taking qualities. He was both talented and astute.

CHAPTER XLIV.

James tries to induce his friends to become Roman Catholics—The King makes a Royal Progress, and touches for the ' King's Evil '—Churchill remonstrates with him for introducing Popish Practices into the ceremony.

CHAPTER XLIV.

1687.

KING JAMES did all he could to induce his personal friends to become Roman Catholics. Many did so simply to please him, others in the hope of preferment.* Indeed, it became the fashion at Court to go to Mass with the King. All who looked for public employment soon realized that the surest road to royal favour was through the Confessional, but this was a road that Churchill was not disposed to follow. James became aware of this in the first year of his reign, and it is almost certain that Churchill's openly-avowed determination on the subject had been communicated to James very soon after he had announced it to Lord Galway. Fond as he was of money, Churchill would not sell his faith for office and its emoluments. He was well aware that, holding the position he did in James's personal esteem and trusted as he had been with the King's political secrets, though no party to his religious schemes,

* Amongst these were Lords Lorne, Melfort, Salisbury and Sunderland. The last-named was the most remarkable. James in Council spoke of his conversion as a matter of great importance, though it is tolerably certain that he was in heart a freethinker of Hobbes's school.

he had only to throw himself warmly into the Roman Catholic interest to become the most powerful subject in the kingdom.

As will be seen later on, Churchill did not hesitate to warn James of the danger he incurred by his Romish practices.* But he advised, he expostulated to no purpose. As a rule, when he sought to convince and win men over, his force of character, coupled with his power of persuasive reasoning, carried the day. But successful as he usually was, he failed to move James in matters of either State policy or religion. James's intolerant mind, ever open to arguments based on superstition, was impervious to those built upon the logic of facts. He lacked the independence of spirit and the magnanimity of mind to appreciate the counsel of a sterling, candid friend like Churchill, and he received his advice with anger and resentment. How and why should the servant he had raised from obscurity to high position presume to advise him—the Lord's anointed, the lawful heir of Saxon Alfred and of Norman William— on a question of conscience which involved his own spiritual welfare, and above all, which concerned the re-establish- ment of the ancient faith, the only true religion, in a matter upon which his mind was irrevocably made up, and on which his confessor thought as he did?

In the autumn of 1687 the King made a royal progress to Portsmouth, Bath, Gloucester, Worcester, Chester, Lich- field, Winchester, Oxford, etc., and Lord Churchill accom- panied him.† As Duke of York, James had been most unpopular because of his religion, and had been roughly handled by the ballad-mongers. He now sought to win the people's favour, and strove to reconcile his subjects to the new order of things which he had instituted. During this progress he touched about 5,000 people for the king's-evil; and at Winchester, to the horror of the Protestants present, the religious part of the rites was performed by two Roman

1⁵ 9, 1687.

---

* Coxe, vol. i., p. 27.
† He started 16, 8, 1687, and returned to Windsor 17, 9, 1687.

Catholic priests.* Walking alone with Churchill in the
Deanery garden before dinner, the King asked him what
the people said 'about this method I have taken of per-
forming the ceremony of touching in their churches.'
'Why, truly,' he replied, 'they show very little liking to
it; and it is the general voice of your people that your
Majesty is paving the way for the introduction of Popery.'
'How!' exclaimed the King in anger. 'Have I not given
them my royal word, and will they not believe their
King? I have given liberty of conscience to others, I
was always of opinion that toleration was necessary for
all Christian people, and most certainly I will not be
abridged of that liberty myself, nor suffer those of my own
religion to be deprived of paying their devotions to God in
their own way.' 'What I spoke, sir,' said Churchill, 'proceeded purely from my zeal for your Majesty's service, which
I prefer above all things next to that of God, and I humbly
beseech your Majesty to believe no subject in all your three
kingdoms would venture further than I would to purchase your favour and good liking; but I have been bred a
Protestant, and intend to live and die in that communion;
that above nine parts in ten of the whole people are of the
same persuasion, and I fear (which excess of duty makes
me say) from the genius of the English nation, and their
natural aversion to the Roman Catholic worship, some consequences which I dare not so much as name, and which
it creates a horror in me to think of.' The King listened
attentively to what, from anyone else, he would have
warmly resented, and then said deliberately: 'I tell you,
Churchill, I will exercise my own religion in such a manner
as I shall think fitting. I will show favour to my Catholic
subjects, and be a common father to all my Protestants
of what religion soever; but I am to remember that I
am King, and to be obeyed by them. As for the consequences, I shall leave them to Providence, and make
use of the power God has put in my hands to prevent any-

* Fathers Warner and Saunders.

thing that shall be injurious to my honour, or derogatory to the duty that is owing to me.' He then went to dinner, during which he talked only with the Dean, who stood behind his chair all the while, the conversation being exclusively on the subject of passive obedience.* This the King did to make Churchill understand how keenly he resented his freedom of speech. Few princes have sufficient wisdom to appreciate the loyalty of those who, like Churchill in this instance, have the courage to tell them home truths. He who ventures on such a course can seldom hope for much royal consideration. But if it be generally hazardous for the courtier to differ from his master, it was doubly so with a King of James's despotic character. It was, moreover, especially perilous to differ from him upon theological points, for, according to his notions, there could be no discussion upon matters which had been settled by an infallible Church. James cared as much for Churchill as a Stewart could care for anyone but himself. In him James knew that he possessed a faithful servant and a prudent counsellor, who, before Charles II.'s death, had saved James from many a scrape into which his obstinacy and bigotry would otherwise have led him. But James felt that Churchill's Protestantism was invincible—a fact of which the priests about the King made much capital —and although it is possible that James would have denied any change of sentiment on his part, still, little by little he did become estranged from his former favourite. It is evident that Churchill never had a high opinion of James's character, or any great personal affection for him. He knew him too well and had too often witnessed his cold indifference to the sufferings inflicted by his orders to have any sincere regard or respect for one who was certainly no

---

* Dr. Maggot was then the Dean. This is related by the author of 'The Lives of the Two Illustrious Generals,' etc., 1713, who says he also stood by and heard the conversation, and was told by Lord Churchill of his conversation with the King in the garden before dinner. See p. 21.

hero to his Gentleman-in-Waiting. Like many a courtier
before and since. Churchill, whilst he served the Prince,
despised the man. James knew how much Churchill's
skilful disposition had contributed to the victory at Sedgemoor; but although he rewarded him, as has been already
mentioned, thenceforward he took him less and less into his
confidence. He told the French Ambassador later on that
he never could put confidence in any man, however attached
to him, who affected the character of a zealous Protestant.*

Churchill fully realized the sacrifices which his staunch
Protestantism entailed upon him, and deliberately chose the
upright course. His resistance to the earnest wishes of the
King regarding a matter upon which James believed that he
had a right to claim obedience—if not from the people at
large, at least from his own household—began the estrange-
ment between them which dates from the overthrow of
Monmouth. That rebellion was always regarded by the
King as a religious rising. He knew that Protestant
London was at the time ripe for a revolt against Popery, and
had not Churchill's soldier-like precautions at Sedgemoor
saved the Royal army from defeat, it is tolerably certain
that Monmouth would have received strong and effective
support from the Protestant citizens of the capital.

* Barillon to Lewis. March 24. 1687; Mackintosh. p. 154.

END OF VOL. I.

BILLING AND SONS, PRINTERS, GUILDFORD.
J. D. & Co.

A List of

New and Standard Works

Works

now in print.

London:

Richard Bentley & Son,

Publishers in Ordinary to Her Majesty the Queen.

1894.

PRINCIPAL ALTERATIONS

SINCE THE LAST ISSUE OF THIS CATALOGUE.

ADDITIONS.

OMISSIONS.

Soups, Savouries, and Sweets, 3s. 6d.

ALTERATIONS IN PRICE.

MAGAZINE DATES OF ISSUE FOR 1895.

(Unless any unforeseen circumstances should arise to cause alteration.)

Monday, January 28.	Friday, July 26.
Monday, February 25.	Wednesday, August 28.
Thursday, March 28.	Thursday, September 26.
Friday, April 26.	Monday, October 28.
Tuesday, May 28.	Wednesday, November 27.
Thursday, June 27.	Friday, December 20.

Copies can be obtained by the public on the following day.

Advertisements will be received to the middle of the month, at 8, New Burlington Street, London (West-End), or at 3, George Yard, Lombard Street, E.C. (City Office); correspondence regarding them should be addressed to Messrs. Ratcliffe, Dunbar and Co., at 3, George Yard, E.C. Charge for an ordinary page in the 'Temple Bar' magazine, £6 6s. Special positions by arrangement.

NOTICES.

*** *Information furnished to Shippers, or others, without loss of time, on inquiry by Telephone to number* **3,730.** *Attendance from* 10 *to* 5 *on Weekdays (Saturdays* 10 *to* 2 *only) general holidays excepted.*

The Closed Days (besides Sundays) in 1895 *are April* 12, 13, *and* 15, *June* 3, *August* 5, *and December* 25 *and* 26.

Attention is drawn to 5 and 6 Victoria, cap. 45, sect. xvii., also 39 and 40 Victoria, cap. 36, sect. xlii., whereby it is made illegal to introduce into this country foreign editions of copyright works, such importations being subject to seizure and penalty.

All works are in one volume unless stated to the contrary.

*** *The present Catalogue supersedes all of earlier date.*

8, NEW BURLINGTON STREET,

LONDON, W.

List—November, 1894.

Ancient History.

BY DR. DUNCKER.

The History of Antiquity.

From the German of the late Professor MAX DUNCKER, by EVELYN ABBOTT, M.A., LL.D., of Balliol College, Oxford. Six vols., demy 8vo. Each Volume can be obtained separately, 21s.

The Ancient Kingdoms of Egypt, Babylonia, Assyria, the Phœnicians, Hebrews, Arabians, the Empires of the Medes, Persians, and Lydians, and the Early History of India.

'A work which should be in the hands of every historical student, not merely for passing reference, but to be carefully read and digested. In all six volumes we may safely say that there is no chapter lacking in interest.'—*The Saturday Review.*

The History of Greece,

From the Earliest Times to the Suppression of the Messenian Rebellion. From the German of Professor MAX DUNCKER. Demy 8vo. (Uniform in size with 'The History of Antiquity.') VOL. I., translated by S. F. ALLEYNE, 15s. VOL. II., translated by S. F. ALLEYNE and Dr. EVELYN ABBOTT, 15s.

BY DR. CURTIUS.

The History of Greece,

From the Earliest Time down to 337 B.C. From the German of Dr. ERNST CURTIUS, Rector of the University of Berlin. By A. W. WARD, M.A. Five vols., demy 8vo., each volume separately, 18s.

[*Vols. I. and III. reprinting.*

'Known to scholars as one of the profoundest, most original, and most instructive histories of modern times.'—*Globe.*

'We cannot express our opinion of Dr. Curtius' book better than by saying that it may be fitly ranked with Theodor Mommsen's great work.'—*Spectator.*

RICHARD BENTLEY AND SON, LONDON.

I

𝕎orks on 𝔸ncient 𝕳istory—(*Continued*).

BY DR. MOMMSEN.

The History of Rome,

From the Earliest Times to the Period of its Decline. By Professor THEODOR MOMMSEN. Translated by WILLIAM PURDIE DICKSON, D.D., LL.D., Professor of Divinity in the University of Glasgow. A new and cheaper edition, revised, and embodying all the most recent alterations and additions made by Dr. Mommsen. In five vols., crown 8vo. (each sold separately, 7s. 6d.), 37s. 6d.

Also, an ABRIDGED EDITION for the use of Schools and Colleges. By C. BRYANS and F. J. R. HENDY. One vol., crown 8vo., 7s. 6d.

'Dr. Mommsen's History increases in interest as he approaches the term of the memorable period he has illustrated with such felicity and genius. . . . His work is of the very highest merit ; its learning is exact and profound ; its narrative is full of genius and skill ; its descriptions of men are admirably vivid. . . . We wish to place on record our opinion that his is by far the best history of the decline and fall of the Roman Commonwealth.'—*The Times.*

The History of the Roman Provinces,

From the time of Cæsar to that of Diocletian. By Professor MOMMSEN. Translated by Dr. P. W. DICKSON. Two vols., demy 8vo., with Ten Maps, 36s.

THE BORDER TRIBES.	GREECE.
SPAIN.	ASIA MINOR.
GAUL.	MESOPOTAMIA AND PARTHIA.
CONQUERED GERMANY.	SYRIA AND NABATHŒA.
FREE GERMANY.	JUDÆA.
BRITAIN.	EGYPT.
THE DANUBIAN PROVINCES.	THE AFRICAN PROVINCES.

'Of all the great scholars of Germany none in our own day rises taller in intellectual stature than Professor Mommsen. . . . Already a kind of legendary halo begins to shine around the head of this "prodigy of literature," as his own countrymen call him, who, so it is said, is able to do with only four hours of sleep, who crowds two working days into one, who is so absorbed in his work that he scarcely knows his own children when he meets them, and so forth. . . . Wherever the student of the history of the Roman people turns his steps he is sure to find that Mommsen has been there before him. Roman coinage, Roman inscriptions, early republican institutions, late imperial chroniclers, the code of Justinian, the story of Coriolanus—everything which has to do in any way with the Seven-hilled City—is part of the vast *provincia* of this Cæsar of history.'—*The Pall Mall Gazette.*

BY PROFESSOR BROWNE.

A History of Roman Classical Literature.

By R. W. BROWNE, M.A., Ph.D., late Prebendary of St. Paul's and Professor of Classical Literature in King's College, London. Demy 8vo., 9s.

'Professor Browne was not only a classical scholar, but one of the most graceful of English modern writers. In clearness, purity, and elegance of style, his compositions were unsurpassed ; and his sketches of the lives and works of the great authors of antiquity were models of refined taste and sound criticism. We esteem very highly the value of a work like this. It is the result of great research and profound study ; but it is also popular and entertaining.'—*Morning Post.*

BY MADAME MIGNATY.

Sketches of the Historic Past of Italy ;

From the Fall of the Roman Empire to the Earliest Revival of Letters and Arts. By MARGARET ALBANA MIGNATY. Demy 8vo., 16s.

RICHARD BENTLEY AND SON, LONDON.

𝔚orks on 𝔐ediæval 𝔥istory.

BY MR. BESANT AND PROFESSOR PALMER.

The History of Jerusalem.

By WALTER BESANT, M.A., and E. H. PALMER, M.A., late Professor of Arabic, Cambridge. Third Edition, large crown 8vo., with Map, 7s. 6d.

Taken partly from the works of the Crusading historians, the travels of the early pilgrims, and other authorities not often consulted ; and partly from the accounts of Mohammedan writers whose works have never before been used for the purpose. Thus, the history is given from two points of view—the Christian and the Moslem.

CONTENTS—The Siege by Titus—From Titus to Omar—The Mohammedan Conquest—The Christian Pilgrims—The Crusades and the Latin Kingdom—Saladin—The Mohammedan Pilgrims—The Chronicle of Six Hundred Years.

BY PROFESSOR GINDELY.

The History of the Thirty Years' War.

By ANTON GINDELY. Translated by Professor ANDREW TEN BROOK. Two vols., large crown 8vo., with Maps and Illustrations, 24s.

'Among the productions of foreign historians which have lately been given us in an English form there is perhaps none that should be received with a warmer welcome than this "History of the Thirty Years' War." Although we are not always able to agree fully with the author's treatment of certain parts of his subject, it would be difficult to point to a single page of his work that is not full of interesting and suggestive matter. The book is in a convenient shape, and is furnished with two useful maps and a number of portraits and charming reproductions of old German plans and pictures of battles and sieges.'—*The Guardian.*

BY DR. STEVENS.

Memoir of Gustavus Adolphus.

By JOHN L. STEVENS, LL.D., Ambassador of the United States Government at Stockholm. Demy 8vo., with Portrait, 15s.

BY THE KING OF SWEDEN AND NORWAY.

Charles the Twelfth : a Memoir.

By His Majesty THE KING OF SWEDEN AND NORWAY. Translated with His Majesty's permission by GEORGE APGEORGE, Her Britannic Majesty's Consul at Stockholm. Royal 8vo., with Two Illustrations, 12s.

BY PROFESSOR CREASY.

The Fifteen Decisive Battles of the World.

Marathon, B.C. 490 ; Defeat of the Athenians at Syracuse, B.C. 413 ; Arbela, B.C. 331 ; The Metaurus, B.C. 207 ; Defeat of Varus, A.D. 9 ; Chalons, A.D. 451 ; Tours, A.D. 732 ; Hastings, A.D. 1066 ; Orleans, A.D. 1429 ; The Spanish Armada, A.D. 1558 ; Blenheim, A.D. 1704 ; Pultowa, A.D. 1709 ; Saratoga, A.D. 1777 ; Valmy, A.D. 1792 ; Waterloo, A.D. 1815. By Sir EDWARD CREASY, late Chief Justice of Ceylon. Thirty-seventh Edition, with Plans. Crown 8vo., canvas boards, 1s. 4d. ; in ornamental cloth binding, with red edges, 2s.

Also, a LIBRARY EDITION. 8vo., with Plans, 7s. 6d.

Also, the LATER DECISIVE BATTLES OF THE WORLD (from Hastings to Waterloo). Crown 8vo., gilt edges, 1s. 6d.

Works of Naval and Military Interest.

BY FIELD-MARSHAL LORD WOLSELEY.

The Life of John Churchill, First Duke of Marlborough.

Vols. I. and II., to the Accession of Queen Anne. By Field Marshal Viscount Wolseley, K.P. In demy 8vo., with Portraits of the Duke and Duchess of Marlborough, James II., William III., the Duke of Monmouth, Duchess of Cleveland, and other Illustrations or Plans, Fourth Edition, 32s.

BY LIEUTENANT LOW.

The Life of Viscount Wolseley.

By CHARLES RATHBONE LOW, F.R.G.S. Crown 8vo., with Portrait, 6s.

EDITED BY THE TWELFTH EARL OF DUNDONALD.

The Autobiography of a Seaman: Thomas, Tenth Earl of Dundonald.

Popular Edition, with a Sequel relating Lord Dundonald's services in South America, and in the War of the Greek Independence, and with an account of his later life and scientific inventions. With Portraits, Charts, and Nine Illustrations on Wood, crown 8vo., 6s.

BY M. LAVISSE.

The Youth of Frederick the Great.

From the French of ERNEST LAVISSE, by STEPHEN LOUIS SIMEON. In demy 8vo., 16s.

BY M. LÉVY.

The Private Life of Napoleon.

From the French of ARTHUR LÉVY, by STEPHEN LOUIS SIMEON. Second Edition, 2 vols., demy 8vo., with frontispieces, 28s.

BY THE DUKE OF TARENTUM.

The Recollections of Marshal Macdonald,

during the wars of the First Napoleon. Translated by STEPHEN LOUIS SIMEON. A New Edition, with Notes and Portrait, crown 8vo., 6s.

BY GENERAL GREELY.

Three Years of Arctic Service, and the Attainment of the Farthest North.

By ADOLPHUS W. GREELY, General U.S. Army, Commanding the Expedition, 1881-84. With Portrait of the Author, over One Hundred and Twenty Illustrations, and Official Charts. Third Edition, 2 vols., royal 8vo., 42s.

BY COLONEL CAMPBELL.

Letters from Camp,

To his Relatives at Home during the Siege of Sebastopol. By COLIN FREDERICK CAMPBELL. Edited, with Notes, by R. B. MANSFIELD and Colonel W. P. L'Estrange, R.A. With Introduction by Field-Marshal Lord WOLSELEY, and a Portrait by LOWES DICKINSON. Crown 8vo., with Map, 7s. 6d.

RICHARD BENTLEY AND SON, LONDON.

(5)

Works of Naval & Military Interest—(*Continued.*)

More about Gordon.

By one who knew him well. Fcap. 8vo., 2s. 6d.

By MISS FITZGIBBON.

A Veteran of 1812.

(The Defence of Canada.) The Life of JAMES FITZGIBBON. By his daughter, MARY AGNES FITZGIBBON, Author of 'A Trip to Manitoba.' Crown 8vo., with Portrait and Illustrations, 7s. 6d.

By MR. JAMES.

The Naval History of Great Britain,

1793 to 1820. By WILLIAM JAMES. With a Continuation to the Battle of Navarino, by Captain CHAMIER, Six vols., crown 8vo., with Portraits of William James, Lord Nelson, Sir Thomas Troubridge, Earl St. Vincent, Lord Duncan, Sir Hyde Parker, Sir Nesbit Willoughby, Sir William Hoste, Lord Hood, Earl Howe, Sir Sidney Smith, Lord Dundonald, 42s. [*See page 7.*

By LIEUTENANT LOW.

The History of the Indian Navy.

An Account of the Creation, Constitution, War Services, and Surveys of the Indian Navy between the years 1613 and 1864. By CHARLES RATHBONE LOW, (late) Indian Navy, F.R.G.S. 2 vols., demy 8vo., 36s.

By COLONEL DAVIS.

The History of the Second Queen's (Royal West Surrey) Regiment.

By Lieut.-Colonel JOHN DAVIS, F.S.A., Author of 'Records of the Second Royal Surrey Militia.' Royal 8vo., with numerous Illustrations. Vol. I., THE ENGLISH OCCUPATION OF TANGIERS, 1661 to 1684, 24s.

By CAPTAIN GOFF.

Records of the 91st Highlanders,

NOW THE 1ST BATTALION OF THE PRINCESS LOUISE'S ARGYLL AND SUTHERLAND HIGHLANDERS, containing an Account of the Formation of the Regiment in 1794, and of its Subsequent Services to 1881. Arranged by GERALD LIONEL GOFF, First Battalion Argyll and Sutherland Highlanders. With numerous Illustrations. Demy 8vo., 30s.

By CAPTAIN BURGOYNE.

Records of the 93rd Highlanders,

NOW THE 2nd BATTALION PRINCESS LOUISE'S ARGYLL AND SUTHERLAND HIGHLANDERS. By Captain RODERICK HAMILTON BURGOYNE, late 93rd Highlanders. A history of the Regiment from its formation to the present time. With numerous Illustrations of dress, etc. Demy 8vo., 30s.

By CAPTAIN WOOLLRIGHT.

A History of the 57th Regiment.

From 1755 to 1881. Including a Record of the Services of the (WEST MIDDLESEX) 'Die Hards,' in the American War of Independence, Flanders, the West Indies, the Peninsula, France, the Crimea, New Zealand, Zululand, etc. By Captain HENRY H. WOOLLRIGHT, Middlesex Regiment. With Coloured Plates, Maps, and other Illustrations. Demy 8vo., 30s.

PUBLISHERS in ORDINARY to HER MAJESTY.

(6)

𝔚orks of 𝔑aval & 𝔐ilitary 𝔈nterest—(*Continued*).

By COLONEL RAIKES.

The History of the Honourable Artillery Company of London.

Including also a brief history of the American Branch of the Regiment founded at Boston in 1638. By Colonel G. A. RAIKES, F.S.A. 2 vols., with Portraits, Coloured Illustrations, and Maps, demy 8vo., 31s. 6d. each.

THE ANCIENT VELLUM BOOK OF THE COMPANY. Being the Roll of Members from 1611 to 1682. Edited, with Notes and Illustrations, by Colonel RAIKES, F.S.A. Demy 8vo., 21s.

THE ROYAL CHARTER OF INCORPORATION GRANTED TO THE COMPANY BY HENRY VIII. IN 1537. Also the Royal Warrants issued from 1632 to 1889, and Orders in Council from 1591 to 1634. Edited by Colonel RAIKES, F.S.A. Thin demy 8vo., 7s. 6d.

The Roll of Officers of the York and Lancaster Regiment.

Vol. I. THE FIRST BATTALION, LATE 65TH FOOT. [*Out of print.*]
Vol. II. THE SECOND BATTALION, LATE 84TH FOOT. By Colonel G. A. RAIKES, F.S.A. Demy 8vo., 21s.

Records of the First Regiment of Militia ;

or Third West York Light Infantry. By Colonel G. A. RAIKES, F.S.A. With Eight full-page Illustrations. Demy 8vo., 21s.

.·. For Colonel FLETCHER'S 'History of the American Civil War,' see page 12.

𝔚orks on 𝔈nglish 𝔥istory.

By PROFESSOR CREASY.

The Rise and Progress of the English Constitution.

By Sir EDWARD CREASY, late Chief Justice of Ceylon. A Popular Account of the Primary Principles, and Formation and Development of the English Constitution, avoiding Party Politics. Fifteenth Edition. Crown 8vo., 6s.

The Fifteen Decisive Battles of the World.

By SIR EDWARD CREASY, late Chief Justice of Ceylon. For Contents see page 3. Thirty-seventh Edition, with Plans. Crown 8vo., canvas boards, 1s. 4d. ; or in cloth gilt, red edges, 2s.

Also, a LIBRARY EDITION. 8vo., with Plans, 7s. 6d.

Also, THE LATER DECISIVE BATTLES OF THE WORLD (from Hastings to Waterloo). Crown 8vo., gilt edges, 1s. 6d.

RICHARD BENTLEY AND SON, LONDON.

(7)

𝕎orks on English History—(*Continued*).

BY MR. JAMES.

The Naval History of Great Britain,

From the Declaration of War by France, in 1793, to the Accession of George IV. By WILLIAM JAMES. With a Continuation of the History to the Battle of Navarino, by Captain CHAMIER. 6 vols., crown 8vo., with Twelve Portraits on Steel, 42s.

'James, one of the most pertinacious of investigators, set a new example. He honestly did his utmost to satisfy himself of the absolute truth of every statement which he submitted to his readers. He wrote hundreds of letters to the surviving actors in the events which he purposed to describe. He read and digested all the despatches, logs, gazettes, previous histories, foreign reports, and private narratives on which he could lay his hands. He carefully balanced conflicting accounts, and arrived in the majority of instances at conclusions the correctness of which has never yet been successfully attacked. He went to immense pains to give the exact Christian names of all officers whom he had occasion to mention, and to analyse the true force of every ship the exploits of which he recounted. Never was there a man more painstaking, more indefatigable, more scrupulously conscientious.'—*Fortnightly Review.*

*** See also page 5.

BY M. GUIZOT.

The Life of Oliver Cromwell.

From the French of M. GUIZOT by Sir ANDREW R. SCOBLE, Q.C. Ninth Edition. Crown 8vo., with Four Portraits, 6s.

BY M. MIGNET.

The Life of Mary Queen of Scots.

From the French of M. MIGNET, by Sir ANDREW R. SCOBLE, Q.C. Seventh Edition. With Two Portraits, crown 8vo., 6s.

BY MISS BRADLEY.

A Life of Arabella Stuart.

By EMILY TENNYSON BRADLEY. 2 vols., crown 8vo., with Portraits and Facsimile, 24s.

BY MR. JOYCE.

The History of the Post-Office.

From its establishment down to 1836. By HERBERT JOYCE, C.B., of the Post-Office. Demy 8vo., 16s.

EARLY POSTS. THE BATTLE OF THE PATENTS. THOMAS WITHERINGS. EDMUND PRIDEAUX AND CLEMENT OXENBRIDGE. WILLIAM DOCKWRA. COTTON AND FRANKLAND. AMERICAN POSTS. THE POST-OFFICE ACT OF 1711. RALPH ALLEN. JOHN PALMER. FRANCIS FREELING. IRELAND.

'A work of great historical value—a work which is not only a history of a particular State Department, but also a valuable contribution to the social history of the seventeenth and eighteenth centuries.'—*The Graphic.*

BY MR. BAINES.

Forty Years at the Post-Office,

1850 to 1890. A Personal Narrative. By FREDERICK E. BAINES, C.B., sometime Surveyor-General of Telegraphs, Assistant Secretary and Inspector-General of Mails. In 2 vols., large crown 8vo., with Portrait, etc.

The Northern and Western Mail Roads—Irish and Scotch Mails—Penny Postage—St. Martin's-le-Grand—The Administration (metropolitan and provincial), with Personal Sketches—Inland Posts—Foreign and Colonial Matters—Electric Telegraphs, Rise (1836), their Transfer to the State (1870), Inland and Submarine—Methods and Management—Blockaded Mails—The Parcel Post—Great Mail-Packet Companies—The Overland Route to India and Australia—The Rail.

PUBLISHERS in ORDINARY to HER MAJESTY.

Works on English History—(*Continued*).

By DEAN HOOK.

Lives of the Archbishops of Canterbury.

See page 16.

By PREBENDARY STEPHENS.

Memorials of the Cathedral of Chichester.

From Original Sources, by the Rev. W. R. W. STEPHENS, Prebendary of Chichester, Author of 'The Life and Times of St. John Chrysostom,' etc. Demy 8vo., with Plan of the Cathedral, and Seven Illustrations, 21s.

By DR. DORAN.

The Queens of England of H. of Hanover.

Sophia Dorothea of Zell (wife of George I.)—Carolina Wilhelmina Dorothea (wife of George II.)—Charlotte Sophia (wife of George III.)—Caroline of Brunswick (wife of George IV.)—Adelaide of Saxe-Meinengen (wife of William IV.). By Dr. DORAN, F.S.A., Author of 'Table Traits and Something on Them,' etc. Fourth and enlarged Edition. 2 vols., 8vo., 25s.

By MR. RUSH.

The Court of London.

By RICHARD RUSH, United States Minister in London, 1819–1825. Edited by his Son, BENJAMIN RUSH. Demy 8vo., 16s.

By MR. COOKE TAYLOR.

The History of the Factory System,

From the Earliest Times down to the present day. By WHATELY COOKE TAYLOR. Introductory volume. Demy 8vo., 16s.

By MISS HILL.

A History of English Dress.

By GEORGIANA HILL. Two vols., demy 8vo., with fourteen Illustrations on steel, 30s.

SAXON-NORMAN PERIOD—PLANTAGENET PERIOD—THE REIGN OF THE ROSES —TUDOR PERIOD—STUART PERIOD—THE HANOVERIAN PERIOD.

HISTORICAL ILLUSTRATIONS OF COSTUME.

Queen Elizabeth.	Prince Rupert, when young.	Queen Victoria.
Mary Stuart at the age of sixteen.	Lady Mary Tudor, daughter of Charles II.	Simon Frazer, Lord Lovat.
Mary Sidney, Countess of Pembroke.	George Villiers, First Duke of Buckingham.	Mrs. Fitzherbert.
Sir Christopher Hatton.	Arabella Stuart.	John Law.
		L. E. Landon.
		Lady Stepney.

'A monument of careful labour.'—*Black and White.*

By MR. P. COURTNEY.

The History of English Whist.

By WILLIAM PRIDEAUX COURTNEY. Demy 8vo., 14s.

Birth and Progress of Whist — Prelates as Whist-Players — Whist at the Universities — Woman's Whist—Celebrated Whist Parties—The Devil's Books and the Devil's Own—Warriors at Whist- Gamblers at Whist—Clubs and Cards—Kings and their Subjects at Whist—Combinations and Superstitions at Cards—The Ideal Whist-Player—The Whist of the Poets—Whist and the Novelists—Books on Whist and their Authors.

A HISTORY OF ENGLISH HORSE-RACING. *See* page 34.

RICHARD BENTLEY AND SON, LONDON.

𝔚orks on 𝔉rench 𝔥istory.

By WALTER BESANT.

The French Humourists, from the Twelfth to the Nineteenth Century.

By WALTER BESANT, M.A., Christ's Coll., Cam. 8vo., 15s.

Rutebeuf—Guillaume de Lorris—Jean de Meung—Eustache Deschamps—Rabelais—Montaigne — Rapin—Passerat—Pithon—Regnier — St. Amant—Benserade—Voiture—Scarron—La Fontaine—Boileau—Molière—Regnard—Gresset—Beaumarchais—Béranger, and others.

By MISS PARDOE.

The Court and Reign of Francis I.

By JULIA PARDOE. 3 vols., demy 8vo., with numerous Portraits on Steel, and a brief Memoir of the Author, 42s.

The illustrations comprise:— Francis the First (two portraits by Titian); Queen Eleanor; The Emperor Charles the Fifth (two portraits by Titian); Duke of Bourbon and Constable of France (by Titian); The Chevalier Bayard; Henry the Eighth (by Holbein); Henry the Eighth embarking for France; Ignatius Loyola (by Wierix); Marguerite de Valois, Catherine de Médicis (two portraits); The Duchesse d'Etampes, Diana of Poictiers, The Duke of Alva (by Schubert); Annas de Montmorency, Constable of France, and Julia Pardoe. The cover of the book is from a design by Diana of Poictiers.

The Court of Louis the Fourteenth.

By JULIA PARDOE. With upwards of Fifty Woodcuts, and numerous Portraits on Steel. 3 vols., demy 8vo., 42s.

PORTRAITS ON STEEL.

Louis XIV. (four portraits). Cardinal Mazarin. Anne of Austria. Madame de Sévigné. Louis, Prince de Condé. Ninon de l'Enclos. Madame de Maintenon (three portraits). Maréchal Turenne. Philippe, Duc d'Orleans. Mdlle. de Vallière (two portraits). Madame de Montespan. Colbert.

The Life of Marie de Medicis,

Consort of Henry IV., and Regent of France during the early years of Louis XIII. By JULIA PARDOE. 3 vols., demy 8vo., with Portraits and Facsimiles, 42s.

ILLUSTRATIONS ON STEEL.

Marie de Medicis (two portraits). Henri de Lorraine, Duc de Guise. The Eve of Saint Bartholomew. Gabrielle d'Estrées. Maréchal de Biron. Duc de Sully. Henri IV. Louis XIII. (two portraits). Maréchal de Bassompierre. Cardinal de Richelieu (two portraits). Anne of Austria. Maréchal de Schomberg. Cardinal Mazarin. George Villiers, first Duke of Buckingham. Marquis de Cinq-Mars.

Works by Lady Jackson.

THE COURT OF FRANCE UNDER FRANCIS I. AND HENRY II.
2 vols., large crown 8vo., with Portraits, 24s.

THE LAST OF THE VALOIS,
And the Accession of Henry of Navarre, 1559—1610. 2 vols., large crown 8vo., with Portraits, 24s.

THE FIRST OF THE BOURBONS.
2 vols., large crown 8vo., with Portraits, 24s.

THE OLD RÉGIME.
2 vols., large crown 8vo., with portraits, 24s.

„ 'Old Paris,' 'French Court and Society,' and 'The Court of the Tuileries' are at present out of print.

PUBLISHERS in ORDINARY to HER MAJESTY.

𝔚orks on 𝔉rench 𝔥istory—(*Continued*).

BY THE DUC D'AUMALE.

Lives of the Princes of the House of Condé.

By the DUC D'AUMALE. Translated by the Rev. R. BROWN-BORTHWICK.
2 vols., 8vo., with two fine Portraits, 30s.

BY MADAME DU NOYER.

The Correspondence of Anne du Noyer

during the Reign of Louis XIV. Now first translated by FLORENCE LAYARD.
2 vols., demy 8vo., with Portraits and Notes, 30s.

BY MADAME CAMPAN.

The Life of Marie Antoinette.

By JEANNE LOUISE HENRIETTE CAMPAN, First Lady in Waiting. With
Memoir of Madame Campan, by MM. BARRIÈRE and MAIGNE. New and
Revised Edition, with additional Notes, and Portrait. Crown 8vo., 6s.

'Madame Campan was first Woman of the Bedchamber to Marie Antoinette, and escaped
almost by a miracle through the Reign of Terror. She died last year, and in her bureau were
found most curious and authentic memoirs of her life during her service about the Queen. We
have suspended the issue of this review to read them, and have read them with delight.'—
Quarterly Review (1822).

BY MADAME JUNOT.

The Court and Family of Napoleon.

By the Duchesse D'ABRANTÈS (Laure Junot). A New and Revised Edition,
with Additional Notes, and an Explanatory List of the Titles of the Persons
mentioned in the Work. 4 vols., crown 8vo., price 36s.

LIST OF ILLUSTRATIONS.

VOL. I.

Andoche Junot, Duke of Abrantès.
Charles Bonaparte, Father of Napoleon.
The Princesse de Lamballe.
Joseph Bonaparte, King of Naples and of
Spain.
Marie Pauline Bonaparte, Princess Borghèse.
Eugène Beauharnais, Viceroy of Italy.

VOL. II.

Napoleon Bonaparte.
Jerôme Bonaparte, King of Westphalia.
General Moreau.
Eliza Bonaparte, Grand Duchess of Tuscany.
Caroline Bonaparte, Queen of Naples.
Lucien Bonaparte, Prince of Canino.

VOL. III.

The Empress Josephine.
Josephine Beauharnais (daughter of the Vice-
roy of Italy), afterwards Crown Princess of
Sweden.
Madame Mère.
Madame Campan.
Louis Bonaparte, King of Holland.
Louisa, Queen of Prussia.

VOL. IV.

Maria Louisa, Empress of France.
Cardinal Fesch, Archbishop of Lyons.
Napoleon II. (The King of Rome.)
Joachim Murat, King of Naples.
Duroc, Duke of Friuli. [Empire.
Prince Metternich, Chancellor of the German

'No person was better qualified than the accomplished writer of these Memoirs for the task
she has undertaken. Allied by blood to the family of Bonaparte, she was in early life accustomed
to meet Napoleon at her father's house almost on the footing of a brother. After her marriage
with Junot, she became one of the leading stars, first in the Consular circles, afterwards at the
Imperial Court, without any interruption to that familiarity with which the Emperor had been
accustomed to treat her when he was only a sub-lieutenant of artillery. The confidential situation
held by her husband, together with her own free access to the Imperial presence, gave her the
opportunity of an occasional peep behind the scenes, and a glimpse now and then of the hand
that set in motion the springs of a policy which, had it been more patriotic and less selfish, would
have established the permanent greatness of the French empire. . . . The gossip of the Duchess
is always delightful, and this work is so full of interesting matter that it would be difficult if we
opened it at hazard to light upon anything unworthy of notice.'—*Athenæum* (1832).

'These Memoirs furnish an admirable view—admirable because to the life—of the interior
of Napoleon's Court. Of the spirit that reigned there, of the characters that were exhibited in
it, and of the genius of the First Consul. Nowhere do we get a nearer or more intelligible view
of Napoleon as a man.'—*Spectator* (1832).

'The best account of the early career of Napoleon yet given to the world.'—*Literary Gazette*
(1832).

RICHARD BENTLEY AND SON, LONDON.

𝔚orks on 𝔉rench 𝔥istory—(*Continued*).

By M. THIERS.

The History of the French Revolution.

By ADOLPHE THIERS. Translated by FREDERICK SHOBERL. With Fifty Engravings and Portraits, on steel, of the most eminent Personages engaged in the Revolution, many engraved by W. GREATBACH. A New and Revised Edition in 5 vols., demy 8vo., 45s.

LIST OF PLATES IN EACH VOLUME.

VOL.
- I. The Attack on the Bastile.
  - Portrait of the Duc d'Orléans.
  - Portrait of Mirabeau.
  - Portrait of Lafayette.
  - Orgies of the Gardes du Corps.
  - Portrait of Marie Antoinette.
  - The King's Return from Varennes.
  - Portrait of Marat.
  - The Mob at the Tuileries.
  - Attack on the Tuileries.
- II. Murder of the Princesse de Lamballe.
  - Portrait of the Princess de Lamballe.
  - Portrait of Madame Roland.
  - Louis XVI. at the Convention.
  - Farewell of Louis XVI. to his Family.
  - Portrait of Louis XVI.
  - Portrait of Dumouriez.
  - Triumph of Marat.
  - Portrait of Larochejaquelin.
- III. Assassination of Marat.
  - Portrait of Charlotte Corday.
  - Portrait of Camille Desmoulins.
  - Condemnation of Marie Antoinette.
  - Portrait of Bailly (Mayor of Paris).
  - Trial of Danton, Camille Desmoulins, etc.

VOL.
- III. Portrait of Danton.
  - Portrait of Madame Elizabeth.
  - Carrier at Nantes.
  - Portrait of Robespierre.
- IV. Last Victims of the Reign of Terror.
  - Portrait of Charette.
  - Death of the Deputy Feraud.
  - Death of Romme, Goujon, Duquesnoi, etc.
  - Portrait of Louis XVII.
  - The 13th Vendémiaire (Oct. 5, 1795).
  - Portrait of Lazare Carnot.
  - Portrait of Junot.
  - Portrait of Bernadotte.
  - Portrait of Massena.
- V. Summoning to Execution.
  - Portrait of Pichegru.
  - Portrait of Moreau.
  - Portrait of Hoche.
  - Portrait of Napoleon Bonaparte.
  - The 18th Brumaire (November 10th, 1799).
  - Portrait of Sièyès.
  - Portrait of Barras.
  - Portrait of Fouché.
  - Portrait of Murat.
  - Portrait of Adolphe Thiers.

By M. DE BOURRIENNE.

Memoirs of Napoleon Bonaparte.

By LOUIS ANTOINE FAUVELET DE BOURRIENNE, his private Secretary. Edited, with Preface, Supplementary Chapters, and Notes, by Colonel R. W. PHIPPS, late Royal Artillery. 4 vols., crown 8vo., with Illustrations, 36s.

LIST OF PORTRAITS.

Napoleon I. (three). Letitia Ramolino. Josephine (two). Prince Eugene. Kléber. Lannes. Talleyrand. Duroc. Murat. Desaix. Moreau. Hortense. Duc d'Enghien. Pichegru. Ney (two). Caulaincourt. Davoust. Junot. Soult. Marie Louise (two). Lasalle. Massena. Macdonald. Suchet. Wellington. Blucher. Gouvion St. Cyr. The King of Rome. Bessieres.

By M. ARTHUR LÉVY.

THE PRIVATE LIFE OF NAPOLEON.

See page 4.

By SURGEON O'MEARA.

Napoleon at St. Helena.

By BARRY E. O'MEARA, Body-Surgeon to the Emperor. A New Edition, with Introduction, copious Notes, and other Additions, and with several Coloured Plates, Portraits and Woodcuts. 2 vols., demy 8vo., 30s.

By MARSHAL MACDONALD.

RECOLLECTIONS OF THE WARS OF THE REPUBLIC AND OF NAPOLEON I.
See page 4.

PUBLISHERS in ORDINARY to HER MAJESTY.

American History.

By MR. WEISE.

A History of the Discoveries of America

down to the year 1525. By ARTHUR JAMES WEISE, M.A. Large demy 8vo., with numerous Maps reproduced in facsimile from the originals, 7s. 6d.

By COLONEL FLETCHER.

The History of the American Civil War.

By H. C. FLETCHER, Scots Fusilier Guards. 3 vols., 8vo., separately, 18s. each.

By CAPTAIN BULLOCH.

The Secret Service of the Confederate States in Europe.

By JAMES D. BULLOCH, late Confederate Navy. 2 vols., demy 8vo., 21s.

By COLONEL RAIKES.

THE ARTILLERY COMPANY OF BOSTON, U.S.A.

See Colonel Raikes's History, described on p. 6.

By MR. GREENHOUGH SMITH.

The Romance of History.

Masaniello—Lochiel—Bayard—Marino Faliero—Benyowski—Tamerlane— —De Laguette—Casanova—William Lithgow—Vidocq—Prince Rupert. By HERBERT GREENHOUGH SMITH. Demy 8vo., 15s.

By MR. JESSE.

Memoirs of Celebrated Etonians.

By JOHN HENEAGE JESSE. 2 vols., demy 8vo., 28s.

EDITED BY JAMES BRINSLEY-RICHARDS.

Seven Years at Eton,

1857-1864. Third Edition. Crown 8vo., 6s.

By THE LATE MR. HUGHES-HUGHES.

The Register of Tonbridge School,

Edited by W. O. HUGHES-HUGHES, M.A. Medium, 6s. ; large paper, 9s.

By MR. FITZGERALD.

Recollections of Stonyhurst College.

By PERCY FITZGERALD, M.A., F.S.A. In demy 8vo. [In the Press.

By REV. J. PYCROFT.

Oxford Memories.

By the Rev. JAMES PYCROFT, B.A. 2 vols., demy 8vo., 24s.

RICHARD BENTLEY AND SON, LONDON.

Political Biography.

EDITED BY PRINCE RICHARD METTERNICH.

The Autobiography of Prince Metternich.

Translated by ROBINA NAPIER and GERARD W. SMITH. Vols. I. and II., 1773-1815, demy 8vo., with Portrait and two Facsimiles, 36s. Vols. III. and IV., 1816-1829, demy 8vo., 36s. Vol. V., 1830-1835, demy 8vo., 18s.

EDITED BY M. PALLAIN.

The Correspondence of Prince Talleyrand and Louis XVIII.

During the Congress of Vienna. 2 vols., demy 8vo., 24s.

BY MR. BALLANTYNE.

The Life of Lord Carteret (afterwards Earl Granville), 1690-1763.

By ARCHIBALD BALLANTYNE. Demy 8vo., 16s.

BY SIR D. LE MARCHANT.

Memoir of Earl Spencer (Lord Althorp).

By the late Sir DENIS LE MARCHANT, Bart. Demy 8vo., 16s.

BY MR. MYERS.

Lord Althorp.

By ERNEST MYERS. Small crown 8vo., 3s. 6d.

EDITED BY MR. LE STRANGE.

The Correspondence of Princess Lieven and Earl Grey.

Translated and edited, with Introduction and Notes, by GUY LE STRANGE. Vols. I. and II., demy 8vo., with Portraits, 30s. Vol. III., demy 8vo., 15s.

EDITED BY LORD COLCHESTER.

A Diary kept while in Office.

By EDWARD LAW, EARL OF ELLENBOROUGH. Two vols., demy 8vo., 30s.

The History of Lord Ellenborough's Administration in India.

Containing his Letters to Her Majesty the Queen, and Letters to and from the Duke of Wellington. Demy 8vo., 18s.

EDITED BY LADY JACKSON.

Diaries and Letters of Sir G. Jackson,

From the Peace of Amiens to the Battle of Talavera. 2 vols., demy 8vo., 30s.

The BATH ARCHIVES. A further Selection from the Letters and Diaries of Sir GEORGE JACKSON, K.G.H., from 1809 to 1816. 2 vols., demy 8vo., 30s.

PUBLISHERS in ORDINARY to HER MAJESTY.

Political Biography—(*Continued*).

EDITED BY MR. MALLOCK.

Letters and Memoirs of the Twelfth Duke of Somerset.

With Selections from his Diaries. Edited by WILLIAM H. MALLOCK and LADY GUENDOLEN RAMSDEN. Demy 8vo., 16s.

BY THE LATE MR. W. M. TORRENS.

Twenty Years of Parliamentary Life.

By WILLIAM McCULLAGH TORRENS, Author of 'The Life of Lord Melbourne.' Demy 8vo., 15s.

BY LORD DALLING AND THE HON. EVELYN ASHLEY.

The Life of Viscount Palmerston.

With Selections from his Diaries and Correspondence. By the late Lord DALLING and BULWER. Demy 8vo. Vols. I. and II., with fine Portrait, 30s. Vol. III., edited by the Hon. EVELYN ASHLEY, 15s. Vols. IV. and V., by the Hon. EVELYN ASHLEY, with Two Portraits, 30s.
ANOTHER EDITION. 2 vols., crown 8vo., each with Frontispiece, 12s.
The 12s. edition contains considerable additional matter and numerous alterations.

BY THE LATE MR. SKENE.

Reminiscences of Lord Stratford de Redclyffe, and the Crimean War.

By JAMES HENRY SKENE, Author of 'Frontier Lands of Christian and Turk.' Demy 8vo., 12s.

BY PROFESSOR FORREST.

Selections from Official Writings of the Rt. Hon. Mountstuart Elphinstone.

Edited, with a Memoir, by Professor G. W. FORREST. Demy 8vo., 21s.

EDITED BY MISS FORSYTH.

Autobiography and Reminiscences of Sir Douglas Forsyth, K.C.S.I., C.B.

Edited by his Daughter, ETHEL FORSYTH. Demy 8vo., with Portrait on Steel, and Map, 12s. 6d.

BY MR. TIMBS.

The Lives of Statesmen :

Burke and Chatham. By JOHN TIMBS, F.S.A. Crown 8vo., with Portraits, 6s.

BY THE EMPEROR OF MEXICO.

Recollections of My Life.

By the late EMPEROR MAXIMILIAN of MEXICO. 3 vols., post 8vo., 31s. 6d.

RICHARD BENTLEY AND SON, LONDON

Legal Biography.

A Memoir of Lord Hatherley.

By the Rev. W. R. W. STEPHENS, Rector of Woolbeding, Sussex, Author of 'The Life and Letters of Dean Hook,' etc. Crown 8vo., with two Portraits, 21s.

BY MISS LEATHLEY.

The Early Life of Sir William Maule.

By his Niece, EMMA LEATHLEY. Crown 8vo., 7s. 6d.

BY MR. NASH.

The Life of Richard, Baron Westbury,

Lord High Chancellor of England. By THOMAS ARTHUR NASH, Barrister-at-Law. 2 vols., demy 8vo., with two Portraits, 30s.

BY SERJEANT BALLANTINE.

Mr. Serjeant Ballantine's Experiences.

A new and cheaper edition (being the fourteenth), crown 8vo., paper cover, 1s., cloth, 1s. 6d. [*Reprinting.*

From the Old World to the New.

Being some Experiences of a Recent Visit to America, including a Trip to the Mormon Country. By Mr. SERJEANT BALLANTINE, Author of ' Some Experiences of a Barrister's Career.' Demy 8vo., with Portrait, 14s.

ANONYMOUS.

Some Professional Recollections.

By a Former Member of the Council of the Incorporated Law Society. Crown 8vo., 9s.

. This work includes some account of the singular career of the Carron Company.

BY MR. THORPE, F.S.A.

The Still Life of the Middle Temple,

With some of its Table Talk, preceded by Fifty Years' Reminiscences. By W. G. THORPE, a Barrister of the Society. Demy 8vo., 15s.

'Westbury, Campbell, Stephen, Huddleston, and a host of other judicial lights appear in these pages as the heroes of a number of funny stories, the whole making up a wonderfully entertaining book.'—*Observer.*

'A very entertaining volume of reminiscences and gossip, associated with a very genial account of the Middle Temple, its life and its ways, ceremonial and social. Mr. Thorpe has lived a life full of varied incidents and experience, and he tells his story with unfailing spirit and good-humour. His fund of anecdote seems to be inexhaustible.'—*Times.*

PUBLISHERS in ORDINARY to HER MAJESTY.

Clerical Biography.

By DEAN HOOK.

Lives of the Archbishops of Canterbury,

From St. AUGUSTINE to JUXON. By the Very Rev. WALTER FARQUHAR HOOK, D.D., Dean of Chichester. Demy 8vo., the following volumes sold separately as shown :—Vol. I., 15s. ; Vol. II., 15s. ; Vol. V., 15s. ; Vols. VI. and VII., 30s. ; Vol. VIII., 15s. ; Vol. IX., 15s. ; Vol. X., 15s. ; Vol. XI., 15s. ; Vol. XII., 15s.

Vol. I. Anglo-Saxon Period, 597-1070.—Augustine, Laurentius, Melitus, Justus, Honorius, Deusdedit, Theodorus, Brihtwald, Tatwine, Nothelm, Cuthbert, Bregwin, Jaenbert, Ethelhard, Wulfred, Feologild, Coelonoth, Ethelred, Plegmund, Athelm, Wulfhelm, Odo, Dunstan, Ethelgar, Siric, Elfric, Elphege, Limig, Ethelnoth, Eadsige, Robert, Stigand.

Vol. II. Anglo-Norman Period, 1070-1229.—Lanfranc, Anselm, Ralph of Escures, William of Corbeuil, Theobald, Thomas à Becket, Richard the Norman, Baldwin, Reginald Fitzjocelin, Hubert Walter, Stephen Langton.

Vol. III. Mediæval Period, 1229-1333.—Richard Grant, Edmund Rich, Boniface, Robert Kilwardby, John Peckham, Robert Winchelsey, Walter Reynolds, Simon Mapeham. [Reprinting.

Vol. IV. Same Period, 1333-1408.—John Stratford, Thomas Bradwardine, Simon Islip, Simon Langham, William Whittlesey, Simon Sudbury, William Courtenay, Thomas Arundel. [Reprinting.

Vol. V. Same Period, 1403-1503.—Henry Chicheley, John Stafford, John Kemp, Thomas Bouchier, John Morton, Henry Dean.

The New Series commences here.

Vol. VI. Reformation Period, 1503-1556.—William Warham, Thomas Cranmer (in part).

Vol. VII. Same Period.—Thomas Cranmer (in part).

Vol. VIII. Same Period, 1556-1558.—Reginald, Cardinal Pole.

Vol. IX. Same Period, 1558-1575.—Matthew Parker.

Vol. X. Same Period, 1575-1633. — Edmund Grindal, John Whitgift, Richard Bancroft, George Abbott.

Vol. XI. Same Period, 1633-1663.—William Laud, William Juxon.

Vol. XII. The Index.

'The most impartial, the most instructive, and the most interesting of histories.'—*Athenæum.*

By PREBENDARY STEPHENS.

The Life and Letters of the Very Rev. Walter Farquhar Hook, D.D.,

LATE DEAN OF CHICHESTER.

By the Rev. W. R. W. STEPHENS, Prebendary of Chichester. 2 vols., demy 8vo., with two Portraits. Fourth Edition. 30s.

Also, The Popular Edition, with Portrait, crown 8vo., 6s.

By THE RIGHT HON. W. E. GLADSTONE, M.P.

Dean Hook : An address.

By the Right Hon. W. E. GLADSTONE, M.P. Demy 8vo., stitched, 1s.

RICHARD BENTLEY AND SON, LONDON.

Clerical Biography—(*Continued*).

RECORDED BY MADAME VON KOBELL.

Conversations of Dr. Döllinger.

Translated by KATHARINE GOULD. Crown 8vo., 6s.

BY DR. THIRLWALL.

Bishop Thirlwall's Letters to a Friend.

By CONNOP THIRLWALL, D.D., Bishop of St. David's, and Edited by Dean STANLEY. A New and Enlarged Edition, with a Portrait, crown 8vo., 6s.

ANONYMOUS.

A Memoir of the Rev. John Russell.

By the Author of 'Dartmoor Days.' With a Portrait, crown 8vo., 6s.

BY DR. GRETTON.

Memory's Harkback over Fifty Years,

1808-1858. By the Rev. FREDERIC E. GRETTON. Demy 8vo., 12s.

BY REV. R. H. D. BARHAM.

The Life of the Rev. R. H. Barham

(Author of the 'Ingoldsby Legends'). By his Son, the Rev. RICHARD H. DALTON BARHAM. A New Edition, with Portrait, crown 8vo., 6s.

BY SIGNOR CAMPANELLA.

Life in the Cloister, at Court and in Exile.

By GIUSEPPE MARIA CAMPANELLA. Demy 8vo., with two Portraits, 10s. 6d.

Letters and Biographies.

THE FOURTH EARL OF ORFORD.

The Letters of Horace Walpole,

Edited by PETER CUNNINGHAM, F.S.A. 9 vols., demy 8vo., with Fifty Illustrations on steel, £5 5s. Hand-made Paper Edition, with Sixty-seven Illustrations on steel, cloth, £10 10s.; vellum, £12 12s.

BY MR. FITZGERALD.

The Lives of the Sheridans.

By PERCY FITZGERALD. 2 vols., demy 8vo., with Six Engravings on Steel by STODART and EVERY, 30s.

EDITED BY LORD BRABOURNE.

Unpublished Letters of Jane Austen.

Edited, with Introduction and Notes, by the Right Hon. LORD BRABOURNE. 2 vols., large crown 8vo., with Frontispieces, 24s.

BY MISS HILL.

Frederic Hill :

An Autobiography of Fifty Years in Times of Reform. Edited by his daughter, CONSTANCE HILL. Demy 8vo., with several Portraits, 16s.

PUBLISHERS in ORDINARY to HER MAJESTY.

2

Letters and Biographies—(*Continued*).

MISS COBBE'S AUTOBIOGRAPHY.

The Life of Frances Power Cobbe.

By HERSELF. With Recollections of Dean Stanley--Matthew Arnold—Mrs.
(Fanny) Kemble—Robert Browning—Sir Charles Lyell—Renan—Archbishop
Longley—Tennyson—Carlyle—Cardinal Manning—Charles Kingsley—Walter
Savage Landor—Dr. Jowett—Lord Shaftesbury—Darwin—John Bright—
Lady Byron—Professor Tyndall—and many other persons of interest. Second
Edition, with illustrations. In 2 vols., square crown 8vo., 21s.

EDITED BY MISS DE MORGAN.

Reminiscences of the Late Mrs. de Morgan.

With Letters addressed to Mrs. and Professor de Morgan. Edited by her
daughter, MARY A. DE MORGAN. In 1 vol., crown 8vo., with Portrait.

BY MR. FITZGERALD.

Memoirs of an Author.

By PERCY FITZGERALD, M.A., Author of 'Recreations of a Literary Man,'
'Lives of the Sheridans,' etc. In 2 vols., demy 8vo., with Portrait, 28s.

BY MR. WOOD.

A Memoir of Mrs. Henry Wood.

Author of 'East Lynne,' etc. By C. W. WOOD, Author of 'Through Holland,'
etc. In 1 vol., crown 8vo., with Photogravures and other Illustrations, 6s.

BY MRS. BISHOP.

A Memoir of Mrs. Augustus Craven

(*Pauline de la Ferronnays*).
With Extracts from her Diaries and Correspondence. By MARIA CATHERINE
BISHOP. In 2 vols., crown 8vo., with two Portraits of Mrs. Craven, 21s.

BY MRS. CROSSE.

Red-Letter Days of My Life

With Reminiscences and Anecdotes of many Persons of Note. By CORNELIA
A. H. CROSSE. In 2 vols., post 8vo., 21s.

BY MR. WATTS.

Alaric Watts.

The Narrative of his Life. By his Son, ALARIC ALFRED WATTS. 2 vols.,
crown 8vo., with Two Etchings, 21s.

BY THE REV. R. H. D. BARHAM.

The Life of Theodore Edward Hook.

By Rev. RICHARD H. DALTON BARHAM. A New Edition. Crown 8vo., 6s.

BY MISS MITFORD.

Recollections of a Literary Life.

With Selections from her Favourite Poets and Prose Writers. By MARY
RUSSELL MITFORD. Crown 8vo., with Portrait, 6s.

EDITED BY HENRY G. HEWLETT.

Henry Fothergill Chorley :

AUTOBIOGRAPHY AND MEMOIR. 2 vols., crown 8vo., with Portrait, 21s.

RICHARD BENTLEY AND SON, LONDON.

Letters and Biographies—(*Continued*).

RECORDED BY LADY BLESSINGTON.

The Conversations of Lord Byron.

With a Contemporary Sketch and Memoir of Lady Blessington. A New Edition, with Notes and eight Portraits. Demy 8vo., 15s.

BY MRS. TOWNSHEND MAYER.

Women of Letters,

Including Memoirs of Lady Morgan, the Misses Berry, Mrs. Opie, Mrs. Shelley, Lady Ann Barnard, Sarah Countess Cowper, and Lady Duff Gordon. By GERTRUDE TOWNSHEND MAYER. 2 vols., crown 8vo., 21s.

BY MR. FRANCIS.

John Francis and the 'Athenæum.'

A Literary Chronicle of Half a Century. By JOHN C. FRANCIS. 2 vols., crown 8vo., with Two Portraits, 24s.

BY MR. SALT.

The Life of Henry David Thoreau.

By HENRY S. SALT. Demy 8vo. With Portrait. 14s.

BY MR. THOMAS ADOLPHUS TROLLOPE.

T. A. Trollope's 'What I Remember.'

Second Edition. Demy 8vo., Vols. I. and II. with Portrait, 30s. Vol. III. 15s.

BY DR. HAKE.

Memoirs of Eighty Years.

By GORDON HAKE. Demy 8vo., 15s.

BY MISS CLOWES.

Charles Knight.

A Memoir. By his Grand-daughter, ALICE A. CLOWES. With Two Portraits Demy 8vo., 12s.

EDITED BY WALTER BESANT.

Charles F. Tyrwhitt Drake, F.R.G.S.

Literary Remains and Memoir. Demy 8vo., with Portrait, 14s.

BY MR. TIMBS.

The Lives of Wits and Humourists:

Swift, Steele, Foote, Goldsmith, the Colmans, Sheridan, Porson, Sydney Smith, Theodore Hook, etc. By JOHN TIMBS, F.S.A. 2 vols. crown 8vo., with Portraits, 12s.

BY MISS WOTTON.

Word Portraits of Famous Writers.

Edited by MABEL E. WOTTON. Large crown 8vo., 7s. 6d.

BY DR. MARTIN.

In the Footprints of Charles Lamb.

By BENJAMIN ELLIS MARTIN. With a complete Bibliography of Lamb's Works, by ERNEST NORTH, and with numerous Illustrations by HERBERT RAILTON and JOHN FULLEYLOVE, quarto, 10s. 6d.

Biographies of Painters and Musicians.

By MR. STORY.

The Life of John Linnell.

By ALFRED T. STORY. Demy 8vo., with Illustrations. 28s.

The Lives of James Holmes and John Varley.

By ALFRED THOMAS STORY, Author of 'The Life of John Linnell.' Demy 8vo.

By SIDNEY COOPER, R.A.

My Life.

By THOMAS SIDNEY COOPER, R.A. Crown 8vo., with Portrait, 6s.

By WILLIAM POWELL FRITH, R.A.

Reminiscences of W. P. Frith, R.A.

Eighth Edition. Crown 8vo., 6s.

FURTHER REMINISCENCES. Third Edition. 8vo., with Portrait, 15s.

By THE REV. C. H. COPE.

Reminiscences of Charles West Cope, R.A.

By his Son, the Rev. C. H. Cope, M.A. Demy 8vo., with Illustrations, 16s.

EDITED BY MR. GOSSE.

Conversations of James Northcote, R.A.

Recorded by WILLIAM HAZLITT. A New Edition, edited, with an Essay on Hazlitt and Northcote, by EDMUND GOSSE. Post 8vo., with Portrait, 6s.

By DR. FLAGG.

Life and Letters of Washington Allston.

By Dr. J. B. FLAGG. With 18 Reproductions of Allston's Paintings. Quarto. 25s.

By JOHN TIMBS, F.S.A.

The Lives of Painters :

Hogarth, Sir Joshua Reynolds, Gainsborough, Fuseli, Sir Thomas Lawrence, Turner. By JOHN TIMBS, F.S.A. Crown 8vo., with Portraits, 6s.

EDITED BY ALFRED SCHÖNE AND FERDINAND HILLER.

The Letters of a Leipzig Cantor.

Moritz Hauptmann to Franz Hauser, Ludwig Spohr, and other musicians. Translated and arranged by A. D. COLERIDGE. 2 vols., thin demy 8vo., 21s.

EDITED BY DR. JENSEN.

The Life of Robert Schumann,

Told in his Letters. Translated by MAY SIMPSON. 2 vols., crown 8vo., 21s.

By THE LATE MR. BEALE.

The Light of Other Days.

Musical Reminiscences of half a Century. By WILLERT BEALE (formerly of Cramer and Co.). 2 vols., demy 8vo., with Portrait, 28s.

RICHARD BENTLEY AND SON, LONDON.

𝕬rt and 𝕾cience, etc.

BY MISS WALKER.

My Musical Experiences.

By BETTINA WALKER. With Reminiscences of Sir Sterndale Bennett, Tausig, Sgambati, Liszt, Deppe, Scharwencka, and Henselt. Crown 8vo., 6s.

BY MR. CROWEST.

The Great Tone Poets :

Brief Memoirs of the Greater Composers—Bach, Handel, Glück, Haydn, Mozart, Spohr, Beethoven, Weber, Rossini, Schubert, Mendelssohn, Schumann, etc. By FREDERICK CROWEST. Seventh Edition. Crown 8vo., 3s. 6d

BY MR. ROWBOTHAM.

The History of Music.

A New Edition. By J. F. ROWBOTHAM. Crown 8vo., 7s. 6d.

BY MR. HARRISON.

Stray Records ;

Or, Personal and Professional Notes. By CLIFFORD HARRISON, the Reciter. A New Edition. Crown 8vo., 6s.

BY MR. WEDMORE.

Studies in English Art.

The SECOND SERIES, containing Romney, Constable, David Cox, George Cruikshank, Meryon, Burne-Jones, and Albert Moore. By FREDERICK WEDMORE. Large crown 8vo., 7s. 6d.

BY MR. WOODWARD.

The Masterpieces of Sir Robert Strange.

Reproductions of twenty of his Engravings in Permanent Photography. With a Memoir and Portions of his Autobiography. By FRANCIS WOODWARD. Folio, 42s.

BY W. P. FRITH, R.A.

John Leech : His Life and Work.

By WILLIAM POWELL FRITH, R.A. Second Edition. 2 vols., demy 8vo., with Portrait and Illustrations, 26s.

EDITED BY MR. GOSSE.

Nollekens and his Times.

By JOHN THOMAS SMITH, formerly Keeper of the Prints in the British Museum. With an Essay on Georgian Sculpture, and a Note on J. T. Smith, by EDMUND GOSSE. Demy 8vo., with a Portrait of Nollekens by JACKSON, and a List of his Works.

BY M. PLON.

The Life and Work of Thorvaldsen.

By EUGÈNE PLON. From the French, by Mrs. CASHEL HOEY. Imperial 8vo., with numerous Illustrations, 25s.

BY M. GUILLEMIN.

The Heavens.

An Illustrated Handbook of Popular Astronomy. By AMÉDÉE GUILLEMIN. Edited by J. NORMAN LOCKYER, F.R.S., and RICHARD PROCTOR, F.R.A.S. Demy 8vo., with over 200 Illustrations, 12s.

𝔄rt and 𝔖cience, etc.—(*Continued*).

BY M. FLAMMARION.

Marvels of the Heavens.

From the French of FLAMMARION, by Mrs. LOCKYER, Translator of 'The Heavens.' Crown 8vo., with 48 Illustrations, 3s. 6d.

BY MR. BYRNE.

Navigation and Nautical Astronomy.

By OLIVER BYRNE, Inventor of Dual Arithmetic. Quarto, 700 pp., 42s.

BY M. FIGUIER.

The Day after Death.

Or, the Future Life Revealed by Science. By LOUIS FIGUIER, Author of 'The World before the Deluge.' With Illustrations, crown 8vo., 2s. 6d.

BY MR. WILLIAMS.

Sketches of Village and Estate Buildings.

From designs by JAMES WILLIAMS, Architect. With Notes. In one Volume, oblong shape, with 30 Illustrations, 15s.

BY MR. WILLIAMS.

Our Iron Roads :

Their History, Construction, and Administration. By FREDERICK S. WILLIAMS. Demy 8vo., with numerous illustrations, 8s. 6d.

The Midland Railway :

Its Rise and Progress. By FREDERICK S. WILLIAMS, Author of 'Our Iron Roads,' etc. Crown 8vo., with numerous Illustrations, 6s.

BY MR. WALKER.

The Severn Tunnel : its Construction and Difficulties, 1872-1887.

By its Constructor, THOMAS A. WALKER. With Portraits on steel and very numerous Sketches and Plans. THIRD EDITION. With an Introductory note by Sir JOHN HAWKSHAW, C.E. Royal 8vo., 21s.

𝔅ooks suitable for 𝔓rizes.

Full information concerning each work will be found on the page named.

RICHARD BENTLEY AND SON, LONDON.

The Drama.

By the late MRS. KEMBLE.

Fanny Kemble's Records of Later Life.

By FRANCES ANNE KEMBLE. 3 vols., crown 8vo., 10s. 6d.

*** Mrs. Kemble's ' Records of My Girlhood ' (3 vols.) are now out of print.

Further Records.

A series of Letters by FANNY KEMBLE, forming a sequel to ' Records of My Girlhood,' ' Records of Later Life,' etc. 2 vols., crown 8vo., with two Portraits engraved upon steel by G. J. STODART. 24s.

By THEMSELVES.

Mr. and Mrs. Bancroft :

Their Recollections On and Off the Stage. Eighth Edition. Crown 8vo., paper wrapper, 1s. ; or in cloth, 1s. 6d.

By MR. PEMBERTON.

Life and Writings of T. W. Robertson,

Author of 'School,' ' Caste,' etc. By THOMAS EDGAR PEMBERTON, Author of ' The Life of Edward Askew Sothern.' With Portrait, Facsimile, and other Illustrations. Second Edition, demy 8vo., 14s.

' This genial and appreciative volume, interesting from cover to cover, brings out a bright, attractive personality, who wins not only our admiration for his stout and brave battle with circumstance, and our esteem for his ready invention, sparkling wit, and lambent humour, but our affection for a kindly, warm, human-hearted brother man.'—*Birmingham Daily Post.*

' There is a good deal in this biography which will be new even to the best informed, and it is particularly rich in personal details, furnished mainly by the playwright's son. All that is recorded of Robertson tends to make his memory sweeter, and it is easy to understand why he was so much beloved by relatives and friends.'—*Globe.*

Edward Askew Sothern :

(' Lord Dundreary '). A Memoir. By T. EDGAR PEMBERTON. Demy 8vo., with Portraits and Facsimiles, 16s.

Also, a NEW POPULAR EDITION, being the Fourth. Crown 8vo., 2s. 6d.

By DR. DORAN.

In and about Drury Lane,

And other Papers. By the late JOHN DORAN, F.S.A. 2 vols., large crown 8vo., 21s.

By MR. FITZGERALD.

The Romance of the Stage.

By PERCY FITZGERALD, M.A., F.S.A., Author of the ' Life of Garrick,' etc. 2 vols., demy 8vo., 24s.

By MR. NEVILLE.

The Stage.

Its Past and Present History in Relation to Fine Art. By HENRY NEVILLE. Demy 8vo., 96 pp., 5s.

PUBLISHERS in ORDINARY to HER MAJESTY.

Poetry and the Drama.

BY THE REV. RICHARD HARRIS BARHAM.

The Ingoldsby Legends.

THE ONLY COMPLETE EDITIONS.

Illustrated by CRUIKSHANK, LEECH, TENNIEL, DU MAURIER, and DOYLE.

'Successful humourists who follow such great masters as Rabelais are generally carried in advance of "the ruck" by some special gift. As Hook owed his great social reputation to unequalled powers of improvisation, so "Thomas Ingoldsby" was borne forward to fame and popularity by his unrivalled command of rhyme. All the wit, humour, and sparkle of the legends would have gone for comparatively little had it not been for the vehicle they were entrusted to. The verse is a thing *per se*, and as Ingoldsby followed no model, so he has had no true successor. He has had imitators ; but none of them have gone beyond imitation. We are told that when in the vein Barham wrote so quickly as to scandalize himself, and lead him to regard distrustfully the work that in every sense had been only play. We should never have doubted it, for nothing but the spell of an exceptional talent could have smoothed away difficulties that must have been proof to any amount of common effort. It was the fable of Orpheus and the beasts over again. Words the most intractable came in to wed themselves pleasantly to the easy ones, and glided by harmoniously to the sound of his magic lyre. What other man would not have given " Mephistopheles " up in despair? or, if he thought a rhyme worth trying for, re nounced it hopelessly after much cudgelling of the brain? How genuine is the humour of the legends is proved by the fact that although many are as freely sprinkled with hits at contemporary history and scandal as a Christmas pantomime, yet they read as pleasantly to-day as ever they did. It was an idea worthy of De Foe, that of evoking the Ingoldsbys, their family, pedigree, property, mansion, and everything that was theirs, that he might weave a series of *vraisemblable* family stories out of their archives. It was realistic as Balzac, the borrowing the very name of his own place, Tappington, and painting from the old Kentish farm. Yet when he went abroad, when he pillaged the solemn convent lore for his grotesque parodies, he was scarcely less successful. There are few we prefer to St. Dunstan, St. Medard, St. Gengulphus, and, above all, the " Jackdaw of Rheims."'—*Pall Mall Gazette.*

A NEW ANNOTATED EDITION, edited, with Notes, by MRS. EDWARD A. BOND, with a brief Memoir of her father, and also a note on the bibliography of the Legends. With the Illustrations on steel of CRUIKSHANK and LEECH, and on wood of TENNIEL, DU MAURIER, DOYLE, etc., and a Portrait of the REV. R. H. BARHAM, also a reproduction of a water-colour by CRUIKSHANK hitherto unpublished. In three vols., demy 8vo. 31s. 6d.

THE CARMINE EDITION. Small demy 8vo., with a carmine border line around each page. With Twenty Illustrations on Steel by Cruikshank and Leech, with gilt edges and bevelled boards, 10s. 6d.

THE EDINBURGH EDITION. An Edition in large type, with Fifty Illustrations by Cruikshank, Leech, Tenniel, Barham, and Du Maurier, re-engraved on Wood for this Edition by George Pearson. Crown 8vo., red cloth, 6s.
*** Also bound in gold cloth, with paper label, same price.

THE POPULAR EDITION. Crown 8vo., cloth, with Sixteen Illustrations on Wood by Cruikshank, Leech, Tenniel, and Barham, 2s. 6d.

THE VICTORIA EDITION. A Pocket Edition, fcap. 8vo., with Frontispiece, cloth, 1s. 6d., or in paper wrapper, 1s.

The Ingoldsby Legends.

ESPECIAL CHEAP EDITIONS.

THE ALEXANDRA EDITION. A new large type Edition, demy 8vo. With upwards of Fifty Illustrations by Cruikshank, Leech, Tenniel, and Barham. Paper wrapper, 1s., or bound in cloth, gilt edges, 2s.

THE PEOPLE'S EDITION. Sixty-four large quarto pages, printed on good paper, with Forty Illustrations by Cruikshank, Leech, and Tenniel, with wrapper, 6d.

RICHARD BENTLEY AND SON, LONDON.

Poetry and the Drama—(*Continued*).

BY THE REV. R. H. BARHAM.

The Ingoldsby Lyrics.

By the Rev. RICHARD HARRIS BARHAM, Author of 'The Ingoldsby Legends.' Edited by his Son, the Rev. R. H. DALTON BARHAM. Crown 8vo., 3s. 6d.

BY VARIOUS CONTRIBUTORS.

The Bentley Ballads.

Selected from 'Bentley's Miscellany.' Edited by JOHN SHEEHAN. Crown 8vo., 6s.

Amongst the contributors are :—Dr. Maginn—Father Prout—Thomas Ingoldsby—Haynes Bayly—Hartley Langhorne—Thomas Love Peacock—Samuel Lover—Charles Mackay—Robert Burns—H. W. Longfellow—J. A. Wade—Albert Smith—Edward Kenealy—Mary Howitt—The Irish Whisky Drinker—W. Cooke Taylor—William Jones—Tom Taylor—G. K. Gillespie—R. Dalton Barham, and many others.

EDITED BY PERCY COTTON.

Selections from the Poetical Works of Mortimer Collins.

Limited to 500 copies (each numbered), printed upon hand-made paper. Demy 8vo., 10s. 6d.

BY MRS. KEMBLE.

The Poetical Works of Frances Anne Kemble.

Crown 8vo., 7s. 6d.

Notes upon some of Shakespeare's Plays.

By FRANCES ANNE (FANNY) KEMBLE. Finely printed in Brown Ink, demy 8vo., 7s. 6d.

ON THE STAGE. MACBETH. HENRY VIII. THE TEMPEST. ROMEO AND JULIET.

BY CHARLES DICKENS.

The Village Coquettes.

By CHARLES DICKENS. A few copies reprinted in fac-simile of the original Edition of 1836. Demy 8vo., sewed, 4s. 6d.

EDITED BY LUCY HARRISON.

Spenser for Home and School Use.

Small post 8vo., 3s. 6d.

BY MISS WALKER.

Poems.

By BETTINA WALKER, Author of 'My Musical Experiences.' Post 8vo., with Portrait, 4s.

PUBLISHERS in ORDINARY to HER MAJESTY.

Poetry and the Drama—*(Continued)*.

BY MRS. WOODS.

Lyrics and Ballads.

By MARGARET L. WOODS, Author of 'A Village Tragedy.' Small 8vo., printed on hand-made paper, 4s.

BY PROFESSOR ROGERS.

Epistles, Satires, and Epigrams.

By JAMES E. THOROLD ROGERS. Crown 8vo., 6s.

BY MR. NEVILLE.

The Stage :

Its History in Relation to Art. By HENRY NEVILLE. Demy 8vo., 5s.

EDITED BY TOM TAYLOR.

Charles Reade's Dramas.

Fcap. 8vo. Sold separately. 1s. 6d. each.
MASKS AND FACES.   THE KING'S RIVAL.   POVERTY AND PRIDE.

BY MR. DUBOURG.

Four Unacted Plays.

By A. W. DUBOURG. Crown 8vo., 7s. 6d.
GREEN CLOTH.   VITTORIA CONTARINI.   LAND AND LOVE.   ART AND LOVE.

Angelica.

Romantic Drama, in Four Acts. By A. W. DUBOURG, joint author (with Tom Taylor) of the comedy 'New Men and Old Acres,' etc. Crown 8vo., paper cover, 3s. 6d.

BY MRS. KEMBLE.

Mr. J. T. Homespun in Switzerland.

By FRANCES ANNE KEMBLE. Demy 8vo., 1s.

BY THE REV. A. BRIDGE.

Poems.

By ARTHUR BRIDGE. Crown 8vo., 7s. 6d.

BY MRS. TINDAL.

Rhymes and Legends.

By Mrs. ACTON TINDAL. Crown 8vo., 5s.

BY DR. DORAN.

In and About Drury Lane.

By JOHN DORAN, F.S.A., Author of 'Their Majesty's Servants,' etc. 2 vols., large crown 8vo., 21s.

. See also page 23 for Biographies of Mrs. Kemble, Mr. Sothern, Mr. and Mrs. Bancroft, etc.

RICHARD BENTLEY AND SON, LONDON.

(27)

Books of Travel, etc.

SCENES IN OUR OWN COUNTRY.

Mr. Hissey's Home Travel.

'The lost art of travelling in one's own country.'—LINNÆUS.

THROUGH TEN ENGLISH COUNTIES.

[Surrey, Hampshire, Wiltshire, Gloucestershire, Worcestershire, Hereford-shire, Shropshire, Warwickshire, Oxfordshire, Buckinghamshire.] The Chronicle of a Driving Tour, by JAMES JOHN HISSEY. In demy 8vo., with sixteen full-page Illustrations by the Author, and a Plan of the route. 16s.

ACROSS ENGLAND IN A DOG-CART:

From London to St. David's and Back. With twenty Illustrations from Sketches by the Author, and Plan of the Route. Demy 8vo., 16s.

AN OLD-FASHIONED JOURNEY IN ENGLAND AND WALES.

Demy 8vo., with Frontispiece, 14s.

A HOLIDAY ON THE ROAD.

An Artist's Wanderings in Kent, Sussex, and Surrey. With numerous Illustrations from Sketches by the Author. Demy 8vo., 18s.

ON THE BOX SEAT ;

Or, From London to the Land's End and back. Demy 8vo., with 16 full-page Illustrations from sketches by the Author. 16s.

*** No copies now remain of 'A DRIVE THROUGH ENGLAND' and 'A TOUR IN A PHAETON THROUGH THE EASTERN COUNTIES.'

BY H.M. THE SHAH OF PERSIA.

Diary of my Visit to Europe in 1878.

By NASR-ED-DIN, SHAH OF PERSIA, and rendered into English by General SCHINDLER and Baron LOUIS DE NORMAN. Demy 8vo., 12s.

BY MR. BARKER.

Wayfaring in France.

By EDWARD HARRISON BARKER. Demy 8vo., with numerous Illustrations, 16s.

'As a description of modern rural France Mr. Barker's book is one of the best we have ever met with.'—*Guardian.*

'The principal merit of Mr. Barker's peregrinations is their unconventional independence. The illustrations are particularly agreeable.'—*Daily News.*

Wanderings by Southern Waters

IN EASTERN ACQUITAINE. By EDWARD HARRISON BARKER. Demy 8vo., with Illustrations, 16s.

Two Summers in Guyenne, 1892-1893.

A Chronicle of the Wayside and Waterside in the Upper Dordogne—Across the Moors of the Corrèze—In the Viscounty of Turenne—In Upper Périgord—In the Valleys of the Vézère and Isle—Riberac and Brantôme—The Desert of the Double—A Canoe Voyage on the Dronne—By the Lower Dordogne—On the Banks of the Garonne. By EDWARD HARRISON BARKER. Demy 8vo., with numerous illustrations, 16s.

PUBLISHERS in ORDINARY to HER MAJESTY

(28)

Books of Travel—*(Continued)*.

BY ADMIRAL DE KANTZOW.

Summer Days in Auvergne.

By Admiral DE KANTZOW. Crown 8vo., with 5 full-page Illustrations, 5s.

BY LADY HERBERT.

A Search after Sunshine :

A Visit to Algeria in 1871. By LADY HERBERT. Square 8vo., with numerous Illustrations engraved by GEORGE PEARSON, 16s.

BY THE REV. MR. ROSE.

Among the Spanish People.

By the Rev. HUGH JAMES ROSE, English Chaplain of Jerez and Cadiz. Author of 'Untrodden Spain,' etc. 2 vols., large crown 8vo., 24s.

BY MR. SCOTT.

Through Spain.

Including a Visit to the Cities of Merida, Ronda, Segovia, Salamanca, Leon, and Oviedo. By S. P. SCOTT. With many Illustrations, 4to., 16s.

BY MR. WOOD.

Letters from Majorca.

By CHARLES W. WOOD, F.R.G.S., Author of 'Through Holland.' Demy 8vo., with nearly 100 Illustrations, 14s.

BY MR. BEAUCLERK.

Rural Italy.

An Agricultural Survey of the Present Condition of the Italian Peninsula and Sicily. By W. NELTHORPE BEAUCLERK, late of Her Britannic Majesty's Embassy at Rome. Demy 8vo., with Map, 9s.

BY DR. WALTERS.

A Lotos-Eater in Capri.

By ALAN WALTERS, Author of 'Palms and Pearls,' etc. Large crown 8vo., with Sketches, 10s. 6d.

BY MR. EDWARDES.

Sardinia and the Sardes.

By CHARLES EDWARDES, Author of 'Letters from Crete.' Demy 8vo. 14s.

BY MR. BICKFORD-SMITH.

Greece under King George.

Population—Agriculture—Industries—Commerce—Internal Communication —Finance—Public Order—Education—Archæology—Religion—Army and Navy—Constitution—Climate—Panhellenism. By R. A. H. BICKFORD-SMITH, M.A., Barrister, late Student of the British School at Athens. Demy 8vo., with Map, 12s.

BY MR. MALLOCK.

In an Enchanted Island.

A Visit to Cyprus in 1889. By W. H. MALLOCK, Author of 'Social Equality,' etc. Third Edition. Crown 8vo., with Frontispiece, 6s.

RICHARD BENTLEY AND SON, LONDON.

𝕭𝖔𝖔𝖐𝖘 𝖔𝖋 𝕿𝖗𝖆𝖛𝖊𝖑—*(Continued).*

BY MR. WOOD.

Through Holland.

By CHARLES W. WOOD, F.R.G.S. Demy 8vo., with 57 Illustrations, 12s.

BY M. HAVARD.

Picturesque Holland :

A Journey in the Provinces of Friesland, Groningen, Drenthe, Overyssel, Guelderland, Limbourg, etc. From the French of M. HENRI HAVARD, by ANNIE WOOD. Demy 8vo., with 10 Illustrations and Map, 16s.

In the Heart of Holland.

From the French of M. HENRI HAVARD, by Mrs. CASHEL HOEY. Demy 8vo., with 8 Illustrations, 15s.

BY MRS. J. H. RIDDELL.

A Mad Tour through the Black Forest.

By CHARLOTTE E. L. RIDDELL, Author of 'George Geith of Fen Court.' Large crown 8vo., 10s. 6d.

BY MR. WOOD.

In the Black Forest.

By CHARLES W. WOOD, F.R.G.S, Author of 'Through Holland,' 'Round about Norway.' Small crown 8vo., with numerous Illustrations, 6s.

Under Northern Skies.

By CHARLES W. WOOD, F.R.G.S., Author of 'Through Holland.' Demy 8vo., with Sixty-eight Illustrations, 14s.

BY MISS DE FONBLANQUE.

Five Weeks in Iceland.

By C. A. DE FONBLANQUE. Small crown 8vo., 3s. 6d.

BY MR. WOOD.

The Cruise of the Reserve Squadron.

By CHARLES W. WOOD, F.R.G.S., Author of 'Through Holland,' etc. Crown 8vo., with 60 Illustrations, 6s.

BY MR. PHILLIPPS-WOLLEY.

Sport in the Crimea and the Caucasus.

By CLIVE PHILLIPPS-WOLLEY, F.R.G.S. Demy 8vo., 14s.

Savage Svânetia.

By CLIVE PHILLIPPS-WOLLEY, F.R.G.S., Author of 'Sport in the Crimea and the Caucasus.' 2 vols., crown 8vo., with Illustrations, 21s.

ANONYMOUS.

Persian Pictures—Safar Nameh.

A Book of Travel in the East. Crown 8vo., price 6s.

PUBLISHERS in ORDINARY to HER MAJESTY.

Books of Travel—(*Continued*).

BY THE LATE CROWN PRINCE OF AUSTRIA.

Travels in the East.

Including a Visit to the Holy Land, Egypt, the Ionian Islands, etc. By His Imperial and Royal Highness the CROWN PRINCE RUDOLF. Royal 8vo., with nearly one hundred full-page Illustrations by PAUSINGER, 31s. 6d.

BY MR. BENTLEY.

The Rock Inscriptions of Sinai.

By GEORGE BENTLEY, F.R.G.S. Demy 8vo., sewed, 1s.

BY PROFESSOR MERRILL.

East of the Jordan.

Travels and Observations in Moab, Gilead, and Basha, 1875-77. By SELAH MERRILL, Archæologist of the American Palestine Exploration Society. Demy 8vo., with 70 Illustrations and Map, 16s.

BY SIR C. WILSON AND SIR C. WARREN.

The Recovery of Jerusalem.

An Account of the Recent Excavations and Discoveries in the Holy City. By General Sir Charles W. WILSON, and General Sir CHARLES WARREN. With an Introductory Chapter by Dean STANLEY. Third Thousand. Demy 8vo., with 50 Illustrations, 21s.

BY MR. RAE.

Egypt from the First to the Third Khedive.

By W. FRASER RAE. In demy 8vo., 16s.

BY MAJOR BARTTELOT.

Diaries of Edmund Musgrave Barttelot,

Late Major 7th Royal Fusiliers Regiment. A Record of his Services in Afghanistan, Egypt, the Nile Relief Expedition, and on the Congo with Mr. Stanley's Expedition. Edited by his brother, Sir WALTER BARTTELOT. Demy 8vo., with Portraits and Maps, Third Edition, 16s.

BY MR. SELOUS.

A Hunter's Wanderings in Africa.

Nine Years amongst the Game of the Far Interior of South Africa, with full notes upon the natural history and present distribution of all the large mammalia, and including accounts of explorations beyond the Zambesi, on the Chobé, and in the Matabele and Mashuna countries. By FREDERICK COURTENAY SELOUS. With Map and nineteen full-page Illustrations by SMIT and WHYMPER. Third Edition. Demy 8vo., 18s.

BY MR. BALDWIN.

African Hunting and Adventure from Natal to the Zambesi,

Including Lake Ngami, the Kalahari Desert, etc., from 1852 to 1860. By WILLIAM CHARLES BALDWIN, F.R.G.S. With Illustrations by JAMES WOLF and J. B. ZWECKER. A Third and Cheaper Edition, with Portrait of the Author and Map. In one vol., demy 8vo.

RICHARD BENTLEY AND SON, LONDON.

Books of Travel—(*Continued*).

By MRS. CUTHELL and CAPTAIN BURRELL.

Indian Memories.

Of the Plains, The Hills, The Temples, Camp Life, Zenanas, The Mutiny, etc. By EDITH CUTHELL and Captain W. S. BURRELL. Crown 8vo., 6s.

MRS. FRANK GRIMWOOD'S NARRATIVE.

My Three Years in Manipur,

and Escape from the Recent Mutiny. By ETHEL ST. CLAIR GRIMWOOD. Fourth Edition. Demy 8vo., with Plan, Illustrations, and two Portraits, 15s.

By GENERAL LE MESSURIER.

From London to Bokhara in 1887.

By A. LE MESSURIER, R.E. Demy 8vo., with Maps and Sketches, 15s.

By DR. WALTERS.

Palms and Pearls ; or, Scenes in Ceylon.

Including a Visit to the Ancient Royal City of Anuradhapoora, and the Ascent of Adam's Peak. By ALAN WALTERS, M.A. Demy 8vo., 12s. 6d.

By MR. WORSFOLD.

A Visit to Java.

By W. BASIL WORSFOLD. With Map and Illustrations from Sketches by the Author. Demy 8vo., 14s.

By GENERAL GREELY.

Three Years of Arctic Service, 1881-84,

and the Attainment of the Farthest North.

By ADOLPHUS W. GREELY, General U.S. Army, Commanding the Expedition. With a Portrait on Steel of the Author, upwards of One Hundred and Twenty Illustrations, and the Official Maps and Charts. Third Edition, 2 vols., royal 8vo., 42s.

By THE HON. MRS. LEIGH.

Ten Years on a Georgia Plantation.

By Mrs. J. W. LEIGH. Demy 8vo., 10s. 6d.

By THE HON. MRS. RICHARD MONCK.

My Canadian Leaves.

An Account of a Visit to Canada in 1864 and 1865. By FRANCES E. O. MONCK. Demy 8vo., 15s.

By MR. BODDAM-WHETHAM.

Western Wanderings :

A Record of Travel in the Land of the Setting Sun. By J. W. BODDAM-WHETHAM. With 12 full-page Illustrations, engraved by WHYMPER. Demy 8vo., 15s.

By MR. PHILLIPPS-WOLLEY.

The Trottings of a ' Tender Foot '

in SPITZBERGEN AND BRITISH COLUMBIA. By CLIVE PHILLIPPS-WOLLEY, F.R.G.S., Author of 'Sport in the Crimea and Caucasus.' Crown 8vo., 7s. 6d.

PUBLISHERS in ORDINARY to HER MAJESTY.

Books of Travel—(*Continued*).

By MR. BADEN-POWELL.

In Savage Isles and Settled Lands:

A Record of Personal Experiences in Europe, Egypt, Ceylon, India, Australia, New Zealand, Java, New Guinea, Borneo, Tonga, Samoa, the Sandwich Islands, and the United States, in 1888-91. By B. F. S. BADEN-POWELL, Scots Guards, F.R.G.S. With Maps, and numerous Illustrations from Sketches by the Author. Demy 8vo., 21s.

'There is hardly a page in the book that does not contain something that is entertaining, in addition to which the descriptions which the author gives of scenery and natives are remarkably good, and we have pleasure in recommending this book to our readers as one of the most pleasantly written records of travel that have come to our notice.'—*Field.*

ANONYMOUS.

South Sea Bubbles.

By the EARL and the DOCTOR. [*Reprinting.*

BY MR. COOPER.

The Islands of the Pacific.

Being an Account of nearly all the Inhabited Islands of the Pacific, their Peoples and their Products. By H. STONEHEWER COOPER. Crown 8vo., 6s.

ANONYMOUS.

Old New Zealand.

A Tale of the Good Old Times, and a History of the War in the North against the Chief Heke. Told by an Old Pakeha Maori. With a Preface by the Earl of PEMBROKE. Demy 8vo., 6s.

BY PROFESSOR NICOLS.

Wild Life in the Australian Bush.

By ARTHUR NICOLS, F.G.S., F.R.G.S., Author of 'Zoological Notes,' etc. With Eight Illustrations after Drawings made for this Work by J. T. NETTLESHIP. 2 vols., large crown 8vo., 21s.

Standard Works on Cookery.

By SIGNOR FRANCATELLI.

The Modern Cook.

By CARLO ELMÉ FRANCATELLI, late *Maître-d'Hôtel* to Her Majesty. Demy 8vo. Twenty-ninth Edition. Containing 1,500 Recipes and Sixty Illustrations, 7s. 6d.

The Cook's Guide.

By the Author of 'The Modern Cook.' 64th Thousand. Small 8vo., containing 1,000 Recipes. With Illustrations, 5s.

'An admirable manual for every household.'—*Times.*

RICHARD BENTLEY AND SON, LONDON.

Sport and Natural History.

By MAJOR FISHER.

Rod and River; or Salmon, Trout, and Grayling Fishing.

By ARTHUR T. FISHER (late Major 21st Hussars). Demy 8vo., 14s.

Through the Stable and Saddle-room.

A Practical Guide for all concerned in the Ownership or Management of Horses. By ARTHUR T. FISHER (late Major 21st Hussars). Crown 8vo., 6s.

The Farrier; or, No Foot, No Horse.

By ARTHUR T. FISHER (late Major 21st Hussars). Author of 'Through the Stable and Saddle-room,' 'Rod and River,' etc. Small crown 8vo., 2s.

By MR. CORBALLIS.

Forty-Five Years' Recollections of Sport.

By JAMES HENRY CORBALLIS. Edited by ARTHUR T. FISHER (late 21st Hussars). Hunting—Shooting—Deerstalking—Salmon and Trout Fishing—Falconry—Golf, etc. Demy 8vo., with Frontispiece, 16s.

By MR. LOWNDES.

Camping Sketches.

By GEORGE RIVERS LOWNDES, Author of 'Gipsy Tents, and how to use them.' In large crown 8vo., with upwards of Fifty Illustrations. 4s. 6d.

By MR. DAY.

The Horse; and How to Breed Him.

The Thorough-Bred, Hunter, Carriage-Horse, Cob, Farm-Horse, Dray-Horse, Pony. By WILLIAM DAY. Second Edition. Demy 8vo., 16s.

The Autobiography of William Day.

With Recollections of the principal Celebrities of the Turf during the present reign. Third Edition. Crown 8vo., paper wrapper, 1s. ; cloth, 1s. 6d.

By COLONEL CORBETT.

An Old Coachman's Chatter.

By COLONEL CORBETT. With Eight Full-page Coaching Sketches on Stone by JOHN STURGESS. Second Edition. Demy 8vo., 15s.

By MR. HARRIS.

The Coaching Age.

By STANLEY HARRIS, Author of 'Old Coaching Days.' With Sixteen spirited Full-page Illustrations on Stone by JOHN STURGESS. Demy 8vo., 18s.

PUBLISHERS in ORDINARY to HER MAJESTY.

Sport and Natural History—(*Continued*).

By MR. BLACK.

Horse - Racing in England, from the Earliest Times.

By ROBERT BLACK, Author of 'Horse Racing in France.' Demy 8vo., 15s.

By MR. WATSON.

Racecourse and Covert-side.

By ALFRED E. T. WATSON, with Illustrations by JOHN STURGESS. Demy 8vo., 15s.

By THE REV. J. G. WOOD.

The Dominion of Man over Animals.

By the Rev. J. G. WOOD, Author of 'Common Objects of the Sea-shore,' etc. Demy 8vo., with numerous Illustrations, 15s.

By FRANK BUCKLAND.

Curiosities of Natural History.

By FRANCIS TREVELYAN BUCKLAND, late Her Majesty's Inspector of Fisheries. Popular Edition, with a few Illustrations. Each Series separately, in small 8vo., price 2s. 6d., as follows :—

1st SERIES.—Rats, Serpents, Fishes, Frogs, Monkeys, etc.

2nd SERIES.—Fossils, Bears, Wolves, Cats, Eagles, Hedgehogs, Eels, Herrings, Whales.

-d SERIES.—Wild Ducks, Fishing, Lions, Tigers, Foxes, Porpoises.

4th SERIES.—Giants, Mummies, Mermaids, Wonderful People, Salmon, etc.

By MR. DIXON.

Our Rarer Birds.

By CHARLES DIXON, Author of 'Rural Bird Life.' With numerous Illustrations by CHARLES WHYMPER. Demy 8vo., 14s.

By MR. PHILLIPPS-WOLLEY.

A Sportsman's Eden.

A Season's Shooting in Upper Canada, British Columbia, and Vancouver. By CLIVE PHILLIPPS-WOLLEY. Demy 8vo., 9s.

WILD LIFE AND ADVENTURE IN THE AUSTRALIAN BUSH.
See page 32.

SPORT IN THE CRIMEA AND THE CAUCASUS.
See page 29.

A HUNTER'S WANDERINGS.
See page 30.

AFRICAN HUNTING.
See page 30.

ANONYMOUS.

A New Book of Sports and Games.

By Various Writers. Crown 8vo., 6s.

RICHARD BENTLEY AND SON, LONDON.

Works on Divinity and Belief.*

₊ See also pages 16 and 17.

`\` See also 'The Recovery of Jerusalem,' 'The Lives of the Archbishops of Canterbury,'
'Life of Lord Hatherley,' 'Memorials of Chichester Cathedral,' 'Rock Inscriptions on Sinai,'
'Life of Dean Hook,' 'Bishop Thirlwall's Letters,' Dr. Duncker's 'History of Antiquity,' 'The
Conversations of Dr. Ignatius von Döllinger,' etc.

By DEAN HOOK.

The Church and its Ordinances.

Sermons by the late WALTER FARQUHAR HOOK, D.D., Dean of Chichester.
Edited by the Rev. WALTER HOOK, Rector of Porlock. 2 vols., demy 8vo.,
10s. 6d.
'One of the clearest, most logical, and most eloquent expositions of the value of ordinances
and the true nature of prayer that have been before the eyes of men.'—*The Daily Telegraph.*

Parish Sermons.

By the late WALTER FARQUHAR HOOK, D.D., Dean of Chichester. Edited
by the Rev. WALTER HOOK, Rector of Porlock. Crown 8vo., 3s. 6d.

Hear the Church.

A Sermon by the late Dean HOOK. Reprinted in demy 8vo., sewed, 1s.

By BISHOP THIRLWALL.

Essays, Speeches, and Sermons.

By the late CONNOP THIRLWALL, D.D., Bishop of St. David's. Edited by
Dr. PEROWNE, Bishop of Worcester. Demy 8vo., 15s.

By DR. KENNEDY.

Ely Lectures on the Revised Version of the New Testament.

With an Appendix containing the chief Textual Changes. By B. H.
KENNEDY, D.D., late Canon of Ely, Honorary Fellow of St. John's College,
Cambridge. etc. Crown 8vo., 4s.

By DR. McCAUSLAND.

Adam and the Adamite;

Or, The Harmony of Scripture and Ethnology. By DOMINICK McCAUSLAND,
Q.C. With Map. Crown 8vo., 3s. 6d.

By PREBENDARY STEPHENS.

Christianity and Islam:

THE BIBLE AND THE KORAN. By the Rev. W. R. W. STEPHENS, Author
of 'The Life of St. Chrysostom,' 'Life and Letters of Dean Hook.' Crown
8vo., 5s.

By CARDINAL MANNING.

Modern Society.

A PASTORAL for LENT. By His Eminence CARDINAL MANNING. 1s.

PUBLISHERS in ORDINARY to HER MAJESTY.

Works on Divinity—(*Continued*).

BY DR. CUMMING.

Works by John Cumming, D.D.

The FALL of BABYLON FORESHADOWED in HER TEACHING, in HISTORY, and in PROPHECY. Crown 8vo., 5s.
The GREAT TRIBULATION COMING on the EARTH. Crown 8vo., 5s. Fourteenth Thousand.
REDEMPTION DRAWETH NIGH; or, The Great Preparation. Crown 8vo., 5s. Seventh Thousand.
The MILLENNIAL REST ; or, The World as it will be. Crown 8vo., 5s. Fourth Thousand.
READINGS on the PROPHET ISAIAH. Fcap. 8vo., 5s.

BY LADY HERBERT.

Devotional Works by Lady Herbert.

ST. FRANCIS of SALES in the CHABLAIS. Post 8vo., 6s.
LOVE or SELF-SACRIFICE. Crown 8vo., 10s. 6d.
WIVES and MOTHERS in the OLDEN TIME. SS. PAULA and OLYMPIAS. Crown 8vo., 6s.

ANONYMOUS.

Letters from Hell.

Newly translated from the Danish. With an Introduction by Dr. GEORGE MACDONALD. Twenty-fifth Thousand. Crown 8vo., 2s. 6d.

'Its awful descriptions are intensely realistic, and hold you by a powerful spell.'—*Christian Guardian*, Toronto.

BY MR. MALLOCK.

Atheism and the Value of Life.

By WILLIAM HURRELL MALLOCK, Author of ' Is Life worth Living?' etc. Crown 8vo., 6s.

BY M. RENAN.

Studies in Religious History.

The Experimental Method applied to Religion — Paganism — Comparative Mythology—Buddhism—The Translations of the Bible—The Teazichs of Persia—Joachim di Flor and the Eternal Gospel—Francis of Assisi—A Monastic Idyl of the Thirteenth Century—Religious Art—The Congregation ' De Auxiliis'—A Word upon Galileo's Trial—Port Royal—Spinoza. From the French of ERNEST RENAN. Crown 8vo., 6s. [*Reprinting.*

ANONYMOUS.

Roots :

A Plea for Tolerance. A New Edition. Small post, 2s. 6d.

BY THE REV. F. ARNOLD.

Turning Points in Life.

By the Rev. FREDERICK ARNOLD. A New Edition. Crown 8vo., 6s.

Essays and Miscellaneous Works.

By MISS HILL.

English Dress.

Saxon, Norman, Plantagenet, Tudor, Stuart, and Modern. By GEORGIANA HILL. With Illustrations. Two vols., demy 8vo., 30s. [See page 8.]

By MORTIMER COLLINS.

Thoughts in My Garden.

Selections from the Papers of MORTIMER COLLINS. Edited by EDMUND YATES. With Notes by FRANCES COLLINS. 2 vols., crown 8vo., 21s.

Pen-Sketches by a Vanished Hand.

Selections from the Papers of MORTIMER COLLINS. Edited by TOM TAYLOR. With Notes by FRANCES COLLINS. 2 vols., crown 8vo., with Portrait, 21s.

By MR. SAUNDERS.

Pastime Papers.

Essays upon Miscellaneous Subjects. By FREDERICK SAUNDERS, Author of 'Salad for the Solitary and the Social,' etc. Small crown 8vo., 4s.

Salad for the Solitary and Social.

Essays upon Miscellaneous Subjects. By FREDERICK SAUNDERS, Author of 'Pastime Papers,' etc. A New Edition, 4to., 7s. 6d.

By MRS. L. LINTON.

The Girl of the Period, and other Essays.

By ELIZA LYNN LINTON. 2 vols., demy 8vo., 24s.

By MR. MALLOCK.

Social Equality.

A Short Study in a Missing Science. By W. H. MALLOCK, Author of 'Is Life worth Living?' etc. Second Edition, crown 8vo., 6s.

By MR. TIMBS.

Doctors and Patients.

By JOHN TIMBS, F.S.A. A New and Revised Edition. Crown 8vo., 6s.

ANONYMOUS.

Conversational Openings and Endings.

With Hints on the Game of Small Talk. In paper wrapper, 1s.

By EDEN WARWICK.

Notes on Noses.

By EDEN WARWICK. A New Edition. Fcap. 8vo., 2s.

PUBLISHERS in ORDINARY to HER MAJESTY.

𝔐iscellaneous 𝔚orks—*(Continued).*

The Spanish Verbs, Pronouns, and Accent.

By F. W. JORDAN, Teacher of Languages and Shorthand. Fcap., paper covers, 6d.

BY PROFESSOR YONGE.

English-Latin and Latin-English Dictionary.

By CHARLES DUKE YONGE. Used at Eton, Harrow, Winchester, and Rugby. This work has undergone careful Revision, and the whole work (1,070 pp.) is now sold for 7s. 6d. The English-Latin Part can be obtained alone for 3s. 6d., and the Latin-English Part alone for 3s. 6d.

' It is the best—we were going to say the only really useful—Anglo-Latin Dictionary we ever met with.'—*Spectator.*

ANNOTATED BY PROFESSOR YONGE.

Virgil.

With copious English Notes. By CHARLES DUKE YONGE. Used at Harrow, Eton, Winchester, and Rugby. Strongly bound, crown 8vo., 6s.

ANNOTATED BY REV. J. EDWARDS AND REV. C. HAWKINS.

The Andromache of Euripides.

With copious Grammatical and Critical Notes ; and a brief Introductory Account of the Greek Drama, Dialects, and principal Tragic Metres. Post 8vo., 4s. 6d.

TRANSLATED BY PROFESSOR STRONG.

The Haunted House.

Translated from the 'Mostellaria' of Plautus. By H. A. STRONG, M.A. Limp cloth, 4s.

Fiction.

SELECTED FROM AMONG THE BEST WORKS OF FICTION OF EACH YEAR.

Bentleys' Favourite Novels.

Each volume can be obtained separately in crown 8vo., cloth, price **6s.,** *at all booksellers' and railway bookstalls in the United Kingdom, and at all the leading booksellers' and importers' in the Colonies, and at the railway bookstalls in India and Australia.*

By "MRS. ALEXANDER."

54

THE WOOING O'T.

"A charming story with a charming heroine."—*Vanity Fair.*
"Singularly interesting, while the easiness and flow of the style, the naturalness of the conversation, and the dealing with individual character are such that the reader is charmed from the beginning to the very end."—*The Morning Post.*

63

HER DEAREST FOE.

"Mrs. Alexander has written nothing better. The book altogether abounds in bright and sparkling passages."—*The Saturday Review.*
"There is not a single character in this novel which is not cleverly conceived and successfully illustrated, and not a page which is dull."—*The World.*

15

WHICH SHALL IT BE?

"No one can read this book without being struck by the more than ordinary ability that it displays. The character of Madeline throughout is of great psychological power, and the way in which, warped by various kinds of outward teaching, she trembles on the confines of terrible faults but is saved by a goodness of nature which cannot wholly be spoilt, shows a power of discrimination not usual in novels. Madame de Fontarce also is a masterly sketch." —*The Saturday Review.*
"A decidedly clever novel."—*The Spectator.*

By JANE AUSTEN.

23

EMMA.

"I am a great novel reader, but I seldom read German or French novels. The characters are too artificial. My delight is to read English novels, particularly those written by women. 'C'est toute une école de morale.' Miss Austen, Miss Ferrier, etc., form a school which in the excellence and profusion of its productions resembles the cloud of dramatic poets of the great Athenian age."—GUIZOT.
"Shakespeare has neither equal nor second. But among the writers who have approached nearest to the manner of the great master we have no hesitation in placing Jane Austen, a woman of whom England is justly proud."—*Macaulay's Essays.*
"Alfred Tennyson talked very pleasantly that evening to Annie Thackeray. He spoke of Jane Austen, as James Spedding does, as next to Shakespeare."—*Sir Henry Taylor's Autobiography.*

By JANE AUSTEN—(*Continued*).

28   LADY SUSAN.—THE WATSONS.

With a Memoir of the Author by the Rev. J. E. Austen-Leigh.

"I have heard Sydney Smith, more than once, dwell with eloquence on the merits of Miss Austen's novels. He told me he should have enjoyed giving her the pleasure of reading her praises in the 'Edinburgh Review.' 'Fanny Price' was one of his prime favourites. I remember Miss Mitford's saying to me: 'I would almost cut off one of my hands, if it would enable me to write like your aunt with the other.'"—THE REV. J. E. AUSTEN-LEIGH.

24   MANSFIELD PARK.

"I have the picture still before me of Lord Holland lying on his bed, when attacked with gout, his sister, Miss Fox, beside him reading aloud, as she always did on these occasions, some one of Miss Austen's novels, of which he was never wearied. I well recollect the time when these charming novels, almost unique in their style of humour, burst suddenly on the world. It was sad that their writer did not live to witness the growth of her fame."—*Sir Henry Holland's Recollections.*

"All the greatest writers of fiction are pure of the sin of writing to a text—Chaucer, Shakespeare, Scott, Jane Austen; and are not these precisely the writers who do most good as well as give most pleasure?"—MARY RUSSELL MITFORD.

"Miss Austen's fame will outlive the generations that did not appreciate her, and her works will be ranked with the English classics as long as the language lasts."—*The Atlas.*

"Jane Austen's novels are more true to nature, and have for my sympathies passages of finer feeling than any others of this age."—SOUTHEY.

25   NORTHANGER ABBEY.—PERSUASION.

"When I was at Trinity College, Cambridge, Mr. Whewell, then a Fellow and afterwards Master of the College, often spoke to me with admiration of Miss Austen's novels. On one occasion I said that I had found 'Persuasion' rather dull. He quite fired up in defence of it, insisting that it was the most beautiful of her works. This accomplished philosopher was deeply versed in works of fiction. I recollect his writing to me from Caernarvon, that he was weary of his stay, for he had read the circulating library twice through."—SIR DENIS LE MARCHANT.

"Read Dickens's 'Hard Times' and another book of Pliny's 'Letters.' Read 'Northanger Abbey,' worth all Dickens and Pliny together. Yet it was the work of a girl. She was certainly not more than twenty-six. Wonderful creature!"—*Macaulay's Journal*, August 12, 1854.

22   PRIDE AND PREJUDICE.

"Ferrier and Austen have given portraits of real society far superior to anything vain man has produced of the like nature. I have read again, and for the third time, Miss Austen's very finely written novel of 'Pride and Prejudice.' That young lady had a talent for describing the involvements and feelings and characters of ordinary life, which is to me the most wonderful I ever met with. Her exquisite touch, which renders commonplace things and characters interesting from the truth of the description and the sentiment, is denied to me. What a pity so gifted a creature died so early!"—SIR WALTER SCOTT.

"One of the best of Miss Austen's unequalled works. How perfectly it is written!"—*The Spectator.*

21   SENSE AND SENSIBILITY.

"I have now read over again all Miss Austen's novels. Charming they are. There are in the world no compositions which approach nearer to perfection."—*Macaulay's Journal* May 1st, 1851.

"First and foremost let Jane Austen be named, the greatest artist that has ever written, using the term to signify the most perfect master over the means to her end. Life, as it presents itself to an English gentlewoman, peacefully yet actively engaged in her quiet village, is mirrored in her works, with a purity and fidelity that must endow them with interest for all time. To read one of her books is like an actual experience of life. You know the people as if you had lived with them, and you feel something of personal affection toward them. The marvellous reality and subtle distinctive traits noticeable in her portraits has led Macaulay to call her a prose Shakespeare."—GEORGE ELIOT.

By RHODA BROUGHTON.

132   ALAS!

"In this novel the author strikes, perhaps, a deeper and truer note of human sympathy than has been audible in any other of her fictions. The interest is not only well maintained, but wholesome and edifying."—*The Globe.*

"Apart from the interest of the plot, 'Alas!' is full of bright word-pictures of Florence and Algiers, and of a pleasant and cultivated appreciation of their beauties which lend an additional merit to its pages."—*The Morning Post.*

By RHODA BROUGHTON—(*Continued*).

149
A BEGINNER.

"The novel displays all the author's power of humorous characterization, her amused sense of the comedy of life. It contains enchanting open-air word-pictures; delightful chatter of children; vivacious dialogue; it throbs with actuality and animal spirits; it is, in short, a characteristic specimen of her work."—*Daily News*.

100
BELINDA.

"Miss Broughton's story 'Belinda' is admirably told, with the happiest humour, the closest and clearest character-sketching. Sarah is a gem—one of the truest, liveliest, and most amusing persons of modern fiction."—*The World*.

18
COMETH UP AS A FLOWER.

"A strikingly original and clever tale, the chief merits of which consist in the powerful, vigorous manner of its telling, in the exceeding beauty and poetry of its sketches of scenery, and in the soliloquies, sometimes quaintly humorous, sometimes cynically bitter, sometimes plaintive and melancholy, which are uttered by the heroine."—*The Times*.

115
DOCTOR CUPID.

"Miss Broughton's new novel is likely to have an even greater vogue than any of its predecessors. It has elements both of humour and of pathos, and once taken up will retain the attention of the reader to the close."—*The Globe*.

"Bright and full of movement as are usually Miss Broughton's novels, few, if any of them, have attained the degree of pathos which gives an especial charm to her latest work, 'Doctor Cupid.'"—*The Morning Post*.

35
GOOD-BYE, SWEETHEART!

"We are more impressed by this than by any of Miss Broughton's previous works. It is more carefully worked out, and conceived in a much higher spirit. Miss Broughton writes from the very bottom of her heart. There is a terrible realism about her."—*The Echo*.

66
JOAN.

"There is something very distinct and original in 'Joan.' It is more worthy, more noble, more unselfish than any of her predecessors, while the story is to the full as bright and entertaining as any of those which first made Miss Broughton famous."—*The Daily News*.

"Were there ever more delightful figures in fiction than 'Mr. Brown' and his fellow doggies in Miss Broughton's 'Joan'?"—*The Daily News* (on another occasion).

140
MRS. BLIGH.

"No one of Miss Broughton's stories has given us so much pleasure as this; not even 'Nancy,' which is probably her best; not even 'Doctor Cupid,' which is no doubt the most interesting of her novels. Rhoda Broughton still takes the form of an analysis of women's feelings, and her greatest successes have been achieved where she has clearly outlined the woman's character, and then limited the rest of the story to circumstances which tend to illustrate that character. In her latest novel she has been truer to this principle than in any other of her works, and it is this quality which makes us say 'Mrs. Bligh' will give more pleasure than any other of the series. The book is a truer picture of woman's love, of her sacrifice of it to a girl, and of the woman's only possible reward, than any Miss Broughton has yet given us. Time, practice, and a sense of literary art have produced in her a form of skill in writing which is apparent upon every page of her new story. How the story is worked out Miss Broughton's readers will see for themselves, and we repeat that she has given them a novel more worthy of remembrance than any she has yet written."—*Pall Mall Gazette*.

53
NANCY.

"If unwearied brilliancy of style, picturesque description, humorous and original dialogue, and a keen insight into human nature can make a novel popular, there is no doubt whatever that 'Nancy' will take a higher place than anything which Miss Broughton has yet written. It is admirable from first to last."—*The Standard*.

47
NOT WISELY, BUT TOO WELL.

"Miss Broughton's popularity in all ranks of society shows no sign of decline. A short time ago Captain Markham, of the *Alert*, was introduced to her at his own request. He told her that in some remote Arctic latitudes an ice-bound mountain was christened Mount Rhoda as an acknowledgment of the pleasure which her tales had given to the officers."—*The World*.

PUBLISHERS in ORDINARY to HER MAJESTY.

By RHODA BROUGHTON—(Continued).

26   RED AS A ROSE IS SHE.

"There are few readers who will not be fascinated by this tale."—*The Times.*

77   SECOND THOUGHTS.

"I love the romances of Miss Broughton; I think them much truer to nature than Ouida's and more impassioned than George Eliot's. Miss Broughton's heroines are living beings, having not only flesh and blood, but also *esprit* and soul; in a word, they are real women, neither animals nor angels, but allied to both."—ANDRÉ THEURIET.

By ROSA N. CAREY.

94   BARBARA HEATHCOTE'S TRIAL.

"Fresh, lively, and, thanks to the skill with which the heroine's character is drawn, really interesting."—*The Athenæum.*

"A novel of a sort which it would be real loss to miss."—*The Daily Telegraph.*

"The story is told by the author with a skilful fascination. If anything, 'Barbara' is better than 'Not Like Other Girls,' and all the girls know that *it* was very good."—*The Philadelphia Times.*

152   BASIL LYNDHURST.

"Miss Carey's pathetic story turns upon a country house in whose life and inmates we come to feel an almost painful interest. We doubt whether anything has been written of late years so fresh, so pretty, so thoroughly natural and bright. The novel as a whole is charming. Tenderness is portrayed without the suspicion of sickly sentiment, and the simple becomes heroic without any sense of effort or unreality."—*Pall Mall Gazette.*

142   FOR LILIAS.

"The materials from which the story has been constructed have been managed, not only with exceedingly delicate and tender handling, but with such unusual ingenuity and fertility of resource, that the result is a novel which not only abounds in graceful and touching passages, but may be fairly said to possess the merit of originality. All the characters are excellently drawn, with strong strokes and in decided outlines, yet always with the utmost delicacy and refinement of touch."—*The Guardian.*

129   HERIOT'S CHOICE.

"Everyone should read 'Heriot's Choice.' It is thoroughly fresh, healthy, and invigorating."—*The York House Papers.*

"'Heriot's Choice' deserves to be extensively known and read. It is a bright, wholesome story of a quiet but thoroughly interesting class, and as such will doubtless find as many admirers as readers."—*The Morning Post.*

147   LOVER OR FRIEND?

"It is a good novel, of the home-life, family-gossip class, in the production of which lady writers specially excel. . . . This is a sensibly and skilfully written book, and the situations at the end show a good deal of dramatic power."—*Pall Mall Gazette.*

"Written with all that delicate charm of style which invariably makes this writer's works pleasant reading. No one could say they are ever dull or commonplace."—*The Academy.*

134   MARY St. JOHN.

"A tale of true love, of self-sacrifice, of loyalty and unselfishness. The story is a simple one, but told with much grace and with unaffected pathos. We are not ashamed to confess that we have ourselves followed the simple and unaffected narrative with an interest and a pleasure which other more exciting and sensational works have failed to arouse in us. The heroine herself is a noble woman, and it is with a sensation of relief that we find her rewarded in the end for the self-sacrifice which is forced upon her. Dollie Maynard, too, is a fascinating young personage, and the way in which she gradually awakens to the merits of her somewhat grave and old-fashioned lover is charmingly depicted. But the most striking and original portrait in the book is that of Janet St. John. This is a masterpiece; and the handsome, worldly woman, so hard of heart in every respect except her love for her husband and her youngest child, must take rank among the few new creations of the modern novelist."—*John Bull.*

74   NELLIE'S MEMORIES.

"A pretty, quiet story of English life, free from sensational incidents, without the shadow of a mystery throughout, and written in a strain which is very pleasing. Miss Carey has the gift of writing naturally and simply, her pathos is true and unforced, and her conversations are sprightly and sharp."—*The Standard.*

RICHARD BENTLEY AND SON, LONDON.

By ROSA N. CAREY—(*Continued*).

108
NOT LIKE OTHER GIRLS.

"The three heroines are quite delightful, and their mother, an excellent person with irreproachable manners and a heart of gold, is also good. Phillis, the second daughter, the brain of the family, is as natural as amusing, and as generally satisfactory a young woman as we have met with in fiction for a long time."—*The Academy.*

"We have a specially grateful recollection of this story—the author's masterpiece."—*John Bull.*

"The story is one of the sweetest, daintiest, and most interesting of the season's publications. Three young girls find themselves penniless, and their mother has delicate health. It relates, in a charming fashion, how they earned their bread and kept themselves together, and left upon the field of strife neither dead nor wounded."—*The New York Home Journal.*

122
ONLY THE GOVERNESS.

"This novel is for those who like stories with something of Jane Austen's power, but with more intensity of feeling than Jane Austen displayed, who are not inclined to call pathos twaddle, and who care to see life and human nature in their most beautiful form."—*The Pall Mall Gazette.*

"One of the sweetest and pleasantest of Miss Carey's bright, wholesome, domestic, stories."—*The Lady.*

124
QUEENIE'S WHIM.

"It is pleasant to be able to place at the head of our notice such a thoroughly good and wholesome story as 'Queenie's Whim.' The plot is very simple, and shows how fair and beautiful a web may be woven by skill and art out of the slightest materials. It is almost impossible to lay the book down without ascertaining what happens to Queenie. Perhaps the subtle charm of the tale lies as much in the delicate but firm touch with which the characters are drawn as in the clever management of the story."—*The Guardian.*

101
ROBERT ORD'S ATONEMENT.

"A most delightful book, very quiet as to its story, but very strong in character, and instinctive with that delicate pathos which is the salient point of all the writings of this author."—*The Standard.*

"Like the former novels from this pen that have had a wide popularity—among them 'Not Like Other Girls,' 'Queenie's Whim,' etc.—this story is of lively interest, strong in its situations, artistic in its character and local sketching, and charming in its love-scenes. Everybody that 'loves a lover' will love this book."—*The Boston Home Journal.*

118
UNCLE MAX.

"In this book Miss Carey has made a very distinct advance; she has cleverly allowed a wicked, selfish, mischief-making woman to reveal herself by her own words and acts—a very different thing to describing her and her machinations from outside. Villains and their feminine counterparts are not characters in which she usually deals, for she sees the best side of human nature. She has made an interesting addition to current fiction, and it is so intrinsically good that the world of novel readers ought to be genuinely grateful."—*The Lady.*

113
WEE WIFIE.

"Miss Rosa Nouchette Carey is one of our especial favourites. She has a great gift of describing pleasant and lovable young ladies."—*John Bull.*

"Miss Carey's novels are always welcome; they are out of the common run, immaculately pure and very high in tone."—*The Lady.*

91
WOOED AND MARRIED.

"There is plenty of romance in the heroine's life. But it would not be fair to tell our readers wherein that romance consists or how it ends. Let them read the book for themselves. We will undertake to promise that they will like it."—*The Standard.*

By MARY CHOLMONDELEY.

127
SIR CHARLES DANVERS.

"Novels so amusing, so brightly written, so full of simple sense and witty observation as 'Sir Charles Danvers' are not found every day. It is a charming love story, lightened up on all sides by the humorous, genial character sketches."—*The Saturday Review.*

"'Sir Charles Danvers' is really a delightful book. Sir Charles is one of the most fascinating, one of the wittiest figures that advance to greet us from the pages of contemporary fiction. We met him with keen pleasure and parted from him with keen regret."—*The Daily News.*

By **MARY CHOLMONDELEY**—(*Continued*).

150
DIANA TEMPEST.

" ' Diana Tempest' is a book to be read. It is more—it is a book to be kept and read again, for its characters will not pass into limbo with this year's fashions. It will stand in the front ranks of fiction for some time to come."—*St. James's Gazette.*

"In this charming book are combined all the qualities, narrative and constructive, that are essential to the achievement of completeness in a model work of fiction."—*Daily Telegraph.*

"One of the brightest novels of modern life that has ever been written."—*Lady.*

"Miss Cholmondeley writes with a brightness which is in itself delightful. . . . Let every-one who can enjoy an excellent novel, full of humour, touched with real pathos, and written with finished taste and skill, read 'Diana Tempest.'"—*Athenæum.*

"A remarkably clever and amusing novel."—*Saturday Review.*

By **MARCUS CLARKE.**

70
FOR THE TERM OF HIS NATURAL LIFE.

"There can, indeed, I think, be no two opinions as to the horrible fascination of the book. The reader who takes it up and gets beyond the Prologue—though he cannot but be harrowed by the long agony of the story, and the human anguish of every page, is unable to lay it down; almost in spite of himself he has to read and to suffer to the bitter end. To me, I confess, it is the most terrible of all novels, more terrible than 'Oliver Twist,' or Victor Hugo's most startling effects, for the simple reason that it is more real. It has all the solemn ghastliness of truth."—THE EARL OF ROSEBERY.

By **MRS. W. K. CLIFFORD.**

143
AUNT ANNE.

"Mrs. Clifford has achieved a success of a very unusual and remarkable kind in this book. She has had the extreme daring to take for the subject of her story the romance of an old woman, and to fill her canvas with this one figure. . . . She and her treatment are quite original and new. She is often laughable, but always touching; her little figure is full of an old-fashioned grace, though grace combined with oddity; her sense of her 'position,' her susceptibilities in that respect, her boundless generosity, are always delightful. Indeed, we do not know when we have met with a more loving and recognisable, as well as attractive, personage in fiction."—*Spectator.*

"One of the most memorable creations of modern fiction. The character of Aunt Anne is not a mere *tour de force*. It is one of those—one is almost tempted to say immortal—creations whose truth mingles so insistently with its charm in every touch that it is hard to say whether it is its truth which makes the charm or the charm which persuades you into believ-ing in its truth."—*Sunday Sun.*

By **MARIE CORELLI.**

126
ARDATH: THE STORY OF A DEAD SELF.

"A daring imaginative conception embodied with marvellous success. The splendours of the city of Al-Kyris the Magnificent; the luxurious, feverish, selfish, ineffectual life of the idolized laureate Sah-lumâ; the gorgeous functions of Zephorânim, the still more gorgeous but ghastly and loathsome festivities presided over by that beautiful fiend the High Priestess Lysia, the varied phenomena of the existence in a community given over utterly to the lust of the flesh, the lust of the eye, and the pride of life; the omens which among all the glories foretell catastrophe and ruin; the catastrophe itself, with all its incidents of strange horror, are painted with an imaginative power which for the time holds us spellbound. The chapters devoted to the fall of Al-Kyris have not often been equalled in English literature for wealth and splendour of lurid invention; some portions of Beckford's 'Vathek' approach them most nearly, but even 'Vathek' is deficient in some of the qualities which give to 'Ardath' its peculiar impressiveness."—*The Spectator.*

117
A ROMANCE OF TWO WORLDS.

"A remarkable work, and whether it be called a novel, or a poem, or a psychological romance, it cannot fail to make a deep impression upon intellectual minds."—*Life.*

"Clever and ingenious."—*The Globe.*

"The author has considerable power of description, and not a little poetical feeling. The book is evidently the outcome of a great deal of serious thought."—*The Saturday Review.*

By MARIE CORELLI—(*Continued*).

144

THE SOUL OF LILITH.

"A weird but fascinating novel, intensely exciting, and deals with a strangeness of character that will give even the jaded and habitual novel reader a thrill and an emotion, and yet the story is one of to-day. . . . It is the best Marie Corelli has yet published."—*Observer.*

"The dominant characteristic of this strange and striking book is its poetic quality. . . . Passages of dignity and melody are of frequent occurrence. Happy metaphor and brilliant illustration spring readily to hand. A keen sense of beauty and refinement in the choice of language and a complete mastery of the writer's technique are constant qualities in the work."—*The Literary World.*

120

THELMA.

"A really admirable novel, pure in spirit, wholesome in doctrine, picturesque, poetical, passionate, pathetic."—*The St. James's Gazette.*

"The rich local colouring, the glowing heat, the vivid and subtle descriptions of surroundings and scenery, all help to make the book one of exceptional merit, as the heroine is one of exceptional beauty and of exceptional talents."—*The Whitehall Review.*

"Nothing can be more vivid and at the same time more delicately coloured than the pictures of the Land of the Midnight Sun."—*The Morning Post.*

114

VENDETTA: THE STORY OF ONE FORGOTTEN.

"Is the weather so very cool, my dear Mr. George Bentley; is ice so cheap; are lemon squashes given away for nothing, that you should send me such a very inflammatory novel as 'Vendetta,' by Marie Corelli? The three tomes of this alarming work are bound in sanguinolent crimson, and figured on each is a hand clutching the hilt of a dagger. Blood! Iago, blood! I am reading 'Vendetta' (figuratively speaking) with a wet cloth round my head, and my feet in a basin of iced and camphorated water; but ere I reach the end of the Signora or Signorina Corelli's appalling romance, dreadful consequences will, I fear, accrue. Possibly, human gore, Naples, the cholera, matrimony (very much matrimony), jealousy, the stiletto, and the Silent Tomb in which brigands have buried their treasures! I shudder; but I continue to read 'Vendetta,' just as when I was a child, I used to shudder over the 'Mysteries of Udolpho.'"—GEORGE AUGUSTUS SALA in *The Illustrated London News.*

131

WORMWOOD: A DRAMA OF PARIS.

"A grim, realistic drama. . . . The effects of love, lawless passion, jealousy, hatred, insanity, all are grouped together round the lost 'absintheur' whom the author has depicted."—*The Athenæum.*

"Like everything heretofore written by this gifted author, it is true to nature. Its pathos, moreover, is sufficiently powerful to sustain the reader's eager interest from beginning to end."—*Galignani.*

By MRS. AUGUSTUS CRAVEN

(Pauline de la Ferronays).

19

A SISTER'S STORY.

"A book which took all France and all England by storm."—*Blackwood's Magazine.*

"'A Sister's Story' is charmingly written, and excellently translated. It is full of fascinating revelations of family life. Montalembert's letters, and the mention of him as a young man, are delightful. Interwoven with the story of Alexandrine are accounts of the different members of the family of La Ferronays. The story of their lives and deaths is beautiful; their letters and diaries abound in exquisite thoughts and tender religious feeling."—*The Athenæum.*

By HENRY ERROLL.

125

AN UGLY DUCKLING.

"'An Ugly Duckling' is not merely a work of the highest promise, it is a finished masterpiece; its author makes what is presumably his début with a work of the very finest quality. Moreover, he has successfully occupied new and supremely difficult ground. It is a novel which is strikingly original, powerful in its reticence, full both of humorous and varied observations and of delicate pathos, true to the subtlest lights and shades of human nature, and unfailingly fresh, interesting and charming from beginning to end."—*The Graphic.*

By MRS. ANNIE EDWARDES.

110   A GIRTON GIRL.

"Mrs. Edwardes is one of the cleverest of living lady novelists. She has a piquancy of style and an originality of view which are very refreshing after the dreary inanities of many of her own sex. The novel is throughout most enjoyable reading."—*The Academy.*

"One of the best and brightest novels with which the world has been favoured for a very long time is 'A Girton Girl.' All the characters talk brightly and epigrammatically, and tell their own stories in their lively conversation."—*The Lady.*

"Mrs. Edwardes tells a story which is full of subtle observation, benevolent sarcasm, and irresistible brightness."—*The Morning Post.*

61   LEAH: A WOMAN OF FASHION.

"'Leah' is the best, the cleverest, and strongest novel that we have as yet had in the season, as it is certainly Mrs. Edwardes's masterpiece."—*The World.*

"Mrs. Edwardes's last novel is the strongest and most complete which she has yet produced."—*The Saturday Review.*

32   OUGHT WE TO VISIT HER?

"To this novel the epithets spirited, lively, original of design, and vigorous in working it out, may be applied without let or hindrance. In short, in all that goes to make up at once an amusing and interesting story, it is in every way a success."—*The Morning Post.*

"Mrs. Edwardes has never done better than in her charming novel, 'Ought We to Visit Her?'"—*Vanity Fair.*

40   SUSAN FIELDING.

"One has not read far into this novel before one feels that the writer is by no means a common person. So true and vivid is the conception of the various characters that we have sometimes a difficulty in realising that we are, after all, only reading the creations of an author's fancy. As to the style, it is excellent. It becomes firmer as the story advances, but throughout it has a delicate grace which it is impossible to define, but of which every reader will be conscious. . . . We hope we have said enough to show that this is no ordinary book. If our readers make themselves directly acquainted with it they will not conclude that we have given it too hearty a recommendation."—*The Globe.*

By JESSIE FOTHERGILL.

133   ALDYTH.

"It is curious that this, which is the most interesting of Miss Fothergill's novels, should also be the least known. Its republication is very welcome, and there can be no doubt that if it were well known it would be more widely appreciated than any of Miss Fothergill's books."—*Observer.*

110   BORDERLAND.

"Miss Fothergill is one of those novelists whose books we always open with assured expectation, and never close with disappointment. We do not say that the quality of excellence is a characteristic of her achievement; she is too much a writer of genius as distinguished from a writer of talent to work upon a dead level. In all her work we find the unmistakable touch of mastery, the imaginative grasp of the creator, not the mere craftsmanship of the constructor, 'the vision and the faculty divine' which displays itself in substance and not in form. . . . 'Borderland' is certain to be enjoyed for its own sake as a story full of the strongest human interest, told with consummate literary skill."—*The Manchester Examiner.*

72   THE FIRST VIOLIN.

"The story is extremely interesting from the first page to the last. It is a long time since we have met with anything so exquisitely touching as the description of Eugen's life with his friend Helfen. It is an idyl of the purest and noblest simplicity."—*The Standard.*

"A story of strong and deep interest, written by a vigorous and cultured writer. To such as have musical sympathies an added pleasure and delight will be felt."—*The Dundee Advertiser.*

By JESSIE FOTHERGILL—(*Continued*).

148

FROM MOOR ISLES.

"'From Moor Isles' is much above the average, and may be read with a considerable amount of pleasure, containing, as it does, many vigorous and affecting passages."—*Globe*.

"The sketches of North-country life are true and healthy."—*Athenæum*.

"Miss Fothergill has written another of her charming stories, as charming as 'The First Violin.' 'From Moor Isles' will distinctly add to Miss Fothergill's reputation as one of the pleasantest of our lady novelists."—*Pall Mall Gazette*.

85

KITH AND KIN.

"In speaking of 'Kith and Kin' it is not necessary to say more in the way of praise than that Miss Fothergill has not fallen below her own mark. None of her usual good materials are wanting. The characters affect us like real persons, and the story of their troubles and their efforts interests us from the beginning to the end. We like the book—we like it very much."—*The Pall Mall Gazette*.

"One of the finest English novels since the days of 'Jane Eyre.'"—*Manchester Examiner*.

76

PROBATION.

"Altogether 'Probation' is the most interesting novel we have read for some time. We closed the book with very real regret, and a feeling of the truest admiration for the power which directed and the spirit which inspired the writer, and with the determination, moreover, to make the acquaintance of her other stories."—*The Spectator*.

"A noble and beautiful book which no one who has read is likely to forget."—*The Manchester Examiner*.

By LADY GEORGIANA FULLERTON.

12

LADYBIRD.

"Lady Georgiana Fullerton has wrought out her plot with power, delicacy occasional depth of thought, and general felicity of language."—*The Athenæum*.

8

TOO STRANGE NOT TO BE TRUE.

"One of the most fascinating and delightful works I ever had the good fortune to meet with, in which genius, goodness, and beauty meet together in the happiest combination, with the additional charm of an historical basis."—"EIRONACH," in *Notes and Queries*.

By RICHARD JEFFERIES.

135

THE DEWY MORN.

"The beautiful description in which the book abounds is what will lend the work its most potent charm. With the pen of a poet and the appreciativeness of a painter he limns in graceful words his pictures of country life with such truth that one can hear the wind among the trees, and see the great clouds flinging their shadows on the sward, as one reads his charming studies."—*Society*.

"'The Dewy Morn' is written from end to end in a kind of English which cannot be imitated, and has rarely been equalled for beauty. The descriptions of scenery and of the aspects of sky and atmosphere are so vitally true as to produce a sense of illusion like that produced by a painting."—*Vanity Fair*.

By JOSEPH SHERIDAN LE FANU.

14

THE HOUSE BY THE CHURCHYARD.

"Le Fanu was one of the best story-tellers that ever wrote English. We protest that, as we write, one fearful story comes to our mind which brings on a cold feeling though we read it years ago. The excitement is so keen that anyone but a reviewer will find himself merely 'taking the colour' of whole sentences in his eagerness to get to the finish. His instinct is so rare that he seems to pick the very mood most calculated to excite your interest. Without explanation, without affectation, he goes on piling one situation on another until at last he raises a perfect fabric. We know not one improvisatore who can equal him."—*Vanity Fair*.

"Le Fanu possessed a peculiar—an almost unique—faculty for combining the weird and the romantic. His fancy had no limit in its ranges amongst themes and images of terror. Yet he knew how to invest them with a romantic charm which ended in exerting over his readers an irresistible fascination."—*The Daily News*.

PUBLISHERS in ORDINARY to HER MAJESTY.

By J. S. Le FANU—*(Continued).*

00 IN A GLASS DARKLY.

"Even 'Uncle Silas,' being less concentrated, is less powerfully terrible than some tales in Sheridan Le Fanu's 'In a Glass Darkly.' This book was long as rare as a first edition copy of 'Le Malade Imaginaire.' Lately it has been reprinted in one volume by Mr. Bentley. It is impossible, unhappily, for an amateur of the horrible to remain long on friendly terms with anyone who is not charmed by 'In a Glass Darkly.' The eerie inventions of the author, the dreadful, deliberate, and unsparing calm with which he works them out, make him the master of all who ride the nightmare. Even Edgar Poe, even Jean Richepin, come in but second and third to the author of 'In a Glass Darkly.' His 'Carmilla' is the most frightful of vampires, the 'Dragon Volant' the most gruesome of romances ; while 'A Tale of Green Tea' might frighten even Sir Wilfrid Lawson into a chastened devotion to claret or burgundy. No one need find Christmas nights too commonplace and darkness devoid of terrors if he keeps the right books of Le Fanu by his pillow. The author is dead, and beyond our gratitude. I cast lilies vainly upon his tomb—*et munere fungor inani.*"—From a leading article in *The Daily News.*

11 UNCLE SILAS.

" We cordially recommend this remarkable novel to all who have leisure to read it, satisfied that for many a day afterwards the characters there portrayed will haunt the minds of those who have become acquainted with them. Shakespeare's famous line, 'Macbeth hath murdered sleep,' might be altered for the occasion, for certainly 'Uncle Silas' has murdered sleep in many a past night, and is likely to murder it in many a night to come, by that strange mixture of fantasies like truths and truths like fantasies which make us feel, as we rise from the perusal, as if we had been under a wizard's spell."—*The Times.*

"The first character is Uncle Silas, that mysterious man of sin ; the next is the ghoul-like goblin of a French governess—the most awful governess in fiction. Then we have the wandering lunatic whom we take for a ghost, and who is even more dreadful. Finally, there is the tremendous scene in the lonely Irish house. No one who has read it can forget it, or the chapters which precede it ; no one who has not read it should have his pleasure spoiled by a description."—*The Daily News.*

By MARY LINSKILL.

130 BETWEEN THE HEATHER AND THE NORTHERN SEA.

" A remarkable book, the work of a woman whose preparation for writing has been her communion with books and nature. This intimacy is wide and apparent. Shakespeare, Milton, Keats, Shelley, Kingsley, Carlyle, Browning, Tennyson, and many more are constantly supplying illustration. The beautiful mottoes to the chapters would make up a choice extract book, and the very names of them are quotations. Her familiarity with nature is as evident as that with books. The grandest passage in the story describes with wonderful vividness and with subtle delicacy the shifting scenes of a great sea storm—we wish we could quote it, but it must not be mutilated—and the aspects of the wild high moorlands ; the lonely, desolate, and reedy marshes ; the rare bits of cornland, the sheltered orchard, whether by night or day, in winter or in summer, or in lovely cheerful spring, in the storm or in the sunshine—all these aspects of nature on the Yorkshire moors and on its dangerous shores are sketched with the same perfect knowledge, the same fine perception of minute differences and changes, and the same sense of beauty."—*The Spectator.*

141 CLEVEDEN.

" The heroine's story is told, and her character drawn with much delicacy of touch, and our sympathy is powerfully enlisted for the timid and affectionate nature that leans upon love, and the religiousness, vague but strong, that bears her through all the dreariness of her desertion by her first lover, and the trust and dependence that drew her gradually towards the less fascinating, but far deeper and stronger nature of the man who becomes her husband. ' Stephen Yorke's ' sketches of dale scenery are beautiful, and clearly the work of one who not only knows them intimately and loves them dearly, but whose tasteful and poetic feeling can appreciate the minuter delicacies of varying seasons and weather, and can gather from Nature in all her aspects her deeper and higher meanings."—*The Spectator.*

157 THE HAVEN UNDER THE HILL.

" In these pages are described many stern battles with the furious and raging sea, when resolute men went under, and ships and life-boats were destroyed as so much matchwood. And the tempest of the ocean finds its counterpart in the tempest of the heart. Dorigen Gower, the heroine, with her strong poetic nature, and brave and noble life, recalls the saint-like characters of the past. . . . . . A fine healthy, breezy novel."—*Academy.*

By MARY LINSKILL—(*Continued*).

139
IN EXCHANGE FOR A SOUL.

"The central figure of the tale is the beautiful fisher-girl, Barbara Burdas. . . . She has the self-restraint, the quiet courage, of the Puritan heroines of old. . . . From first to last she is an original as well as fascinating creation."—*Morning Post.*

145
TALES OF THE NORTH RIDING.

"If Miss Linskill had written only her fine 'Tales of the North Riding,' they would have been sufficient to fix her title of Novelist of the North. Her characters are portraits of northern folk, as they who have lived among them will recognise, and her scenery is precisely what one's memory recalls."—*Sheffield Daily Telegraph.*

"What Mr. Hardy is to the Wessex country, Mary Linskill might have become to the North Riding of Yorkshire, had her life been spared a little longer. The 'Tales of the North Riding' gives many evidences of her real ability, and, in the second story, 'Theo's Escape,' Miss Linskill rises to the level of her best novel, and in it she displays the strongly artistic faculty which is never absent from any of her books."—*Manchester Examiner.*

By MAARTEN MAARTENS.

146
GOD'S FOOL.

"The Story of Elias, God's Fool, is in some respects beautiful, in all curious, and thickset with gems of thought. The picture of the creature with the clouded brain, the missing senses, the pure and holy soul, and the unerring sense of right, living in his deafness and darkness by the light and the law of love, is a very fine conception, and its contrast with the meanness and wickedness of his surroundings is worked out with high art."—*World.*

"A very interesting and charming story. Elias Lossell only became a fool gradually, as the result of an accident which happened to him in early youth. Gradually the light of this world's wisdom died out for him ; gradually the light of God's wisdom dawns and develops in him. The way these two lights are opposed and yet harmonised is one of the most striking features of the book. As a subtle study of unusual and yet perfectly legitimate combination of effect, it is quite first-rate."—*Guardian.*

136
AN OLD MAID'S LOVE.

"A picture of a Dutch interior. Cool shadows, fine touches, smooth surfaces, clear outlines, subdued meanings, among these sit Suzanna Varelkamp, the old maid, exactly as you may see in a Dutch picture an old lady in a prim room knitting a stocking and looking as if she and dust had never known each other. The book is fresh, vivid, original, and thoroughly interesting."—*The Saturday Review.*

151
THE GREATER GLORY.

"A number of various types are introduced, sketched with remarkable clearness of touch. Some belong essentially to the soil, but the majority are specimens of those to be met with in all cultivated communities. The plot is one of singular interest, marked by dramatic contrasts and a strong vein of pathos. It would be difficult to conceive figures more touching than those of the old Baron and Baroness Rexelaer, nor, in a different way, than the pair of young lovers, Reinout and Wendela, charming creations of a poetic fancy."—*Morning Post.*

138
THE SIN OF JOOST AVELINGH.

"A masterly treatment of a situation that has an inexhaustible fascination for novelists, but which very few are strong enough to treat worthily. An admirable novel. Has throughout the merits of Dutch art . . . combined with a most delicate loveliness."—*The Guardian.*

"Maartens has inherited many of the special gifts which once distinguished his great countryman—but that is not all. 'The Sin of Joost Avelingh' has qualities of imagination which Dutch pictorial art hardly ever achieved, save on the canvases of Rembrandt."—*The Manchester Examiner.*

From the French of HECTOR MALOT.

83
NO RELATIONS.

"A cheap edition of a book which, within the short space of a year, has reached the almost unprecedented sale of 200,000 copies in France, and which has been there awarded the valuable Academical prize of M. Monthyon, cannot fail to meet with appreciation in this country."—*Preface.*   [*Reprinting.*

By HELEN MATHERS (Mrs. Reeves).

50   ## COMIN' THRO' THE RYE.

" A clever novel ; never dull, and never hangs fire."—*The Standard.*
" There is a great deal of power in ' Comin' thro' the Rye.' There is originality in the tragic plot, and an unceasing current of fun which saves the tragedy from becoming sombre."
— *The Athenæum.*

By FLORENCE MONTGOMERY.

88   ## MISUNDERSTOOD.

" Read ' Misunderstood '; very touching and truthful."—*Diary of Dr. Wilberforce, Bishop of Winchester.*
" This volume gives us what of all things is the most rare to find in contemporary literature
- a true picture of child-life."—*Vanity Fair.*

89   ## SEAFORTH.

" In the marvellous world of the pathetic conceptions of Dickens there is nothing more exquisitely touching than the loving, love-seeking, unloved child, Florence Dombey. We pay Miss Montgomery the highest compliment within our reach when we say that in ' Seaforth' she frequently suggests comparisons with what is at least one of the masterpieces of the greatest master of tenderness and humour which nineteenth-century fiction has known. ' Seaforth' is a novel full of beauty, feeling, and interest."—*The World.*

37   ## THROWN TOGETHER.

" This charming story cannot fail to please."—*Vanity Fair.*
" A delightful story. There is a thread of gold in it upon which are strung many lovely sentiments."—*The Washington Daily Chronicle.*

By W. E. NORRIS.

112   ## A BACHELOR'S BLUNDER.

" We have endeavoured in noticing some previous books of this author to express our high appreciation of his graphic powers and his right to be reckoned one of the leading English novelists—one who has been compared to Thackeray in reference to his delicate humour and his ready seizure of the foibles as well as the virtues of mankind, and to Anthony Trollope in a certain minuteness of finish in the depicting of people and of scenes. This story of a natural and unsophisticated girl in the midst of the intense worldliness of modern English society, and of a marriage deliberately viewed in advance and by both parties as one entirely of convenance, affords an excellent field for his characteristic modes of treatment."—*The Boston Literary World.*
" Exceedingly good reading, as Mr. Norris's novels nearly always are. The situation is, so far as we know, original, which is a rare merit."—*The Guardian.*

119   ## MAJOR AND MINOR.

" The author's fidelity of analysis throughout this clever book is remarkable. As a rule he here deals with ordinary sentiments, but the more complicated characters of Gilbert Segrave and Miss Huntley are drawn with the subtle touch of the accomplished artist. These merits are familiar to the readers of Mr. Norris's former works, but in none of these is to be found a vein of such genuine humour as in ' Major and Minor.' The irrepressible contractor Buswell, Mr. Dubbin, and the fair Miss Julia, whose admiration for poor Brian lands him in a more than awkward dilemma, are each and all as life-like as they are diverting. In this, his latest book, Mr. Norris remains the elegant and slightly caustic writer he has ever been, while his knowledge of the world and sympathy with human nature have become wider and more real."
— *The Morning Post.*

126   ## MISS SHAFTO.

" The books of Mr. Norris are worth reading, not because he recalls this or that distinguished predecessor, but because he has a charming manner of his own which is rendered recognisable not by eccentricity or whim, but by a wholesome artistic individuality, and one does not nowadays often read a fresher, brighter, cleverer book than ' Miss Shafto.' "—*The Academy.*

RICHARD BENTLEY AND SON, LONDON.

By W. E. NORRIS—(*Continued*).

123

THE ROGUE.

"Mr. Norris is just now to the fore. He is probably one of the first amongst rising novelists. Mr. Lang speaks of him as 'the Thackeray of a later age.'"—*The World.*

"Mr. Norris is always an artist. Tom Heywood is by no means the author's only triumph. Lady Hester and Stella are in their way almost equally, and Mr. Fisher, the unscrupulous financier who is prompted by his one unselfish emotion to a heroic act of self-abnegation, is even better; but our space is exhausted, and we must content ourselves with a hearty commendation of one of the cleverest and brightest novels of the season."—*The Spectator.*

By MRS. NOTLEY.

73

OLIVE VARCOE.

"A sensational story with a substantial fund of interest. It is thoroughly exciting."—*The Athenæum.*

"Among the pleasures of memory may be reckoned the impression left by a perusal of 'Olive Varcoe,' a story sufficiently powerful, picturesque, and original to raise hopes of still more excellent work to be achieved by the writer of it."—*The St. James's Gazette.*

By FRANCES M. PEARD.

106

NEAR NEIGHBOURS.

"The home life of the Dutch, | And the story is such
Sketched with eloquent touch, | That you'll find there is much
Forms the scene of Miss Peard's latest | To like in her pleasant 'Near Neighbours.'"
labours. | *Punch.*

"'Near Neighbours' is an excellent novel. It is a story of modern life in the Netherlands, and it reminds one of a gallery of Dutch pictures without their coarseness."—*The Saturday Review.*

By MRS. J. H. RIDDELL.

104

BERNA BOYLE.

"In 'Berna Boyle' this very clever author has broken new ground. A more fiery, passionate, determined, and, we must add, more uncomfortable lover than Gorman Muir could hardly have been 'evolved out of the consciousness' of Emily Brontë herself."—*The Standard.*

"'Berna Boyle' is one of the best of Mrs. Riddell's novels; certainly the best I have read of hers since 'George Geith.'"—*Truth.*

109

GEORGE GEITH OF FEN COURT.

"Rarely have we seen an abler work than this, or one which more vigorously interests us in the principal characters of its most fascinating story."—*The Times.*

"The author carries the reader with her from the first page to the last. And of all the girls we can call to mind in recent novels we scarcely know one that pleases us like Beryl. She is so fresh, so bright, so tender-hearted, so charming, even for her faults, that we fall in love with her almost at first sight. The subordinate characters are sketched with great felicity, and considerable skill is displayed in the construction of the plot. We like, too, the thoughts, pithily and eloquently expressed, which are scattered throughout the volume."—*The Fortnightly Review.*

By MAJOR HAWLEY SMART.

80

BREEZIE LANGTON.

"A capital novel, full of sweet English girls and brave, open-hearted English gentlemen. It abounds with stirring scenes on the racecourse and in the camp, told with a rare animation, and a thorough knowledge of what the writer is talking about."—*The Guardian.*

"We predict for this book a decided success. Had the author omitted his name from the title-page, we should unhesitatingly have credited Mr. Whyte Melville with his labours. The force and truth of the hunting and racing sketches, the lively chat of the club and the barracks, the pleasant flirting scenes, and the general tone of good society, all carry us back to the days of 'Kate Coventry' and 'Digby Grand.'"—*The Saturday Review.*

By the BARONESS TAUTPHŒUS (née Montgomery).

4

THE INITIALS.

"One of those special and individual tales the coming of which is pleasantly welcomed. It must please all who love character in persons lower than Antonys and Cleopatras. No better humoured or less caricatured picture of life in Germany has ever been executed by an English pencil."— *The Athenæum.*

7

QUITS !

"'Quits!' is an admirable novel. Witty, sententious, graphic, full of brilliant pictures of life and manners, it is positively one of the best of modern stories, and may be read with delightful interest from cover to cover."— *The Morning Post.*

By ANTHONY TROLLOPE.

10

THE THREE CLERKS.

". . . Trollope's next novel was 'The Three Clerks,' which we have always greatly admired and enjoyed, but which we fancied had come before the ecclesiastical fictions. The sorrows, the threatened moral degradation of poor Charlie Tudor, the persecution he underwent from the low money-lender—all these things seemed very actual to us, and now we know that they were photographs reproduced from the life. The novel seems to have been a special favourite of its author's, and perhaps he places almost higher than we should be inclined to do the undoubtedly pathetic love-scenes of which Kate Woodward is the heroine. He declares elsewhere, if we remember aright, that one of these scenes was the most touching he ever wrote. And he says here, 'The passage in which Kate Woodward, thinking she will die, tries to take leave of the lad she loves, still brings tears to my eyes when I read it. I had not the heart to kill her. I never could do that. And I do not doubt but that they are living happily together to this day.'"— *The Times (reviewing Anthony Trollope's Autobiography).*

From the German of E. WERNER.

121

FICKLE FORTUNE.

"Werner has established her claim to rank with those very few writers whose works are, or should be, matters of interest to all readers of cultivation throughout Europe."--*The Graphic.*

"The tale partly resembles that of Romeo and Juliet, in so far as the hero and heroine fall in love almost at first sight, and discover that they belong to families which are at deadly feud, but such deadly feud as can be carried on by means of lawyers and lawsuits. The style of writing is excellent, of the easy, lucid, vivacious sort, which never induces weariness and scarcely allows time for a pause."— *The Illustrated London News.*

65

SUCCESS, AND HOW HE WON IT.

"'Success, and How He Won It' deserves all praise. The story is charming and original, and it is told with a delicacy which makes it irresistibly fascinating."— *The Standard.*

"A book which can hardly be too highly spoken of. It is full of interest, it abounds in exciting incidents, though it contains nothing sensational; it is marvellously pathetic, the characters are drawn in a masterly style, and the descriptive portions are delightful."— *The London Figaro.*

By the HON. LEWIS WINGFIELD.

LADY GRIZEL.

"On putting down Thackeray's 'Esmond' we seem to come back suddenly from the days of Queen Anne, and on closing 'Lady Grizel' one is almost tempted to believe that one has lived in the reign of George III."— *The Morning Post.*

"A clever and powerful book. The author has cast back to a very terrible and a very difficult historical period, and gives us a ghastly and vivid presentment of society as it was in Chatham's time."— *Vanity Fair.*

Bentleys' Favourite Novels.

Each Work can be had separately, uniformly bound, price **6s.**

The most Recent Additions to the Series have been:

DIANA TEMPEST. By MARY CHOLMONDELEY.
THE GREATER GLORY. By MAARTEN MAARTENS.
BASIL LYNDHURST. By ROSA NOUCHETTE CAREY.

RICHARD BENTLEY AND SON, LONDON.

Recent Works of Fiction
IN LIBRARY FORM.

I.

The Vicar of Langthwaite. By LILY WATSON. In 3 vols., crown 8vo.

II.

Speedwell. By LADY GUENDOLEN RAMSDEN. In 1 vol., crown 8vo.

III.

The Greater Glory. By MAARTEN MAARTENS, Author of 'An Old Maid's Love.' In 3 vols., crown 8vo.

IV.

The Romance of Shere Mote. By PERCY HULBURD, Author of 'In Black and White.' In 3 vols., crown 8vo.

V.

A Devoted Couple. By J. MASTERMAN, Author of 'The Scotts of Bestminster.' In 3 vols., crown 8vo.

VI.

Eve's Apple. By MARY DEANE. In 2 vols., crown 8vo.

VII.

The Daughter of the Nez Percés. By ARTHUR PATERSON, Author of 'A Partner from the West.' In 2 vols., crown 8vo.

VIII.

Thorough. By Mrs. ALFRED MARKS (MARY A. M. HOPPUS), Author of 'Masters of the World.' In 3 vols., crown 8vo.

IX.

If Men Were Wise. By E. L. SHAW. In 3 vols., crown 8vo.

X.

The Power of the Past. By ESMÉ STUART, Author of 'Joan Vellacott.' In 3 vols., crown 8vo.

XI.

Victims of Fashion. By A. M. GRANGE. In 2 vols., crown 8vo.

XII.

A Troublesome Pair. By LESLIE KEITH, Author of 'Lisbeth,' 'A Hurricane in Petticoats,' etc. In 3 vols., crown 8vo.

XIII.

An Interloper. By FRANCES MARY PEARD, Author of 'A Country Cousin,' 'The Baroness,' etc. In 2 vols., crown 8vo.

XIV.

In a Cinque Port: A Story of Winchelsea. By E. M. HEWITT. In 3 vols., crown 8vo.

XV.

Mrs. Romney. By ROSA NOUCHETTE CAREY, Author of 'Nellie's Memories.' In 1 vol., crown 8vo.

XVI.

Wedded to a Genius. By NEIL CHRISTISON. In 2 vols., crown 8vo.

XVII.

The Adventuress. By ANNIE EDWARDES, Author of 'Archie Lovell,' 'Ought We to Visit Her?' etc. In 1 vol., crown 8vo.

XVIII.

The Old Old Story. By ROSA NOUCHETTE CAREY, Author of 'Lover or Friend?' 'Wooed and Married,' etc. In 3 vols., crown 8vo.

XIX.

The Intended. By H. DE VERE STACPOOLE. In 1 vol., crown 8vo.

XX.

The Princess Royal. By KATHERINE WYLDE, Author of 'Mr. Bryant's Mistake.' In 3 vols., crown 8vo.

ALSO IN THE PRESS.

Toddle Island. Being the Diary of Lord Bottsford of England. In 1 vol., crown 8vo.

AND

A Family Arrangement. By the Author of 'Dr. Edith Romney,' 'Evelyn's Career,' etc. In 3 vols., crown 8vo.

AND

Lady Jean's Vagaries. In 1 vol., crown 8vo.

PUBLISHERS in ORDINARY to HER MAJESTY.

Standard Works of Fiction.

'In respect of the novelists of the past, Mr. Bentley is an especial benefactor. He has published the only tolerable edition of the works of that great genius, JANE AUSTEN, who, if she had belonged to any other country than England, would have had *éditions de luxe* as the sand of the sea in number. He gave us not many years ago the first general edition of a writer, second only to her among those whom for some inscrutable reason the public taste has not adopted, THOMAS PEACOCK. And now he has given us Miss FERRIER'S books in a form in which they can be read.'—*Pall Mall Gazette.*

JANE AUSTEN'S NOVELS.

(Messrs. BENTLEYS' are the ONLY COMPLETE EDITIONS.)

LIBRARY EDITION.

VOL. I.—SENSE AND SENSIBILITY.
,,   II.—PRIDE AND PREJUDICE.
,,   III.—MANSFIELD PARK.
,,   IV.—EMMA.

VOL. V.—NORTHANGER ABBEY, AND PERSUASION.
,,   VI.—LADY SUSAN, THE WATSONS, ETC. (With a Memoir and Portrait of the Authoress.)

In Six Vols., crown 8vo., 36s.

'I have now read over again all Miss Austen's novels. There are in the world no compositions which approach nearer to perfection.'—*Macaulay.*

'Ferrier and Austen have given portraits of real society far superior to anything vain man has produced of like nature. Miss Austen had a talent for describing the involvements and feelings and characters of ordinary life, which is to me the most wonderful I ever met with. Her exquisite touch is denied to me.'—*Sir Walter Scott.*

'Jane Austen's novels are more true to nature, and have for my sympathies passages of finer feeling than any others of this age.'—*Southey.*

THE COLLECTED WORKS OF

THOMAS LOVE PEACOCK.

Including his Novels, Fugitive Pieces, Poems, Criticisms, etc.   Edited by Sir HENRY COLE, K.C.B.   With Preface by Lord HOUGHTON, and a Biographical Sketch by EDITH NICOLLS.   3 vols., crown 8vo., 31s. 6d.

HEADLONG HALL.
MELINCOURT.
NIGHTMARE ABBEY.

MAID MARIAN.
MISFORTUNES OF ELPHIN.

CROTCHET CASTLE
GRYLL GRANGE.
ETC.

'His fine wit
Makes such a wound the knife is lost in it ;
A strain too learned for a shallow age,
Too wise for selfish bigots ; let his page

Which charms the chosen spirits of the time
Fold itself up for a serener clime
Of years to come and find its recompense
In that just expectation.'—*Shelley.*

A NEW LIBRARY EDITION OF

MISS FERRIER'S NOVELS.

(THE EDINBURGH EDITION.)

Six Volumes, small crown 8vo.   The Set, 30s., or separately as under :—

MARRIAGE - 2 vols., 10s.   **THE INHERITANCE** - 2 vols., 10s.
DESTINY - 2 vols., 10s.

This Edition is printed from the Original Edition corrected by the Author, of whom a short Memoir is prefixed in 'Marriage.'

'Miss Ferrier's novels are thick-set with specimens of sagacity, happy traits of nature, flashes of genuine satire, easy humour, sterling good sense, and, above all—God only knows where she picked it up—in mature and perfect knowledge of the world.'—*Professor Wilson.*

'On the day of the dissolution of Parliament, in the critical hours between twelve and three, I was employed in reading "Destiny." My mind was so completely occupied on your colony in Argyleshire that I did not throw away a thought upon Kings or Parliaments, and was not moved by the general curiosity to stir abroad until I had finished your story. It would have been nothing if you had so agitated a youth of genius and susceptibility, prone to literary enthusiasm, but such a victory over an old hack is worthy of your notice.'—*Mackintosh* (to Miss Ferrier).

RICHARD BENTLEY AND SON, LONDON.

Cheap Editions of Works of Fiction.

BY MRS. WOODS.

A Village Tragedy.

By MARGARET L. WOODS, Author of 'Lyrics and Ballads.' Second Edition. Small post 8vo., 3s. 6d.

BY DR. KENEALY.

Molly and her Man-o'-War.

By Dr. ARABELLA KENEALY, Author of ' Dr. Janet of Harley Street.' Crown 8vo., 6s.

ANONYMOUS.

An Australian Girl.

By 'Mrs. ALICK MACLEOD.' The Second Edition in crown 8vo., 6s.

BY MISS BETHAM EDWARDS.

The Parting of the Ways.

By M. E. BETHAM EDWARDS, Authoress of 'Kitty.' In crown 8vo., 6s.

BY MR. W. H. MALLOCK.

The Old Order Changes.

By WILLIAM HURRELL MALLOCK. New and Cheaper Edition, with Frontispiece, crown 8vo., 6s.

BY MISS MONEY.

A Little Dutch Maiden.

By E. ERNLE MONEY. A New and Cheaper Edition, crown 8vo., 6s.

BY MR. LISLE.

The Ring of Gyges.

By CHARLES W. LISLE. Crown 8vo., 6s.

BY MISS BLYTH.

The Queen's Jewel.

The Little Duke of Gloucester. By M. P. BLYTH, Author of 'Antoinette.' With Ten Illustrations by WILLIAM LANCE, quarto, 6s.

BY MR. JEPHSON.

He would be a Soldier.

By R. MOUNTENEY JEPHSON, Author of 'The Girl he left behind him,' etc. Eighth Edition, with Four Illustrations, crown 8vo., 2s. 6d.

BY MRS. ORLEBAR.

H. S. Limpness the Moonfaced Princess.

By F. ST. JOHN ORLEBAR. With numerous Illustrations, quarto, 3s. 6d.

BY MISS WARDEN.

Those Westerton Girls.

By FLORENCE WARDEN, Author of 'The House on the Marsh,' etc. Third Edition, in fcap. 8vo., paper wrapper, 1s.

PUBLISHERS in ORDINARY to HER MAJESTY.

Cheap Editions of Works of Fiction—(*Continued*).

BY CHARLES ROBERT MATURIN.

Melmoth the Wanderer.

By the Author of 'Bertram.' Reprinted from the Original Text, with a Memoir and Bibliography of MATURIN. In 3 vols., post 8vo., 24s.

'Célèbre voyageur Melmoth, la grande création satanique du révérend Maturin. Quoi de plus grand, quoi de plus puissant relativement à la pauvre humanité que ce pâle et ennuyé Melmoth?'—C. BAUDELAIRE.

BY THE HON. MRS. HENNIKER.

Sir George.

By the Hon. MRS. HENNIKER, Author of 'Bid me Good-bye!' A New and Cheaper Edition. Crown 8vo., 2s. 6d.

BY A NEW WRITER.

A Chronicle of Two Months.

Reprinted from THE TEMPLE BAR MAGAZINE. Crown 8vo., 2s. 6d.

BY COLONEL BURNABY.

Our Radicals.

By the late Col. FRED BURNABY. A New Edition. Crown 8vo., 2s. 6d.

BY MR. GOODMAN.

Too Curious.

By E. J. GOODMAN. A New and Cheaper Edition. Crown 8vo., 2s. 6d.

BY THE AUTHOR OF 'SIR CHARLES DANVERS.'

The Danvers Jewels.

Fcap. 8vo., paper wrapper, 1s.

BY MR. HARDINGE.

Out of the Fog.

By WILLIAM MONEY HARDINGE. Fcap. 8vo., paper wrapper, 1s.

Florence Montgomery's Stories.

A new story by Miss Montgomery, entitled 'Colonel Norton,' is now in the press.

I.
MISUNDERSTOOD. Twenty-fourth Edition. With 6 Illustrations, by Du Maurier. Crown 8vo., 6s.

II.
THROWN TOGETHER. Twentieth Thousand. Crown 8vo., 6s.

III.
SEAFORTH. Ninth Thousand, with Frontispiece. Crown 8vo., 6s.

IV.
TRANSFORMED. Fourth Thousand. Crown 8vo., 5s.

V.
THE BLUE VEIL, AND OTHER STORIES. Small crown 8vo., 3s. 6d.

RICHARD BENTLEY AND SON, LONDON.

MRS. HENRY WOOD'S NOVELS.

The 3s. 6d. Edition.

EAST LYNNE. (Three Hundredth Thousand.)
THE CHANNINGS. (One Hundred and Tenth Thousand.)
MRS. HALLIBURTON'S TROUBLES. (Eighty-eighth Thousand.)
THE SHADOW OF ASHLYDYAT. (Fiftieth Thousand.)
LORD OAKBURN'S DAUGHTERS. (Fifty-eighth Thousand.)
VERNER'S PRIDE. (Forty-fifth Thousand.)
ROLAND YORKE. (Eightieth Thousand.)
JOHNNY LUDLOW. First Series. (Thirty-fifth Thousand.)
MILDRED ARKELL. (Fiftieth Thousand.)
ST. MARTIN'S EVE. (Forty-fifth Thousand.)
TREVLYN HOLD. (Fortieth Thousand.)
GEORGE CANTERBURY'S WILL. (Fiftieth Thousand.)
THE RED COURT FARM. (Forty-second Thousand.)
WITHIN THE MAZE. (Sixty-fifth Thousand.)
ELSTER'S FOLLY. (Thirty-fifth Thousand.)
LADY ADELAIDE. (Thirty-fifth Thousand.)
OSWALD CRAY. (Thirty-fifth Thousand.)
JOHNNY LUDLOW. Second Series. (Twenty-third Thousand.)
ANNE HEREFORD. (Thirty-fifth Thousand.)
DENE HOLLOW. (Thirty-fifth Thousand.)
EDINA. (Twenty-fifth Thousand.)
A LIFE'S SECRET. (Thirty-fifth Thousand.)
COURT NETHERLEIGH. (Twenty-sixth Thousand.)
LADY GRACE. (Sixteenth Thousand.)
BESSY RANE. (Thirtieth Thousand.)
PARKWATER. (Twentieth Thousand.)
THE UNHOLY WISH, etc. A New Edition.
JOHNNY LUDLOW. Third Series. (Thirteenth Thousand.)
THE MASTER OF GREYLANDS. (Thirtieth Thousand.)
ORVILLE COLLEGE. (Thirty-third Thousand.)
POMEROY ABBEY. (Thirtieth Thousand.)
JOHNNY LUDLOW. Fourth Series.
ADAM GRAINGER, etc. (Tenth Thousand.)
JOHNNY LUDLOW. Fifth Series.

'The power to draw minutely and carefully each character with characteristic individuality in word and action is Mrs. Wood's especial gift. This endows her pages with a vitality which carries the reader to the end, and leaves him with the feeling that the veil which in real life separates man from man has been raised, and that he has for once seen and known certain people as intimately as if he had been their guardian angel. This is a great fascination.'—*The Athenæum.*

Each Volume is in crown 8vo. size, scarlet cloth, lettered on the side and sold separately, price 3s. 6d.

PUBLISHERS in ORDINARY to HER MAJESTY.

Albert Smith's Stories.

ETCHINGS BY LEECH.

The Adventures of Mr. Ledbury.

A New Edition, with upwards of Twenty humorous full-page Illustrations on Steel by JOHN LEECH. Royal 8vo., 21s.

The Marchioness of Brinvilliers.

A New Edition, with Fourteen spirited full-page Etchings on Steel by JOHN LEECH. Royal 8vo., 21s.

EDITED BY JOHN RUSKIN.

Portraits of the Children of the Mobility.

Drawn from Nature by JOHN LEECH. With Portrait of Leech, and Prefatory Letter by JOHN RUSKIN. Reproduced in Autotype. Quarto, 10s. 6d.

ETCHINGS BY CRUIKSHANK.

Old 'Miscellany' Days.

Stories by Various Authors. Reprinted from 'Bentleys' Miscellany.' Royal 8vo., with 33 full-page Illustrations on Steel (only once worked fifty years ago) by GEORGE CRUIKSHANK. 21s.

BENTLEYS' EMPIRE LIBRARY.

The price of each Volume is Half-a-Crown, bound in cloth.

By MRS. ALEXANDER.
RALPH WILTON'S WEIRD.

By MRS. EDWARDES.
A BLUE STOCKING. | A VAGABOND HEROINE.

By HELEN MATHERS.
AS HE COMES UP THE STAIRS.

By RHODA BROUGHTON.
TWILIGHT STORIES.

By CHARLES DICKENS.
THE MUDFOG PAPERS, etc.

RICHARD BENTLEY AND SON, LONDON.

EDITED BY CHARLES W. WOOD.

THE ARGOSY MAGAZINE.

Monthly of all Booksellers, 6d. (the December and June numbers, 1s.). The Midsummer numbers, published each year from 1884 to 1892 inclusive, 6d. each.

THE BACK NUMBERS, with exception of the undermentioned, which are out of print, can be obtained at the same price :—

Nos. 1 to 24, December, 1865, to November, 1867.		No. 143, October, 1877.
No. 51, February, 1870.	No. 83, October, 1872.	,, 144, November, 1877.
,, 65, April, 1871.	,, 88, March, 1873.	,, 157, December, 1878.
,, 71, October, 1871.	,, 97, December, 1873.	,, 172, March, 1880.
,, 74, January, 1872.	,, 133, December, 1876.	,, 180, November, 1880.
,, 75, February, 1872.	,, 135, February, 1877.	

THE VOLUMES (of which there are two in each year) can be obtained, price 5s. each, with exception of Vols. 1, 2 (for 1866), 3, 4 (for 1867), 9 (in 1870), 11, 12 (for 1871), 13, 14 (for 1872), 15, 16 (for 1873), 22 (in 1876), 24 (in 1877), 26 (in 1878), and 30 (in 1880), which are out of print.

CASES for binding the Volumes can be had, price 1s. 6d. each.

TO CORRESPONDENTS.—All MSS. and Communications must be addressed to the SUB-EDITOR of THE ARGOSY, 8, New Burlington Street, W. From the large number of Articles received, it is impossible to return them unless accompanied by stamps. The Publishers will not be responsible for Articles accidentally lost.

TO ADVERTISERS.—Advertisements and Bills are requested to be forwarded to Mr. NELSON, Advertisement Contractor, 23, Laurence Pountney Lane, Cannon Street, E.C., by the 10th of each month.

The Publication days are shown on page inside cover at beginning.

The Volumes for 1895 are Nos. 59 and 60.

LIST OF SERIALS IN 'THE ARGOSY.'

1866.—**Griffith Gaunt**, by Charles Reade.

1867.—**Robert Falconer**, by Dr. George Macdonald.

1868.—**Anne Hereford**, by Mrs. Henry Wood. **Buried Alone**, by C. W. Wood.

1869.—**Roland Yorke**, by Mrs. Henry Wood.

1870.—**Bessy Rane**, by Mrs. Henry Wood.

1871.—**Dene Hollow**, by Mrs. Henry Wood.

1872.—**Within the Maze**, by Mrs. Henry Wood.

1873.—**The Master of Greylands**, by Mrs. Henry Wood.

1874.—**In the Dead of Night**, by Thomas Speight.

1875.—**The Secret of the Sea**, by Thomas Speight. **Parkwater**, by Mrs. Henry Wood.

1876.—**Edina**, by Mrs. Henry Wood.

1877.—**Gabriel's Appointment** by Miss A. H. Drury.

1878.—**Pomeroy Abbey**, by Mrs. Henry Wood.

1879.—**Called to the Rescue**, by Miss A. H. Drury.

1880.—**The Mystery of Heron Dyke**, by Thomas Speight.

1881.—**Court Netherleigh**, by Mrs. Henry Wood.

1882.—**Mrs. Raven's Temptation**, by Mrs. Fyvie Mayo.

1883.—**Winifred Power**, by Miss B. Duffy.

1884.—**The White Witch**, Anonymous.

1885.—**The Mystery of Allan Grale**, by Mrs. Fyvie Mayo.

1886.—**Lady Valeria**, by Major Moberly.

1887.—**Lady Grace**, by Mrs. Henry Wood. **The Missing Rubies**, by Miss Sarah Doudney.

1888.—**The Story of Charles Strange**, by Mrs. Henry Wood.

1889.—**The Village Blacksmith**, Anonymous. **Featherston's Story**, by Mrs. Henry Wood. **Divided**, by Katharine Carr.

1890.—**The House of Halliwell**, by Mrs. Henry Wood, and **Stories by Johnny Ludlow**.

1891.—**The Fate of the Hara Diamond**.

1892.—**Ashley**, by Mrs. Henry Wood, and **A Guilty Silence**.

1893.—**The Engagement of Susan Chase**, by Mrs. Henry Wood; and **Mr. Warrenne: Medical Practitioner**. (An Old Story retold.)

1894.—**The Grey Monk**, by the Author of 'The Mystery of Heron Dyke.'

RICHARD BENTLEY AND SON, LONDON.

INDEX.